PENGU

GO

Jenny Newman grew up in Cumberland and at the age of eighteen became a nun in a French order. Five years later she left the convent and went to university. She is now a lecturer and lives on Merseyside. She is the editor of *The Faber Book of Seductions* and co-editor of *Women Talk Sex: Autobiographical Writing on Sex, Sexuality and Sexual Identity*. *Going In* is her first novel.

Going In

JENNY NEWMAN

PENGUIN BOOKS

PENGUIN BOOKS

Published by the Penguin Group
Penguin Books Ltd, 27 Wrights Lane, London W8 5TZ, England
Penguin Books USA Inc., 375 Hudson Street, New York, New York 10014, USA
Penguin Books Australia Ltd, Ringwood, Victoria, Australia
Penguin Books Canada Ltd, 10 Alcorn Avenue, Toronto, Ontario, Canada M4V 3B2
Penguin Books (NZ) Ltd, 182–190 Wairau Road, Auckland 10, New Zealand

Penguin Books Ltd, Registered Offices: Harmondsworth, Middlesex, England

First published by Hamish Hamilton 1994
Published in Penguin Books 1995
1 3 5 7 9 10 8 6 4 2

Copyright © Jenny Newman, 1994
All rights reserved

The moral right of the author has been asserted

Printed in England by Clays Ltd, St Ives plc

For Dave

With grateful thanks to Elizabeth Mavor, for her illuminating initial suggestion; to P. B. Parris and Barry and Aira Unsworth for reading the manuscript and suggesting many improvements; and to David Evans, who helped at every stage.

ONE

———

Sister Monica was the youngest nun on the staff of St Cuthbert's School for Girls, and her bold and bright mosaics lit up its pea-green corridors and panelled classrooms. She had a pale, smooth skin, dark eyes and a wide, curving mouth. Every Friday I would tell her about my week while we tidied the art room. Usually she listened patiently, but this afternoon she stopped me short.

'It's high time you told your mother, Biddy,' she said, waggling a paintbrush in my direction.

'Why should I? It's you I tell things to, not her.'

'She still has a right to know,' replied Sister Monica, smiling. 'And besides, Mother Wilfred wants to speak to her.'

Mother Wilfred was the Superior, tall and stern. She knew my mother from the two embarrassing terms she'd worked here as a cleaner, until a row over some unwashed toilet seats.

'So you want to be one of us?' Mother Wilfred had boomed when I stuttered out my news. 'Well, we'll have to see.' And with that she'd flapped off down the corridor. I was hurt by her lack of enthusiasm, hurt and surprised, because I was the only pupil who'd responded to her regular appeals for what my friend Lorraine called penguin material.

'Let us pray that one girl here today will become a Bride of Christ,' Mother Wilfred would intone every Friday, her pale eyes raking our assembled heads. Automatically we cast down our eyes and began the formula. *The harvest is great, O Lord, but the labourers are few* ... Couldn't she see it didn't work? It was years since a St Cuthbert's girl had become a nun.

Then, one day in sixth form, I had realized what we were praying for. 'Dear God, please don't let it be me,' I muttered, my skin coming out in goose bumps. To spend my life behind walls, with a shaven head under my wimple, and a cell for a bedroom. I bought some make-up straight away, and set out to find a boyfriend.

Until the sixth-form retreat the previous summer I'd thought I was safe. Hadn't I been in love with Jonathon Maule? Besides, it wasn't girls like me Mother Wilfred had in mind, but the ones from good homes and Catholic backgrounds. But during that retreat I learnt another kind of love.

The retreat house had once been a stately home, with terraced gardens falling away to the Cheshire plain, and alleys where the few remaining peacocks still strutted. To my surprise I enjoyed the sunlit hours in chapel, and the sense of peace and order. While my classmates giggled in the dormitory at night, I lay silent, pondering the words of the young retreat priest.

'To God, the soul is feminine,' he'd told us. 'You, my dear little sisters, by weeding out every act of impurity and self-love, can turn your souls into a beautiful garden, where the Good Lord will love to wander.'

On the third day, when the others were packing their bags to go home, I went for a last walk round the ornamental lake. I'd been to the country before, but never had the skies looked so high, and the colours so bright. Sister Monica would call that sky *cobalt*, I decided, pausing to gaze at its reflection in the water. Taking a few deep breaths, I watched the emerald grass begin to wiggle and swim before my eyes, and heard a roaring in my ears. For a few seconds I thought I was going to faint – but no, the grass grew steady again, and whatever wind there was must have dropped, because the sun was still warm on my shoulder-blades. These new sensations come not from feeling faint, but from prayer, I decided, gazing at a water-lily, prayer and silence. During my retreat the world had grown fresh, and new, and full of possibilities – of what I didn't quite know, but my sense of well-being was complete.

Trying to postpone the moment when I would have to climb on the coach and return to Liverpool, I wandered round the other side of the lake and down to the grotto. There was more to life than working for exams, and going home every evening to a house full of clutter. I too could be holy, I thought with excitement, and have a special relationship with God. Then these new feelings might come more often. I wouldn't do anything extreme, of course. Why shut down on life when I was on the brink of finding out about it?

I had just taken out my rosary beads when Sister Monica appeared at my side. Anxious not to break silence, I carried on with the Joyful Mysteries as she fell into step beside me. 'Holy Mary, Mother of God . . .' Sister Monica took up the refrain, 'Pray for us sinners, now and at the hour of our death, Amen.'

When we had finished the decade she turned to smile at me. 'Have I guessed right?' she asked. Three days in the fresh air had brought the colour into her cheeks, and her brown eyes were brighter than ever.

'I don't know what you mean,' I stuttered.

A peacock's wail broke the silence. 'This might come as a surprise to you, Brigid,' said Sister Monica slowly, 'but I've been wondering for some time if you have a vocation.'

The sun beat down through a laburnum tree to glimmer and dance round her head. 'How can you tell?' I asked, flattered and frightened at the same time.

'One learns the signs over the years,' she replied. 'Some girls suddenly grow thoughtful – or spend a little more time in prayer. Others try and drown God's voice in alcohol, or pop music. God doesn't only choose goody-goodies.'

'How did *you* know you were meant to be a nun?'

Lorraine and I had often wondered what had made this beautiful, lively young woman take the veil. Had it been a rash promise made to God, in exchange for the health of some relative? Or was it a secret grief, like unrequited love? None of our theories seemed to fit, but close as I felt to her, I had never dared ask until now.

'I felt . . . chosen, as though God wanted me for His own. For years I tried to put Him off – then one morning I woke up knowing He'd be content with nothing less than everything.'

I thought of working in the same community as Sister Monica, and other women like her, sharing their serenity and sense of purpose. 'I sometimes feel like that too,' I confessed, 'but I've been trying to ignore it.'

'It's no good, Brigid,' remonstrated the nun gently. She had picked a spray of lilac, and was absently crushing its petals between her fingers. 'If God wants you for a nun He will never let you forget it.'

'Couldn't I wait a few years?'

'You can postpone an earthly wedding, Brigid – but you can't postpone a heavenly one. You might lose your vocation.'

'Then I could go to college.'

'It's strange how often the Lord asks us for the only thing we're afraid to give up,' mused Sister Monica. 'You can't fob Him off with second best.'

My nostrils caught the scent of lilac, sharp and cloying. 'But why is living in the world second best?'

'If you really have a vocation, the world will never make you content,' said Sister Monica, slipping an arm around my shoulders. 'Don't worry,' she added, 'the Lord will repay you a thousandfold. Look at me, and see how happy I am. I gave up being an artist, and now I'm painting every day!'

I had gone home that night with a holy picture tucked

inside my missal. On the back Sister Monica had copied out a poem about a nun taking the veil:

> I have desired to go
> Where springs not fail
> To fields where flies no sharp and sided hail . . .

Try as I might not to think about it, my thoughts kept turning to the idea like a tongue to a loose tooth. Soon I was going to chapel at lunchtime, instead of gossiping with the other girls. There I would tell God every detail of my day, begging Him to stop me feeling jealous of Elisabeth Bavidge, and help me pass my A levels. I quickly forgot about Jonathon Maule, and, no longer worried about being a swot, began getting top marks. The only thing I hadn't managed to do was confront my mother.

'Madge will say I should have more fun,' I told Sister Monica now, picking up a discarded paintbrush to sluice it under the tap.

'Madge?'

'It's what I call my mum – ever since Dad disappeared down to London.'

Sister Monica glanced across, her brown eyes sympathetic. 'Just because your mother says it doesn't mean it's wrong.'

'Do *you* think I'm too withdrawn?'

'Well, Brigid,' said Sister Monica, standing back from her easel to gaze in my direction, 'you do take life rather *seriously*.'

'But it is serious,' I replied, restoring the washed brushes to an empty jam-jar. 'If I don't pass my exams I'll end up a lay sister.'

'All work has meaning when it's offered up to God,' said Sister Monica with a hint of reproach.

'Try telling that to Madge.'

'Why not ask Lorraine to help you? She's your best friend, isn't she? And she gets on well with your – with

Madge. She'll know how to explain why you want to be a nun.'

'I could try,' I said doubtfully, 'but Lorraine's a lapsed Catholic, too. She and Madge think alike on these things.'

'Lorraine might surprise you,' said Sister Monica. 'Yes, I know she's fiery – but she's generous – and very loyal.'

My friend and I lived in the same street, and often walked home together. 'I'll tell her tonight,' I promised.

Nodding her approval, Sister Monica smoothed down her veil and detached a bundle of keys from her belt. 'Come and see me tomorrow,' she said, locking the door, 'and let me know how it went.'

Ten minutes later, Lorraine and I were pushing our way through the crowd of schoolgirls at the bus-stop, the younger ones with swinging plaits and pony-tails, and others, like Lorraine, with hair hastily backcombed before leaving the cloakroom, under the very nose of Sister Bosco. Beside us scampered Maureen, Lorraine's little sister, legs and arms flying as she dribbled her football along the kerb.

'Go away, Mo – you're getting on my nerves,' said Lorraine, rolling up her brown velour hat to stuff it in her pocket. Next she turned up her collar, unbuckled her belt, yanked it round her waist and pulled it tight, then hitched up her skirt to expose two plump knees. Her boyfriend was at the secondary modern along the dual carriageway, but she was never averse to a few stray glances.

On the far side of the road I saw Jonathon Maule striding towards the bus-stop, and looked away quickly.

'Tighten your belt, Bid,' said Lorraine out of the side of her mouth. 'You look such a *square*.'

I kept my uniform as it was. Unlike Lorraine, I'd been made a school prefect, and wanted to set a good example.

'Why should I go away?' asked Maureen.

'She can stay if she likes,' I said. Surely Sister Monica couldn't expect me to speak in front of a twelve-year-old.

'Mo! Scram!'

For once the young girl sped off obediently through the winter dusk, to join a gang of lads marking out their goalposts under the trees with two piles of anoraks. Lorraine and I tramped over the Little Jordan and across the park.

Soon the sodium lights were behind us, and Lorraine shifted her bulging satchel from one shoulder to the other, and started to talk about the night ahead at the Beverly Hills ballroom, where she would plonk her handbag on the floor and dance round it till chuck-out time. She had long stopped asking me to come with her. Claiming I needed more time to study, I had taken to spending Friday nights in my bedroom, saying the rosary.

Already we had passed the giant Palm House, its panes clouded by frost. Not noticing my silence, Lorraine slowed to a saunter, dug in her satchel for a packet of Number 6, and selected the least bent. As the match flared I glimpsed her face, round and intent. Inhaling sharply, she began on her plans for college – where she would live, and what clothes she'd buy when she got there. With a numb mind I waited for her to stop talking.

'I wouldn't be seen dead in a duffel-coat or a stupid college scarf,' she said happily as we passed the aviary, 'but I could do with some new flares – oh yes, and one of those hipster skirts in red bouclé . . .'

My future as a nun, so plausible up in the art room, felt flimsy alongside this wealth of detail. And Lorraine was supposed to help me tell my mother! My resolution was melting like butter. By the time my friend had twice modified her new wardrobe and set us up in a student flat, we were nearing the ring of houses on the far side of the park and my tongue was still clamped to the roof of my mouth. Ahead of us the rush-hour traffic was roaring through the big stone gates and on to cocktail hour in the suburbs.

'Mo!' yelled Lorraine. 'Mo! Come on – it's time for tea.'

We trailed through the maze of streets leading down to the Holy Land, with Maureen bobbing alongside us, a pale face in the gloom. 'What's your favourite Beatles song, Brigid?' she asked. 'Your very, very fave?'

Down on the river a foghorn lowed lugubriously. David Street, Jacob Street, Isaac Street, Moses Street. Maureen darted up the O'Shaunessys' front path and into the house. Within seconds, 'Twist and Shout' was roaring out into the evening air. Emboldened by the music, I blurted out my news.

'I'm going to be a nun.'

'Are you buggery!' laughed Lorraine, shifting her satchel to the other shoulder. 'By the way – can I borrow that sweater dress?'

'I know it seems sudden – but I mean it.' I curled my fingers round the front gate to stop them trembling.

'Is this a new way of catching Jonathon?' asked Lorraine. 'Making yourself unavailable in the hope he'll appear just before you take the veil? You can't expect me to spread such a silly rumour.'

'I couldn't care less about Jonathon – or any other boy.'

Lorraine's mouth turned into a small red 'O' of disbelief. 'You must be mental.'

'I'm saner than I've ever been – and I'll do it, if they'll have me.'

'I knew there was something up – all this hanging round Sister Monica, and not coming to the Bevvy. But I didn't think you'd be this stupid.'

'What's so stupid about being a nun?'

'It means giving up college – and travel – and clothes – and boyfriends.' Lorraine leant against the gatepost, looking dazed.

'Those things don't count if you have a vocation.'

'Vocation?'

'A sense of purpose – spiritual purpose.'

'But you wanted to be a teacher!'

'And end up married to some boring man in a semi-detached – or else a spinster, like Miss Vavasour?'

'Better than ending up a fucking sadist, like bloody Bosco.'

Trust Lorraine to drag in Sister Bosco. She had hated her ever since the old nun had caned her in front of the whole class during Lent. Sister Bosco had put up a mass chart with the name of every girl in the class down one side, in alphabetical order.

We each had to put a tick opposite our name whenever we went to church. Girls from good Catholic homes scored the most points, and were allowed to stay inside at dinner-hour to fill the inkwells and clean the mouse's cage. The rest of us peppered our columns with enough ticks to look respectable, and hoped not to be found out – all except for Lorraine, that is, whose line remained defiantly blank.

'Come out here, child,' snapped Sister Bosco one morning.

Heaving an exaggerated sigh, Lorraine wiggled her way to the front like Marilyn Monroe. Even at that age she was lad mad.

'Kneel down, you bold girl,' snapped Sister Bosco, 'and tell me why you haven't filled in your mass chart.'

'That's my business.'

'Remember this, my girl – if you haven't been to mass you're in a state of mortal sin.'

'So what?' said Lorraine, getting a sharp crack with the ruler for her pains.

'How do you think you'll find a decent Catholic husband?' gobbled Sister Bosco.

'Same as you did,' smirked Lorraine.

The old nun's eyes turned to boiled gooseberries, and beads of sweat broke out on her upper lip. Thwack went the

9

ruler again, and Lorraine was made to spend the whole of the first period kneeling in front of the blackboard, as a penance. At the end of term Sister Bosco reported her to the parish priest. 'It's my business, not yours,' was all that Lorraine would say to either of them, and they had to be content with that.

'I'm not going to be like Sister Bosco,' I countered. 'I'm going to be popular and dedicated, like Sister Monica.'

'Fat chance,' snorted Lorraine. 'I know I smoke, and swear, and like going with lads, but I'd make a better nun than you. There's something about you, Brigid – something weird. You can act the goody-goody and the creep, but underneath you're selfish as hell – and they'll crucify you when they find out.'

'For an atheist you use a lot of religious language.'

'So what?' Lorraine looked as though she was about to lose her temper.

'Please don't be cross – we'll keep in touch. I feel so confident, and so at peace – as though everything's taken care of.'

'You sound like a selfish baby.'

I swallowed the insult, remembering that God understood me even if my friend didn't. 'It's the bravest thing I've ever done,' I told her, opening the gate. 'Please come in – I want you to help me tell Madge.'

'I'll do nothing of the sort, you cracked mare,' Lorraine blazed back at me through the dusk. 'Do your own dirty work.'

I'd never seen my friend so angry. 'No, don't talk to me until you've seen sense,' she shouted. 'There's a whole wide world out there – and you're too chicken to take it on.'

If she didn't stop yelling soon I wouldn't need to tell Madge, because she'd hear us from the back kitchen. 'Brainwashed into joining a gaggle of penguins!' Lorraine drilled on.

'I might have guessed you wouldn't understand,' I hissed, backing up the path.

'I understand why you've gone cold and posh.'

'I'll pray for you,' I whispered, sliding my key in the lock. It was all I could think of.

'Don't you bloody well bother!' cried Lorraine as I skidded inside. 'If you so much as mention me in that place I'll – I'll fucking well sue you!'

TWO

'Was that Lol's voice?' asked Madge. She was reading the *Echo* at the kitchen table, her long form curved like a question mark over the horoscopes.

'Lorraine – er – can't come in,' I said. 'She's got to iron a blouse.' I scrutinized my mother's lank grey hair and gaunt, rather untidy features to see if she'd overheard us shouting, but she seemed more intent on Lady Luck.

'*Scorpio!*' she crowed happily. 'That's me. *With Jupiter in the ascendant and Mercury in your very own House, you can expect some welcome news from a loved one.* What do you say to that, Biddy? *Family ties will grow closer.*'

As she rustled on to the crossword, joggling the saucer of cigarette butts at her elbow, I felt a pang of guilt at her unsuspecting face. Ever since my dad had left, she'd supported me as best she could, cooking, cleaning, doing whatever came to hand. I looked round the cluttered little kitchen, with its rows of carrots, onions and tomatoes on wallpaper that had looked so gay and continental when my dad put it up in the fifties, and now was stained and torn. There was the cushion for the kitten she had bought when I passed the eleven-plus, and in that old armchair she'd held me all night during a childhood bout of bronchitis. And now I was about to say I was leaving her for good. Not even Sister Monica had been told about the sacrifices Madge had made, in case she said my duty lay not in the convent but at home with my mother.

'You forgot the washing-up liquid,' I said loudly, rolling up my sleeves, 'and there's no hot water.'

I knew I should feel grateful for everything she'd done,

but recently we'd begun to argue. I was irritated by the way she'd taken to sitting in the kitchen all day reading love stories and picking at Mars bars and bacon sandwiches, when she wasn't off down to the Wellington Vaults, or poisoning the air with Player's Extra Strong.

For her part, Madge had grown satirical about my long hours of homework, and lack of boyfriends. 'What's up with you?' She raised her voice above the babble of the Light Programme. 'Got bad marks?'

While I thought of Sister Monica, and how disappointed she'd be if I didn't break the news, Madge lit a cigarette, and tossed the match into a saucer. 'Make us a cuppa, will you, Bid?'

My mouth dry, I put the kettle on the stove and asked Madge to turn down the wireless. She ignored me, and carried on reading. If Lorraine had been here she would have jollied us both along, while I tidied up and Madge read out the titbits from the paper. Then I would have found the right moment to confide in Madge over tea. As it was, I stalked over to the wireless and snapped it off myself. It was now or never.

'I'm going to be a nun,' I remarked into the silence.

Madge raised her watery blue eyes to mine. 'Did Sister Monica put you up to this?' she inquired calmly.

'Certainly not,' I said, nettled. 'The idea came from God.'

'Did He come down from heaven to tell you so Himself?' said Madge satirically. 'Or was it a vision of Our Lady on the corpy tip – like in *The Song of Bernadette*?' Her eyebrows arched towards her hairline. 'Let's hope God will soon inspire you to light the gas, so we'll get that cup of tea.'

Taken aback by my mother's composure, I groped for the matches. 'It was nothing like that,' I replied, 'just a little voice that wouldn't go away.'

'The girl's off her chump,' she remarked to a passing smoke ring. 'It's all this studying!'

First Lorraine, and then Madge – no one was taking my vocation seriously. 'I know I always wanted to go to college,' I plunged on, trying to sound convincing. 'But it's not enough any more.'

'You should get a proper boyfriend,' said my mother, 'and forget this stupid plan.'

'Sister Monica says being a nun is as normal as getting married.'

'Not round here it isn't.'

I thought of Madge, working as a cleaner to support us both. 'What's so wonderful about living round here?' I asked.

'You've got a crush on Sister Monica,' retorted Madge, ignoring my question, 'and she's taking advantage of it.'

'She wouldn't do such a thing,' I replied indignantly.

'Why not? They're short of recruits, aren't they?'

'Only because women aren't answering God's call,' I replied, trying unsuccessfully to recapture my earlier certainty.

'What makes you think you're so special?' snorted my mother.

'I've told you – God wants me for Himself.' I stared fixedly at a row of discoloured carrots and onions.

Madge gave a smug smile as she stubbed out her cigarette in a tangle of bacon rinds. 'That's not what Mother Wilfred thinks.'

'Mother Wilfred?' I gaped. No wonder Madge hadn't been surprised by my news.

'She rang me up last week,' said Madge with a glint of triumph. 'She says I've not got to worry. You may not have the makings of a nun.'

A lump rising in my throat, I stirred a puddle of bacon fat with the toe of my shoe. Mother Wilfred should be on my side and not my mother's.

'What you need is some fun.'

14

'I hate fun,' I muttered, staring into the back yard. Ahead of me stretched life outside the cloister, blank and purposeless, with no swishing habit and air of dedication.

And then I realized: Mother Wilfred was just testing me. Every vocation was put to the proof. It was my job to stay firm.

Turning back to her crossword as though the matter were concluded, Madge took out a biro. 'A word for smartly dressed,' she said. 'Four letters, the second one an H.'

And to think I'd been afraid of hurting her feelings. She snapped her fingers, and began to write with a flourish. 'And don't stand there like one o'clock half-struck,' she added. 'I still haven't had my tea. If you were really cut out to be a nun, I wouldn't have to keep on asking.'

THREE
—

As soon as my mother left for the Wellington Vaults after Saturday dinner, I tracked back across the park to Sister Monica. The frost had long melted, and the glass of the Palm House was glinting at a pale February sun. Some boys had strung up a net on one of the tennis courts, and were knocking a ball back and forward.

St Cuthbert's School for Girls was a semi-detached extravaganza in orange brick, with a mock-Tudor front door and many spires and Jacobean chimneys. The whole house had been built for two Victorian merchants and their families, but the seaport was in decline by the time the Joubertian Sisters reached Liverpool in the 1930s, and the merchants' descendants had long since migrated to the Wirral.

The nuns could easily afford the semi nearest the iron bridge, and the octagonal turret room over the front door soon became Sister Ursula's study, and the first-floor drawing-room a dormitory. As their school expanded the community living quarters shrank to the attic, and their oratory was moved to the little room that now served as a stock cupboard. By the time I passed my eleven-plus at the end of the fifties, the nuns were doing well enough to buy the other semi – but it was occupied by a dentist who showed no signs of moving.

At assembly Mother Wilfred instructed us to pray for more space: it was the bulge year, and classes were being squeezed on to the upstairs landing. Dutifully we bowed our heads and offered up three Hail Marys. Next month the dentist dropped dead of a heart attack.

'It's a miracle,' announced Mother Wilfred. 'We nearly turned away twenty-five new pupils.' She paused to bow her head over her joined hands. 'And now, girls, let us pray for the soul of the departed dentist. The poor man died without making his Easter Duties. *Eternal rest, grant unto him, O Lord* . . .'

The new chapel, once the dentist's waiting-room, was deserted apart from an old lay sister, who glanced up from her Stations of the Cross as I tiptoed down the aisle. Wondering if she knew about my vocation, I knelt down, crossed myself devoutly, and gazed at the sanctuary.

It was a familiar sight: the tabernacle and altar beneath were draped in green silk, lovingly embroidered by Sister Ligori; above it hung an ebony crucifix, illuminated by a flickering sanctuary lamp. After the sixth-form retreat I had begun slipping in here at lunchtime, as much to escape from the superior stare of my rival, Elisabeth Bavidge, as to pray. Once here, I would gaze at the sanctuary lamp until I forgot about Elisabeth and Jonathon; or else I would take out Sister Monica's holy picture, and stare at the words until my eyes watered: *I have desired to go* . . .

Lulled into a daydream by the sibilant prayers of the old nun, my mind drifted towards the other boys – the Kevins and Garys and Josephs from the Catholic secondary modern, who had sometimes made cautious advances through Lorraine. I had agreed to a few double dates, hoping against hope that I would fall in love with an available boy. But the evenings were always a failure. How could I love some sweaty-handed boy whose idea of conversation was to bore me with his football heroes? Worst of all was the long walk home from the bus-stop, when Terry would steer an acquiescent Lorraine into a shop doorway and pin her against the plate glass. While she panted and squirmed with pleasure, I would hang around on the pavement, trying to stop Kevin or Gary or Joseph from inserting a slimy tongue between my lips, or sliding his hand inside my waistband. If I couldn't have Jonathon, I didn't want anyone, and eventually I came to prefer the taunt of Frigid Brigid to their amateurish groping.

Coming to with a start as the old nun clumped into the sacristy, I gathered my wandering thoughts. Despite not backing down the night before, I had gone to bed dismayed by Lorraine and Madge's incredulity. Now, in the peace of the little chapel, I knew once more that my vocation was to be taken seriously. My life must have a meaning, and it was better, I reflected, to turn to God than wait for some unsatisfactory man to sort it out. With that I made the sign of the cross with extra devotion, and left the chapel.

Sister Monica was bent over a drawing-board by the art room window. 'Brigid!' Her face lit up as I entered the room. 'You did it. Well done!'

'Madge knew all along,' I said. 'Mother Wilfred phoned her last week.'

'I guessed as much. Even so, it was time you spoke.'

'Mother Wilfred says I may not have a vocation.'

'It isn't her who decides,' said Sister Monica cheerfully. 'It's Mother General.'

'Who's that?'

'The Head of all the Joubertians,' said the art teacher. 'Soon she'll be coming from France on a pastoral visit.'

'Will I be able to see her?'

'It is compulsory. She'll want to see if you've a genuine vocation.'

'How will she know?'

'She'll talk to you at length – and ask a few questions. She made me go to art school first, and I nearly died of impatience.' Sister Monica smiled a private smile. 'But she was right – I was far too flighty.'

'Will she make me go to college?'

'I doubt it – you're the quiet type. Mother General is one

of the old guard, so it will stand you in good stead. She'll be interested in your mother's opinion, too. You must win her round by good behaviour.'

'But Madge gets on my nerves.'

'Then you must learn to be more charitable. Mother General will want to know if you can live in community.'

'When I'm a nun I'll be nice to everyone – even Sister Julian.'

'Then you can start practising straight away, because she's coming up to see you.'

'It's too soon,' I cried in panic. Our English teacher had the most sarcastic tongue in the school.

'She was the first to guess you had a vocation,' Sister Monica said reproachfully.

'But she thinks I'm stupid.'

'Not at all – she says you're very intelligent.'

'Then why does she keep picking on my accent?'

'She wants you to get ahead,' explained Sister Monica. 'People in the world can be very prejudiced.'

Before I could say any more, the door opened and there stood Sister Julian herself. She was only a few years older than Sister Monica, but tall and thin, with a high forehead and roman nose. Closing the door behind her, she sauntered across the room.

'So this is our new postulant.' Her words were clipped and carefully articulated like a foreigner's, and it was impossible to tell if she meant them seriously. I sprang to my feet as she bent to embrace me, accidentally nudging the starched cheek presented to mine.

'Mother Wilfred says this is only a phase,' I mumbled.

'Tsch – Mother General will soon put her right. We need more brains in the order.'

'Sister Julian!' expostulated the art teacher. She was laughing, but I detected a hint of nervousness. 'God doesn't only call the clever.'

'Of course not,' said the other nun lazily, 'but if they offer themselves . . .'

'I wish you would speak to my mother – and Lorraine,' I said.

'Lorraine O'Shaunessy's a little madam,' said the English teacher. 'You mustn't let her hold you back.'

'She doesn't want to hold me back,' I protested. 'She wants me to go to college with her.'

'College!' Sister Julian smiled. 'You can do better than college, Brigid. How would you like to go to university?'

'It's early days,' put in Sister Monica, looking anxious again. 'First she must go to the Mother House.'

'Ah! the Mother House! Imagine, living in the Languedoc – and next door to the greatest Romanesque cathedral in France.' I'd never seen Sister Julian so animated. 'Do you know what the Romanesque is, Brigid?'

Romanesque – the word made me think of Sister Julian's nose. 'I think I'll like it,' I said.

'Like's not the right word,' she said austerely, 'but you'll certainly have an aesthetic experience – n'est-ce pas, Monica?'

'There's more to the Mother House than its beauty,' said the art mistress, fiddling with the scissors and paste on her desk. 'It's our spiritual home.'

'It was before the Vatican Council,' replied Sister Julian, 'but now those French nuns are out of date. All the new stuff's coming from Holland. This is a good time to become a nun, Brigid – despite the death of Pope John.'

'Oh – if you're talking theology,' said Sister Monica, 'but the Mother House goes back to the Middle Ages.'

'Quite so. And if this new Pope gets his way, it'll stay there.' Yawning, Sister Julian stretched out her arms. 'God knows why the Church is so scared of change, Brigid. It's time we got things moving.' I caught a glimpse of white linen under her cape, and looked away. 'What are you doing there, Monica? One of your collages? How nice.'

'The Bishop wants it by teatime,' explained Sister Monica. 'I must get on.'

'And I must get back to the stock cupboard,' said Sister Julian, rather reluctantly, I thought. 'Come and see me next week, Brigid. Berbiers is rich in legend. I'll tell you about Simon de Montfort, and the sack of the Cathar cathedral.'

'She's very well educated,' said Sister Monica after the door had closed, 'and her mind moves fast. But she expects everyone to think as she does.'

'She gets impatient in class, too,' I said, thinking of the green-grey eyes that turned pale as a hawk's if any girl failed to keep up.

'She's devoted to her subject, and she's right about Berbiers – it *is* beautiful. But the best thing about being a nun is the sense of community.'

We began cutting up milk-bottle tops to make mackerel for the Feeding of the Five Thousand, each fish no bigger than a silver splinter. The winter sun shone down on Sister Monica's pale face as she bent over her work, her neat rows of paints and brushes to hand. There was still a lot to be done.

'Good heavens! Is that the time?' she cried as the chapel bell tolled its four strokes. 'I'm late again, Brigid. Will you tidy up? Thanks, you're an angel.'

Her veil was slightly askew, and I was relieved to see a wisp of dark hair sticking out from the white linen beneath. I still hadn't dared ask her if nuns shaved their heads.

'It'll soon come right with Lorraine,' she promised as she headed towards the door. 'And I'll pray for your mother, too. Remember, if the Good Lord wants you for His own, she'll soon come round to His point of view.'

'When does Mother General arrive?'

'August.'

'That gives me plenty of time to improve,' I called to Sister Monica's retreating back. 'By then I'll be a new person.'

FOUR

———

Late spring gave way to a hot May and June. Soon I had sat my A levels and left school. But the hoped-for transformation in my behaviour was slow in coming. Because Mother Wilfred said it was my duty to stay with Madge for what might well be my last few weeks, I turned down Lorraine's suggestion of a last fling on the Costa Brava. Better to have gone. As the summer yawned on through late July and August, I merely got on my mother's nerves. To escape her radio noise and ever-thickening clouds of cigarette smoke, I would tramp for hours along the deserted promenade.

'Haven't you got anything better to do than mope around Liverpool?' she would demand as I clumped in, my hair sticky from the sea fret. I hadn't. Most of the upper sixth had already found holiday jobs.

Or 'Why can't you make your way in the world,' my mother would say, looking up from her latest love story, 'like I did? Instead of sitting here with your head stuck in the Third Programme.'

'If you call this making your way,' I gestured round the untidy little front room, 'you can keep it.'

'You're a spiteful girl,' replied Madge, her voice thickening. 'I've always done my best for you since your dad pushed off. But you just won't see it.'

I stared at her face, with its watery grey eyes and roughened skin. 'I wish you hadn't bothered,' I declared. 'I hate it here.'

Madge had lost her air of triumph, and now seemed disposed to believe in my vocation, swinging from tears to irritation and back to tears again many times through that long, dark summer.

It was no use trying to tell her how I felt on the inside, I thought, staring at her red eyes and drooping mouth. The prospect of entering a convent was the only thing that kept me going. 'Please, Biddy,' she would say, her face leaking at me, 'don't lock yourself away for life. You're all I've got left.'

The A level results came out in mid-August. Thanks to the help of her new boyfriend, the results of Elisabeth Bavidge, my one-time rival, were nearly as good as mine, and Lorraine's were even better.

My results only gave more ammunition to Madge. 'When I think what I would have done with your chances,' she would remark acidly as I plodded upstairs to bed, cocoa in hand, 'that is – if I'd been lucky enough to have them.'

Sometimes she would tap on my bedroom door on one pretext or another as I sat reading, or saying my rosary. 'Aren't nuns supposed to be happy people?' she would ask in innocent tones, glancing in mock disbelief at my solemn face. The waiting was beginning to get on my nerves.

'I'm not a nun yet.'

'I hardly know what you are any more, Brigid,' she would say as she banged out of the room. Or worse still, she would add, 'I don't know what your Mother General will make of all this.'

With my mother constantly reminding me how much she disliked convents, I hoped she would refuse to see Mother General, rather than destroy my future by some damaging revelation. When the invitation did finally arrive it was, to my surprise, addressed to both her and her brother, David, our only male relative.

My uncle was the opposite of Madge – bachelor-neat, and steady in his opposition to all whims and fancies. He had been appalled when, twenty years earlier, his sister had converted in order to marry an unreliable-looking Londoner. When my dad disappeared and Madge lapsed soon after, he tried to persuade her to take me away from St Cuthbert's. But I wanted to stay with my friends, and Madge didn't want to fork out for a new school uniform.

Despite my insistence on going to mass every Sunday, Uncle David had always remained fond of me. Thinking to cheer me up, he overcame his deep suspicion of priests and nuns, and persuaded Madge to accept.

'It'll be difficult for both of us,' he said to her, fiddling nervously with his tie. He disliked standing up to his outspoken elder sister. 'But it's the least we can do for our Brigid. Can't you see her mind's made up?'

'Hers is,' said my mother, 'but theirs isn't, I'll be bound.'

Mother General was to begin by seeing me on my own. I set out across the park, leaving my uncle giving a final polish to his two-tone Hillman Minx, and Madge staring moodily at the kitchen wallpaper. They were to come by car in half an hour.

Mother Wilfred made no secret of the fact that she didn't like me, so it seemed a bad omen when she met me at the door. 'Too goody-goody by half,' I'd overheard her remark to Sister Bosco, 'and what a family background!'

It was the first time I'd been inside the convent proper, so its silent air, heavy with furniture polish, was new to me. Its layout was the reverse of the high school in the next door semi, so I was troubled by a sense of rooms turned the wrong way round. I followed Mother Wilfred down the corridor into a little parlour where the fifth-form cloakroom should be, half-expecting to find Lorraine backcombing her hair.

'Go on in, child.' Mother Wilfred gave me a little shove.

Mother General was seated by the empty fireplace, her hands clasped on a notebook and black propelling pencil. 'So this is the little Brigid,' she said as I bobbed clumsily in front of her. She pronounced my name in the French fashion, making me think incongruously of Brigitte Bardot.

Mother Wilfred hovered at the door for a few seconds, then disappeared as Mother General gestured me to a seat on the other side of the fireplace. To think I was in the presence of the Head of all the Joubertians! Not quite knowing what to do with my handbag, I jammed it down the side of my chair, and struggled to sit up straight.

She was about the same age as Mother Wilfred, but her blue eyes were dark where Mother Wilfred's were pale, and her manner was gentle, almost motherly. 'Now tell me, my dear,' the old nun began without preamble, 'when were you called to the religious life?'

Encouraged by her voice, which sounded warm and faintly guttural, I stared at her across the hearthrug. Although I wanted to please her more than anything else in the world, my mind remained obstinately blank. What could be the right answer? The day I was born? Two months ago? Or that I still wasn't quite convinced? She smiled encouragingly as the silence grew intense.

'Last year,' I said at random.

Mother General nodded. 'And how did the Good Lord make his will known to you? Through a dream, perhaps? Or a vision?'

'No, Mother.' I shook my head.

'And when did you last have a mystical experience?' pursued the old nun. 'Two months ago? Or was it a fortnight? Or even this morning?'

'I don't think I've ever had one,' I said unhappily.

'No swoonings? Or moments out of time? No messages from Our Lady or signs of the stigmata?'

Again I shook my head, sorry to be such a disappointment.

After pausing to write in her little black notebook, Mother General changed tack. 'And have you ever had a boyfriend?' she asked with a kindly air.

After my dearth of spiritual experiences I tried to be forthcoming. 'Er – yes – I mean no,' I gabbled. 'Nobody I ever liked; that is – not except – for one – who I didn't really have . . . because somebody else . . .' my words trailed away.

'I see,' said Mother General. Aware that our interview was not going well, I prayed that she didn't.

'So how exactly *did* you decide you had a vocation?' the old nun said at length.

I nerved myself to be honest. 'Er – I never wanted to be a nun. It was just that I couldn't – stop thinking about the convent. And all the rest,' I gestured towards the window, 'well, it seems so pointless. Nothing to live for – except God – and doing it all for Him.'

I noticed that Mother General looked paler than when the interview had begun, and her features were drawn. 'Over the years I have learned to mistrust young visionaries with their dreams and forebodings,' she told me in a tired voice, her Polish accent growing more noticeable. 'So arrogant! And so very manipulative! The still, small voice of the Lord is heard oftener in quiet humility than in pseudo-mystical experiences.' The old nun leaned back in her chair and shut her eyes. 'Yours are all the signs of a genuine call,' she pronounced slowly.

So I was being praised for my very ordinariness, the side of me that everyone else had overlooked. If only Lorraine could have heard this.

'You have much to offer the Joubertians,' Mother General went on, ignoring my stupid grin, 'and we, I believe, will prove your spiritual home. It remains now to see your mother.'

As though on cue, Mother Wilfred swung open the door, and there were Madge and Uncle David, clattering awkwardly through the hall.

'Mrs Murray,' smiled Mother General, her air of weariness

vanished. 'How very kind of you to come. And Mr Hedges. You are very welcome.' Rising to her feet, she stretched out a hand.

'Pleased to meet you,' said Madge. Although she liked poking fun at my school elocution lessons, she herself kept a special voice for nuns and social workers. She was wearing a turquoise suit, turban, and white peeptoes bought for the wedding of a distant relative. She thought they made her look like one of the royal family, but the effect was spoiled by her lank hair and dipping hemline. Ignoring my vacated chair, she positioned herself on the far side of the room, her head cocked like a wily old pigeon's. I prayed she would say nothing to change Mother General's mind.

After a glance in my direction, the old nun coughed gently and began to speak, while Mother Wilfred passed round coffee and biscuits. First she acknowledged my mother's generosity in allowing a daughter to dedicate her life to God, assuring her that it was a great blessing to have a child called to be a Bride of Christ. Earthly husbands sometimes took women away from their families only to let them down, or even abandon them altogether. But the Heavenly Bridegroom would never abandon a nun who had given herself to him.

Although Uncle David was obviously still too nervous to risk speaking, he seemed to be overcoming his dislike of nuns, because he began nodding eagerly at everything Mother General said. Madge shot him a disapproving glance, which was intercepted by the old nun. Aware that my mother was proving the greater challenge, Mother General began addressing herself solely to her, going on to say that her own first prayers every morning were for her mother and father at home in Cracow, just as my first prayers would always be for my mother and uncle here in Liverpool.

Madge was manifestly losing concentration. Cramming a second biscuit into her mouth, she began to munch abstractedly while rummaging in her handbag. Mother Wilfred compressed her lips, and glanced at Mother General, who seemed unruffled. I knew Madge was looking for a cigarette, and could only hope she wouldn't find one. But yes, out came a crumpled packet, to be laid on the arm of her chair. When she began slapping her pockets for matches, Mother Wilfred rose to her feet and placed an ashtray out of reach on the sideboard. Madge gave her a look of violent dislike.

Undeterred by the fidgeting, Mother General spoke on. Yes, there were times when my mother and Uncle David would miss me. After my Clothing the following May, when I would receive the Holy Habit, they wouldn't be allowed to visit me for a whole year. I would only have permission to write home once a month, and not at all during Lent and Advent, and when I was on retreat. But good nuns made dutiful daughters. After God and the Joubertians, my mother would have pride of place.

Madge was clearly reluctant to come second to either God or the Joubertians. As Uncle David went on smiling and nodding, she swallowed hard and stared obstinately at a row of begonias outside the window. I glanced at Mother Wilfred, but her blue eyes remained expressionless.

Mother General gave a little shrug. 'Brigid will show you,' she said, 'what a joy it is to be the mother of a nun. Won't you, dear?'

The conspiratorial tone was too much for Madge. Cutting across my reply, her voice trembled with anger. It was the moment I'd been dreading.

'There's a lot you don't know about Brigid,' she said ominously. She had now located a box of matches, and rattled them distractedly.

'Perhaps you will tell me,' murmured Mother General.

'Well ... her temper has hardly improved since she's decided to become a nun,' replied my mother, pretending a reluctance to speak she may not have felt. 'We've had some very unpleasant outbursts over the last few weeks. And she's turned very moody.'

Mother Wilfred cleared her throat, but mercifully Mother General ignored her to gaze steadily at my mother.

'God does not always call the most likeable women to be His Brides – or the most worthy,' pronounced the old woman. 'You will already know, Mrs Murray, that many of us nuns struggle with unfortunate temperaments.' She glanced at Mother Wilfred. 'Soon Brigid will be getting guidance from her novice-mistress. In the meantime, she must pray to Our Dear Lord for the gift of patience.' She gave me a little smile before adding, 'Brigid is a good girl, Mrs Murray – a very good girl. I've heard all about her from Sister Monica.'

But Madge wasn't giving up easily. 'She's my only daughter,' she was quavering to Mother General. 'I can't manage without her.'

Can't find anyone else to clean up the kitchen, more like, I thought, keeping my eyes down.

'Have a word with Mrs Bavidge,' Mother General was telling her. 'The poor woman was heartbroken – but now she has granted her blessing. Elisabeth will prove a source of great joy –'

I was too horrified to worry about being rude. 'Elisabeth Bavidge – from here in Liverpool?' I interrupted, as though there were thousands of Elisabeth Bavidges.

'She wanted to tell you weeks ago,' said Mother General, 'but her mother begged her not to. Now that Mrs Bavidge is reconciled, you are the first to know.'

I was aware of a sick fluttering in my stomach, and the day growing darker and somehow wrong. Elisabeth Bavidge, with her ice-blue eyes, and shiny-straight hair worn like a badge of good breeding.

'Her A levels are nearly as good as yours,' Mother General went on as I struggled to stay calm. 'And her French is excellent. I believe her family has a holiday home near Orléans. And you, Brigid, have a Grade B. That is good, because French is compulsory in the novitiate. Some of our postulants-to-be have to learn it specially.'

My mother sniffed. She had no liking for the Bavidges, so the news confirmed her worst impressions. Elisabeth's father had been a consultant, and Madge had been sent to him just before he died. She found him bossy, and ignored his recommendations on principle.

'A heart surgeon who drops dead,' she'd jeered. 'Good job I didn't stick to *his* diet!'

And now she was pointedly asking Mother General how Mrs Bavidge would manage without her daughter, while I sat with my mind in a whirl. So Jonathon and Elisabeth had split up. If only I'd waited – but no: I had a vocation; and no man who liked Elisabeth would ever turn to me.

Before the old nun could reply to Madge, our attention was drawn to Uncle David, who obviously wanted to speak.

'Is that the young girl we saw in the theatre?' he stammered out.

I nodded. He'd only met Elisabeth the once, when he'd taken my mother and me to see *The Norman Conquests* on Madge's birthday. Elisabeth, lounging in the seat next to him in a minuscule suede skirt and matching thigh boots, had been quick to let us know she'd been given comps.

'A beautiful girl like that, wasting her life,' Uncle David went rushing on. 'Somebody ought to stop her.'

And Elisabeth hadn't even tried to be nice to him. 'You never wanted to stop me . . .' I told him, my voice tailing away in embarrassment as Mother General's gaze switched from him to me.

'The Lord is never outdone in generosity,' the old nun put in. 'He will repay Elisabeth and her dear mother a hundred-fold. Just as he will repay you, Brigid, and you, Mrs Murray.' Her tone made it clear our interview was drawing to an end.

My mother and me, Elisabeth and Mrs Bavidge – two widows and their mites. But what a difference between the mites. With the news of my rival's vocation the importance had drained out of the afternoon. Because Elisabeth was so much more beautiful than me, Mrs Bavidge was that much more generous. My mother, outclassed, knew defeat when she saw it.

'I'm in for a very lonely old age,' she said as we rose to our feet.

Mother Wilfred ushered her rapidly to the door. Glad of the chance to escape, the rest of us followed her out of the parlour. But the old nun drew me aside before I could slide away.

'You think Elisabeth should not be a nun, yes? Because she is a débutante with a French manor house?' she said once the others were out of earshot. 'The Good Lord was a carpenter – but he is not prejudiced – oh no. He chooses girls from all walks of life – rich and poor, pretty and plain – all kinds hear his call.' The old nun chuckled. 'Make no mistake about Elisabeth. Beneath the glamour she is very spiritual.'

So Mother General thought I was jealous of Elisabeth Bavidge – and charity prevented me from telling her that far from being spiritual, Elisabeth would do anything to be noticed – even abandon Jonathon Maule. And instead of leaving her behind, I would be with her all the time – in the refectory, at prayers, in the dormitory at night and first thing in the morning. And everyone would prefer her to me, because she was pretty and sophisticated, and had given up her handsome boyfriend for God. It would be worse than when she got him in the first place.

By the time I escaped from Mother General, my mother and uncle had already reached the car park. Glad to be unobserved, I slipped into the back seat and felt my face slacken after the strain of looking cheerful. As the plane trees flickered past the window, I leant back wearily, trying not to think of my rival.

'What a charming woman!' Uncle David was saying to Madge. 'I have to admit I was wrong about nuns.'

'Charming?' she replied. 'Yes, I suppose she was – if you say so.'

'What do you mean by that, Madge?'

'I mean,' said my mother, 'that those old buzzards are desperate for recruits, and no one can see it but me. Brigid, a good girl! She's too green to know any different. But if she's made up her mind to throw away her life, then that, I suppose, is that. As for me, I want a drink. For God's sake let's stop off at the the Welly.'

'I don't want to go to the pub,' I said to the back of her neck.

'Bloody typical,' said my mother. 'Rigid to the end.' She swivelled round in her seat. 'If you're so sure you're doing the right thing,' she said, 'why won't you celebrate?'

'You can drop me off at the house,' I replied. 'I have other ways of celebrating.'

Before the car had left the street I had run inside, slammed the door and opened the telephone directory. Luckily there was only one Maule. I picked up the phone and dialled. No answer. In case I had a wrong number, I dialled again, imagining a bell shrilling through a deserted hall, ruffling the scent of a pot-pourri, and echoing up the stairs to a first-floor balcony and on into the attic, and a deserted study bedroom.

Still no answer. I'd known long ago he didn't fancy me and never would. But that night I tried his number over and over again – wanting to say goodbye, to round things off, and most of all, wanting to find out why on earth Elisabeth Bavidge was entering a convent – until my mother returned from the Welly at half-past eleven, which put a stop to my attempts.

FIVE

I had fallen in love with Jonathon Maule the year his voice broke. He was at All Hallows, the Catholic boys' school in the city centre. St Cuthbert's took girls who passed the eleven-plus – like Lorraine and me – along with girls who had failed but were too genteel for the secondary modern, and paid school fees. Although respectable, it was far inferior to All Hallows, with its classics masters, rugby matches and Saturday morning school.

Each year All Hallows mounted a Gilbert and Sullivan operetta. To our chagrin, the monks refused to involve us in their productions, so the soprano parts were taken by the junior boys. The year I fell in love it was *Patience*, and Jonathon played Bunthorne. As usual, we girls had saved up our pocket money to suffer each night's performance from a bench in the gallery. Soon we knew all the tunes off by heart:

> And every one will say
> As you walk your mystic way . . .

There was Jonathon, far below in the spotlight, a dashing, dark-haired figure wooing a small boy dressed as a milkmaid. We all wanted to talk to the star performer after the show, but he was surrounded by a bevy of adoring first-form boys, and it was hard to catch his eye. Painfully aware of our sprouting underarms and bulging thighs, we gloomily conceded that Carruthers Minor, clear of complexion and slim of hip, made a prettier Patience than any of us would.

Lorraine put Jonathon's indifference down to snobbery, warning me that he'd have a posh girlfriend tucked away at the tennis club. But I knew he was too intelligent for that. Jonathon was ignoring the prettier girls in my form because he needed a soulmate. If only we could start talking, my lank hair and thick waist wouldn't matter. He was the first boy I'd ever wanted to get to know.

Each night that week I lay awake, devising ways of falling into conversation with him. I soon found out that he lived in Cressington Park, which luckily was at the end of my bus route. Lorraine would have teased me for having a crush, not understanding that for me sex with Jonathon was hardly relevant. I shook her off by pretending I was staying behind to revise, and began hanging around the bus-stop.

Mostly he was engrossed in conversation with Edward, a boy I later knew to be the brother of Elisabeth Bavidge. But once in a while he'd arrive early, and I would turn as though surprised to see him and begin gabbling about anything that might arrest his attention – how much I'd enjoyed his performance, a Beethoven concert on the Third Programme, and, on one disastrous occasion, my deep desire to learn the violin.

For once I had his full attention. 'Then you've no time to lose,' he told me. 'I began at five on a half violin.'

'A half violin?' I'd echoed confusedly. 'How could you play on that?'

He stared back in puzzlement before a smile spread over his features. 'That means a *half-size* violin – not one half of a violin,' he explained kindly. And off he went to his friend at the other end of the queue. A moment or two later they were chuckling together over my *faux pas*.

Undeterred, I found out from another boy that Jonathon liked Sartre, and I pored over the pages of *Being and Nothingness*, trying to dream up questions without understanding half of it. And music – I'd already listened to three Beethoven symphonies, so perhaps we could discuss them . . . Then, grown far too self-conscious for casual conversation, I asked him where he was going to university. Perhaps I could apply to a college in the same town.

'I shall stay here,' he said, gesturing at the Victoria Building. 'Liverpool's a great place to be a student.'

I stared in amazement at the dirty street, while the wind whipped exhaust fumes, dust, and fish and chip papers into a rancid cocktail.

'What a friendly place!' Jonathon was saying enthusiastically, 'and the locals are wonderful.'

'Friendly! Wonderful!' mimicked Lorraine, who had just appeared. 'You haven't met my dad!'

Mr O'Shaunessy, his mouth downturned by years of disapproval, had divided his front bedroom into two malodorous bedsits which he rented to a succession of university students who, like gaudy birds of passage, alighted on the city for three years before fluttering back to their middle-class lives.

'They think they'll find a poet in every pub,' he would say satirically, 'when what they'll find is a puddle of sick. Silly buggers! Call us all la and wack and think they know the locals.'

There were more like him in the Dingle. Far from being friendly and wonderful, they would watch each reckless batch of freshers identify themselves by swinging a university scarf round their necks, only to be set on by a gang of yobs the moment they left the Wellington Vaults.

'Well, I think they're wonderful,' said Jonathon. 'And I'm having a great time already.'

Queueing for the number 86 bus, I would listen to him and Edward planning their evening. The city, which had never opened its doors to me, appeared to them like a giant pleasure dome. A takeaway at Wang's Oriental Supper Bar on the way to the Somali night-club, a late-night ferry across the river, a new production at the studio theatre – everything they did had its glamour.

I longed to be invited, but they never seemed to notice me sitting behind them. Sometimes, in desperation, I would persuade Lorraine to adopt one of their ideas.

'Let's spend the day on the Birkenhead ferry,' I'd say, as though the thought had just struck me. 'Bring your copy of *The Rape of the Lock*.'

Reluctantly she'd agree, and turn up at the right time, and we'd spend the day sitting on the top deck in the sun. She'd roll up the sleeves of her T-shirt and rub in Ambre Solaire, and, when I insisted, even take a turn in reading out loud. Or else I would plan a *fête champêtre* in the Palm House, and we would spend all our pocket money on French bread and *pâté de foie gras*. But these occasions always seemed to fall flat.

'This wine's giving me a headache,' Lorraine would say. Or else the bread would be stale or the sun went in half-way across the Mersey, because Jonathon and Edward had already moved on to something more exciting.

They spent a lot of time planning their lives after graduation. Their ideal society was an Oxbridge college, they told us, and that was where they wanted to end up – as fellows of a place like All Souls. There they would live in the company of their peers – like Roland and Oliver in the *Chansons de Geste*. To me that seemed an odd ambition, but I soon grew reconciled. If Jonathon didn't fancy me, better that he didn't fancy anyone else.

Elisabeth Bavidge didn't appear until the upper sixth. The first thing Lorraine and I noticed at the beginning of the new term was a girl with chiselled features and a shiny bob, lounging across a desk as though she owned the place.

'If Daddy hadn't sent me to such a stupid school,' she was saying to the room at large, 'I would have got decent A levels.'

'Who on earth is that?' I asked, staring in fascination at the skinny legs in their mulberry-coloured tights.

'That,' came the reply, 'is none other than Elisabeth Bavidge – the consultant's daughter.'

She had, it seemed, just returned from finishing school in Lucerne, where she'd failed her A levels with éclat. Now her father, who had recently been appointed to the Royal, was refusing to spend any more money on her education.

At first we all tried to make her feel welcome, resolving not to mock her preposterous accent, her insistence on the fancy, foreign spelling of her name, and her talk of 'Mummy and Daddy'. But far from looking grateful, she spurned our invitations to the Expresso Coffee Bar and the Beverly Hills ballroom.

'Bet you she goes to Ascot,' said Lorraine, 'and thinks she's a cut above the rest. Lah-di-dah!'

I watched Elisabeth saunter out of school in her little black pumps, too unsure of myself to ask what she did at weekends, or where she bought her clothes with their cindery rusts and purples. I too found coffee bars and dance halls boring, but had never dared say so. Then one day she sat down beside me on the bus from the city centre.

'What – Marks & Spencer!' she sang out, glancing at my carrier bag.

I knew already it would look wrong. 'Er – just a pleated skirt,' I stuttered, 'for around the house.'

'You should make more of yourself.' Her eyes narrowed, as though she was painting my portrait. 'If you lost some weight and got an urchin cut you'd be a *jolie laide*.'

'A what?' I stuttered.

'That's French for pretty-ugly.'

Pretty ugly. I turned to stare out of the window, red to the roots of my hair.

Lorraine was not so acquiescent.

'Your skirt is too short,' Elisabeth told her at our end-of-term party. 'Too short and too tight. Why not try something looser – in a plain, dark shade?'

'Why should I dress like you?' my friend said truculently. 'The boys don't like your granny graveclothes, Elisabeth, and I don't blame them. Baggy brown and boring bloody black!'

'Mulberry and ginger,' corrected Elisabeth. 'Haven't you heard of Biba?'

No, it seemed, we hadn't.

'She thinks we're common,' said Lorraine, her beehive nodding angrily. 'Well, let her. Dowdy little snob.'

Nor was Elisabeth liked by the staff. '*Such feeble work*,' proclaimed Sister Julian's italics at the end of Elisabeth's first essay, '*after such an expensive education.*' Sister Bosco banished her outright from maths, and even Sister Monica grew impatient with the newcomer's lazy ways.

So it had never occurred to me that Jonathon Maule would show an interest. Then, one snowy afternoon towards the end of term, I walked down to the city centre after school. As usual I had gone round by his bus-stop, more from habit than from any real hope. Over the last week or two he seemed to have changed his schedule, and Edward was often there alone.

After leaving the bookshop at the top of Bold Street, I paused, feeling tired and lacklustre, to gaze at the carpet of snow in the bombed church. Even though we were about to sit our mocks, I was finding it hard to concentrate. How was I going to read the great tomes in my satchel? Disconsolately I turned into the Kardomah, where I'd arranged to meet Lorraine.

She was nowhere to be seen in the warm, plush-coloured fug, but to my irritation there was Elisabeth in a little alcove. Pretending not to notice her, I crossed to the other side of the café. It was only then that I saw she was with a shaggy, dark-haired boy, sitting with his back to the room. Dismay ran through me like an electric shock. Scanning the menu distractedly, I tried to believe I was wrong – then

Shaggy-hair presented his profile. The high cheekbones, the curved upper lip – there could be no doubt about it. Elisabeth was out to tea with Jonathon Maule.

At that moment Lorraine walked in.

'Look, Bid – there's Bunthorne,' she said.

'I wish you wouldn't call him that.'

'Fascinating,' Lorraine went on. 'He's talking to La Bavidge. And he says he doesn't like girls.'

'He's probably helping her revise.'

'Then why is he holding her hand?'

'I couldn't care less,' I replied quickly. 'And now, would you mind if we placed our order? I want a Russian tea.'

'Cut it out, Bid,' said Lorraine, 'we've been friends for too long. I know why you pretended to work late all last term, and why you made us freeze to death on the Birkenhead ferry, and pose in the Palm House, instead of going to the pictures like we used to.' She admonished me with the menu. 'You're trying not to cry because Jonathon Maule has tapped off with a dingy little snob from finishing school.'

I could feel my cheeks turn the same hue as the surrounding plush. 'You're talking rubbish,' I said huskily. 'He's too bright to bother with her for long.'

'Since when did boys want brains?' asked Lorraine satirically. 'Mine's a cup of filter coffee, please – oh, yes, and a knickerbocker glory.'

I was proved wrong, and Lorraine right, because Jonathon did continue to bother with Elisabeth. From then on they were often seen heading off to revise in the library, or going for a walk in the park. Predictably, Elisabeth's essay marks showed a sudden improvement. Thanks to Mo, Lorraine's little sister, the news that I was going to be a nun leaked out in the spring term, but Jonathon and Elisabeth seemed too absorbed in each other to take much notice.

'At least he can't pass her exams for her,' I said to myself as we huddled on the examination room steps before our French A level. It was a cold June day, with a smell like rotten eggs drifting downriver from the chemical works. Elisabeth's accent was far better than Sister Kevin's, who hadn't been to France since the novitiate, and she'd done well in the oral; but her written work was poor. Even though it was a sin, I hoped she'd fail.

'It's okay for you, wanting to be a nun,' said Lorraine. 'But if I get a low grade, I've had it.'

Elisabeth and Jonathon were standing together near the door, with Jonathon exhorting her in low tones. To my surprise, Elisabeth was looking pale and strained, with dark circles under her eyes. I watched Jonathon give her a kiss on the cheek as the doors opened. 'Thank goodness,' I said to myself, 'I shan't be seeing them again.'

But I did see Elisabeth once more, before the meeting with Mother General. I'd been wandering disconsolately round the city museum, and had taken a short-cut back to the bus-stop through the make-up section of a big department store.

As I passed the Chanel counter a smart woman in a grey suit and lavish eye make-up called me by name. It was a moment before I recognized her.

'Sorry about all the slap,' said Elisabeth with a grimace. 'This is the best job I could get. I promised Mama to pay off my overdraft by D-day.'

D-day? I was too surprised by the sight of this new, friendly Elisabeth to take in more than half of what she said. Why didn't I come home with her and meet her mother? She was just about to stop work, and we may as well, she concluded, learn to be friends.

'If you like,' I replied, bemused by her insistent manner. None of us had ever been invited to the Bavidges' before. A few minutes later she had joined me outside the store, and was steering me towards her bus-stop.

They lived in a large house in the street next to the Maules. Elisabeth led me into what she called the drawing-room, introducing me first to her mother, an elegant woman with eyes as blue as her daughter's; and then to an elder brother called Timothy. Jonathon was there, playing chess with Edward, but apart from volunteering to make a fresh pot of Lapsang Souchong, he said little. All four wore tea-cosies on their heads, though nobody told me why, and I felt too embarrassed to ask. After I'd sat down on the sofa, Timothy explained he'd been living at home since his father died. I remembered that Mr Bavidge had had a heart attack – or was it a coronary? – on his American lecture tour, because Elisabeth had missed a week of school.

My visit was not a success. Edward began to tease Timothy about his new job at the Museum of Natural History, where he was to have special responsibility for the prehistoric mammals. The younger boy put on a record called 'Monster Mash' and Elisabeth whipped a pink plastic model of a dinosaur out of her pocket and made it cavort round the coffee table in time to the tune. I could only surmise that it was their way of coping with grief. Thoroughly out of place, I choked down the smoky brew they'd given me to drink and left with a mumbled excuse.

A few weeks later, Mrs Bavidge sent me an invitation to her daughter's eighteenth birthday party. I didn't want to see Jonathon playing the devoted boyfriend, and decided not to go. Besides, I reasoned with myself, why should I bother to please them, when they didn't like me? And how would I fend off their questions about my future? The Bavidges were just the sort of people to find a vocation funny.

SIX

—

Madge was up before me the day I left for France. I hadn't slept well, spending half the night counting over the things I would need for going abroad – passport, English money, boat ticket, train ticket, French francs. The last three items had come direct from the Mother House, together with a map of Berbiers. Because I'd never been out of England, Mother Wilfred had arranged for me to travel with Elisabeth. We were to meet in the morning at Lime Street station.

I hadn't seen Elisabeth since our meeting in the department store. 'She's gone to the château,' explained Mrs Bavidge over the phone. 'Poor darling – she's making the most of every moment. I'm all on my own for the next fortnight. Why don't you bring your mother round to tea? I'm sure we have oodles to talk about.'

I didn't see Madge in the world of Lapsang Souchong and oodles, so pretended there was too much to do. Since then I'd heard nothing.

By the time I was dressed, Madge was down in the kitchen, prodding two fried eggs with a fish slice. She had put on her smartest slacks, and laid a place for me in our chilly little parlour, where I sat down to eat with my stomach clenched like a fist.

'This'll set you up, Bid,' she said, slapping down a greasy plate. 'Better than paying a fortune on British Rail.'

Knowing it was too late to admit I hated leaving her alone, I tried to fix my mind on the photograph of the late Pope John while shifting a half-chewed lump of bacon fat from one side of my mouth to the other.

'I don't suppose you'll get many breakfasts like this in the convent,' said Madge.

'I don't suppose I will,' I replied, plucking a grey hair out of my beans and forking down the last of the egg. 'No more, thanks, Madge. That was delicious.'

'Don't drop grease on your new suit,' said this new, solicitous mother. I glanced down at the lemon yellow corduroy stretched across my thighs. She had bought it for me only the week before.

'I know it's a waste of money,' she'd told me as she counted out the notes to the sales assistant, 'because you might only wear it the once. But you'd better look chic in France.'

Uncle David was taking us to the station, and when the doorbell rang at nine o'clock prompt I pushed back my chair with relief and ran upstairs. My bedroom wore a subdued but friendly air in the morning light, like an underestimated relative. The pink candlewick bedspread, the bulky old wardrobe – they would be waiting there in the hope of my return. The wardrobe was empty – Lorraine had come round the night before and helped herself to what she wanted for college. Without really forgiving me for going away, she had decided to call a truce.

'I'll have that,' she'd announced, riffling through my clothes with expert hands, 'and that – white T-shirts are always useful. No, not the pleated skirt, thank you very much. It's too long.' The rest of my clothes had been stuffed in the bin along with my A level notes.

For the tenth time I ran through the list sent by the Mistress of Novices. Four pairs of black lace-up shoes; three pairs of corsets; toothbrush, flannel and hairbrush – all stowed away in my suitcase along with my missal, a copy of *The Imitation of Christ*, rosary beads, a statue of Our Lady given me by Sister Monica, and a little crucifix. No other personal possessions were allowed.

Snapping my suitcase shut, I looked round for the last time then hurried downstairs.

'Have you got your passport?' said Madge.

I rummaged once more through my handbag.

'Hurry up, Brigid,' said Uncle David. 'Or you'll miss that train.'

My mother thrust a plastic carrier bag into my hands. 'There are some ham sandwiches in there,' she said, 'and a chicken portion, and half a fruit cake. You never know what you'll get to eat on foreign trains.'

'Come on, Madge, we're late.'

'I'm not coming with you to the station,' she said, her voice starting to quiver. 'I don't think I could bear it.'

The last time I'd see her for years and still the spasm of irritation. Anybody would think it was her sacrifice and not mine. 'Then it's goodbye,' I said, giving her a peck on the cheek. The held-back tears sandpapered my eyes as I walked down the little path.

'Goodbye, Brigid,' called Madge as she peered after me. 'You will write, won't you?'

'As soon as I get permission,' I replied, and with that Uncle David gave a last flick of the duster at an already gleaming windscreen, and we moved off down the street.

As soon as we entered the station I began looking for Elisabeth – but my attention was caught instead by a sturdy figure darting across the platform like a kingfisher.

'Lorraine!' I exclaimed. She was wearing my turquoise sweater dress.

'Hope I'm not in the way,' she said, 'but I thought you might like to see it on me.' She twirled around on a pair of white stilettos. 'I know it looked better on you,' she added, glancing down at her hips.

'You're burning your boats, our Brigid – giving away your clothes like this.' Uncle David was only half joking. 'What'll you do if you leave?'

I remembered Mother Wilfred's warning on my last visit to St Cuthbert's. 'Going in takes courage,' she'd said, 'but coming out takes more. Don't be afraid to leave if you find that you haven't a vocation.'

'Where's Elisabeth?' I changed the subject hastily. Up and down the platform porters were slamming the doors shut. Lorraine maintained a significant silence. Since finding out that Elisabeth was entering the Joubertians too, she had ostentatiously refrained from criticizing her.

'No sign of her,' said my uncle. 'I hope she gets on at Runcorn. You're too young to be travelling alone.'

'Don't be silly – I'm eighteen years old,' I retorted, more brusquely than I meant.

'Let me know if she makes your life a misery,' said Lorraine, 'and I'll come and rescue you. You can even have your dress back.'

'She'll never crack on,' said Uncle David mournfully. 'She's got that look in her eye. She was just the same as a little one – never telling anyone what was up . . .'

'It won't be a misery – and it's time to go,' I said hastily, kissing Uncle David first and then Lorraine. Why ever had I longed to leave home?

'For a clever girl you can be bloody stupid.' Lorraine squeezed my arm as the whistle blew, her eyes moist.

'Goodbye,' I called from the train window, my throat lumpy. 'And thanks for seeing me off.'

I was shaking as the train pulled through the cuttings and the two little figures, one bright, one dark, disappeared from view. Digging my nails into palms running with sweat, I flopped back against the seat, glad to be alone. Feelings don't count, I reminded myself, quoting Mother Wilfred. And if I wasn't looking forward to entering the convent – why then, that was all the more proof I was doing God's will and not my own.

As the train rattled over the rooftops of Penny Lane I

glanced down at a street full of women that God had allowed to be ordinary – taking their children to school, going to the butcher's, deciding what to have for tea. Lucky them, I thought, not to have a vocation. And they don't even realize they're free.

A slice of green between two houses followed by a glimpse of lake across the park, and then St Cuthbert's flickered into view. Down there was the bus-stop where I used to hang around Jonathon. How stupid I'd been. He was out of my class and always would be. As the train sped through the suburbs, I wondered yet again why he and Elisabeth had parted. Perhaps she'd explain on the way down to London. But she failed to appear at Runcorn, and my eyes closed on the Cheshire plain. I hadn't slept for nights, and was oblivious within five minutes.

At Victoria there was still no sign of Elisabeth. While waiting for the boat train I chewed on an undercooked chicken portion, pleased by her non-appearance. By dusk the ferry was gliding across a sea smooth as oil towards the lights of Boulogne, and I was filled with a wild hope that Elisabeth's vocation had been a hoax, an elaborate ruse orchestrated by Mother General to test my determination.

My distress at leaving home had evaporated. If Elisabeth didn't turn up, no one need know I was a cleaner's daughter from the Dingle, and once infatuated with Jonathon Maule. Picturing myself swishing down a sunny cloister, I resisted a pâtisserie from the station buffet and sipped a glass of mineral water instead, while workers in bright blue overalls wandered around the platform. It was gassy, with an after-taste of aspirin, and I wanted to savour every mouthful. This is the real France, I thought with a burst of elation. Elisabeth can keep her silly old château.

I chose a smoking compartment on the night train because it seemed more decadent. Surely such a small act of daring wouldn't endanger my vocation. After all, there were only a few hours to go before the novitiate, and I wanted to make the most of them. As I settled into the frowsty plush opposite a woman with a cat in a wicker basket, I thought of Lorraine and how if she was here now she'd be egging me on to do something mad – like flirting with those Frenchmen in their blue overalls. But that would be going too far, I reflected, reaching for my *Imitation of Christ*. I wanted to enjoy myself – but not too much. I opened my book and began reading.

By Dijon the Frenchwoman was sleeping so soundly that she didn't even stir when three young Americans piled into the apartment, calling to each other volubly. I struggled to keep my face blank, hoping to pass for French. The first two were hippy types – a red-haired man and a dark woman – with matching loons and grubby-looking feet stuffed into moccasins. I couldn't decide whether the second woman was their travelling companion, or had just got dragged into the conversation. Probably the latter, to judge from her crisp shirtwaister and gleaming cap of blonde hair, poles apart from the hippy woman's greasy ringlets.

It was one in the morning when the train rolled out of the station. I pulled up my blind as we clattered through the outskirts of Dijon, to glimpse a furnace lighting up a tiny street, and a man leaning on his bike at a level crossing, before a row of shuttered houses. The three Americans were settling down to sleep, and so should I. Tomorrow was to be the most significant day of my life.

As the train wheels rattled insistently through my mind – don't ever forget, don't ever forget – images from the day kept flickering through my mind: my mother's sad face, Lorraine twirling across the platform, the lights of Boulogne. I pushed them aside and courted sleep.

At first I thought the cat was trying to escape from its basket, but the little animal was curled up peacefully. The noises were too regular for someone having a nightmare, a panting and gasping I couldn't quite place. Anxiously I peered across the gloom.

A brown hand on a white back, two bodies intertwined on the seat – now I knew what was going on. The hippies were snogging, as we called it in school. The muffled grunts, the sighs, the furtive sucking noises – they took me back to the things Lorraine did with her boyfriend, Terry, when he propelled her into a shop doorway after a night at the Beverly Hills. Now the man was unzipping the woman's jeans and trying to slide them over her hips. I could even see the cleft of her bottom. At an especially loud moan I stirred in my seat and cleared my throat.

For a moment the couple lay still, while I located my rosary beads and began fingering the first decade. When they resumed their moaning and panting, I glanced across at my fellow passengers. The Frenchwoman still appeared to be sleeping soundly, and, as far as I could see, the American in the shirtwaister was staring straight ahead, although the other woman's feet were by now dangerously close to her thigh. It wasn't that I minded people kissing, I reasoned with myself, trying to emulate the blonde woman's composure. It was just that sex should be a private matter, not an uncontrolled fumble in a railway compartment.

No longer able to concentrate on my rosary, I turned my attention to the sun coming up over the empty fields, until the pair fell fast asleep somewhere south of Orange. Too tired to care whether I slept or not, I gazed at their unconscious forms in the dawn light. With their shaggy manes and tangled legs they looked young and innocent as twin foals. I began to feel more kindly towards them, and wondered what it was like to be carried away. Perhaps the girl was to blame. In school Sister Bosco had told us that boys had a stronger sex drive than girls, so it was our responsibility to stop them.

Besides, Sister Bosco had added, her cheeks a brighter

shade of puce, any sin against chastity was a mortal sin. That meant that with every impure deed – or even an impure thought – we risked an eternity in hell. This had worried me. Once a boy had put his hand inside my bra, pinching the flesh hard before caressing the nipple. That night I'd lain awake for hours, unable to stop myself touching my breast the way he had, while knowing that what I was doing was just as much a mortal sin as going all the way. The next morning I had crossed the road with extra care. If I was run over by a bus or dropped down a manhole I risked eternal damnation – unless I contrived to make a sincere act of contrition before I died. In chemistry I handled the Bunsen burners with extra caution. The next lesson was in the gym, where I refused point blank to climb the wall bars. Suddenly the whole timetable seemed fraught with hazard. By four o'clock I could stand no more. I had to go to confession. `

I had awaited my turn in the parish church, half-aware of Father Gorman's intermittent drone from the confessional, and the occasional raised voice of a penitent. On the days when he forgot to switch on his hearing-aid you had to shout quite loudly. In no time at all I was pulling the curtain behind me. 'Bless me Father for I have sinned . . .' I muttered, then proceeded with a few makeweight items to camouflage the real one: I answered my mother back twice, I swore three times, I cheated in a chemistry test. Father Gorman murmured softly after each admission, as though in approval. Soon I had run out of other sins. 'And,' I raced on, 'I've committed a sin against purity.'

The old man's head bobbed up on the far side of the grille.

'What was that you said, child?'

'I've committed a sin against purity,' I muttered.

'I can't hear you. For the Lord's sake, speak up,' piped the priest.

'I'VE COMMITTED A SIN AGAINST PURITY.' Everyone in the church would know by now.

'And what sort of sin was that?' he wheezed.

I'd been counting on his accepting the fact in silence. 'I – I touched myself,' I stuttered out.

'Where, child?'

'In bed, Father.'

'I meant, whereabouts on your body?' the old man rasped back.

'On the breasts – while I – er, thought about my boyfriend.'

'And were you alone when you did this?'

'Yes, Father,' I replied, wondering who on earth would do such a thing with someone else.

Mercifully, he seemed satisfied. 'Go and beg forgiveness of Our Blessed Lady, Virgin most pure and mother of all the faithful,' he droned. It was his standard form of absolution. He ended by giving me three more Hail Marys than usual, and I stumbled back to my pew vowing never to think about sex again. Better to go to hell than to confession.

The couple opposite stirred. In the rosy morning light I could see her hand move up the purple-clad thigh, coming to rest lightly in the fork between his legs. I turned my attention to the fields outside the window, where sunburnt labourers were climbing down from a trailer. We had reached the Midi, where the grape harvest had begun. Grappling for the rosary in my handbag, I forced myself to pray.

SEVEN

I didn't open my eyes until the train pulled into Berbiers. All around me was the chatter of French voices, quite unintelligible after the careful conjugations of Sister Kevin. Dogs barked and babies squalled as the passengers queued to leave the train. It was the end of the line.

The blonde American was still asleep, her hands folded over her paperback. Rubbing my eyes, I glanced at my watch. Nine o'clock in the morning. I must have fallen into a doze instead of saying my rosary. The Frenchwoman scooped up her cat basket and jumped off while the hippies were yawning and stretching. I checked my suitcase was locked tight before dragging it from the rack, not wanting all those black shoes to come tumbling out. Not that anyone would ever guess what they were for, I thought, pushing my way off the train.

A flight of pigeons was wheeling and dipping in the pale green air of the roof. I had made it to Berbiers, and was ready to get the most out of my last hour and a half in the world. Glancing round once more for Elisabeth, I crossed the platform and stepped out into the morning.

It was like opening the door of an oven. This was nothing like the warmth of an English September, this was the hot south, beating on the pavement and throbbing in front of the shops and cafés. The garish yellow of my corduroy suit, so cheerful in the English afternoon where it was bought, was beginning to attract curious glances, and soon I was sweating profusely. Within everyone else in shorts and T-shirts, it felt like fancy dress.

I paused under a plane tree to take off my jacket and

consult the map. Yes, this was the Place Jean Moulin and the convent was only five minutes away through that little maze of streets; there was the dome of the cathedral poking up above the rooftops. I would locate it first, and then I might have time for a cup of coffee. Fixing my eyes on the big bronze dome, I plunged down the nearest alleyway.

The houses were smaller and darker than any I'd seen in the Dingle. Washing hung in rows overhead, and women were calling from first-floor windows to their friends down in the street. '*T'as pris ton pain ce matin?*' Some fell silent as I passed, but others carried on talking in twanging, nasal tones. Feeling dwarfed by the medieval façades, I clumped down one alley and then another, glancing at window-sills bedecked with geraniums and the rooms beyond, often empty apart from a stove, bed and chest of drawers.

Disoriented by the maze of tiny streets, I was about to try and retrace my steps to the Place Jean Moulin for another look at the map when I saw the cathedral rise up ahead of me, its dome gleaming. And that must be the convent, huddled in its shadow. Before I left Liverpool, Sister Julian had explained how the cathedral of St Cyprien had been built on the site of a Roman temple, a Celto-Hibernian church, and a medieval cathedral razed to the ground by Simon de Montfort. Dutifully I read a plaque commemorating the fifteen thousand murdered Cathars, and stared up at the windowless, rose-red brick.

Reluctant to enter the dusky interior on such a bright morning, I wandered round the east end to a bluff overlooking the river. Over to my right was a high wall, with trees visible over the top, which I knew from Sister Julian surrounded the convent park. Beyond it the Languedoc was spread out in the sun, mile after mile of vineyards, with straggling bands of pickers bent over the symmetrical green rows, and in the distance rocky white mountains, with here and there a cross glinting on a summit.

A sudden wave of exhaustion swept over me. Glancing at my watch, I saw there was only half an hour to go – I must have spent longer than I thought in the old town. In front of the cathedral was a little café, Au Pavillon d'Algers, its tables spread in the shade of a horse-chestnut. Before ordering a coffee I plunged into the next door tabac and chose two postcards, one of the cathedral for my mother and a street scene for Lorraine. '*Et un pacquet de Gauloises, s'il vous plaît, Madame,*' I heard myself say. Me, buying cigarettes! I must remember to tell Madge.

Soon I was washing down the hot breath of nicotine with an espresso so strong it made my ears roar and my stomach clench in a griping pain. The woman at the next table was drinking brandy, used by Madge for medicinal purposes. I summoned the waiter again, and when my drink arrived, downed it in one gulp. Feeling muzzier than ever, I left the last of my francs in a little pile on the table, and made my way to the toilet at the back of the café.

There was no sign on the door itself. Not knowing how to ask the waiter if this was the ladies' or the gents', I pushed my way inside.

I must have entered the wrong one – but there seemed to be no other. There was one large hole in the ground and two small platforms either side. The door didn't have a lock. What if a man came in as I straddled the stinking hole?

Embarrassed at my mistake, I darted out of the café. There was an iron pincer at my right temple and my feet felt preternaturally large, as though they had sprouted platform soles. Perhaps if I arrived early the nuns would let me lie down for a few minutes. Gripping the handle of my suitcase, I made my way across the square. The sun was bouncing on the cobbles to deliquesce in pools of yellow sherbet. As I stood on the kerb waiting for a break in the traffic my stomach began to churn at the stench from a nearby drain. Suddenly I was floating in a cassoulet of Berbiers, swirling with garlic, coffee, cognac, the smell of urine, and the dirty reek of nicotine forcing its way up through my lungs. I felt an urgent need to retch and the pressure on my bladder was intense. As I stared at the face of my watch the pavement pulsated into points of light before sweeping up to swipe me in the face.

'Brigid! Brigid!' The finishing-school vowels drilled into the pit where I was lying and dragged me back to reality. Reluctantly I opened my eyes on a tanned face close to mine.

'Elisabeth! Where have you been?' I gasped, torn between dismay and relief.

'I stayed on at the château – and Mummy came out to join me. Sorry to have left you in the lurch.'

'I seem to have fainted,' I mumbled. 'The sun . . . no breakfast.' Of all people to come to my rescue.

'The door's over here,' she said, helping me to my feet. 'Mummy had just dropped me off when you keeled over.' She started to dust me down. 'Goodness, what a smart suit.'

'Thanks,' I replied, feeling hopelessly overdressed by comparison with Elisabeth in her denim jeans and striped blue T-shirt. 'You won't tell anyone what happened?'

'Of course not,' she replied, brushing the hair from my eyes and producing a mirror and comb. Her breath smelt of garlic, and her perfume was so dark it was almost feral.

I held her little mirror to my face, pasty in the heat, with a dribble of spit down the right side of my mouth. Hastily I licked my handkerchief and wiped it away.

'We're a little late,' Elisabeth went on, steering me through the traffic, 'so we'd better get a move on. I say, why didn't you come to my party? I was going to make it a joint announcement. If other girls have a coming-out party, why shouldn't we have had a going-in party?' she grinned.

I nodded without following her drift.

'You're still looking a bit peaky,' she said. 'Lean on me and we'll soon be there.'

We made our way through the big double doors opening on to the street, and across a cobbled courtyard. The front door opened as if by magic, and there stood a stocky little nun at the top of the steps. 'Hurry up, *mesdemoiselles*,' she called out, 'you have already missed the address of Monsieur l'Aumônier.'

'We'll hear him again, I dare say,' whispered Elisabeth in my ear. Clucking, the portress ushered us inside, and slammed the door behind us.

Inside the front hall were twenty or more young women, mostly chattering with their relatives in small groups. Everyone seemed more vivid and excitable than me, with eager faces and glowing skin. Some were dressed, like Elisabeth, in jeans and T-shirt – others in flowery summer dresses. Already they looked at home in these austere surroundings, and not at all worried, as I would have been, about what their parents might say or do next. Even those on the verge of tears seemed unembarrassed, as though crying was a natural thing to do.

Their families, too, were making the most of the ritual parting. Fashionably dressed mothers were plying their daughters with last-minute gifts, or hugging them convulsively while the fathers stood to one side, exchanging jokes. Everyone seemed to be acquainted. Feeling more out of place than ever, I followed Elisabeth through the babel of French, German, and was that Portuguese or Spanish? As though by instinct, she stopped in front of a nun with grey eyes and a sallow face, who was talking animatedly to a dapper little priest in a cassock.

'Excuse me,' Elisabeth interrupted her, 'we have arrived a little late, after a long journey. Is there any chance of a coffee?'

I stood back a little to dissociate myself from such brash behaviour.

Turning, the nun turned looked us both up and down,

Elisabeth with her rucksack slung casually over one shoulder, and me wiping the beads of sweat from my face with a paper tissue. Before we could introduce ourselves, the nun said with a faint air of amusement, 'No, this is not a café. *La petite Elisabeth* must wait until lunchtime.' The grey eyes sparkled. 'Ah yes,' she went on, 'I know who you are. The chic Elisabeth Bavidge, and her friend Brigid Murray – who is a little shy, and a little homesick, I see.' She struck our names from a list.

I could barely follow what she said, let alone reply. 'Er – *oui – mais –*'

'And where are your parents?' she asked.

'Mummy can't bear saying goodbye,' said Elisabeth in French, 'so she dropped me off outside. And Brigid's mother stayed in Liverpool.'

'So you came unchaperoned?' The little woman turned her gaze on me as I nodded my head. 'You English – so calm and independent. And now that independence must be surrendered, yes?' Elisabeth nodded. 'I am your novice-mistress, Mother Chantal. You will call me Mère-Maîtresse. Mother-Mistress, you would say in English.'

'No, we wouldn't,' whispered Elisabeth in my ear. Ignoring her, Mère-Maîtresse summoned a bespectacled novice in her forties. 'This is Sister Bon Pasteur, the Senior Novice. As the oldest of her year, she acts as my assistant. In a few moments we will show you to the dormitory, where your postulants' dresses are waiting on your beds. Coffee will come later.'

Before I could follow Sister Bon Pasteur and Elisabeth towards the stairs, a cheerful American voice rang in my ear. 'Hi there! Do you remember me?'

I turned to see the neat blonde woman in the shirtwaister.

'Eleanor Chase,' she said, extending her hand.

'My name is Brigid Murray,' I replied, 'I'm English.'

'I thought so.'

'Actually, I was trying to catch your eye on the train.'

'Why was that?'

'Well . . . that couple on the seat beside you – did you see what they were doing?'

'You mean Scott and Mary Lou?' replied Eleanor. 'Sure. It was their last night together.'

'Their last night? You mean that she's also . . .?'

'Mary Lou's my cousin. What a character! She vowed to be a nun at nine years old – then persuaded me to join her! We came down together. Hi! Mary Lou! Come over here, will you?'

The dark woman with the greasy curls made her way from where she was talking to Elisabeth by the big stone fireplace.

'My God, you reek of smoke and liquor,' she said in a heavy drawl, worlds apart from her cousin's rapid delivery. 'What a relief. We had you down as a real stiff.'

'And I thought I was anonymous.'

'Not in that suit, honey,' she said, the bells on her smock jangling as she moved. 'We knew where you were headed.'

'My mother said I should wear classic clothes,' I explained awkwardly. 'She thinks – or rather hopes – that some day I'll come to my senses and leave. And my suit will – would – still be in fashion.'

'Fashion!' chorused the two Americans and burst out laughing.

To my relief, Mère-Maîtresse was signalling for us to join the queue of nervous newcomers in her wake as she led the way to the dormitory. Soon I was standing by my bed, unbuttoning the embarrassing suit for the very last time, as the other young women were divesting themselves of jeans, dirndls and mini-skirts, of tartan and denim and broderie anglaise, all to be borne by Sister Céline, the portress, to the linen-room, where they would hang, explained Sister Bon Pasteur, until the day we died.

By every bed stood a novice, waiting to show us how to wear our postulant's garb. I peeled off stockings damp with sweat, and struggled into my corset, and a pair of knickers so large they could only be called bloomers. Then I clawed my clumpy black shoes out of my case, glad that the novice was averting her eyes, and thus unlikely to notice the crumpled packet of cigarettes underneath. Finally, I pulled my postulant's dress of brown serge over my undeodorized body, and the novice, smelling faintly of starch, showed me how to drape the *pèlerine* or light cape over my shoulders, and tie the little veil behind my head.

When we were all dressed, Mère-Maîtresse announced that it was time for chapel.

'Can't we bathe first?' came an anxious American voice.

'You will wash before going to bed.' Mère-Maîtresse indicated the row of basins at the top of the dormitory. 'Bathday only comes round once a week – for you it will be Thursdays.'

The American groaned out loud. Shocked, I turned round to see who it was. Yes, it was Mary Lou, who looked as though she only washed once a year. I scrutinized Mère-Maîtresse's face to see what she thought of such behaviour, but it was impossible to tell.

'We have half an hour between now and lunch. You may thank the Good Lord for your safe arrival in Berbiers,' she continued, 'and then you can examine your consciences in His presence.'

I flopped into a pew, feeling ragged, nauseous, and – yes, Mère-Maîtresse was right – a little homesick. How dare Eleanor and Mary Lou laugh at the suit my mother had saved up for weeks to buy? This was not the new beginning of my Liverpool dreams. My fingers still smelled disgustingly of tobacco, and my veil, tied too tight by the novice, had turned into a glowing band round my temples. Worse still, Elisabeth Bavidge had a vocation after all, and was kneeling at my side.

Her eyes were shut, the lashes dark against the thin, tanned cheek. Why, out of all the schools in Liverpool, had her father chosen St Cuthbert's? For months she had sat in the same classroom as me, and listened to the same teachers. And after falling, like me, for Jonathon Maule, she too had to be a Joubertian! Now that she was in my life for another two years at least, any further struggle to avoid her seemed not only pointless, but against God's will. Closing my eyes again, I prayed for the grace to accept His plan.

Perhaps she would keep her word, and say nothing about my collapse in the street, and be discreet about my ramshackle mother, my absentee father, and my infatuation for Jonathon Maule. Pressing my palms against my throbbing temples, I glanced covertly at the motionless figure beside me, and tried hard to feel convinced.

EIGHT

—

After chapel, Mère-Maîtresse led us to the refectory, a long room with a tiled floor and wooden table with benches either side. Unsure about what to do next, we straggled after her. Ahead of me a French girl was crying unashamedly into her handkerchief. I had noticed her in the front hall – and felt sympathetic because, like me, she looked awkward and out of place, with her round face and little girl's pinafore dress. 'I'll never stand it – I know I'll never stand it,' she had sobbed, clinging to a father even shorter and stockier than she was. 'I want to go back to Boujac.'

'She'll have us all started in a minute,' muttered Mary Lou while we waited to say grace. Already her postulant's veil had slipped down over her forehead, making her look like a young Apache.

'Your places have been allocated in order of age,' explained Mère-Maîtresse. 'Jütta Schmidt and Fatima Alves are the two youngest, yes? You will sit on my right and left hand. Next are Theresa O'Mahoney and Nathalie Lim Kee. Brigid Murray, you will sit between Elisabeth Bavidge and Eleanor Chase. And you four will go down to the bottom.'

The snivelling French girl was joined by three others at the foot of the table – two Irish, and one Portuguese.

'Why do they have to sit down there?' asked Eleanor.

'Those are the lay postulants,' explained Sister Bon Pasteur. 'That means they are not educated, and unlike us choir nuns would find it difficult to read Latin or train as teachers. They usually come from peasant families.' Eleanor opened her mouth to protest, but Sister Bon Pasteur carried on smoothly. 'They will soon be joined by the lay novices –

and the choir novices will fill up the gaps.' They filed in as she spoke, habits swishing, to take up their places in silence. With their downcast eyes and white veils, they were impossible to tell apart. Involuntarily, we straightened our backs – apart from the little lay postulant, who was blowing her nose into a large white handkerchief.

'Quiet – Mère-Maîtresse is waiting to speak,' Sister Bon Pasteur hissed at her.

'Meals are usually taken in silence,' explained the novice-mistress, 'but today I will give you Benedicamus – so the novices can show you what to do.'

'Benedicamus? What on earth is that?' asked Mavis Sterne, a middle-aged New Zealander with a tight perm.

'*Benedicamus domino.* Let us bless the Lord. That's how Mère-Maîtresse gives us permission to talk,' explained Sister Bon Pasteur, her gravel-coloured eyes glinting behind her bifocals. 'We answer *Deo gratias.* Thanks be to God. It's quite a treat.'

After grace we were told to feel in the small locker by our place under the table top. In it was a knife, fork and spoon, already engraved with our initials. Beside them was a white linen table napkin and a small tea towel, with our name tags sewn on. Two of the novices were placing a tomato the size of a melon on our platters.

'I'm starving,' Mary Lou broke the silence. 'Hi, Elisabeth! Snag me a piece of bread, will you?'

Elisabeth was just about to comply, when another novice, shorter and plumper than Sister Bon Pasteur, cut in. 'Please – it is forbidden to ask for food. You must wait to be offered.'

The American glowered at her. 'But what if no one knows you're hungry?'

'You may proffer the dish to your sister – so. Then she offers it to you in return.'

'What if she doesn't feel like it?' asked Elisabeth, waving the dish just out of Mary Lou's reach.

'I guess you kick her under the table,' said Mary Lou.

'Certainly not,' replied the plump novice. 'If you fail to attract a sister's notice by attending to her needs, then you must remain hungry. We in the Mother House try never to leave the table without an act of mortification.'

'Well, we can speak today,' said Mary Lou truculently, 'and I'm going to get a hunk of that bread. Hey, Elisabeth!'

I remained silent while Elisabeth and Mary Lou wrestled over a long white loaf, pleased they were making such a bad impression. The refectarians were pouring us each a glass of wine – from the convent vineyard, explained a thin novice with a shy laugh – last year's vintage.

'But I've taken the pledge,' wailed an Irish girl, pointing to the jubilee pin in her cape. The thin novice nodded sympathetically, and I wondered if I too should declare a hatred for alcohol.

'Then you must untake it,' said Mère-Maîtresse from the top of the table. She seemed to have an uncanny knack of overhearing our remarks to one another, even when they were in English. 'Otherwise you break the Rule by being singular.'

I hastily raised my glass and took a gulp. The peppery red liquid coursed down the back of my throat, washing away the rancid taste of tobacco, and making my eyes water. Soon I would be drinking more than my mother. Apprehensively I watched the refectarians dispensing cuts of dark brown meat – two to each plate – except for the lay sisters, who were given four. Opposite me, Elisabeth was dousing her neatly sliced tomato in olive oil. Catching my eye, she asked if I felt better. I nodded hastily, and before she could continue turned to Mary Lou, who was staring gloomily at the next course. 'What the hell is this?' she asked, stabbing at it with her knife. 'Some kind of beef?'

'Horsemeat, I imagine,' replied Elisabeth, chewing unconcernedly. 'The van came this morning.'

'You're pulling my leg!' shrieked Mary Lou, dropping her fork. 'Mère-Maîtresse, tell me it's not possible!'

The novice-mistress glanced down the table. 'All this concern over food is not seemly,' she chided. 'Elisabeth, will you please stop making mischief?'

'We don't eat horses in Texas,' expostulated Mary Lou. 'We ride them.'

'Horses do not have immortal souls,' said Sister Bon Pasteur. 'We may eat them if we wish.'

'It's no worse than eating bird – or pig,' remarked Eleanor.

Unconvinced, Mary Lou pushed the meat to the side of her plate and began to pick at a lettuce leaf. The salad was served separately, and for pudding we helped ourselves to apples and grapes. I wondered how Madge would have managed, with her aversion to fruit and vegetables. Instead of lettuce, the lay sisters were given a large pile of pasta, which they ate hungrily before mopping their plates with hunks of bread. Their table manners were not good. I was glad to have passed my A levels – or I too would be shovelling down stodge at the bottom of the table, with nothing ahead but work in a convent kitchen.

'What wouldn't I give for a doggy bag,' said Mary Lou.

'Doggy bag? What is that, please?' said a German voice.

'It's for left-overs –'

'We wash up at table,' Sister Bon Pasteur cut short the American's reply. 'During dessert, the refectarians bring us big jugs of hot water. First you fill your tumbler – putting a fork in, so that it doesn't crack. That's right, Brigid. After washing and drying our cutlery – using our individual tea towels – we pour the water on to our platter, swirl it round and then tip it into one of those large enamel basins.'

'Where's the washing-up liquid?' asked Mavis.

'Your platter is for your use only – so it is not necessary.'

'At home we had a dishwasher,' said Franny, a Californian blonde.

'So did we,' said Eleanor. 'More hygienic.'

'These postulants!' said Sister Bon Pasteur to one of her fellow novices. 'So very full of themselves.'

I thought of our kitchen in Moses Street, with the washing-up teetering on the draining-board and the smell of damp, and was glad to see these rich and confident new-comers rebuked.

The plump one nodded. 'We know better than to question these things,' she said. 'If you want to be a nun, you must do as you are told.'

Choking down the last piece of horsemeat, I carefully wiped my lips.

'Please do not get grease on your napkin,' said Sister Bon Pasteur. 'You must now wrap it round your knife and fork.'

'Sorry, Sister,' I said meekly.

'Please – it is not necessary to say "Sister" all the time,' said the thin novice kindly, 'only on formal occasions – or when there are lay people present – or as a mark of respect to older religious.'

Embarrassed to have forgotten her name already, I nodded dumbly. 'You will soon get used to the ways of the Mother House,' she went on with a shy smile. 'After lunch Mère-Maîtresse will show you round, and you will see for your-selves how beautiful it is.'

'I'd rather sit and talk,' said Frannie. I disagreed, glad when the meal and its pointless chatter was over. The novices had two hours' silent study stretching ahead. The sooner we began following their timetable, the better, I reflected, as we clumped out of the refectory after grace, the unaccustomed length of our postulants' dresses flapping against our calves.

'In the novitiate we live apart from the professed nuns,' explained Mère-Maîtresse, 'in one wing of the main court-yard. It is forbidden to leave it without permission. I'll begin by showing you the novitiate room.'

She glided off down the cloister, her hands tucked inside her sleeves and her eyes downcast, looking as though she'd been born here. We followed her through a pair of double doors into a high room with rows of oak desks reflected in a polished floor.

'Normally this is a place for silent study – except when it's raining. Then we use it for recreation.'

'You mean you *relax* in here?' Frannie burst out, gazing incredulously at the bare white walls.

'In winter we push back the desks and dance to get warm.' Mère-Maîtresse gestured to an old gramophone in the far corner, where Mary Lou was already riffling through a pile of 78s in shabby cardboard sleeves.

'Folk music!' Mary Lou exclaimed to Eleanor in disgust, then wandered across to Frannie, who was staring gloomily out of the window at a square of white dust.

'These Americans!' whispered Jütta. 'They should stick to their Hiltons and their doggy bags.'

I nodded, wondering if Mère-Maîtresse was going to utter a rebuke – but all she did was say mildly, 'You'll find you enjoy recreation. You can talk – or stroll – or garden – or sew.'

I followed close on her heels as she led us out of the room and across the courtyard to a little doorway. Stooping slightly, we plunged down a steep flight of steps into a cool stone corridor.

'We are now in a tunnel under the main road,' Mère-Maîtresse explained as a car roared overhead, 'and about to enter the most beautiful part of our grounds . . . the convent park!' She paused dramatically at the top of another flight of stone steps.

Even Elisabeth seemed impressed by the sunlit expanse dissected by gravel alleys. 'Oleanders!' she exclaimed, waving at a riot of pink and red blooms. 'Mummy's tried to grow them for years.'

'In fine weather we come here for recreation,' explained Mère-Maîtresse, leading us down the central alley to a point where the wall had crumbled away. Sloping off to the right was the convent vegetable garden, where a gardener was assiduously hoeing a row of beans. Then there was a sharp drop to the river below, and rising up across the little gorge the cathedral ramparts I had visited just six hours ago. The shadows were lengthening in the vineyards beneath as the stubby little tractors roared into life after the siesta.

Behind us the Americans were still grumbling – this time joined by Elisabeth and an English-speaking Frenchwoman. Some Brazilian and Portuguese women were jabbering at each other about the view, and in the middle Jütta Schmidt was haranguing the tall Austrian who had arrived in a dirndl.

'Sisters! Sisters!' exclaimed Mère-Maîtresse. 'Remember – French is the native tongue of our Mother Foundress. To speak anything else is to break our Holy Rule.'

'What's she on about?' Mary Lou asked Eleanor.

'In French, please,' interrupted Mère-Maîtresse. 'You were told to learn the language before you came.'

'But I didn't have time!' grumbled Mary Lou when Eleanor translated. 'I was working as a cocktail waitress.'

'You have plenty of time now,' replied Mère-Maîtresse, in French. 'No, Eleanor, please do not translate. Mary Lou must learn the virtue of obedience.'

'I've backpacked my way round the whole goddam world,' muttered Mary Lou as we paused to admire an acacia grove, 'and never needed one word of a foreign language.' But you do in Berbiers, I thought to myself, pleased at her discomfiture.

My clumsy black shoes were pinching my toes as we made our way back to the convent, and the half-chewed meat lay heavily on my stomach. Although I hated the thought of the dormitory, with its twin rows of beds in hospital white, I was longing to lie down and close my eyes.

Instead, trying to conceal a yawn, I listened to a girl from Donegal with shadows under her eyes and a drawn face. She explained over supper in her halting French that she had been *en route* for two days. It had been her first train journey, and she hadn't dared sleep a wink.

We were sent upstairs mercifully early, after a brief visit to chapel. Sister Bon Pasteur motioned me to the same pew as this morning – third row from the front, on the right-hand side. This would be my place for the whole novitiate. To my left Elisabeth once again knelt motionless – every inch the model postulant. Trying to ignore the fidgeting of Mary Lou on my other side, I stared at the flickering sanctuary lamp and struggled to gather my thoughts into a final act of thanksgiving.

Upstairs I undressed with due modesty, as instructed by the senior novice, and hung my new garb on a hook by my bed. Too shy to wash properly at the row of basins, I ignored the tang of sweat from under my arms and between my legs, and slid quickly between the cool white sheets.

From the other side of the dormitory came a clatter, followed by muffled laughter. I made the sign of the cross, and focused my mind on the Four Last Things: Death, Judgement, Heaven and Hell. I must be sure in the future to have nothing to do with those Americans. When Mère-Maîtresse reprimanded them – as soon she must – I didn't want to be compromised.

After lights out I sensed rather than saw the senior novice move silently down the dormitory to open the shutters. I thought of Lorraine and Uncle David on the platform at Lime Street, half a world away.

And my mother – was she missing me? or already ensconced in the Welly, drinking to my departure? After the sun, the wine and the long journey, nothing was going to keep me awake. Dimly aware that somebody was crying three beds down, I turned on to my side and fell asleep.

NINE

While knowing that pride came before a fall, I couldn't help feeling pleased about the way I adapted to novitiate life, not going home at the end of the first week like the girl in the dirndl, nor mocked by the senior novice for crying myself to sleep every night, like Lucie Péreyre.

Secure in my new knowledge that every second had a purpose, I soon learned to love the long, orderly days. For me it was no sacrifice to rise at the first stroke of the bell, wash in cold water and, with no worries about what to wear, don my brown serge dress while murmuring the prayers led by the senior novice. Unlike the other postulants, I never bemoaned the lack of mirrors. I liked not being reminded of my thin hair and plain face. I didn't even mind Fridays, when we would kneel at our bedside to use the little discipline of knotted rope, firmly enough to sting the back and legs, but not so hard as to make a mark.

Far from finding the rooms impersonal and under-furnished, I relished their clean surfaces and lack of clutter, so different from Moses Street. I began practising custody of the eyes, and would mortify my curiosity by looking down-wards as I crossed the courtyard, instead of allowing my gaze to rove around the tops of the plane trees to the blue sky beyond. I studied each door handle to learn how to turn it silently, and learned to greet a fellow postulant not with 'Hi!' or 'Hello!' but with the words '*Vive le Seigneur*', to which she would answer '*Que son nom soit béni*' – blessed be His name.

I now knew never to call out a sister's name during silence, but to attract her attention with a gentle tug of her sleeve; to walk with my hands tucked in my sleeves; to stand up and apologize if I dropped my cutlery; and to drop to my knees and kiss the floor if I was late to chapel or the refectory. And I soon adopted the Berbiers practice of making, unknown to anyone else, an act of mortification before the end of every meal. If we had horsemeat or garlic or snails it was easy – I simply offered the dish to my neighbour and then, when she proffered it in return, accepted a second helping. And if there was nothing on the table I disliked, I, who hated sugar, could always stir three spoon-fuls into my coffee.

These little acts of mortification, which I'd so dreaded before entering the novitiate, were not, I now saw, ends in themselves, but ways of leading me to God. It now seemed incredible that anyone could dread having a vocation. My new life was far, far superior to anything I'd ever known before. 'All this and heaven too,' I would think in the early morning, gazing around the sunlit park as we settled down for recreation. When I was a schoolgirl my relationship with God had been tumultuous, a matter of furtive prayers in my bedroom and secret visits to chapel. Now the time for adolescent outpourings was past. I was no longer a gushing young girl, but one who aspired to become a Bride of Christ and understand the holy observances of His house.

At times His presence seemed almost physical – a gentle, approving gaze as I churned the butter, or watered the flowers in the novitiate garden, or, strongest of all, when I poured out my heart to Him in chapel, knowing He surpassed any earthly lover, and thanking Him every day for the blessing of a religious vocation.

My mother wrote at surprisingly regular intervals – long, rambling, inconsequential letters, sometimes talking about her youth in the Second World War, other times about her married life, seldom about the present, but always affection-ate. Uncle David wrote once or twice, and Lorraine quite often – threatening to come and get me the moment I admitted to making a mistake, full of her course in business studies, and begging for gossip about 'La Bavidge'. We in the novitiate were only allowed to write one letter on the first Sunday of every month. I wrote first to Madge and then to Uncle David – so it was the beginning of November before I settled down to write to Lorraine.

There were plenty of things to tell her – about the beauties of the park, and how the novices were not so intimidating, now I could tell them apart; and that, far from making a mistake, I was happier than ever before.

Even so, I felt constrained. Mère-Maîtresse had warned us not to divulge too much about convent routine, because lay people were insatiably curious about nuns, and even Catholics sometimes misunderstood our rituals. Once an Irish sister's letter home had fallen into the wrong hands, and her description of kissing the floor had been taken up by the tabloids. Our letters were submitted to Mère-Maîtresse with the envelopes left open, for her to seal, weigh and dispatch. We never knew if she read them or not.

I felt safe describing my fellow postulants, and began with Mary Lou, not because I liked her best, but because Lorraine would. Omitting any mention of the boyfriend, I said that we'd travelled to Berbiers together, and, trying not to sound smug, explained how the American refused to speak anything but English, and could only remember our novice-mistress's title by thinking of a mare and a mattress. 'Every morning we form a queue – the line, Mary Lou calls it – outside Mère-Maîtresse's little study, to go in one by one, drop down on one knee, and ask for what we need – soap, writing paper, sanitary towels or toothpaste.'

I paused, wondering if Lorraine would find this act of humility a contemptible lack of independence, then brushed aside my doubts and scribbled on. 'At first Mary Lou lived on what she had in her rucksack – and then she got Frannie or Eleanor to ask for her – until Mère-Maîtresse forbade it. Now she is trying to mime what she wants – but Mère-Maîtresse just ignores her.'

I paused again, this time to ask myself how much I dared say about Mère-Maîtresse. It would all be favourable, of course. She was the most inspiring person I had ever known, and meticulous in her observance of our Holy Rule. As a schoolgirl I'd thought the nuns who taught me were models of self-discipline. Now I could see they'd grown lax. Mother Wilfred should have forbidden Sister Ursula to stay up so late marking exercise books, and shouldn't Sister Bosco have learnt to control her temper? Even Sister Monica, who had most recently left the novitiate, sometimes failed to respond to the first stroke of the bell – and once she'd sworn in front of the fourth form. Mère-Maîtresse would never do any of those things, but she wasn't bossy, like Sister Bon Pasteur, or aloof, like Sister Ursula. She set a constantly good example, and I said as much to Lorraine.

Then I wrote a paragraph or two about Frannie Messmer and Lucie Péreyre, who had stopped crying and grown cheerful and loquacious. Of course there was no one as nice as Lorraine – and we weren't allowed to have special friends – or particular friendships, as they were called here. But Fatima, a Portuguese girl from Coimbra, had been especially kind; and so had Eleanor Chase, when she wasn't fooling around with the other Americans.

In my mind's eye I saw Lorraine flicking impatiently to the next page. Why was I fobbing her off with Mary Lou and Frannie Messmer and a list of others she would never meet? I should tell her about 'La Bavidge'. Sighing, I wiped my pen on my blotter and gazed out of the window. Lorraine would love to hear how Elisabeth had shocked us all. But that would mean telling her about our Chapter of Faults.

At the end of our first week Mère-Maîtresse had issued

each one of us with a little black notebook, explaining that we were to examine our consciences twice daily, and mark down any misdemeanours. Every Wednesday after lunch we would follow her to chapel. Mère-Maîtresse would turn round her prie-dieu to face us at the top of the centre aisle; then we would confess out loud any infringements of the Holy Rule, and beg our sisters' forgiveness.

One by one we listed our faults. 'I broke the general silence six times, washed a blouse without permission, ran once in the courtyard, and broke a plate through inattention. I failed to answer the rising bell immediately, wasted some embroidery silk, and went to the dormitory during the day without permission.' Then Mère-Maîtresse would tell us to kiss the floor in penance.

As well as confessing our own failings, it was our duty, explained our novice-mistress, to help a sister who, from absent-mindedness or human respect, omitted to mention an infringement of the Rule. Far from being sneaky, such behaviour was proof we had a sister's spiritual welfare at heart. At the end of every Chapter, Mère-Maîtresse would pause and, scanning our faces from left to right, ask if anyone wanted to add something. No one ever did. I was often aware of my sisters' omissions: Lucie never confessed to chatting in between the Stations of the Cross, one of the novices was frequently late for chapel, and none of the Americans saw that grumbling about food infringed our rule of poverty. But I never dreamed of pointing these things out, because I was afraid of being called a goody-goody and a creep.

And then, last Wednesday, it had happened. How I longed to tell Lorraine. We had begun as usual by listing our faults, first the novices, and then the postulants. Elisabeth had been strikingly honest, and I almost admired her for enumerating in that small, clear voice the sort of failings no one else ever mentioned. She confessed to being vain about her French, and using it three times to exclude other sisters at recreation. Then she explained how she had been carried away by vanity this week, and made a hurtful remark about another sister's figure; I knew then it was me she was talking about, and wondered if I had to reply. But no, Elisabeth was going on to say that she begged my forgiveness, and the forgiveness of any other sisters she had offended, asking us to believe that she would in future try harder to control her quick tongue. Even Mary Lou understood enough to sense something unusual was going on, and knocked her missal to the floor with a crash. Behind me Lucie Péreyre giggled nervously.

Elisabeth, by this time drawing to a conclusion with an admission of moral cowardice, was not to be deflected. Her cheeks bore two bright spots of red, and her voice began to tremble slightly, but even when she explained how she had often given in to human respect by not pointing out a sister's failing, we still weren't warned. Sister Bon Pasteur was nodding approvingly, and I was too busy thinking of my own turn to follow, which now seemed lazy and superficial.

'Kiss the floor, Elisabeth,' said Mère-Maîtresse. Was I mistaken, or was her tone friendlier than for the rest of us? Mary Lou and I stuttered our way through our lists, and then as usual Mère-Maîtresse asked if anyone was going to help another sister. Mary Lou had already put away her notebook, and placed a hand on the rail, ready to rise, when Elisabeth said in that same small, clear voice, that yes, she had something to add.

Again the shuffling stopped and the silence grew more intense. My heart began to race as I remembered that she had seen me break the Grand Silence last night, when I whispered a request for two aspirins to Eleanor. I knew my headache didn't count as an emergency – and besides, Eleanor was not meant to have the aspirins in the first place, she had failed to surrender them on arriving in Berbiers. We would both get into trouble through my lack of mortification.

But Elisabeth was not staring at me, but at the senior novice, who failed to grasp what was happening, and nodded encouragingly.

'Yes, Mère-Maîtresse, I have something to add. Sister Bon Pasteur has forgotten on several occasions this week that we are all equal in the sight of God.'

Sister Bon Pasteur stopped her nodding and cocked her head on one side, like a dog with water in its ear. 'What do you mean?' she breathed.

'I know I am younger than you in the religious life,' continued Elisabeth with manifest humility, 'but I have noticed that you discriminate between us and the lay novices and postulants – especially Lucie Péreyre.'

'What do you mean?' croaked the novice, turning putty-coloured. Even though we were supposed to be gazing floorwards, all eyes swivelled in her direction.

'In recreation – you always send her on errands – and never anyone else. And you failed in charity by mocking her when she was homesick.'

I surreptitiously turned my head and saw that, in the back row with the other lay postulants and novices, Lucie was gazing at Elisabeth with her lips apart.

'I was doing what I judged best,' said Sister Bon Pasteur. 'You have no right to interfere. Lucie needs to learn discipline.'

'I have every right,' said Elisabeth. 'I have heard you call her *péquenaude* – peasant.'

Sister Bon Pasteur went from putty colour to ash. 'I beg pardon of God, of you, Mère-Maîtresse, and you, my sisters, for my unedifying behaviour,' she mumbled.

'Kiss the floor,' said Mère-Maîtresse. Shaken, the rest of us filed out of chapel, as the novice-mistress beckoned the senior novice to one side, and led her into her office.

It was a subdued little group that met in recreation. Mère-Maîtresse was still closeted with Bon Pasteur, so we wandered up and down the alleys of the park. Nobody dared broach the subject of our Chapter of Faults until Mary Lou spoke up.

'Gee, Lizzie, did you see Bon Pasteur's face? She looked like she was going to have a heart attack.'

'You should have waited,' said Eleanor soberly, 'and got her on her own.'

'I was doing what we've all been told to do,' replied Elisabeth, 'by the Holy Rule.'

While agreeing with Elisabeth in principle, I thought she was mad to speak out against the senior novice. It was not the sort of thing people forgot.

'Remember that it is forbidden to speak of our Chapter of Faults in recreation,' said Mavis, our senior postulant. The novices were walking a little apart from us that afternoon, as though closing ranks. It was the first time a postulant had challenged their authority.

'I don't care if it is forbidden,' said Lucie loudly as the novices moved off towards the acacia grove. We turned in surprise, because the lay postulants seldom addressed the whole group. She cleared her throat, her round face shining. 'I thank you, Elisabeth,' she glowed. 'What you did takes courage. You notice what happens – and pouf, you say out loud.'

'I agree,' said the Irish postulant at her side. 'B.P. is a bully, and we're a bunch of cowards.'

Elisabeth gave Lucie's cape a little tweak. 'I don't suppose Sister Bon Pasteur knew what she was doing,' she said, adding, as though to close the subject, 'and now, Sisters, it's time we did something useful. Let's pick some runner beans for Sister Alphonse.'

Nodding her head in agreement, Mavis began moving towards the vegetable garden, to be followed by Elisabeth, with the grateful little Lucie in tow. After a few moments' hesitation, the rest of us followed in their wake.

Sister Bon Pasteur emerged from Mère-Maîtresse's study at teatime, still paler than usual but no less composed. No one had mentioned the episode since. Drawing a jagged line down the edge of my blotter, I thought how the story would confirm Lorraine's worst suspicions. To my left sat Elisabeth with bent head and racing pen, covering page after page. I had noticed an envelope on her desk already addressed to Jonathon Maule, and wondered if next Wednesday she'd confess to writing to her ex-boyfriend. It seemed unlikely.

Turning to a fresh sheet, I picked up my pen, and began describing our Chapter of Faults. If Elisabeth was doing what she pleased, so would I. Mère-Maîtresse's English was not good, and she would never find time to read all our letters.

TEN

Pale as a communion wafer, the sun floated through the mist above the cathedral ramparts. Each carrying a workbag and a folding chair, we followed Mère-Maîtresse to the convent park. Even in November it was still warm enough to sit outside.

It was my favourite time of day, when the convent lay inviolate in the pearly morning light, with the beginning roar of the rush-hour traffic on the far side of the wall only heightening the solitude. On the acacia tree above our heads a solitary leaf was waiting to be drawn down to earth. The sole sign of life came from the convent gardener, whom I now knew to be called Hercule, coaxing a plume of smoke from a bonfire at the far end of an alley.

We arranged our chairs in a circle and took from our workbags a strange array of garments and undergarments, most of which I would not have recognized three months earlier. I now knew that nuns didn't wear wimples, but coifs, with the white linen caps to go underneath them known as *serre-têtes*. To save washing, our bodices had detachable sleeves with hooks at the top. Under the bodice went a white cotton shift, and over it a cape, or *pèlerine*.

Although it was months before our Clothing, we had already begun making our habits – which was just as well, given my slow progress. Wishing I'd taken needlework more seriously at school, I threaded a needle and stuck it into a band of white linen – every stitch, said Mère-Maîtresse, should be a perfect act of dedication to our Heavenly Bridegroom.

To my left sat Fatima, her little brown hand flying down

a seam to leave almost invisible stitches in its wake. She would willingly have done mine too, but Mère-Maîtresse insisted I learn for myself. No Joubertian was ever supposed to waste time, not even at recreation. The devil, she said, soon finds work for idle hands.

I wasn't afraid of the devil – but I did want to please Mère-Maîtresse. Within five minutes I'd jabbed myself in the thumb and smudged the white linen with blood. Luckily she was concentrating on Mary Lou, who was taking her first turn to read aloud. It was only a few days ago – after running out of supplies – that she had joined the line to stutter out her requests in French – *des serviettes hygiéniques, du savon, du pâte dentifrice* – which to Elisabeth's amusement she called *pâté*. Now she could occasionally join in at recreation. Hunched over the book, her brow furrowed by her effort at comprehension, the young American stammered her way through Anne Joubert's memories of her First Holy Communion. Mère-Maîtresse's tongue clicked in irritation as her hands worked automatically on a piece of palest blue cambric.

'*C'était ice – ici – qu'elle re – ren – rencountray . . .*'

'*Ren – con – tra,*' said the novice-mistress impatiently, as though she was spelling it out for an idiot. A Parisian by birth, she was in no doubt about the importance of good French, nor where it originated. Nor did she stop at correcting Mary Lou. The Portuguese and Irish lay sisters, the German nuns, even native French speakers like Marie-Noëlle from Quebec and Lucie from the Languedoc itself – all had benefited from Mère-Maîtresse's lessons in pronunciation.

'*Elle . . . quitta . . . la gair . . .*' The novice-mistress could bear it no longer. Snatching the book from Mary Lou's grasp, she handed it to Eleanor, at work on my right.

We had reached the point where our Foundress, aged twenty-four, realized her life was incomplete. 'Mademoiselle Joubert could no longer deny that she wanted God more than she wanted any earthly lover,' intoned the blonde American. Despite her dowdy brown dress and woollen stockings, she looked as neat and crisp as on the train to Berbiers. I sat up straighter, having resolved not to lean back in my chair for the whole of that week, an act of mortification I was offering up for the return of my mother to the Church.

'Six months after her return to Berbiers she sought permission from the Holy See to found her very own religious order,' Eleanor went on, turning a page. After listening to the official biography for ten minutes at the beginning of every morning recreation, we had found out a lot about Anne Joubert. Every foundation, explained Mère-Maîtresse, has a bequest from its Foundress, a unique gift to be perpetuated by each new generation of religious. We in the Mother House were specially responsible for keeping alive the spirit of the Blessed Anne, manifested in her selfless dedication to the young girls in her charge.

Having already been through the biography three times, we knew exactly how she set up a school for the daughters of the local bourgeoisie, to deter them from wasting their time card-playing and theatre-going. By 1803 a steady stream of pupils were graduating from her academy as rational, well-educated young women who could earn their living as governesses instead of throwing themselves at the first available suitor. Soon we would hear once again how the Blessed Anne's co-workers had become known as the Joubertians, and how, after her death, the spread of her order worldwide and no fewer than three accredited miracles had led to her beatification.

But there was more to her life than this. I glanced round our little circle, and wondered if anyone else was aware that our Foundress had lived in revolutionary Paris at the same time as the English radical, Mary Wollstonecraft, and flirted with the Girondin Jacques de la Rivière. While browsing in the Liverpool library one rainy August day before I entered, I had come across a book about the Godwins, and there it all was: the friendship between the two young women, the French and the English, and how in 1793 both were sporting the tricolour in their bonnets and discussing the New Philosophy through a series of spring nights.

Mary Wollstonecraft was then in the middle of her disastrous love affair with an American army captain called Gilbert Imlay, and read Anne her *Thoughts on the Education of Daughters* while her lover was away in Le Havre. She tried hard to convince her new friend that nothing was so inimical to peace of mind as platonic relationships between the sexes. Anne disagreed, saying it was sexual love that caused havoc, and the two women quarrelled outright over Anne's refusal to lose her virginity to Jacques. When Mary left Paris three days later in pursuit of Gilbert Imlay, she didn't even say goodbye.

Here in the novitiate we were given a more edifying version of Anne's life, which dwelt on the pieties of her childhood, all but excised the Parisian episode, and gave a detailed account of her life after she had taken the veil. I was on the side of our Blessed Foundress, and wondered if she felt vindicated when Mary bore an illegitimate daughter to the irresponsible Gilbert. How foolish to have sex before marriage. As so often during this part of the story, my thoughts turned to Lorraine, and the way our lives were drifting apart. In her last letter she had told me about her new boyfriend, Rick, the leader of the students' union. She had moved in with him while they were organizing a sit-in, whatever that was. Now she had taken to wearing denims, and had stopped backcombing her hair. 'You should see my new gear, Brigid,' she wrote. 'I look just like a women's libber.'

Madge, too, had written this week. Her letters were growing less cheerful, and she'd begun bemoaning the fact that she would never have grandchildren. I couldn't imagine why she was wishing a husband on me, I thought sourly, when her own experience of marriage was so unhappy. All that Mills & Boon must have gone to her head.

With an effort I wrested my thoughts away from Moses Street, and back to our Blessed Foundress. She never saw Mary again. Nor did she ever recommend *Thoughts on the Education of Daughters* to her nuns, despite their growing expertise as teachers. In the rules she laid down for the Joubertians, politics was a forbidden topic, and sexual expression went unmentioned.

'With the profit from her first small school, the Blessed Anne bought the big house by the cathedral in 1797.' I could tell by her voice that Eleanor was drawing to the end of a chapter. I also knew that Mary Wollstonecraft had herself retired from active politics by this time. Disillusioned with the French Revolution, she – the ex-apostle of free love – married William Godwin on finding she was pregnant again. A few months later, on 15 September, the Foundress attended the first requiem mass in her new chapel. It was for her one-time friend, Mary, who had died only a few days after the birth of the baby girl who was to become Mary Shelley.

I was glad we didn't have to hear about Dr Poignand ferreting in Mary's womb for the broken placenta, and the puppies placed at her breasts to draw off the milk. But I did sometimes wonder if Our Holy Mother Foundress ever missed her old friend – or did Mary's painful death simply reaffirm her views about the hazards of sex?

'*Benedicamus domino*,' said Mère-Maîtresse. It was the signal for Eleanor to stop reading.

'*Deo gratias*,' we chorused in reply. Morning recreation had begun. Eleanor closed the book, placed it carefully on the grass, and took out her workbag.

'If the Blessed Anne Joubert hadn't founded the Joubertians,' remarked Fatima, 'we wouldn't be sitting here today.'

'I'd have joined the Poor Clares,' said Frannie. 'I like the habit.'

'But ours is better,' said Lucie from her place next to Elisabeth. She was cobbling a potato in the heel of a thick black stocking, which she waved around absently as she talked.

'Let's hope you'll learn to look after it,' replied Mère-Maîtresse. 'Your postulant's dress has oil stains down the front.'

'It's not oil, Mère-Maîtresse, it's butter – from when the machine got stuck,' faltered Lucie. It would have been better to accept the rebuke without making excuses, and her reddening cheeks proclaimed that she knew it.

'I entered the convent because it was the last thing anybody expected,' said the clear voice of Elisabeth into the silence.

I tugged my grubby thread extra hard at the inevitable ripple of laughter that followed. Her attack on Sister Bon Pasteur in the Chapter of Faults had only served to make her more popular. The postulants still gathered round her at recreation, and Lucie adored her outright. Even Bon Pasteur had thawed out after a couple of days.

By comparison with Elisabeth I seemed typically English, a cold girl who kept her mouth shut at others' expense, and preferred silence to recreation. Only that morning Fatima had remarked that Elisabeth was nice enough to be Portuguese. It was the highest compliment she could pay, and I knew she would never dream of saying any such thing to me.

Worst of all was that Elisabeth pretended to like me. She'd been at pains to reassure me that she would never tell the others about Jonathon, or how I'd fallen down drunk outside the convent. Next she began saving her chocolate bars for me, and leaving holy pictures on my bedside locker. When she took to choosing the chair next to mine at recreation, I found myself longing for the snobby old Elisabeth of our schooldays.

Staring across at her self-satisfied little smile, I caught the novice-mistress's wide grey eyes fixed on mine, and hastily returned to my needlework. A few days earlier I'd pushed aside my desire to be thought well of, and told her in private about my antipathy. My confession only made matters worse. Telling me to rise from my knees, she motioned me to the chair beside her, and reminded me about the Little Flower, St Thérèse of Lisieux, who had a particular dislike for one of the nuns in her community. The saint decided to mortify herself by cultivating that nun's friendship; so convincing were her efforts, that eventually the despised one asked her what it was about her that specially appealed.

'But that's dishonest,' I retorted, remembering with a blush Elisabeth's attempts to be kind. 'Duping that poor nun into believing she was liked, when she wasn't!'

'We didn't come here to be popular. There are great opportunities for mortification in community life.'

'I just can't bring myself to make up to her.'

With a little shrug, Mère-Maîtresse told me about the pebbles on the beach – gloriously smooth from all the chafing. In the days that followed I tried to follow her advice, and accept Elisabeth's little gifts with gratitude. But my words never rang true, because I was uncomfortably aware that by making me the object of her charity, Elisabeth was getting ahead in the spiritual world at my expense.

Finally Mère-Maîtresse suggested I pray for grace to the Blessed Anne. As I bowed my head that morning in recreation, dimly aware of the quiet chatter going on around me, I murmured an aspiration to our Mother Foundress, who lost her friend Mary for ever. Elisabeth was more to me than a friend: she was my sister in religion, and I would make it my business to love her.

ELEVEN

It was the last week of March, and the novitiate felt strangely deserted. Monday had been the Feast of the Annunciation, the day the novices exchanged their white veils for brown and made their First Vows. From the front benches of the novitiate chapel, at right angles to the sanctuary, we watched them swear at the altar rail to live poor, chaste and obedient for the following year; and then Bishop Eugene hung a little wooden cross inscribed with a J round each of their necks. They were no longer novices, but young professed.

For the next five years they would renew those vows on exactly the same date. Then, if Mother General judged fit, they would take them for life, and become Joubertians proper. After that, any nun who changed her mind would need a papal dispensation.

We, the postulants, gathered for recreation on our own. The newly professed had gone over to the convent to receive a sealed envelope from the hands of Mother General herself. Among the young Joubertians these missives were nicknamed *billets-doux* – love letters. Inside, written in italics on a card of cream vellum, was a single place name.

To Rio or Reykjavik, Lusaka or Llangollen – next morning the recipients would be leaving Berbiers for convents all round the world – except for Sister Augustine and Sister Bon Pasteur. Sister Augustine was a thirty-eight-year-old ex-civil servant who had been sent home to Malta. We were never told why she had been judged unsuitable for the religious life, but speculation ran riot: she couldn't understand Latin, her mother was ill, she was too morose, she had cancer, she used to giggle during the Chapter of Faults.

Then Mavis reminded us we weren't supposed to speculate, and that was the end of that.

As for Sister Bon Pasteur, she was to join the community in the Mother House. We still saw the former senior novice each morning as we knelt in the novitiate chapel when she glided up to the communion rail, gravel-eyed as ever; and sometimes we glimpsed her at the far end of the main cloister, as we crossed between the novitiate room and the refectory. Extroverts like Lucie and Mary Lou would wave, but Sister Bon Pasteur never waved back. We knew why not. Postulants were forbidden to speak to professed nuns without special permission.

On that first night Mère-Maîtresse had allowed us to put on a record and dance to Portuguese folk-tunes, but it wasn't the same without the novices. They were our elder sisters in religious life, the ones who'd comforted us when we were homesick and saved us their chocolates when we were depressed. It was the novices who'd shown us how to adjust our veils in the glass of the dormitory door by hanging a towel on the other side; and how to warm up our feet at bedtime by chafing the soles with a hairbrush. Even Sister Bon Pasteur had been known to plead for us to have an extra hour in bed, or to be allowed to talk during dinner. Now they were gone we felt older and more responsible.

We would get used to it, said Mère-Maîtresse. When the next batch of postulants arrived it would be our job to keep their spirits up. In the meantime there was our Clothing to prepare for. If we didn't wish to dance we could take out our sewing.

By the beginning of May even poor needlewomen like Mary Lou and me had finished our habits, and it was time for us all to go on retreat: for the seven days before our Clothing we were to live without recreation, letters and conversation. The retreat master was a robust little Dominican called Father Albert. We could air any last-minute doubts or spiritual problems with him, or Mère-Maîtresse, and nobody else.

On the morning before our retreat was due to begin, we were told to go in threes to the linen-room, where Sister Nicole, the community seamstress, would be waiting.

The novices had tried to warn us about her before they left. 'She's a bit of a dragon,' one of them had said when Mère-Maîtresse was out of the room, 'so you'd better be polite – or you'll end up looking a fright.'

Looking a fright? We didn't understand.

'You have to dress up for the first part of your Clothing ceremony,' Sister Bon Pasteur interrupted smoothly, 'before you change into your habit.' She turned to the other novices. 'And now, Sisters,' she said, 'I think we've worried the postulants quite enough. Why don't we all take a turn in the garden?' And with that she swept out of the novitiate room.

'Dress up as what?' Mary Lou said to the puzzled knot of fellow postulants that hung behind. 'Urban guerrillas?'

'Perhaps we play at being the Blessed Anne Joubert,' suggested Eleanor, 'or Mary Wollstonecraft.' I had told the others about our Foundress's secret life in Paris.

'Bags I be Jacques de la Rivière,' said Elisabeth. 'He must have had a wonderful peruke.'

'Why does nobody ever tell us anything?' said Eleanor as we trailed after the novices. It was a common complaint, because we never knew what was in store for us.

'I'll have a word with Auntie Céline,' promised Lucie. 'She's always ready for a gossip.'

Lucie's Auntie Céline was known to the rest of us as Sister Céline Marie, the portress. Sometimes Lucie contrived to be sent on errands around the convent. If the front hall was empty she would dart across to her aunt's little kiosk by the front door and spend a few minutes listening to the latest gossip.

The next time the novices were at their theology lecture,

Lucie told us the news. 'You're not going to believe this,' she spluttered, her face red with suppressed laughter, 'but we dress up as brides: white dresses, white veils, white stockings, white shoes: the lot.'

'How very virginal,' murmured Elisabeth.

'But I'm not a virgin,' said Mary Lou.

Mavis shot her a reproving look.

'Auntie Céline said she'd never had such a shock,' Lucie was rattling on. 'The dresses are all falling apart, and if Sister Nicole takes against you she'll give you one that doesn't fit. When Auntie took a deep breath at the altar rail she nearly burst out of her bodice. And you wear what shoes you're told to wear. Hers weren't even the same size.'

When the dreadful summons came it was Mavis, the fifty-five-year-old New Zealander, who rose first from her seat at a nod from Mère-Maîtresse and walked resignedly out of the community room, to be followed by Elisabeth and me.

Usually Mavis took her role as senior postulant very seriously, walking down the Great Cloister with lowered eyes and hands tucked under her *pèlerine*. But today she looked worried, and obviously eager to talk.

'I've been dreading this for weeks,' she muttered.

'Why is that?' asked Elisabeth as she strolled along the Great Cloister, hands in pockets.

'Because I can't *stand* dressing up,' answered the New Zealander. 'I even refused to be my sister's bridesmaid.'

'I've always loved it,' replied Elisabeth. 'And now I have one last chance.'

'I agree with Mavis,' I said. 'It's a stupid custom and should be discontinued.'

'At least no one you know will be there to see you,' remarked Elisabeth over her shoulder. 'Mama's insisting on putting in an appearance.'

'Mine too,' said Mavis. 'It'll cost her a fortune. All the way from Auckland.'

'That's nice,' I said automatically. When I'd told Madge the date of our Clothing, she'd written a letter back full of excuses for staying away – she couldn't afford the fare, she hadn't been feeling well.

I didn't believe in this over-convenient illness; and as for the money, Uncle David would gladly have lent it to her. In some moods I feared she was just stalling, and would turn up at the last minute to disgrace me, getting drunk at the reception, or telling embarrassing stories about my childhood. At other times I yearned for her presence. After all, everyone else's parents were making the effort.

'You can share my family, Brigid,' said Elisabeth. 'Edward will be coming over – and Timmy. They're longing to see you again.'

For the first time I was stirred by her readiness to lie. Perhaps she really was trying to be friends. I felt a wave of affection towards her, and tapped on the linen-room door feeling more cheerful than usual.

'Come in,' cried a muffled voice.

The early morning sunshine was flooding into a room crammed with racks of habits in every state of repair – torn, faded or nearly new. Perched on a ladder-back chair by the window was a frail old nun with a tape measure round her neck. Her coif stood out from her head like a large shell, dwarfing the fine-boned face. Everything about Sister Nicole had shrunk to a point – except for her eyes, which were round and violet-coloured, and her hands, still broad and capable as any couturier's. She had been trained by none other than the great Molyneux.

'Good morning, Sister Nicole,' sang out Elisabeth. 'We've come to be measured.'

The shrivelled little mouth broke into a smile. Ever since Elisabeth had said her grandmother had once worked for Norman Hartnell, the seamstress had seen her as a kindred spirit. It was Sister Nicole's job to check our habits as we were making them. Where mine had frequently been sent back because the stitches were too big, Elisabeth's was often returned with an extra bit of sewing done for her, a sleeve impeccably turned, or the hem on a veil so finely stitched it was invisible.

'*Ah! La petite anglaise!*' she said. 'Come to be dressed by a real couturier.'

With Elisabeth the barbed wit that had reduced scores of postulants to tears never went beyond gentle teasing. 'Hartnell,' Sister Nicole would murmur, glancing mischievously at her favourite from under heavy lids. 'He was all very well in his time – but try as he might, he could never be a Frenchman.' And she would tilt her head on one side and peer at Elisabeth out of her coif like a little owl.

Then Elisabeth would ask in mock innocence, 'But wasn't Molyneux an Englishman too, Sister Nicole?'

And Sister Nicole would reply, 'I do believe he was, my dear. But he came to France, you know – like all the best ones.' She nodded complacently. 'They all come to France in the end.'

The old woman was clearly delighted to be fitting out her favourite. 'I have just the dress for you, *chérie*,' she said, 'but first you must choose yourself a pair of shoes from that pile in the corner. No, not you, Mavis,' Sister Nicole added sharply. 'You will have to be measured. You have an awkward shape.'

Reluctantly Mavis moved towards her. 'And you can stop making those silly faces,' added the seamstress, looking up sharply. 'You are old enough to know better.'

'That's precisely the point,' retorted Mavis. 'I'll be mutton dressed as lamb.'

'You will be the Bride of Christ,' replied the old nun severely, wrapping her tape measure round Mavis's bust, 'and with a figure like yours you can count yourself lucky.'

Mavis bit her lip as Sister Nicole selected a long dress

from the rack beside her. The humiliation was to be worse than she'd feared; her bridal gown was yellow with age, as though it had been cut out in sepia, with dusty flounces and a sagging hem. With it went a heavy, floor-length veil.

'Do I have to wear that?' said Mavis, her voice rising. 'It smells musty.'

'It is just the dress for you,' replied Sister Nicole uncompromisingly, 'cleverly designed for the pear-shaped figure.'

As the old nun showed Mavis how to attach the veil, Elisabeth wandered over to a rack of coloured clothes in the far corner. This was the room where our secular outfits were held in storage against the day of our death or departure.

'Here are Mary Lou's purple flares,' she said. 'Don't those bells look weird?'

'Such an unflattering style,' put in Sister Nicole, her mouth full of pins. 'I dare not think what Monsieur would have said.'

Elisabeth and I gazed at clothes in every style and hue, ranging from the psychedelic sixties to long ago taupes and eau-de-nils.

'There's your denims,' I remarked.

'They're so faded – especially next to your suit. You wouldn't think we came from the same country.'

'Why do you keep them all?' I asked Sister Nicole. 'They take up so much space.'

'If a nun returns to the world she has a right to everything she brought with her.'

'She'd look a bit odd in this,' said Elisabeth, pulling out a wasp-waisted suit in fifties puce. 'Especially if she'd put on weight.'

'There will be plenty of selvedge on that,' said the seamstress, with an expert glance across the room, 'I would be able to let it out.'

While Mavis was trying on her dress, Elisabeth and I

riffled our way down the rack, pulling out this and that for closer inspection. Soon we had left the fifties reds and blues and were in among the wartime clothes, serviceable wear economically cut, with no foreign labels.

'All these boring browns and beiges,' murmured Elisabeth as she moved on. She had clearly forgotten her enthusiasm for Biba. A moment or two later she stopped with a faint cry in front of an organza dress with a square neck and floating panels. As she plucked it from its hanger a scent of iris and palest vanilla ruffled the air around our heads.

'Shalimar – how divine!' she murmured, raising one dove-grey sleeve to her nostrils. 'Who did this one belong to?'

'Sister Julian,' said the seamstress.

'Our old English teacher?' I asked in astonishment. It was hard to imagine her clad in the gossamer fabric.

'Who else?' said the old nun curtly.

Elisabeth picked up a fox fur draped on the next hanger.

'Did this belong to Sister Julian too?' she asked.

'No, certainly not. That belonged to Sister Elisabeth of the Trinity.'

'She must have worn Shalimar too,' said Elisabeth in surprise, as she laid her cheek against the fur. 'What a coincidence!'

'No coincidence at all,' said Sister Nicole. 'They were the best of friends – before they entered, that is.'

'What happened then?' asked Elisabeth. 'Did they quarrel?'

'Not at all. They were separated.'

'Why was that?' Elisabeth pressed on.

'You know the rule about particular friendships,' replied Sister Nicole.

'But I still don't understand what they did wrong,' persevered Elisabeth.

'Neither did they.' Sister Nicole pursed her lips. 'That is

why they have never been allowed to see each other since. Now stop bothering me with all these questions – and put that fox fur back on its hanger, *chérie*. I think it has fleas.'

'Poor little animal,' I said, stroking the moth-eaten pelt, 'spending the rest of its days in the linen-room.'

'It will do nothing of the sort,' said Sister Nicole. 'I will be taking it to the charity shop tomorrow. And about time, too. *Il est vilain comme tout!*'

'Shouldn't it stay here – in case Sister Elisabeth decides to leave?'

'There is no chance of that,' said the seamstress. 'She died last week in the Congo.'

A wail rose from behind the screen. 'Come out at once, Mavis,' said Sister Nicole sharply, 'and let us see what can be done.'

We turned to watch the senior postulant walk out stiffly, two hectic spots of embarrassment in her cheeks. Elisabeth stifled a giggle.

I could see why. Mavis cut an extraordinary figure. Her hair, snipped monthly by Mary Lou, who claimed to have once held a Saturday job in a salon, stuck out in a frizzy halo round her anxious face. Where a younger woman might have looked virginal, the white satin made Mavis look as though she'd been laid out to dry in the sun. She was glancing down in dismay at her small bosom, which was lost in a row of bulky pleats. Around her ample hips the seams were ominously tight.

'I'm going to die of embarrassment,' she moaned. 'Sister Nicole, can't you do something?'

'The great Molyneux himself could do nothing with a shape like that,' said Sister Nicole. 'You will have to make the best of it. Now, try on this pair of shoes.'

While Mavis forced her feet into a pair of narrow T-straps, Sister Nicole handed a flouncy creation to Elisabeth.

'At least it will hide my skinny legs,' said Elisabeth.

'It will do more than that,' said the seamstress proudly. 'Go and try it on.'

Turning to me, Sister Nicole ran an expert eye over my waist. 'Eighty-five centimetres! You have been eating well.'

'I must start to cut down,' I replied, embarrassed.

'Do not be so stupid,' said the old nun. 'If you had seen what I have seen . . .' Her cape rose as she shrugged her bony little shoulders.

We all knew what she meant. She had spent the Occupation in a small convent in Lyon, where they lived on the verge of starvation. The community's struggle to survive had become legendary, and so had Sister Nicole's ruthless streak. On one occasion the seamstress, then a very young woman, told her Mother Superior that the convent handyman had presented her with a rabbit – a rare luxury. Could she spend the morning concocting a stew? She trotted down to the herb garden for a sprig of thyme, a bay leaf and a bunch of parsley. Then she told the rest of the community she was going to the kitchen, and did not wish to be disturbed.

Sister Nicole proved a talented cook. The stew was dark, and aromatic with garlic. It wasn't until Mother Superior congratulated the young woman on their first square meal for months that she was told she had just eaten Esaü, the convent tabby.

'My God,' Mother Superior had moaned. 'It's not possible. I loved him like a son.' And bending double, she regurgitated her stew on the refectory floor.

'What a pity,' Sister Nicole had remarked philosophically as she fetched a bucket and mop, 'with you so emaciated. If I had known you would waste the poor cat, I would never have told you.'

Nowadays Sister Nicole was determined never to go hungry again, and Mother General turned a blind eye to the old woman's hoard of biscuits. When she thought nobody was looking the seamstress would pull out her tin and select a sable or a bourbon cream. From where I stood behind the screen I could hear her munching, along with the sound of Hercule raking monotonously at the gravel outside the window. Undoing the hooks and eyes of my postulant's dress and veil as quickly as possible, I slid into the white dress, shivering a little despite the heat of the May morning. By comparison with the nubbly brown serge of the last nine months the satin was cold against my skin, bringing my arms out in goose pimples. It was the sort of material you couldn't forget you were wearing.

Elisabeth and I emerged at the same time. I stared in envy at her tiny bodice tapering into a V-shape over her stomach before falling to the floor in a cascade of gauzy frills. With her fringe swept back under a mist of tulle to reveal her high, narrow brow she looked innocent and merry, like a child bride in Dickens.

'I made it for my own Clothing the year war broke out. Tulle was tulle in those days,' said Sister Nicole proudly, 'and nobody has worn it since. You don't get many women with figures like ours.' She smiled fondly as Elisabeth pirouetted across the room. 'And now,' she said, turning to me, 'what shall we do about Brigid?'

What indeed, I asked myself, my early morning elation quite vanished. I stared down at the jaundiced cloth draped over my bulging stomach, as though for a shotgun wedding. A stale smell rose from the armpits, and I wondered which other women had sweated into the fabric, and what had become of them since. Had any of them felt beautiful on the day of their Clothing, I wondered, or were they all as fat and clumsy as me?

'It's a good job you and I have been granted a vocation, Brigid,' said Mavis as she watched Sister Nicole pin and tuck, 'because I can't see many men racing us to the altar. It would have been all right for you, Elisabeth,' she added.

Elisabeth laughed. 'I have my doubts,' she said.

'That,' I told her, raising my arms at a prod from Sister Nicole, 'is the second time today that you've lied out of sheer good nature.'

'I wasn't aware I was lying,' replied Elisabeth. 'Perhaps I'm not as good-natured as you think.'

'Stop chattering, *mes enfants*,' interrupted Sister Nicole, 'and start getting changed.' She walked over to the window and rapped sharply on the pane. 'Away with you, Hercule!' she scolded. 'You have been raking that gravel for long enough.' She watched the gardener slouch off, dragging his rake. 'A typical Basque,' she remarked over her shoulder, 'always hanging around where he is least welcome.'

At length I was able to climb out of the sallow dress and follow Mavis and Elisabeth back to the novitiate. Soon the next trio of postulants was on its way to the linen-room. By the end of the afternoon all sixteen of us had been fitted with a wedding-dress and veil, and there was nothing ahead but our retreat.

'All we can do is pray to look prettier,' whispered Mary Lou as we filed into chapel for Father Albert's first lecture. I knew that she was dreading the unbroken silence of the next week. As for me, I would be only too glad to roam the garden in solitude. And it would be a relief to stop expecting a letter from Madge. From now on there was no point in speculating about whether or not she would change her mind and come to the ceremony. I would just have to wait and see.

The whole park was trembling on the brink of summer. As I walked up and down the alleys, saying the rosary or reading my office, I would allow myself to pause every now and again to admire the beds of antirrhinums and blue plumbago, pansies and geraniums. Banksia roses twined up the trunks of the acacias to riot over the topmost branches and glow against the sky, or cascade earthwards in a shimmer of palest yellow. As I stood gazing, my rosary forgotten, I would feel a keen anticipatory happiness – of what I didn't quite know – as though I was on the brink of falling in love again, but this time successfully, triumphantly even. And so I was, I reminded myself. I was on the threshold of a love affair with God which would last for all eternity.

We were given the opportunity to consult Father Albert about any last-minute doubts, but I didn't feel the need. Once during the seven days I saw Elisabeth emerge from Mère-Maîtresse's study with a tear-stained face, and wondered why. Like everyone else in the novitiate, I knew that Jonathon had been writing to her once a week. At first Mère-Maîtresse had kept most of the letters unopened. But soon there were too many envelopes bulging with Basildon Bond to fit in her tiny bureau. She consulted Mother General, who said that the postulants were there to make up their minds, and Elisabeth had better be acquainted with what her suitor had to say.

The letters tailed away. And then, the day we went on retreat, Jonathon wrote to say he'd left university and joined the BBC, and was doing research on the Cathars. Could he bring the camera crew to Berbiers, and film our Clothing? After speaking to Mère-Maîtresse, Elisabeth had written back saying he was welcome to come to the ceremony, but he couldn't have permission to film it. As far as I knew he hadn't replied.

Perhaps he had decided to stay away. I no longer cared one way or the other, but was sorry to see Elisabeth upset. It must have been hard to turn him down. I would never have found the strength, but knowing about Elisabeth's sacrifice had helped me put him in perspective. I no longer awoke with the rising bell to realize I'd dreamed of him all night, or caught myself thinking about him in chapel. Yes, thanks to Elisabeth it was a matter of indifference to me whether I saw him again or not.

TWELVE

On the day of our Clothing we ate breakfast in silence as usual, and then went into the garden to recollect ourselves before the ceremony. Cars were drawing up on the far side of the wall, and the doorbell was ringing every few minutes. Sister Céline would be run off her feet.

Mère-Maîtresse was already in the parlour entertaining those visitors who'd arrived early. None of us postulants had spoken for seven days. With every knock on the door Frannie and Mary Lou would glance up sharply, as though the temptation to break silence was almost unendurable.

Soon it was time to go and change into our dresses under the sharp eye of Sister Nicole. 'Good luck, child,' she said, giving me a little pat as she adjusted my veil. 'You don't look too bad at all.' I smiled back, but before I could catch her eye to see if she meant it she'd moved on to Eleanor.

Teetering slightly in our unfamiliar shoes, we processed from the linen-room along the Great Cloister, entering the chapel from the west end. As we moved slowly down the aisle the *lycée* choir sang '*Veni, Sponsa Christi*' – Come, Bride of Christ – and somehow the imperfect haircuts didn't matter any more, and the dresses no longer looked noticeably yellow. Ahead of me was Elisabeth, her narrow back erect. Beside her was Mavis, and far from being eclipsed, she looked as dignified as any other bride. To my right was Mary Lou, not laughing now but silent and absorbed. From the corner of my eye I scanned the backs of the visitors. Surely that was Mrs Bavidge, dabbing at her eyes with a lace handkerchief. And those two young men flanking her in summer suits must be Edward and Timothy. They seemed to have grown taller. With an effort I turned my eyes from the congregation. This was the most important day in my life, and I wanted to stay composed. No matter if Madge was here or not.

The sunlight streamed through the big east window behind the altar, lighting up the honey-coloured stone of the sanctuary and splashing the flagstones with red and blue from the stained glass. One by one we left our pew to prostrate ourselves on the sanctuary floor.

'My daughter, what do you seek?' Bishop Eugene's voice hovered over me in the shape of a question mark.

I paused for a moment, my face pressed against the cold stone. 'Take your time,' Mère-Maîtresse had instructed us. 'It's your ceremony, not the Bishop's.'

Slowly I rose to my knees, like the others before me, and heard my voice come out clear and disassociated: 'My Lord Bishop, I seek admission to the Holy House of Joubertians.'

Beside Bishop Eugene stood the Sister Sacristan, bearing a pair of silver scissors on a velvet cushion.

'Your request is granted,' said the Bishop.

As he picked up the scissors the Sister Sacristan leaned forward to raise my veil a little, so that he could snip the statutory lock of my hair. Then I made my way back to my pew, aware of the silence, and everyone's eyes upon me. A lot of the postulants had younger sisters present. Were they hoping they wouldn't be called upon to renounce the world, like we had? Or were they just a little bit envious of the grandeur of the occasion, and the clarity and importance of our lives? Suddenly I felt worthy of the day and the music, and held myself erect as we filed out of the chapel to the sound of an organ voluntary.

In a classroom specially converted for the purpose, Sister Nicole helped us change into our habits, moving among us to adjust a *pèlerine* here and there, or pin up a sleeve. 'Hurry up, child,' she said as I struggled to cram my hair under my *serre-tête*. I now knew that nuns didn't have to shave their heads; but that night in the dormitory the senior novice would take out her scissors and hack off the rest of our hair. It was a sign of vanity to worry about the cut.

'Everyone's waiting,' said Sister Nicole. Impatiently she seized the tapes of my *serre-tête* with her bony fingers and pulled them tight. As she slid on my coif with practised hands I felt the weight of my veil – white, to show I was a novice – drag down my back.

Blinkered by the wings of my coif, I turned my head slowly to see the other novices gathering by the door. Sister Nicole gave me a little push towards the line of white veils. But which one was my partner, Mary Lou? That tall one, standing with her back to me? No, that was Eleanor. I remembered how hard I'd once found it to tell the novices apart. Now we were just as anonymous. That small one tying up her shoe must be Elisabeth – no, it was Lucie. And now Mary Lou was tugging at my sleeve, her grey eyes dancing. Side by side we set off for chapel. Without her tumbling ringlets she looked clean-cut and vivacious, like someone from *The Sound of Music*.

The organ music died away as we took our places. The moment had come for the Bishop to bestow on us our names in religion. Some of us hoped to keep our baptismal names; others wanted a saint's name, but there was no guarantee we'd get our wish. Sometimes Mother General bestowed a name not asked for, as a means of mortification.

'Mavis Sterne, from henceforth you will be called Sister Raphael.' Lucky Mavis, that sounded nice. I knelt in the pew with my eyes downcast, as the Bishop's voice rolled on. Lucie Péreyre was to keep her baptismal name and be known as Sister Lucie, Elisabeth was to be Sister Elisabeth of the Trinity. Oh yes, the nun who'd used Shalimar and died in the Congo. With a thudding heart I awaited my turn.

'Brigid Murray, from henceforth you will be called Sister Brigid.' Not the change of name I had asked for, but it could be worse. The bishop's voice continued to intone one name after the other. Eleanor Chase was to become Sister Georgina . . . Mary Lou Moton was to become . . . the name was drowned by a muffled groan.

After the ceremony we gathered outside to pose for photographs with our families. Before I had time to decide whether or not I was sorry that Madge wasn't there, Elisabeth – that is, Sister Elisabeth – had hold of my arm and was steering me towards her family.

'Brigid – or should I call you Sister Brigid now? – how lovely to see you again! And don't you make a lovely nun!' Mrs Bavidge, more glamorous than ever in a summer coat of some floating material and a garden party hat, waved a glass of white wine in my direction. 'Are you allowed a drink, darlings? No? What a shame. You must be so hot, the pair of you.' She gazed at Sister Elisabeth and me in concern. 'What does it feel like in those heavy habits?'

'It feels strange and somehow . . . dignified,' laughed Elisabeth. 'Don't worry, Mummy. You'll soon grow used to us.'

'Elisabeth!' A tall young man with horn-rims accosted her – it was Timothy, her elder brother. 'I shall never be able to tease you again. And is this Brigid? Nearly unrecognizable!' He bent his face towards me, blue eyes twinkling and the scent of his skin strangely familiar: a blend of wine, aftershave and tobacco, a tweedy, worldly smell I'd almost forgotten.

'Your mother sends you lots and lots of love, Brigid,' said Mrs Bavidge, gazing at me solicitously, 'and she's so very sorry not to be here.'

I didn't ask Mrs Bavidge why Madge hadn't been able to make it, because there seemed no point. While I was thanking her for including me in her group, Mary Lou detached herself from a group of Americans even taller than she was, and strode across to where we stood, her skirts flapping. Already her coif was slightly askew, and a wisp of brown hair was poking out from beneath her *serre-tête*.

'Come and join us,' said Mrs Bavidge, extending her hand. 'Your name is . . .?'

'Sister Boniface, worse luck,' groaned the young American. 'Wouldn't you know I'd be called after some guy no one's ever heard of?'

Jütta Schmidt, newly named Sister Nicholas, paused on her way past to stare reproachfully. 'There is great devotion to St Boniface in Westphalia,' she said in heavily accented English. 'In my country he is a very important saint.'

'But to me he sounds like a cross between an emperor and a skeleton,' responded the American, unabashed. 'I don't know where to start with him.'

When the last guest had departed we sat down to a lavish meal in the refectory. There was no spiritual reading – we were allowed to chatter throughout the meal, which was lit by little candles illuminating the dusk which crept through the refectory windows. I glanced up and down the table with its twin rows of faces radiant with happiness.

Even I found plenty to talk about during recreation. We strolled up and down the gravelled alleys – in twos, threes, any number we wished. As we passed the acacia grove I found Elisabeth at my side.

'Thank you for letting me share in your family,' I said awkwardly. 'If it hadn't been for you I'd have felt out of things – with my mother not coming. You were all very kind.'

'Not kind at all – just pleased to have you with us,' she replied, giving my elbow a gentle squeeze. 'I'm glad you had a nice day.'

'One of the best.'

As the others moved in a chattering band towards chapel

and Compline, I paused for a moment at the bottom of the park to gaze over the low stone wall. To my left were the cathedral ramparts, floodlit in the spring dusk. Out in the darkening countryside one or two cowbells tinkled as the animals were driven in from pasture. Even though nine o'clock was already clanking out from the bell tower, I lingered in front of Hercule's greenhouse to admire a bed of peonies. It was then I caught sight of a shadow regarding me from inside the glass door, tall and serious, the shadow of a young nun. For a moment I stared back without realizing it was me. And then, without thinking, I raised my hand in a sacerdotal blessing, like Bishop Eugene at the end of our ceremony.

From behind me came a sound I hadn't heard for many months: a long, low wolf whistle.

'Mary Lou!' I cried, whirling round.

'Sister Boniface to you, kid,' she replied, with a grin. 'Oh yes, I saw you posturing in front of the glass. Well, you're right to posture, and so am I.' She caught me by the waist and whirled me round, then steadied me again to gaze at our twin reflections. 'They've turned us into holy nuns,' she said, 'and no mistake!'

THIRTEEN

—

It was the hottest summer ever known in Berbiers. Each morning at five we would wake to find the sun blazing through the shutters. As I knelt in chapel the moisture would trickle down my back to soak the elasticized waist of my baggy blue knickers, and I would try not to think enviously of Lorraine, who had recently sent me a postcard from the Costa Brava. She had bought her first bikini, a pink one, and was tanning nicely.

Sister Fatima began to faint regularly during mass, keeling over with a soft thump somewhere between the Offertory and the Sanctus – unless Mère-Maîtresse, aided by Sister Raphael, managed to catch her in time, sit her up and stick her head between her knees. After the attack had passed she would totter up to the communion rail, her olive skin tinged with green and her coif askew.

By the end of breakfast the courtyard had turned into a tank of broiling light. Mère-Maîtresse never seemed to feel the heat – but with a glance of mingled pity and amusement at our faces moustached with sweat and our dampening *serre-têtes*, she would lead us to a patch of shade where we could sit in a circle and sew.

Sister Céline had whispered to Lucie that the novices were always granted a fortnight's holiday at this time of year – in an old château out in the *maquis*, or scrubland. Had we heard anything yet? Our hopes were fanned like a forest fire – but no one dared ask Mère-Maîtresse. She disliked unseemly curiosity, and was well capable of calling the whole thing off if we stood in need of mortification.

As our needles skidded in and out of sewing damp with

sweat, we exhumed the approved topics of conversation: neither the future nor the past but the convent present: the forthcoming Feast of the Assumption, Sister Lucie's plans for the vegetable garden, and the lectures of Father Bonaventure, the Carmelite. At nine o'clock sharp the *baccalauréat* class from the *lycée* would file through the garden on their way to the library, talking animatedly. 'Ssshh!' their teacher used to admonish them as they passed our little circle. 'You will distract the novices.' And momentarily they would drop their voices before bursting into chatter again the moment they rounded the corner. One of these young girls was Sister Bon Pasteur's niece, but I never knew which. We were to lower our eyes as the crocodile passed, so I gained no more than a confused impression of long brown legs and bright satchels.

The heat grew worse as we did our charges, or domestic duties. Every morning we dispersed to different parts of the convent for an hour or two of manual labour. As senior novice, Sister Raphael held the most privileged post, that of sacristan, with two lay novices acting as assistants; Sister Boniface, to whom Mère-Maîtresse invariably gave the messiest jobs, had taken over the butter machine from Sister Lucie; Sister Fatima was head refectarian, in charge of five others; and I was one of the four novices delegated to clean the dormitory, lavatories and upstairs washbasins under the sharp eye of Sister Killian, before going out to water the courtyard.

As Madge's daughter, I had grown smug about my ability to fry bacon without spilling grease on the floor, and fold a newspaper after reading it. Housework was easy, and I'd despised the girls who chose to learn domestic science at school instead of Latin. Here in Berbiers I learnt better. Why had I never noticed the rings of brown slime at the bottom of taps, and the dustballs lurking under beds? Sister Killian always did.

'Sister Brigid!' she would hiss, 'you've forgotten the struts on the banisters. And that door-knob needs polishing.'

As I returned, humbled, to the ill-done charge, I began to feel a grudging respect for my mother. Housework was bad enough, I would reflect, on struggling to make a bed with perfectly mitred corners, if you could offer it up to God; if you couldn't, why bother?

To stain our garments during these tasks, or wear them out unnecessarily, signified a lack of respect for our Holy Habit. Before our Clothing Mère-Maîtresse had shown us how to keep our skirts out of the dust by gathering them up behind us as we walked downstairs; how not to wear them to a shine by sitting on them, but to tuck them up behind us and sit on our underskirts instead; how to detach our sleeves from the little hooks on the shoulders of our bodice when doing manual work, and to pin back our capes and veils.

They were lessons that Sisters Boniface and Lucie never managed to learn. If they remembered to pin back their veils, there was sure to be dust or grease on the fingers that did the pinning; splinters would reach out to snag their skirts, candles would tilt to deposit their wax, and in the refectory olive oil would splash from plate to skirt before they had even sat down. Other novices, such as Sisters Elisabeth and Georgina, always looked immaculate. The rest of us teetered on a fine line between disrespect and simply feeling grubby.

I soon stopped noticing the smell of dried sweat emanating from the day before yesterday's blouse, the grime on my collar, and the indelible yellow stains at the armpits of my vest. We were only allowed to bath once a week, and even then deodorants and talcum powder were forbidden luxuries. Every morning we scrubbed our skin in cold water, crouching over the row of basins in a struggle to observe due modesty while washing armpits, feet and crutch under the cover of our dressing-gowns.

Some of the postulants had arrived with a supply of tampons. These disappeared from their bedside lockers at the first week. When questioned, Sister Bon Pasteur said they were unsuitable for religious. Although some of the Americans pretended they couldn't see why, not even Mary Lou felt like challenging Mère-Maîtresse on the subject. After three months we all began asking for sanitary towels at the same time. On the fourth occasion, Sister Bon Pasteur explained to us how expensive they were, and how wasteful. Then she issued each one of us with a dozen triangles of white cotton – and showed us how to fold them – so.

'But how,' stammered Mary Lou in her deficient French, 'do we dispose of them?'

'Dispose of them, no,' replied the senior novice. 'That would be wasteful. You are to put them in the bin inside the lavatory door. Each one is marked with your initials. The lay sisters will wash and return them to you.'

'But we can't expect them to do that,' replied Mary Lou, her face reddening. 'It's uncivilized!'

'They are used to it,' replied Sister Bon Pasteur impassively. 'Please do not deny them an opportunity for mortification.'

From then Lucie bore a binful of bloody *serviettes hygiéniques* to the convent laundry once a month, and spent the morning scrubbing. The cleansed triangles were often to be seen drying in the back yard, and then were left, neatly folded, on our beds the next day. We soon got used to it, and to the smell of menstrual blood from the damp linen between our legs. Coping with knickers which could be changed twice a week was not so easy; *serre-têtes*, coifs and veils were changed only once. The habit itself wasn't to be laundered until the end of the year, just before we took our First Vows. Then all five yards of material would be unpicked stitch by stitch and soaked in a great stone trough in the laundry.

My last job every morning was to water the courtyard – a custom designed to settle the dust and cool the atmosphere. Despite the heat, it was considered better to work outdoors than in, because lapses were less likely to be noticed. My pleasure in criss-crossing the yard between the rows of palm trees, turning the dust from white to a satisfying coffee-colour, was not marred even by the bulky loops and folds of my habit – or not, that is, until Hercule began to turn up.

The convent gardener was a thickset man with a louring grin that I had once thought simple-minded, but now knew was crafty. To him the novitiate courtyard was out of bounds, but there was nothing, it seemed, to stop him from lounging in the gateway and staring while I did my charge. Soon I would begin fumbling under his gaze, tripping over the hose as I lugged it across the yard, and blushing to the rim of my *serre-tête* whenever I splashed myself.

Nor did my contact with Hercule end there. For Lucie and me the last charge of the day was to help him water the vegetables. Straight after evening recreation we would make our way to the edge of the park, where he would be waiting for us by his potting-shed. From the start he had made it obvious that I was only a hindrance, with my foreign upbringing and ignorance of gardens; but with Lucie it was a different story.

'Eh, Hercul-es!' she used to cry as soon as she spotted him, pronouncing his name in the fashion of her native village, which lay just over the border from Hercule's own and, like his, spoke Basque. And his stubborn leer would moisten into a grin.

'Eh, Luci-a!' he would bellow back joyfully, ignoring me completely. 'Let's go, my girl!'

Then Sister Lucie would hoist the skirts of her habit and race him to the big stone basin on the topmost of the garden's four terraces. Mostly he would let her win. Once there, she would plunge her arm into the water and pull out the plug, mindless of Mère-Maîtresse's instructions about removing the sleeve.

Each terrace had its own system of irrigation channels waiting for the cascade of water from the basin. Our job was to pile up a little dam of mud at the end of each runnel as it filled, so that the water would flow on to irrigate the next level. If we failed to move fast enough the method would fail, and the whole garden would be in danger of flooding.

Hercule always worked in his bare feet, moulding the mud with prehensile toes, but Lucie and I were supposed to wear galoshes. To my dismay she peeled off her shoes and stockings on the very first evening, right there in front of the grinning gardener.

'It's the best way,' she had shouted over her shoulder as she chased down to the next terrace. 'I used to help my father do this.' By the time it reached the bottom the water was flowing with less force, and sometimes she would dance around in the mud, chirruping at Hercule in a mixture of French and Spanish as he laboured to catch her up.

Despite the fact that Hercule was forbidden to enter the enclosure, he seemed to have gleaned a lot about convent life. When he was in an especially good mood he would mince around the garden trailing an imaginary skirt and mouthing, 'Your habit's in a shocking state, Sister Lucie. Kiss the floor.' And instead of rebuking him, Lucie would toss back her veil with muddy fingers and laugh delightedly.

I soon came to resent their fooling. On one occasion, after racing each other to the stone basin, they left it too late to come and help me, and I, gouging clumsily at the mud in my galoshes, couldn't move fast enough to prevent the flood of water from racing down to swamp the terraces.

'Idiot!' Hercule had yelled at me, his face purpling with

rage as the bottom tier collapsed in a heap of stones and muddy vegetables. 'Why can't you work at it like a woman?'

He had to labour all night to restore it, and refused to so much as glance at me for weeks afterwards, despite all Lucie's efforts to sweeten his temper. But the next day the pair of them were racing each other for the basin just as before.

FOURTEEN

Hercule's contempt didn't stop him from bothering me during my morning charge. No longer content with lounging in the corner of the courtyard, he had started slouching across to where I stood with the hose.

One morning in mid-June he was at my elbow within the first five minutes. 'Here in the Midi water is dearer than wine,' he growled at me in Basque. I glanced anxiously towards the novitiate. As usual, he had chosen a time when Mère-Maîtresse was busy elsewhere.

'Dearer than wine,' he said again. 'Do you hear me, Sister Brigid?'

'Yes,' I nodded, my fingers tightening on the hose-pipe.

'Then why do you waste it?'

I pointed out in my careful French that watering the yard was a waste in the first place, but he affected not to understand. After a pause, he mooched, hands in pockets, back to his viewing-point, while I flung the hose in the corner without stopping to coil it, and hurried back to the novitiate.

Pausing on the threshold, I sighed gratefully at the air of peace, the thick walls, and the shutters closed against prying eyes. At least Hercule couldn't follow me here.

It was then that I noticed my letter, unexpected because our mail was first opened by Mère-Maîtresse, and appeared on our desks at irregular intervals. Slowly I moved towards my place, vaguely aware of the other novices returning to the community room in ones and twos, pausing on the threshold as I had done to unpin their habits and tidy their veils. Most novices longed for news from home, so those who also had letters quickened their stride.

For several minutes I sat fingering the acid-blue envelope with its address in blobbing biro, while around me the others read with absorption. Elisabeth had already scanned several pages of cream vellum, and was leafing through a pile of press cuttings, while Lucie, unable to keep anything to herself, was waving a photograph of a donkey beneath the nose of Sister Fatima.

I envied them both for getting letters they longed to read; but most of all I envied Sister Georgina, the former Eleanor Chase, and the last to arrive at her desk. She sat down heavily, her normally pale face red from waxing the refectory floor. As usual, her desk top was bare. Her family, Boston Episcopalians, had cut her off when she entered the convent, and she hadn't received a letter since arriving in Berbiers.

Madge hadn't bothered to come to my Clothing. Now it was too hot for reading about her swollen ankles, or lack of grandchildren. Quickly I raised my desk lid and wedged my envelope beneath a copy of *The Imitation of Christ*, earning an undeserved nod of approval from Sister Raphael. To defer reading a letter was an approved act of mortification. I smiled shamefacedly and opened my *Lives of the Saints*.

That day the temperature climbed to an unprecedented 105 degrees Fahrenheit. At lunch it was a struggle to fork down my greasy chicken and pile of pasta as my sisters' table manners chafed like a heat rash. Fatima with her mouth agape and Georgina gnawing endlessly on a drumstick – did they have to look so stupid? Half-way through, Mère-Maîtresse gave us permission to speak, and everyone except Georgina and me began to chat about their letters. Lucie's father had just bought a new mule; and Elisabeth's letter was from Jonathon, who apologized for missing our Clothing. He had been sacked from the BBC but was still considering a visit to Berbiers. Before I could ask why he'd lost his job, Sister Killian reminded us not to talk about our pasts. Normally I would have agreed, but today I glanced up in irritation. The Irish nun was toying with the base of her wine glass, so I knew what was coming next, and my irritation mounted.

'You spoil it by doing that,' Elisabeth remarked as Killian sloshed some tap water into her glass. 'This is a nice little wine – from the old Carignan vines in the park. Try it neat.'

'Certainly not. 'Tis the devil's drink.'

As she continued to fidget, I raised my own wine to my lips. It tasted strong and acidic, with a tang of sun and soil.

It was then that Sister Killian took up her goblet.

'For the conversion of England,' she announced loudly. Elisabeth looked smug. Since discovering that her grandmother – she who had supposedly worked for Hartnell – had been born in Dublin, Elisabeth had taken to proclaiming herself Irish. With a triumphant glance in my direction, Killian tilted back her head and drained her wine to the last drop.

The conversation rose and fell like the sound of birds in the trees as I struggled to remind myself that God had His plans for each individual soul, and it was not my job to question whom He had called and why, or fret because they sounded stupid. High above the rest soared the Texan vowels of Sister Boniface.

'Mère-Maîtresse! We're melting!' she called down the table, her forkful of meat suspended in mid-air, 'and we've heard about the château from Lucie's auntie – Sister Céline. Tell us – are we going there or not?'

A silence descended as Mère-Maîtresse gazed ominously in her direction. Trust Bony to ruin everything. But our novice-mistress replied calmly enough, 'Wait and see, Sister Boniface. That is the perfect course of action – to leave it in the hands of the Lord. He will take care of your holiday. And,' she added, turning to Lucie, 'you may tell the same thing to Sister Céline. She's old enough to know better.'

And that was all our novice-mistress would say on the subject, no matter how much Bony begged and pouted.

'For goodness' sake shut up,' ordered Killian in the end. 'It's a waste of time.'

Like everyone else, I knew the Irish nun was right, but that didn't stop me from dreaming about the château for the rest of that long, hot day. In recreation, struggling to sew altar cloths damp with sweat, I conjured up a river gorge rushing with green water. In Bible study I was wandering down country lanes with dust white as talcum, until the exhaust fumes from the cars of homecoming commuters drifted over the convent wall to hang flatly in the enclosure and remind me it was time for evening meditation.

After supper, Lucie and I helped Hercule as usual, and left him smoking his pipe on the bench outside his potting-shed. There were only a few minutes left before Compline, so Lucie raced ahead to change her muddy apron, leaving me at leisure to watch the last rays of light fade from the cathedral walls. How I was longing to climb the narrow stone stairs to the dormitory and prepare for bed. Soon I would be able to unpin my veil, slacken the strings of my *serre-tête*, and peel off my habit layer by layer before slipping in between the sheets.

Suddenly Sister Alphonse, the convent cook, appeared out of the gloom.

'Be a good child, Sister Brigid,' she wheezed, 'and run down to the kitchen garden for me. I need a bunch of shallots to give Monsieur l'Aumônier's housekeeper.'

I wasn't supposed to leave the courtyard unaccompanied, and we both knew it. But the old nun looked flustered, so it seemed an act of charity. Besides, at nineteen I could surely run a little errand like that without special permission.

Silently I moved across the courtyard and down the stone steps into the tunnel. By the time I was descending the path to the vegetable garden twilight had gathered. At first I thought Hercule had retired for the night – but no, there he was, only a couple of yards away, standing motionless by the path. Why, I wondered idly, was he hosing down Sister Alphonse's shallots in pulsating splashes of tobacco colour – and so late at night? And then I saw the spindle of tawny flesh dangling between his thumb and forefinger.

As the blood surged to my face, I cried out without meaning to. The splashing stopped abruptly, and Hercule turned round, still fumbling at his groin. But instead of buttoning his flies as I expected, he took two slow steps towards me, fanning his fingers down the stiffening flesh. Soon his face was so close to mine that I could smell the wine and garlic on his breath. I tried to avert my eyes from his but couldn't, as I sensed rather than saw the obscene flapping in the region of his crutch.

'Why do you stare so, Sister?'

'I don't know,' I stuttered. And forgetting all about Sister Alphonse and her shallots, I turned on my heel and ran for the novitiate.

My sisters, be sober and vigilant, for the devil, your enemy, is roaming the earth like a ravening lion, searching for someone to devour. We were half-way through Compline before my heart stopped racing, but I still couldn't banish the memory of the gardener's sly smile, and the disgusting red sausage swelling in his hand. Any sin against chastity was a mortal sin – even the merest daydream, if it was indulged. And here was I in the presence of the Blessed Sacrament, picturing Hercule. This was the fruit of my disobedience – but how would I find the right words to confess it in French, I wondered, when I hardly knew in English?

It wasn't until I was climbing the stone stairs to the dormitory that I remembered my letter. Too late to read it now. Re-entering the community room after Compline was forbidden, and I had broken enough rules for one day. Tomorrow would be time enough.

FIFTEEN

___

Sister Killian appeared at the far end of the gravelled alley, moving as fast as she possibly could without breaking into a trot. By the time she reached us she was out of breath, and her broad face was flushed with heat. Hastily she dropped down on to one knee.

'There's a lady from England to speak to you, Mère-Maîtresse,' she panted, 'in the parlour.'

'Now?' demanded the novice-mistress sharply, as though the visitor had come expressly to plague her.

It was the hour of Mère-Maîtresse's weekly English lesson, and she and I were sitting in a little gravelled square surrounded by a privet hedge. Soon she was to be sent to an English-speaking country – she didn't yet know which. As an unusual concession, Mother General had given her permission to learn the language in advance.

I had felt flattered to be chosen as Mère-Maîtresse's teacher, when everyone had predicted it would be Elisabeth. I especially liked sitting alone with her in the park, watching her normally austere expression soften as she struggled to recite the lists she insisted on learning by heart, and I chipped in every now and again with a correct pronunciation. In the novitiate English was a forbidden pleasure, and here was I, licensed to indulge in a whole hour of it.

We had been loaned two dog-eared textbooks by the *lycée*, and were working through them systematically. When Sister Killian arrived we'd just finished the months of the year. I stared in irritation at the young Irish nun, whose beaming face suggested a special pleasure in interrupting us. Resignedly the novice-mistress laid aside her book.

'Very well,' she sighed, 'I'll go and see.'

As the two figures, one white-veiled and the other brown, toiled their way towards the tunnel, I scanned the park for any sign of Hercule. Even though he hadn't appeared in the courtyard since that night in the vegetable garden, I still couldn't blot out the shameful memory of what had happened. Surprisingly, Sister Alphonse had never inquired after her missing shallots, and in our Chapter of Faults I confessed to going without permission to the vegetable garden, and nothing more. But I still worried – irrationally – that Hercule himself might report me.

After making sure he wasn't around, I wandered towards the edge of the garden. From the general direction of the station rose the noise of a shunting engine; closer to hand a family squabble lanced the summer air. This, I reflected, was all I knew of Berbiers, and probably all I would ever know. The streets I'd seen on the morning of my arrival had faded into a distant, headachy dream.

Suddenly I became aware of heavy footsteps marching up behind, too staccato for Hercule. It was Sister Killian, smiling no longer.

'Mère-Maîtresse wants you in the parlour, Sister Brigid. You're to put on your Sunday sleeves and new *pèlerine*, and hurry up, please.' The sweat was still gleaming below the tightly-stretched *serre-tête*. The moment she'd delivered her message she put her finger to her lips and stumped back across the garden, leaving me to follow in her wake.

I'd had similar messages before, when the visitor – the parent of a prospective postulant, perhaps, or a visiting priest – only spoke English. Quietly I made my way through the cool of the tunnel and out into the blinding light of the courtyard. Since I'd watered it that morning the shade from the palm trees had shrunk to tight aureoles around their base, and the tiny lizards scuttled from the novitiate steps into a hot white dust.

On my way up to the dormitory to change, I met Sister Lucie. Even though we were in silence, she paused to whisper, 'Killian's told me the news. Make sure you have a good time.'

How sweet of Lucie to tell me to enjoy myself. If our lesson hadn't been interrupted, I would have been doing just that. I smiled back at her, letting her think that I didn't want to break silence, and passed on into the dormitory.

The Mother House had never looked so serene as it did that afternoon. By the time I reached the cloister, the community had dispersed about its afternoon tasks, so nothing disturbed the sunlight falling in golden slabs on the polished floor. Across one of the arches was emblazoned our Mother Foundress's favourite text:

If any man come to me, and hate not his father, and mother, and wife, and children, and brethren, and sisters, yea and his own life also, he cannot be my disciple.

I paused to savour the sunny, impregnable silence, then hurried on across the front hall to the parlour, and tapped gently at the door.

Silence. I knocked again, more loudly this time. Mère-Maîtresse did not take kindly to her novices bursting into rooms uninvited. Still no reply. Cautiously I pushed open the door.

There was no sign of our novice-mistress, but at the far end of the room, in the dim light filtering through the shutters, I could discern a grey-haired woman standing with her back to me. Somebody's mother. I closed the door quietly and moved into the room.

'Brigid!' The woman swung round. 'You gave me a start, creeping up on me like that.'

'Madge!' I cried. 'What on earth are you doing here?'

She was looking older than I remembered her, and even more unkempt, with a greasy wisp of hair hanging in front of her ear. Her turquoise linen coat, last worn at Mother General's visitation, was creased and grubby.

She took a few steps forward, clearly undecided as to whether or not she should hug me. I stayed where I was, my hand clutching the back of one of the parlour chairs.

'How did you travel?'

'By overnight coach. Quite a marathon.'

That would explain why she looked so tired. 'I saved up fifty pounds,' she was rattling on, the colour in her cheeks mounting, 'and your Uncle David lent me the rest.'

'I can't believe it,' I said, wishing I could feel something besides a dull weight.

'All that way on my own,' she replied, clearly pleased with herself. 'Not bad, for a first trip abroad.' With that she lurched, rather than stepped, towards me, with the air of someone plucking up courage. She smelled different, with sweat, cigarette smoke and travel mingling with a new, sickly-sweetish odour I couldn't identify. I wished I could hug her in return, and say that seeing her was the best thing in the world, but I couldn't. Unable to move a muscle, I sensed rather than felt the pressure of her cheek through the side of my coif and veil.

'If only you knew how much I've longed to see you,' she said, flinching a little, 'especially after missing that ceremony of yours – when you got your habit. Briony Bavidge showed me the photographs. We've got quite pally.'

I pulled out the parlour's only upholstered chair – it would have been a mistake to call it easy – and sat on a mahogany stool close by.

'That's nice.'

'You look so hot in all that gear,' Madge swept on. She was plucking at the imitation gold chain round her neck, which was coming out in big red blotches. 'It must be murder. The temperature's up in the nineties.'

'Why didn't you tell me you were coming?'

'I wrote to you ten days ago,' she said in surprise, 'saying that if you didn't write back to say no I would be on my way. Didn't you get the letter?'

The letter! For the first two days I had postponed reading it; and then forgotten it altogether. It was still lying un-opened at the bottom of my desk.

'Er – no – that is, yes – I mean, I haven't had time to read it.'

'You mean they wouldn't let you read it,' said my mother, her eyes bright with suspicion. 'They've been censoring your mail.'

'It's not like that at all,' I said, feeling irritation and guilt at the same time. 'I meant what I said – I haven't had a spare moment. We're very busy.'

'Busy!' echoed Madge. 'Doing what, might I ask?'

I stared at a framed photograph of the Mother General before last, reminding myself how far my mother had come to see me. 'Well,' I replied after a moment or two, 'we're in the middle of our canonical year, you know. That means we're preparing to take our First Vows. And then there's housework – and gardening – and private study. And a Carmelite priest comes to lecture on Bible history twice a week.'

'Surely you can take that in your stride,' said Madge, her forehead puckering, 'after doing so well at school.'

'How did you get permission to see me?' I asked, attempt-ing to change the subject.

'With great difficulty, because your portress hardly speaks English. When she saw I can't speak a word of French she got hold of a young Irish nun and asked her to translate.'

So that was why Sister Killian had stopped smiling. If only she knew.

'It's very awkward, Mother,' I said. 'Canon law forbids us to have visitors for twelve months.'

'I knew they wouldn't turn me away, not after I'd travelled

all this distance. After all, you're hardly likely to be going anywhere.' She began fumbling in her handbag.

'Do you have to smoke?'

'There's an ashtray on the sideboard,' she said. 'I found it before you came in. So they must allow it.'

'What did Mère-Maîtresse say?'

'She was at a loss,' said my mother gleefully, 'what with me speaking no French and her speaking no English.'

I could see that Mère-Maîtresse would need more than the months of the year to cope with Madge.

'I think she's gone away to make me a hotel booking,' Madge rattled on, puffing out a long stream of smoke, 'but I'm not sure. She might let me stay here – you've got enough room.'

'We're not allowed to sleep under the same roof as a lay person.'

'Surely I can't do you much harm – I'm only your silly old mother.'

'It's not about harm,' I tried to explain, 'it's because I've dedicated my life to God, and this is the one time I can concentrate on Him alone.'

'I didn't even know you believed in God until you got this idea of being a nun,' said my mother testily.

'Not that old argument again,' I pleaded. 'I'm here to stay, and that's that.'

During the last part of our conversation Mère-Maîtresse had been gliding in and out of the parlour, loading crockery from the corner cupboard on to a tea-tray. I wanted to ask her how I should behave, and how long I had to stay, but I couldn't catch her eye.

'Why does she have to keep barging in and out?' asked my mother conspiratorially.

Before I could reply, Mère-Maîtresse advanced with a tray laden with cheese, baguettes, fruit, and a decanter of wine. I rose quickly to my feet. '*Mère-Maîtresse . . . vraiment je regrette l'arrivée de ma mère,*' I stumbled out. '*Je n'avais aucune idée . . .*'

Mère-Maîtresse nodded briefly in my direction while point-edly removing my mother's ashtray from the arm of her chair and pulling out a gate-legged table. 'I'm sure you are as surprised as I am, Sister Brigid,' she said. 'We will talk about it later. For the moment, make sure your mother gets enough to eat.'

Madge was listening to us both intently. 'So you've learned to parleyvoos, Brigid,' she said to me, ignoring my novice-mistress. 'You sound like a native.'

Mère-Maîtresse poured my mother a glass of wine, and handed it to her with a faint smile. '*Pour vous, Madame Murray*,' she said. '*A la vôtre!*'

'What's she on about?' asked my mother.

'She's saying the food is for you, and she hopes you enjoy it.'

'On my own? In here?' cried Madge. 'Why can't I eat with the rest of you?'

I glanced at Mère-Maîtresse, who shook her head.

'We're not allowed to,' I said awkwardly.

'Not even with your own mother? I can't believe it.' Madge seized a plate of bread and waved it in my direction. 'Why don't you sit down, Bid? It can't do any harm, just this once. I'll never manage all this on my own.'

'We can't eat with lay people.'

'You may miss evening meditation,' Mère-Maîtresse was saying to me, 'and stay here until supper-time. But no longer.' With that, she nodded to my mother and withdrew from the parlour.

'Thank goodness she's gone,' said my mother. 'A bit too high-falutin for my taste – mincing around with downcast eyes.'

'It's just a little inconvenient – you coming so unexpectedly.'

'At least we're on our own again,' said Madge philosophi-cally. She began prodding at one of her baguettes with a fork. 'Pooh, garlic,' she exclaimed triumphantly, waving a slice of salami in the air. 'Good job I'm not travelling back on the coach tomorrow.'

'How long are you planning to stay?' I asked neutrally.

'Until my money runs out,' she said, with surprising sang-froid. 'I'm going to make the most of this. It's my first trip abroad, and may be my last.'

I was touched. Her shoes were down at heel, and one of her stockings was laddered. I knew how economically she lived.

'Don't use up all your savings,' I said. 'I'll probably be back in England soon.'

'I'm not counting on it. It would be just like them to send my girl to darkest Africa. I've made it to France – but I don't see myself sleeping in a mud hut.' She chuckled, pleased by her sense of adventure.

There was another long silence, then my mother cleared her throat.

'What is it?' I said.

'To be honest, I'm not just here for the trip, Bid,' said my mother at last. 'I'm here because I'm worried about you – and so's your Uncle David. Your letters have grown so stiff – as though you don't remember who we are.'

'It's hard only writing once a month,' I tried to explain. 'There's so much to say that I never get started.'

There was yet another long pause, while my mother continued to munch steadily.

'What are you worried about?' I tried again. 'Can't you see that I'm happy?'

'You don't seem happy to me, dear, and that's that,' she said sharply. 'If you were, you wouldn't look so pale and puffy.'

My temper snapped. 'Looks matter to some of us very little,' I said. 'I know it was different when you were young.'

She paused a moment before saying quietly, 'At least I didn't turn my back on the world, Brigid. I loved life – you seem almost to hate it.'

'Not at all,' I replied sharply, 'I just see it differently.'

'But why the self-denial? It seems so joyless.'

'It's what I want to do,' I replied firmly. 'It's not my fault you can't understand it.'

I rose to my feet at a tap on the parlour door. Outside stood Sister Céline, her face aglow with curiosity.

'I have booked your mother into the Hôtel Métropole,' she said, 'and here is a little map of how to get there. It is a good place, very clean and quite cheap – run by the uncle of Sister Bon Pasteur.'

'Thank you very much,' I replied, aware that the portress had heard us quarrelling and was longing to know why. 'My mother is very grateful.'

'She speaks no French,' Sister Céline went on, craning her neck. 'It must have been difficult, travelling all that way. When I opened the door, I thought she was asking for money. It was only when she repeated your name that I thought, this must be the mother of Sister Brigid.'

'It was good of you to invite her in,' I replied awkwardly.

'*Tiens!* She looked so hot and tired, and a little bit lost. It was the least I could do.'

At that a bell began tolling. 'Is that the time?' I cried. 'I'm going to be late for supper.'

'I will show your mother out,' said the plump little nun eagerly. 'Look, I give her the map. A chance to practise my English, no?'

'Where are you going?' said my mother, looking startled, as I moved off down the corridor.

'I'm late for supper,' I replied. 'I'm sorry you haven't finished eating. Sister Céline will show you out.'

'Just a moment, Bid. There's something I want to give you.'

As I stepped into the parlour again, puzzled, she slid a little object wrapped in paper tissues into my hand. 'Go on, take a peek,' she said. 'I want to see your face.'

Unwrapping it hastily, I saw two little glass cats with spiky whiskers, one of them blue, the other pink.

'They're cute, aren't they?' she said. 'There's one for you and the other for Elisabeth – I mean, Sister Elisabeth. A little keepsake.'

I turned over the little ornaments in my hand. My mother had no way of knowing that neither Elisabeth nor myself would be able to keep these presents. Personal gifts were always surrendered to Mère-Maîtresse at the end of a visit, and the little glass cats would end up in a jumble sale.

'Don't you like them?' said Madge.

'They're beautiful,' I told her. 'Sister Elisabeth will be delighted.'

'I thought so. A souvenir of Liverpool.'

'I'll see you tomorrow,' I said, sliding the little package into my pocket as I moved swiftly towards the door, already five minutes late. 'I'm sure that it will be all right, now that you're here.'

'That's just what I think,' said my mother. 'I'll be back in the morning.'

Following the lead of Mère-Maîtresse, no one asked about my mother during evening recreation, not even Sister Boniface. Everyone knew that visitors were forbidden. It was a problem for our novice-mistress to resolve, not me, and she would do it in her own time. Whatever her decision, I would have to accept it.

At the tolling of the bell for Compline, I gave Sister Elisabeth her little tissue-wrapped present. She opened it and smiled.

'But Brigid,' she cried, 'I've hardly met your mother. She really shouldn't have bothered.' Then we each put our little package on Mère-Maîtresse's high, wooden desk.

For the first time that day the tears pricked at my eyes. I knew how much it had cost my mother to come, so why couldn't I behave like a proper daughter? For a few moments I lingered in the darkened community room, dabbing at my eyes before heading for chapel. To my surprise, Mère-Maîtresse suddenly emerged from her study and moved towards me through the gloom. I stood motionless, expecting a rebuke – for the arrival of my mother, for failing to read her letter, for being late to supper, for crying, for what else I didn't know. Instead she nodded in the direction of the chapel.

'Your mother has no right to bother you now,' she murmured in my ear as we paced side by side down the Grand Cloister. It was the only time I'd ever known her break the Grand Silence.

'She's come a long way,' I replied.

'Nevertheless, it is time you detached yourself.'

'It isn't that easy,' I said. 'She means well.'

'But she would like to rule your life, no?' said the novice-mistress.

'No – I mean yes – I mean, perhaps that's right.'

'People think that convent walls are built to keep daughters in, Sister Brigid, but it is not always so. They are there to keep mothers out – especially over-possessive ones. Remember that tomorrow morning.'

I knelt down to pray with Mère-Maîtresse's words ringing in my ears. How on earth was I going to cope? I felt extraordinarily tired – almost too tired to get undressed, much as I longed for bed. By the time I climbed between the sheets most of the novices were already lying down, and Raphael was moving along the dormitory opening the shutters. I gazed out at the night and thought of Madge. Perhaps she was lying awake in the Hôtel Métropole, and staring, like me, at the southern stars spangling down at odd angles. When she comes tomorrow, I thought, I'll be nicer to her. We'll chatter about the past – the happy bits, not the others, and I'll be relaxed and friendly, convincing her I've made the right choice.

But I didn't see my mother the next day, or the day after that. The following morning, Mère-Maîtresse rose from her place as usual at the end of breakfast. Instead of leading us out to the garden for recreation, she stood stock still at the bottom of the table. Twenty faces turned to her expectantly.

'Sisters,' she said, her grey eyes bright beneath her dark brows, 'you are to go straight to the dormitory, and pack a fortnight's change of linen. After that you may collect your books from the community room and assemble in the front hall. Your summer holiday has begun. We are about to depart for Château le Bignan.'

SIXTEEN

Up and down the dormitory the other novices were selecting clean veils and *serre-têtes* from their lockers. I hurried down the centre aisle to the room at the far end, beyond caring that it was forbidden to visit the lavatory without permission. It was the only place you were sure of being alone.

Diving into the nearest cubicle, I slammed the door behind me. Mère-Maîtresse was right: my mother must learn I had a life of my own. The château was an escape route, and Holy Obedience meant me to take it.

I closed the lavatory lid and sat down heavily. Abandoning my mother in Liverpool was one thing, countered a nagging little voice; leaving her in Berbiers is another. Mère-Maîtresse is an ambassador's daughter, and her family travel all over Europe; she won't understand that it's Madge's first trip abroad, that she mightn't even have enough money to get back. I would have to explain.

Mère-Maîtresse was in the front hall talking to Sister Céline. Without waiting for her to finish I burst out, 'I can't possibly go to the château this morning. My mother is coming to see me.'

Sister Céline clucked sympathetically.

'That will be all, thank you,' Mère-Maîtresse told her, then turned to me as the portress shuffled off reluctantly. 'You have been forbidden to enter the foyer without permission, Sister Brigid. Please go and finish your packing – and don't forget to straighten your *serre-tête*.'

'But Mère-Maîtresse,' I begged. It was the first time I had ever demurred. 'Can't my mother come to the château?'

'Sister Céline will tell her that we have gone on a

community holiday,' said Mère-Maîtresse. 'Besides, the place needs to be cleaned. Don't worry, Sister – the Lord will take care of your mother.'

'I'm an only child,' I said feebly.

'The Church is your mother, too,' replied Mère-Maîtresse, 'and you now have obligations to her – more than to any earthly mother.'

'Yes, Mère-Maîtresse,' I mumbled, too troubled to know whether or not I agreed.

'Dry your tears, Sister Brigid, for your sisters' sake. You don't want to spoil their holiday.'

'No, Mère-Maîtresse,' I replied, my tears flowing all the faster.

She dismissed me with a brief nod. As I made my way down the corridor, I was choked by a sudden anger. Why should my mother overturn my life? Especially after not bothering to come to my Clothing. Serve her right to be left alone for a few days.

Excited chatter filled the community room. For the next fortnight we were dispensed from our rule of silence. Desks were banged open and shut as the novices gathered their few possessions from the desks and shelves. Already Sister Boniface had pulled down my workbag, in case I forgot it, and Elisabeth had gone to fetch my missal from the chapel. Only Sister Killian looked sour.

'You are making things very awkward for Mère-Maîtresse,' she snapped. 'Can't you see she's got enough on her plate?'

Trying to ignore her, I scooped a pencil and notebook from the bottom of my desk, accidentally dislodging my mother's letter. I didn't know when I would see her next, so I shoved it in my case. The least I could do was find out what she'd had to say.

By the time I climbed on board the minibus, Sister Patrice, the convent driver on loan from the main community, was revving up the engine. Within seconds we were lurching across the cobbled yard and through the main gates, the ancient vehicle blowing a cloud of exhaust fumes over the customers at the pavement café.

A tall, heavily built woman with a rubicund face, Sister Patrice was cousin to the famous Jean-Paul Briquet, hero of the Resistance. As a young girl she had driven an ambulance for the Maquis, and there were tales of her going up into the hills under cover of night to rescue some wounded Frenchman from under the noses of the Nazis.

Blinkered by her big starched coif, she swung out into the Rue Jean Moulin without pausing to look left or right. A grimy dustbin lorry bore down on us, its horn blaring as it passed us on the inside. Overtaking it again, we joined the dual carriageway.

'*Mon dieu*, Sister Patrice . . .' came Mère-Maîtresse's faint protestation from the front passenger seat.

'The less you see the better these days,' Sister Patrice replied jovially, as the driver of a large Citroën raised his fingers in an obscene gesture. The speedometer needle hovered at ninety-five. In the back seat Bony made the sign of the cross in mock terror as the minibus shot across the flow of traffic into the fast lane. The château was a good half-hour out of Berbiers.

To our relief we soon turned off the highway and began the long climb into the hills. The sun was blazing down on a scrubland pierced here and there by white outcrops, and the town shrank to a cluster of matchbox houses through the rear window. Sister Fatima reached across and took my hand.

'It is sad for you, no,' she murmured, 'to leave your mother alone?'

I nodded, embarrassed that my palm, cradled in her small dry grasp, was damp with sweat.

'You will see her again soon,' she went on with a little

squeeze. 'The château has not been occupied for many months. Mère-Maîtresse will want us to clean it up before we have visitors.'

I nodded, willing myself to believe her. How my mother would love to see a real French château. I'd read about Le Bignan in the life of our Foundress, and in our refectory there hung a daguerrotype of Nathalie Sémichon, who had bequeathed it to our order in the mid nineteenth century, for use as a holiday home. A stiff little figure in a silk crinoline, she stood in front of her beloved orangery, surrounded by silver tubs of myrtles and tuberoses.

Cool air blew through the windows as we plunged down a narrow lane running through a forest of oak trees. I was beginning to feel better.

'We'll soon be getting our first glimpse,' said Sister Patrice, 'over to the right.' Killian took out her rosary beads as the minibus lurched towards the edge of a ravine.

'Slow down, Sister Patrice!' came Lucie's anxious voice. 'The gendarmes are on our tail!'

'I wish I was out of here,' moaned Bony. 'I'm going to be sick.'

Through the rear window I could see two fresh-faced countrymen in a police van, their blue caps tilted jauntily.

'Pouf! It is only Hubert and Jean-Baptiste,' replied Sister Patrice, glancing for the first time in her rear-view mirror. 'They know better than to arrest a Briquet.' She crashed into third gear and pulled away up the hill, keeping well in the middle of the road. Putting on a spurt, the gendarmes drew abreast, then overtook us on a sharp bend.

'What would you?' said Sister Patrice with a shrug as they winked their lights in an ironic salute. 'Nice boys, both, but so in love with their uniform.' She accelerated down the road after them.

'There it is, everybody!' shouted Bony, pointing out of the window, 'There's Château le Bignan!'

I caught a glimpse of a rococo fantasy perched on the far side of a gorge, utterly out of place against the austere backdrop of the Languedoc. Then it disappeared again behind the oak trees which had been encroaching on its pleasure grounds for centuries. A few minutes later, and Sister Patrice was turning between a pair of tall, wrought-iron gates.

'How beautiful it must have been,' murmured Elisabeth. As we wound up the long white drive I pictured the garden in its heyday, with the fountains, dry and dusty now, plashing before the mossy assembly of pagan gods and goddesses lining the terrace. And there at the top of the drive was the famous orangery, no longer crammed with fruit, but its peach-pink brick still bright in the morning sunshine. The first Madame Sémichon had supervised the planting of the parterres in the reign of the Sun King, in patterns transcribed by herself from fashionable embroidery books. The colours had long grown jumbled, and the silver tubs had disappeared decades ago into the homes of the local peasants, but the tuberoses, jasmines, myrtles, pinks and irises still grew in profusion.

Sister Patrice slewed to a halt in the centre of the carriage sweep and, helped by Sister Raphael, unloaded a big box of groceries and some dusters and brushes. A wan-looking Mère-Maîtresse descended from the front passenger seat, while the rest of us gathered by the two semi-circular flights of stone steps that fanned out on either side of the front door.

'You mean we're going to live in there for two weeks?' asked Sister Georgina, gazing up at the peeling shutters.

'Of course you are,' said Sister Patrice, dumping a bucket and mop at her feet. 'The community are coming here on retreat in three weeks' time. You make it nice and cosy for us, do you hear?'

Almost reluctantly, our little group followed Mère-

Maîtresse up the steps. She unlocked the door with a huge iron key produced from her pocket, and we were enfolded by the silent space of the great hall, the château's only concession to local architecture. The tattered banners and dusty hunting trophies of the early Sémichons gloomed at us down from the walls, surrounded by masks of mangy animals grinning through dusty teeth.

'Hurry up, please,' said Mère-Maîtresse, the colour returning to her cheeks. 'There will be no stopping before we've opened up the rooms. Sister Lucie, you will go downstairs and light the range. Sisters Georgina and Fatima will begin by sweeping the hall and passage. Sister Killian will beat the carpets. And Sister Boniface, you can go outside and clean the dovecot. Here's a shovel and brush.'

My charge was to convert the six big rooms on the first floor into our sleeping quarters. Lugging a polythene bag full of sheets, I made my way up the great staircase. Lunch was simple – a baguette apiece as we worked, distributed by Lucie. By mid-afternoon my back was aching and my hands were sore and cracked as I toiled on through the heat, disturbing dust that had settled last summer. Some holiday, I thought to myself.

The only person who didn't get hot was Lucie, struggling to light the range in the dank basement. It was eight-thirty before dinner was ready. After evening prayers in an oratory improvised from the Sémichons' dining-room, we assembled round the kitchen table for a meal of cassoulet followed by goat's cheese and fresh figs. The novices' spirits were high, but I didn't feel like joining in their banter, so slipped out as soon as I could to do my last charge of the day, which was locking up the château.

Elisabeth and I had been instructed to share the large room over the front door. 'It's high time you English got to like each other,' Mère-Maîtresse had said. Wondering if the other novice felt as sceptical as I did, I loitered as long as possible before making my way upstairs, gazing down the drive which still glimmered whitely in the dusk.

One of the fountains, repaired by Killian that afternoon, was splashing in the darkness, and fireflies were dancing over the lily pond. But try as I might to focus on their tiny points of light, an image of my mother's disappointed face hung between me and the southern night. Where is she now? I wondered, my early anger evaporated. Speeding northwards on the night coach, her big adventure over? Or hanging on in Berbiers, to be consoled, perhaps, by the uncle of Sister Bon Pasteur, who in my imagination spoke accurate if stilted English.

'Really, Madame,' I heard him say, leaning a little further over the bar, 'I pity you, having a daughter like that. After coming all this way!'

A yellow square of light hit the gravel at my feet, and a sash window squeaked open.

'Psst! Sister Brigid,' came a stage whisper from the first floor. 'You're to stop moping and come to bed.'

Elisabeth. I climbed the perron and locked the big front door behind me.

By the time I reached our bedroom she was kneeling beside her pillow, her head bowed over a pile of frothing, peach-coloured underwear, not very neatly folded. She looked up as I gave the door a little bang, then made the sign of the cross and rose to her feet.

'I've just found out how to work them,' she said, gesturing at the three crystal chandeliers. 'They're all on the same switch, so I can't economize. Doesn't the room look good?'

I didn't agree. That afternoon I had spent over an hour washing the chipped, primrose-painted pine and curly gilt chairs of the first Madame Sémichon, so knew how tawdry it all looked by daylight – not the sort of place where young nuns should be sleeping, even on holiday.

'Where did you get those?' I asked, staring at a pair of

cami-knickers. There was a tacit understanding that we weren't required to observe the Grand Silence as strictly as usual, because there was no Chapter of Faults for the entire fortnight. Nevertheless, we kept our voices low.

'Janet Reger,' replied Elisabeth casually, doing up the buttons of her voluminous white nightdress. 'Jonathon bought them for me – a whole set as a farewell present. I made sure I wore them all before leaving Liverpool. Then I persuaded Mère-Maîtresse that it would have been wasteful to leave them behind. One can hardly give one's used knickers to the poor.'

Unused to undressing in front of anyone else, I removed my habit as quickly as possible and climbed into bed.

'Look at that.' Elisabeth pointed at the ceiling, where some aristocrats were disporting themselves at a *fête galante*.

'Not very edifying, is it?' I remarked.

'At least it makes a change from the Four Last Things.'

Above my bed a trio of ladies in pale blue silk were frolicking on a swing, their breasts popping out like candied fruit. 'There's something I've been meaning to ask you,' I said, fixing my eyes on a powdery white wig and trailing ribbons.

'Fire away.'

'I've often wondered – before you entered – er, how could you bear to leave Jonathon Maule?' The question hung awkwardly in the air over our twin beds.

'Quite easily,' replied Elisabeth after a short pause. 'We were just good friends, as they say.'

'But you were inseparable,' I protested, trying to needle her. 'All those long, intense conversations . . .'

'I used to talk about my vocation,' she said simply. 'He was the only one who understood.'

More spiritual airs and graces. Determined to call her bluff, I adopted a cool, woman of the world tone. 'But he was so obviously in love with you.'

'In love with me?' She burst out laughing. 'Nonsense. He only had eyes for Eddy.'

'Eddy?'

'Edward. My brother. Not that Jonathon got very far.' She paused when I failed to respond. 'Couldn't you see that he was homosexual?' She asked at length.

Homosexual? Handsome, sexy Jonathon Maule? My mind swirled. I had never known any homosexuals. Weren't they supposed to be effete and somehow . . . different? I remembered Nigel Green at King Street Juniors, with his milksop's face, too scared to jump on a moving bus or play last across the road, being called a queer, a cissy and a poof. But Jonathon wasn't in the least like Nigel Green, who had married and had three children.

Above my head the white-wigged lady simpered behind her fan.

'I never noticed,' I answered dully, recalling those wasted months of infatuation, and my jealousy of Elisabeth – when all the time Jonathon preferred the gangling Edward Bavidge to both of us. At least I hadn't wasted time moping, I thought, turning on to one side. God must have seen that a foolish girl like me needed protecting, and out of His goodness called me to be a nun.

'There's something else you haven't noticed.' Elisabeth's voice cut across my reflections. Following her gaze I saw the little glass cat my mother had given me – the pink one – on the locker beside my bed. The blue one was on the shelf beside Elisabeth.

'How did they get here?'

'Mère-Maîtresse came in while you were locking up. She left them as a surprise.'

'They don't exactly go with the chinoiserie, do they?' I gestured at a cabinet of Sémichon porcelain. Suddenly I felt like crying again.

'Maybe not. But I'm glad we've got them back. It's nice to get presents.'

Nice. Perhaps Mère-Maîtresse would ask my mother to the château. That would be really nice.

'Switch off the chandeliers, will you?' After a few minutes' silence, Elisabeth's voice came sleepily from the next bed. 'And for heaven's sake don't lie there worrying. You'll hear from your mother tomorrow.'

But no news came the next day or the day after that, and soon I was forgetting about my mother for hours on end. When the cleaning was complete our holiday proper began, and we spent whole hours wandering down narrow white lanes, gorging ourselves on grapes from the wayside vines, and picnicking in the forests. It was good to be free from routine – and just at the point when my nerves had been stretched to snapping point. As I lazed in the shade of some oak tree after lunch and gazed up into its leaves I began to see how lucky I was to get such a holiday. Who would have thought convent life was so luxurious?

On the afternoon of the third day I had run up to the attic for some empty jam-jars. Lucie and I were to go blackberrying. Clutching the dusty glass to the front of my cape, I paused for a moment to look out of the little round windows in the roof. Shrunk to the size of an insect, Killian was attacking the weeds on the gravel below with a hoe. Beyond her was Bony, her habit girded, moving slowly through the lily pond by the main gates. Wearing a giant pair of waders she'd found in the bottom of the dovecot, she was clearing the leaves from its surface with a long steel prong. Pausing now and again to gaze abstractedly into the moss-agate waters, she looked like nothing so much as a big brown heron.

It was then I saw the minibus speeding towards the château, with Sister Patrice at the wheel and a little figure clinging to the seat beside her. It screeched to a halt outside the gate and turned in sharply.

The idea struck me suddenly. I would try and catch Sister Céline on her own. She was bound to have seen my mother, or at the very least to have heard if she'd returned to England. I dumped the dusty glass jars and sped down three flights of stairs, my hand sweeping the mahogany banister polished to a high shine that morning by Sister Georgina.

They were gathered in the front hall, Sister Céline, Sister Patrice and Mère-Maîtresse. As I descended the last flight of stairs they suddenly stopped talking, and a triangle of faces – one pale, one sallow and one rubicund – turned up towards me.

'Brigid,' said Mère-Maîtresse solemnly. It was the first time she had failed to call me Sister since our Clothing, and I stared at her in surprise.

'Brigid!' she repeated. 'Come over here.' The little triangle parted to let me in.

'I have some very sad news for you,' said my novice-mistress quietly as Sister Céline put her arm round my shoulder. It was only then I noticed she was crying.

'Am I to leave the château?' I guessed blindly, panic-stricken at their solemn faces. 'To see my mother?'

'No, my child,' said Mère-Maîtresse. 'There is no need for you to leave the château, not for today. Sister Patrice has just told me. Your mother died two hours ago of a heart attack.'

SEVENTEEN

They buried her in the convent cemetery, next to Nathalie Sémichon, in a special corner reserved for lay people closely associated with the order. After trying, without success, to contact my father, Uncle David flew out from England. Monsieur l'Aumônier presided over a requiem mass where the only other mourners were novices and nuns.

For weeks afterwards everyone treated me very gently, carefully avoiding any mention of the holiday that had been cut short. Soon summer was inching its way into autumn, and there was a faint chill in the air as we rose for Matins, but I took no pleasure in the sparkling September skies.

When the new batch of postulants arrived with the grape harvest, I resented the upheaval, too fatigued to adapt to new people. As senior novice, Sister Raphael was responsible for showing them round the novitiate. Her opening address was drowned by the stubby little tractors roaring in from the surrounding vineyards to deposit their grapes in the cooperative at the bottom of our street.

Like everyone else, I sat next to one of the newcomers at mealtimes, and showed her how to ask for more bread or a second serving in silence, and how to wash her knife, fork and spoon in the tumbler of hot water poured by the refectarians. It was strange to think that a year ago we had looked like them, a weepy and ill-assorted little bunch with their tear-stained faces and inexpertly tied veils.

During the winter I began to recover my spirits. By Christmas I was noting with an emotion close to relief that my first thoughts on waking were not necessarily to do with my mother, and was finding myself able to concentrate again – on my prayers, on spiritual reading, and on manual work. There was no longer any need to water the courtyard, so I was transferred inside to work the butter machine. Sometimes whole mornings or afternoons passed without my pausing to reproach myself. But I still took care to visit my mother's grave at least once every two or three days, usually towards Vespers.

I was haunted by a sense of waste. It had been weeks before I could bring myself to open Madge's last letter, that luckless, neglected letter in which she explained why she hadn't turned up for my Clothing. She had been in hospital then, she told me – nothing serious, only a mild heart attack. Mrs Bavidge had promised not to breathe a word – they neither of them wanted to spoil my day.

I forced myself to read on as the lines blurred. My mother knew she didn't have long to go, and wished to see me for one last time. Could she come and visit me in the Mother House? Uncle David had lent her the money. Unless I wrote to stop her, she would be with me in ten days. It was to be her first trip abroad, and she was longing to get a glimpse of Berbiers. I folded the letter carefully, and slid it into my missal, where I would never forget it again.

The cemetery was close to hand, in a corner of the park, and Mère-Maîtresse had given me permission to go there as often as I wished. The only person to witness these visits was Hercule, who would still hang around watching, but without trying to disconcert me. He had grown subdued since the days Lucie used to race him for the *bassin*, and I was glad never to have told anyone else about the embarrassing incident in the vegetable garden. If Hercule remembered it he gave no sign, and neither did I. From time to time he would approach with a gift from his greenhouse, early irises, perhaps, or a precious pot of begonias, and I wondered how I could ever have felt afraid of him.

'My poor little Sister!' he would murmur as he wandered

off to trim the graves or brush away any leaves that had drifted on to the gravel paths. Far from finding his sympathy intrusive, I liked him pottering around in the winter twilight as I gazed down on the little mound of earth adorned with hothouse flowers, and wondered what my mother would have made of her last resting-place.

In the spring we prepared to take our First Vows. The ceremony was simpler and more austere than our Clothing, and the congregation was restricted to Joubertians only. In the middle of the service we filed out to exchange our white veils for brown; then Bishop Eugene placed round each of our necks the little wooden cross marked with a 'J' that we would wear every day for the rest of our lives as a reminder that we had vowed to live poor, chaste and obedient.

At recreation that night our talk was muted, as though the momentousness of the occasion hadn't quite worn off. Beside me sat Sister Boniface, bent over her embroidery, her face pale from the long winter and unusually late spring. Slim and serious, she looked a model nun, unrecognizable as the greasy-ringleted hippy I'd first seen entangled with her boyfriend. Putting the finishing touches to a pale pink petal and neatly snipping the silk, she broke the silence that had descended on our little group.

'Well, Sisters,' she said in her now exemplary French. 'This is the end of us.'

We all knew what she meant. The following morning it would be our turn to receive our *billets-doux* – those cards delivered to each newly professed nun from the hand of Mother General herself.

'I dread leaving Berbiers,' sighed Lucie, 'yet in the beginning I was so unhappy.'

'So was I,' sighed Fatima. 'And now I know I will never be so happy again. I would give anything to be you, Brigid.'

Each year one of the young professed was elected to stay in the Mother House – as Sister Bon Pasteur had done last year. Usually the nun singled out for this honour was French; but this year Sister Céline had told her niece in confidence that I had been chosen instead – she'd overheard Mother General tell Mère-Maîtresse. Lucie – who as a lay sister was not herself eligible – couldn't resist telling the rest of us, first me, and then the others. It was, they all agreed, a good decision. My French was fluent and, unlike most young nuns, I had no relatives anxiously awaiting my return home. Uncle David and I had never been close. And with my mother buried here, it seemed more fitting I should stay close by.

I glanced round the little circle of faces – Sister Lucie, Sister Raphael, Sister Fatima, Sister Elisabeth. Apart from my uncle, they were the only family I had. Tomorrow they would be dispersed around the globe, and it was unlikely I would see any of them again.

On my other side sat Mère-Maîtresse. On the day of my mother's funeral I'd vowed never to forgive her. If she hadn't ignored my pleading, my mother might not have died a lonely death in a French hotel. But I soon saw my mistake. The blame was mine, for failing to read my letter; not Mère-Maîtresse's, who had done her best according to her lights. Confronted with an importunate parent, she had only tried to uphold canon law. After tomorrow she would no longer be responsible for my spiritual welfare – but I felt glad she would be close by, ready to be consulted.

Over the past few months she'd taken to seeing me alone for an hour or two each week, beckoning me into her study after lunch. Under the pretext of giving her more English lessons, I was allowed to speak in my own language – it improved her ear, she said. We still had the dog-eared textbooks from the *lycée*, but these days we seldom bothered with any grammar. Mostly she encouraged me to talk about my past – that hazy and undistinguished past I'd once been so eager to forget. I treasured those periods of intimacy, when the shutters were closed against the glare, and the postulants were upstairs having their siesta; and I never dared question why she had decided to ignore the rules, for fear she might stop. Mostly I told her stories about my mother, embellished with dimly recalled details about her job as a ward orderly during the Blitz, and my father's tortuous courtship. We seldom spoke about her death, because there seemed no point.

'See it as a special sign of God's favour,' Mère-Maîtresse had told me soon after the funeral. 'Far from leaving you an orphan, Sister Brigid, He will place you more than ever under His protection.'

Mère-Maîtresse had been right. After my grief had abated, I felt closer to God than ever before, and often meditated on Sister Monica's words: if God takes away what we most prize, it is only to bind us to Him all the more.

The morning after our First Vows we were summoned, one by one, to Mother General's office. The procedure was simple: we were to knock and wait until the old nun bade us enter. After kneeling at her feet we would accept from her extended hand a card bearing a single word. We were free to read it if we chose, but a model nun would kiss the floor without so much as a glance at the name of her future home, murmuring as she arose the statutory words of response: 'Be it done unto me according to thy word.'

Ahead of me was Elisabeth, in and out of Mother General's office in no time, her eyes dancing. My turn next. Trembling slightly, I knelt at the old woman's feet, awed by her grave stare. I tried not to read the word on the card, but my eyes were drawn down against my will. No matter: I knew already where I was going. *Liverpool*. The spidery italics began to jiggle and hop before my eyes. I'd been given the wrong *billet-doux*.

The old nun's eyes widened in amazement as I attempted to hand it back. Never, she said sternly, had any Joubertian done the like.

'But I'm staying in Berbiers,' I heard myself stutter.

'To stay in the Mother House is a great privilege,' said Mother General, 'and I had to make sure you were worthy. During your final retreat I observed you closely, and soon saw that you were not. A good nun practises detachment, Sister Brigid. She does not spend her time as you do, staring at the sky, or contemplating the flowers instead of her prayerbook. You must conquer your love of places.'

'But this is the first place I have ever loved!'

'Then let it be the last,' responded Mother General. 'I am told you do not love Merseyside; that is why I am sending you back. You are to teach in St Cuthbert's.'

I opened my mouth to speak, but Mother General held up her hand.

'I know you have no qualifications, but your A levels are good. You must use them now in God's service. Sister Monica has been taken ill, and they are very short-staffed.'

'Sister Monica – ill?' I said. 'What's the matter with her?'

'I have told you more than enough for one morning,' responded Mother General. 'You are a Joubertian now, and must go where you are told.' Then she added more kindly, 'Don't cry, Sister Brigid. You are young, and think you won't survive away from the blue skies of the Midi. I once felt like you on returning to Cracow. But it passes. In the meantime,' she said, holding up a crooked forefinger, 're-member to thank the Good Lord daily for your suffering. It is a special token of His favour.'

Did He really want me to live just across the park from my home in the Dingle, and everything I'd tried to leave behind? The whole community would remember me from the first form – with my scouse accent, and the wrong school blazer bought cheap. Uncertainly I rose to my feet.

'But the ceremony is incomplete!' cried the old nun.

Blushing, I dropped back to my knees, and pressed my lips to the cold tiles. Raising my head, I got a glimpse of

Mother General's shoes, impersonal as any man's, and polished to a high shine.

'Be it done unto me according to thy word,' I mumbled.

'Please tell Sister Boniface to come in next.'

'Wish me luck!' whispered the young American as she slid past me into the room.

Still clutching my card, I turned towards the chapel. Before I'd advanced more than two paces, Elisabeth came hurtling out of the community room, her skirts flying.

'Guess what!' she said as she skidded to a halt. 'I'm going to Rome to study art history. Eddy will be green with envy – and as for Mummy –' she checked herself at once, and dropping her eyes, noticed the name on my card.

'Back to square one!' she said sympathetically. 'Poor you.'

The parlour door opened wide again and slammed shut. Bony was at our side.

'Well, kids, it's the missions for me,' she said, lapsing into English. 'I'm off to the Congo. That means another three languages at least. I give up.'

'What do you say? Speak in French, please.' Without noticing, we had been joined by Sister Fatima. 'Ah! The missions. What luck. Me, I go to Coimbra to study mathematics.'

Coimbra on the Mondego. One of the postulants had gone to school there. From the convent windows you could see the storks' nests floating on a sea of ochre roofs, and at night the black-gowned students serenaded each other in the cobbled streets. Yet Fatima longed to go on the missions.

'And all I want,' moaned Boniface as we moved towards the dormitory to strip our beds, 'is to work in an inner city – like you, Brigid.'

Although I'd longed to escape my mother, I could scarcely bear the thought of going back without her.

'I'll write to you from Rome,' promised Elisabeth. 'And Mummy will come and visit you – and so will Timmy, and

Jonathon – I'll insist. And Lorraine will be home in the holidays. It won't be so bad.'

Elisabeth's plane was in two hours' time, so I left her to finish packing while I visited the cemetery. As I passed through the novitiate room, Mère-Maîtresse beckoned me into her study.

'So you are going back to your old home, Sister Brigid.'

I tried to sound stoical. 'I'll write when I need advice.'

'If Mother Wilfred gives you permission,' my novice-mistress reminded me gently. 'From now on she will be your spiritual director.'

'I was afraid of her in school.'

'She's a disciplinarian – but very fair-minded. You must remember what you've learnt, and be a credit to me.' For a few seconds Mère-Maîtresse looked touchingly young and vulnerable.

'I don't know how I'll manage without you.'

'You can always turn to your beloved Sister Monica for support and advice.'

'She's been taken ill,' I said. 'I don't even know what's wrong with her.'

'Monica has a generous spirit, and will find time for her protégée whatever the matter is.'

'It's a pity she won't be in school, to help with my teaching.'

'You can always ask Sister Ursula – she's a fine head-mistress. And Sister Ligori is good, too. And Sister Bosco – yes, I know she has her faults – but there's a warm heart hidden under the bluster.'

'It's Sister Julian who's head of English,' I said.

Mère-Maîtresse's gaze clouded for a few seconds. 'I've been praying about this ever since I heard your destination,' she said slowly. 'I'm going to take a risk, Brigid – and depend on you not to let me down.'

Swallowing hard, I nodded.

'Change is on the way,' she said, 'and, believe me, some of us have prayed for it. But one can go too far, too fast.'

I stayed silent, only aware that I didn't want any changes. I wanted everything to stay the same.

'Sister Julian is sure of herself,' Mère-Maîtresse went on, 'too sure, perhaps – and I fear she may lead others astray. Then her considerable intellect – one of God's greatest gifts – would serve to undermine our order.'

'I'll be sure and avoid her,' I promised, without quite understanding what was meant.

'You needn't go to extremes,' said my novice-mistress with the flicker of a smile, 'or you will neglect community life.'

There was a knock at the door. Elisabeth and Boniface were leaving for the station. The rest were going in an hour. Putting Mère-Maîtresse's words to the back of my mind, I helped carry the luggage downstairs, then stood with her at the top of the perron as the minibus roared across the cobbles. Soon I too would be gone. It was time to visit the cemetery.

Hercule was nowhere to be seen, but my mother's grave was piled high with spring flowers – narcissi, jonquils, irises and orange blossom. I knew she was in heaven, despite her lack of faith. But it felt like deserting her yet again, and I gazed with a heavy heart at the little mound with the plain wooden cross at its head.

On leaving the graveyard I bumped into Lucie, who was racing back to the novitiate, her skirts held high around her knees. I looked at her in envy. She it was, not me, who had been chosen to stay in the Mother House; Lucie the tomboy, with her patois and disorderly ways, was the first lay sister ever to be granted this honour.

'Yes, I know I'm out of bounds,' she panted, 'but I wanted to give Hercule my good news. By the way, he sends you his deepest respects. He promises to tend your mother's grave daily; and so will I.' She paused to clear her throat, and then went on, her voice forlorn. 'I wish you were staying here with us, Brigid. In the summer we would water the garden again, all three of us — you, me and Hercule. It would be like old times.'

'It is better that I return to Liverpool,' I replied. 'I learnt nothing in a beautiful place, so now I must go to an ugly one.'

It was the first time Lucie had heard me speak like this, and her brown eyes widened. 'Please, it is too late to grieve,' she said as we began walking back across the park. 'Obedience is always best.'

My luggage was waiting in the front hall. Soon Sister Patrice would be revving up the minibus one more time. On the steps stood Mère-Maîtresse, holding out my suitcase, and Sister Céline, who was glancing at her watch. It was getting late.

'Goodbye, Sister Brigid,' said Mère-Maîtresse, plucking lightly at my sleeve. It was her only gesture of affection. 'You are bearing your new sisters a breath of air from the Mother House. Remember that the Lord loves a cheerful giver.'

'Goodbye, Mère-Maîtresse,' I said, and jumped as Sister Patrice sounded her horn. 'Goodbye, Sister Céline. Goodbye, Lucie.'

The young nun seized my suitcase and heaved it on to the back seat. 'I'll pray for you every day,' she said, her eyes brimming.

'Hurry up!' cried Sister Patrice. 'The train will leave in just seven minutes!'

Before I'd slammed the door shut, the minibus was lurching over the cobbles. Instead of waving back at the three minuscule figures in the wing mirror, I forced my eyes to the road ahead, in tune for once with Sister Patrice's driving.

Sister Lucie was right to say it was too late for grief, I thought, as we sped down the dual carriageway. But she was not right to say obedience was always best. Madge had been my responsibility and nobody else's, and I'd backed down when I should have spoken out.

I willed the rush-hour traffic to part before us. Mère-Maîtresse was an admirable nun, but she'd divided me from Madge at a critical moment. And far from helping me accept my guilt, my sisters in Christ had tried to gloss it over with talk of Holy Obedience.

I climbed on the train a few seconds before it pulled out of the station, and after watching Sister Patrice climb back into the minibus I stayed in the corridor to catch a last glimpse of Berbiers.

The cathedral ramparts were ablaze in the setting sun, with the convent nestling in their shadow. As the train rumbled over the viaduct and away from my mother's grave, I vowed never again to stay silent when I should speak out. I had important lessons to learn, and returning to a Liverpool without Madge in it was the best way of beginning to learn them.

EIGHTEEN

—

The train pulled in to the same dingy platform where Lorraine and Uncle David had waved me off two years ago. I half expected to see them both, my uncle stiff and sombre, and Lorraine twirling around in my turquoise sweater dress. Then I remembered: no one would have told them of my arrival. Instead there was Mother Wilfred, the breezy, authoritarian Superior of St Cuthbert's.

She was the tallest woman I had ever seen. When I was in school a criminal had happened to escape from Walton jail. Three hours later two policeman spotted Mother Wilfred striding along the boulevard in the winter dusk, six foot three and square of shoulder. Convincing each other she was the convict in disguise, they trailed her back to St Cuthbert's, refusing to go away until Sister Ursula appeared and swore to her Superior's identity.

Tonight she towered over the little cluster of people waiting at the ticket barrier. 'Sorry about your mother, child,' she boomed as she strode towards me, her skirts flapping. 'I told her not to go to Berbiers, but she would have her own way.'

Seizing my case, she bundled us both into a waiting taxi. Within seconds we were swinging out of the concourse and past the amusement arcade.

'Mind you, we none of us knew how ill she was,' Mother Wilfred ran on. 'We could have done something, if only she'd said. Sister Annunciata would have been only too happy to nurse her.'

I pictured the convent infirmarian tripping upstairs to the stale-smelling little bedroom. 'She hated being a trouble,' I lied, then turned to look out of the window. There was the department store where we'd gone to buy my suit.

'I'm glad you're bearing up,' barked my new Superior. 'There's a busy term ahead, and I don't want any more collapses.'

We whirled past the Kardomah, where I'd first seen Elisabeth with Jonathon Maule. She would have arrived in Rome by now, and he was said to be filming in Tangier. Liverpool was shabbier than I remembered, and the people looked pastier than ever. I stared at the façade of the coffee shop, puzzled by the absence of tables and chairs outside. And then I remembered: this was England, and everyone drank indoors. Understandably, I thought, with the sunlight strained through a haze the colour of dirty milk, and the air wafting through the window rancid with hot dogs. Even though it was May I felt chilly, and shivered slightly as we left the city centre, to nose our way down the boulevard.

'Sister Ursula will be glad of your help,' said Mother Wilfred, 'now that Sister Monica is ill.'

'What's the matter with her?'

The Mother Superior nodded impatiently at the back of the taxi driver's neck. I should know better, said her look, than to ask such a question in the presence of a layman. People loved gossiping about nuns. 'We don't know,' she replied. 'It's a mystery.'

Soon we were entering the park. For the first time I saw that it had been laid out on French principles, with its paths and drives based on circles, ellipses and their tangents. As a child I had loved the park-keeper's lodge because it was like the gingerbread house in *Hansel and Gretel*. Now I could see it was meant to be a *cottage ornée*. But what a jumble of styles! With its Tudor veneer and over-embellished red brick clashing with the lobster granite of the gateway, it looked not so much fanciful as vulgar. And where was the bright ornamental foliage of France? Avenues not of acacias but of heavy English oaks destroyed the perspectives, and the palm house was blotted out by clumps of rhododendrons in a travesty of Le Nôtre.

I hovered awkwardly at the convent gates while Mother Superior paid the fare, then followed her through the big pseudo-Tudor front door and down the hall, past the little parlour where I'd first met Mother General.

'Your sisters are waiting in the community room,' said Mother Wilfred as we plunged down a dark corridor to one side of the stairs, to emerge in a tiled hall at the back of the house. On the left-hand side was a stout mahogany door. It was the furthest I had ever been into the convent.

There was a fluttering noise as Mother Wilfred turned the handle, and the assembled nuns rose quickly to their feet.

'You're very welcome, Sister Brigid,' somebody said sweetly, to be echoed and re-echoed by the others: 'Welcome home, Sister Brigid . . . You're very, very welcome.'

They embraced me one by one – first Sister Ursula, thinner and paler since I saw her last, and then Sister Bosco, her complexion more mottled than ever. 'We're glad to have you with us,' she said gruffly. 'We could do with a bit of young blood.' And then came Sister Julian, with her aquiline nose and over-refined accent, grazing my cheek gently with her coif. Why did Mère-Maîtresse think her dangerous? Next was Sister Ligori, who had retired many years ago, but continued to help with music classes, and finally Sister Kevin, my old French teacher, who clasped my hand warmly. 'The girls are longing to see you, Brigid. It will be good for them – being taught by a past pupil.'

'I hope so,' I said apprehensively. Tucking my hands in my sleeves, I tried to look as different as possible from the schoolgirl of two years earlier.

Mother Wilfred took me by the elbow and steered me towards the huddle of lay sisters by the door. 'And these, my dear, are the really important members of our little community – Sister Gonzaga, Sister Columba, and Sister Annunciata.'

Most familiar to me was Sister Gonzaga, who used to ladle out our school dinners with a cross face, and insist that everyone ate their Spam; and I had often seen Sister Columba hurrying between convent and school with messages for the teaching nuns. Sister Annunciata would only be summoned when a girl had a bad nosebleed or a dizzy spell.

'You're very welcome, Sister Brigid,' the three of them chorused, but none of them said whether they remembered me or not, or offered to embrace me. I sensed it wouldn't have been appropriate.

'How is everyone in Berbiers?' Sister Ursula asked as I rejoined the others. 'Mère-Maîtresse? And Sister Céline? And dear old Sister Nicole? I did so love it there. Holiness oozes out of the very walls.'

'Well, the walls don't ooze much at St Cuthbert's,' intervened Mother Wilfred, 'unless it's a bit of rising damp. We're none of us saints here, Sister Brigid, and we've no high-falutin notions. Just ordinary working women.' She raised the lid of an empty desk. 'I've put you next to Sister Bosco. And this is your locker, fourth from the right on the top row.'

The community room was smaller and more cluttered than the one at Berbiers, with heavy curtains instead of shutters. I was surprised to see a television set in one corner, and beside it a magazine rack holding copies of the *Radio Times*. The room looked out over the playground, or would have, were it not for the frosted glass, which had provoked a lot of speculation when we were in school. Lorraine thought it was where the nuns used to flagellate themselves, while Patsy McCann, who had an aunt in the Carmelites, maintained it was where they kept their coffins. If only we'd known it was so ordinary.

'It's time I took you to your cell,' announced Mother Wilfred. 'You can get your unpacking done before Vespers.'

She climbed ahead of me to the attic, which had been subdivided into eleven cubicles, each big enough to contain a bed, a locker, a chair and a narrow wardrobe.

'Here you are, next to Sister Bosco,' she said, panting slightly. 'I've told her to look after you.'

I was relieved to see that we each had our own cubicle. 'Who sleeps on the other side?' I asked. Often, while waiting at the bus-stop as a schoolgirl, I had gazed at the row of skylights, and wondered whose was which.

'Sister Monica.'

'Is she in there now?'

'She's been moved to the infirmary. You may go and see her tomorrow, if Ursula can spare you.'

'Yes, Mother,' I said, as meekly as I could, then turned to my unpacking. But instead of leaving me alone, the Superior stayed looming in the doorway. 'I hope you're going to stand up to all this,' she said as I opened my case. 'What's that you have there, a glass cat? I'm surprised your novice-mistress let you keep it.'

I slid the little ornament into the locker drawer for fear of confiscation.

'To put it frankly,' Mother Wilfred carried on, 'we asked for somebody older – and more experienced. Mother General agreed – then changed her mind at the last moment. A pity, in my view. This community isn't the place for a young nun.'

'Why not?'

'We're overstretched as it is, and have no time to help a greenhorn.'

'I'll do my best to fit in.'

'It's unfortunate you've had no training, because the children will be watching you to see how far they can go,' she said, 'especially girls like Maureen O'Shaunessy who knew you well. Don't get over-familiar.'

I nodded politely. My lack of experience had suddenly

stopped bothering me. Only two years ago I'd been one of Mother Wilfred's pupils, and knew just how boring she could be. There wasn't much I didn't know about St Cuthbert's girls, and I felt ready to take them on – the bright ones, the lazy ones, the ones obsessed with boys and make-up. I would make them love reading as much as I did.

'Don't flatter yourself you'll turn them all into bookworms,' added Mother Wilfred, as though reading my mind.

At least I wouldn't bore them all with Lamb's *Tales from Shakespeare*, I thought, remembering the Superior's readings from the nineteenth-century classics.

'Most of them come from good Catholic homes,' the Superior was saying, 'so their respect will stand you in good stead. It is your job to sustain that respect.'

After Mother Wilfred had sailed away down the stairs, I tried to shake off the feeling I was out of bounds by arranging my belongings on top of the bedside locker, with the little pink cat in pride of place beside my missal and crucifix. Out of the window, I could see some boys, stripped to the waist, playing tennis in the park; and beyond them a jumble of roofs and television aerials silhouetted against the distant hills. For the first time in my life as a nun I felt confined – back in Liverpool, but shut away in a convent. Between me and those high Welsh hills lay the Dingle, and I wondered whether Lorraine had spent the summer in Moses Street, and why she hadn't written. It must be hard, corresponding with a nun. Half the time you didn't get an answer – and when you did, the letter was so stilted it was hardly worth it. Lorraine had probably given up in disgust.

After breakfast the following morning, Sister Bosco led me through the big panelled door that separated the convent from the school.

'Mother Wilfred governs our community life, but once we're on this side of the door, Sister Ursula is boss,' she explained jovially. 'I told her I'd show you the ropes.'

I nodded as politely as I could, eager to get on with my charge. But the Deputy Head was in no hurry. 'There are big changes on the way,' she told me. 'The Bishop has decreed that from now on we will spend our breaks with the secular staff, instead of on our own in the stockroom. He wants us to be more – involved.' She sniffed. 'Personally I disagree with him. The lay teachers have their concerns, and we have ours. It's better for both sides to keep their distance.'

Big changes? These were nothing but details. Impatiently I waited for her to finish. After she'd given me a full account of the parent–teacher association I could contain myself no longer. 'Please, Sister, when may I see Sister Monica?'

'You are in a rush, aren't you?' said the other nun. With a quick glance at my face she added more kindly, 'I dare say you can go up around mid-morning, if she's sitting up. But you'd better get some work done first. Come with me, and I'll tell you what to do.'

My charge was to scrub the downstairs school corridor, clean out the lower school cloakroom, and the three adjacent classrooms, which included my own. They were all quite clean now, explained Sister Bosco, because the exams were on. Normally I would set to work in the evening, after class. But today a quick sweep and dust would suffice. Then I must go to the stockroom and copy down my timetable.

'I remember your dear mother working here,' went on Sister Bosco, opening the broom cupboard. Her tone came as a surprise. She had often taken it upon herself to run a finger along a banister or windowsill and complain about skimped work. Madge could hardly have been a satisfactory cleaner, and had most certainly hated St Cuthbert's. 'Too many old maids,' she used to say, 'with nothing else to fuss about.'

I had never given much thought to my mother's job, apart from wishing she worked somewhere else. Now, as I picked up a broom and started to sweep, I wondered how she'd felt cleaning in the school where I was a pupil. I'd always dreaded doing what she did – yet here I was, working my way down the same corridors. Then I remembered that nothing was worthless or menial if offered up to God. If not, it may as well be done for a man, or for money, I told myself, glad to be working for neither.

Next I went to the stockroom, which was little more than a cubbyhole looking out on the lower corridor, with bookshelves lining the walls and a Belfast sink in one corner. Sister Julian was sitting in the middle, counting out copies of *Flush*.

'Ah! The return of the native,' she said, looking up over her glasses.

'I've come to get my timetable,' I told her, too constrained to admit I didn't grasp her allusion.

'I suppose you're worried about your new classes?' she said. 'No? That's good – because everyone else is. Heaven knows why – you can hardly be worse than old Bosco.'

I had my own view of Sister Bosco's teaching – but it didn't seem right for one nun to criticize another.

'Oh, dear – I've shocked you,' said Sister Julian. 'Apologies.'

'Teachers can't always be interesting,' I said.

'Maybe not – but they shouldn't be bullies, either. There's no need to look so prim, Brigid – I can see what you think.'

No wonder Mère-Maîtresse had warned me about her. 'I'm going to visit Sister Monica,' I told her.

'Now?' asked the English teacher, her eyebrows arching towards her coif.

I nodded. 'Mother Wilfred has given me permission.'

'In that case . . .' she shrugged. 'It wouldn't do for us to disappoint the invalid. Here, take your timetable. Let's hope you speed her recovery.'

Glad to escape from the strange, satirical woman, I made my way to the infirmary.

'Come in,' cried a voice. I entered a room with a large fireplace, four high beds with white coverlets, and an expanse of pine floorboards. The infirmarian was bending over the bed farthest from the door, plumping the pillows of Sister Monica, who was smiling gratefully. Her hands, thin and blue-veined, were clasping a little sheaf of letters.

'Brigid!' she exclaimed, looking up, 'or Sister Brigid, I should say. How lovely and brown you look!'

She was wearing the regulation nightcap, a white linen bonnet which covered her hair, all except one dark lock which lay coiled on her neck. Round her shoulders was a crocheted shawl. She looked smaller without her coif, and more ordinary. Suddenly embarrassed, I tried to avert my eyes.

'Sister Monica,' I stammered as the nurse bustled away. 'What is the matter with you?'

'Nobody knows,' she replied, sadly. 'They've run test after test. I keep on having these violent fits, and they think I might be epileptic.'

'But you can't stop teaching!' I exclaimed.

'I might have to – just imagine, if I had a fit in class.'

'It's a waste – you were brilliant.' Sister Monica had made art the most popular subject in the school.

'The doctor has ordered complete bed-rest. If that doesn't work, they'll give me another job elsewhere – cooking or library work. It's a shame. I so wanted to be on my feet by the time you arrived – to help you acclimatize.'

'I'll come up and see you often,' I said.

'Yes, you must,' said Sister Monica. Her skin had a waxy pallor, and her eyes looked tired and slightly swollen. 'I want to hear all about the Mother House. Does Sister Nicole still tyrannize over the linen-room? And did Hercule teach you to water the garden? I long for a good gossip. It feels so lonely up here – especially during term-time.'

I felt reluctant to embark on my Berbiers adventures with Sister Annunciata hovering around. 'I'll come a little later,' I said awkwardly. 'Shall I bring you something to read?'

'Nuncy keeps me well supplied with library books. The trouble is, I get so drowsy on these phenobarbs. You must forgive me if I seem muzzy.'

'I wish you were still in school,' I said.

'So do I, Brigid. I know it's wrong to be attached – but I miss my pupils. Look, they've been writing to me.' She shuffled the little pile of envelopes.

'I'll try and make it up to them.'

Sister Monica nodded seriously. 'Yes, that's important. The girls need someone young to confide in – and so do you, Brigid. There are some fine nuns in this community, but they've been here a long time, and are set in their ways.'

'Don't worry about me – I prefer talking to older people.'

Sister Annunciata, who had been fussing around the bed proprietorially, bore down on Sister Monica with a glass of water and some tablets.

'Brigid's a sensible girl – so don't you be turning her against us,' she scolded. 'There's life in us yet.'

'There's plenty of life in *you*, Nuncy,' said the invalid affectionately. 'It was some of the others I was thinking of.'

'There are queer fish in any community,' said the nurse, 'and they must be our cross.'

'And so must I,' said Sister Monica, 'lying here idle when there's so much to be done.'

The infirmarian gave a reproachful click of her tongue. 'The sick are a great blessing,' she said, twitching a sheet. 'The Good Lord will reward us all on your account.'

'I'm sure He will, Sister, if you tell Him to,' laughed the young nun. 'And look at Sister Brigid, come to join us. A nun fresh from the Mother House is a great blessing. And if I was well she wouldn't be here.'

'You've been chatting long enough, Sister Monica,' said the infirmarian. 'You mustn't over-exert yourself.'

'I suppose you're right, Nuncy,' said Sister Monica, looking paler than ever. 'Thanks for coming to see me, Brigid. Better run along now, or you'll have Sister Julian after you.'

I opened my mouth in surprise. How did she know that Sister Julian had objected to my visit?

'You don't have to tell me,' said the invalid, waving aside my silent query. 'I know she disapproves of me. Oh dear, what am I saying? These tablets make me feel so heavy.' She lay back against the pillow and closed her eyes.

Sister Annunciata followed me as I tiptoed out of the infirmary. 'It's hard on Monica, laid up like this,' she whispered once we had reached the corridor, 'and Sister Julian has no right to cast aspersions. A great affliction is a sure sign of the Lord's favour. Monica's a living saint, that's what. And don't let anyone tell you different.'

NINETEEN

It was break-time on the last Monday of term. The domestic science mistress, a big woman with a face like a floured bun, had tacked up some paper decorations left over from the fifth-form party. Each time the door opened the orange, blue and yellow fluting gave a tired rustle and then subsided. The sky looked grimy through the windows, which were too high to be cleaned from the outside. But I could sense the day was bright, with a dome of royal blue over the halberd hedges and frosty chrysanthemums in the park. In ten days' time it would be Christmas.

'Chuck us a fag, Margie,' said Miss Vavasour, a lanky woman in her fifties with an iron-grey crop and weathered skin. Sport was not highly regarded at St Cuthbert's, because the nuns thought it unladylike and best left to Protestants. But Miss Vavasour continued to coax and cajole her pupils on to the pitch. Although as a girl I had never liked games, I had always liked Miss Vavasour.

Margie Manifold, who had joined the staff only last term, rummaged in her handbag and tossed the games mistress a packet of Gold Leaf.

'Cheers.' The older woman lit up and inhaled deeply. 'How you survive without smoking, Sister Brigid, I can't imagine. But then you always were a good child.'

'She never got the habit,' said Mr Bethany, the music teacher. In the seven months since my arrival this had become a familiar staffroom joke.

'Don't you take any notice, Sister Brigid,' said Miss Vavasour. 'I'm glad you've joined us. It's a change for the better.'

'I agree – nice and sociable,' crooned Mrs Tarn, the French teacher. As a girl I had disapproved of Lavinia, as she encouraged the older girls to call her. She was too easy to sidetrack during General Studies, with stories about her days on the Boul' Miche, and holidays in the Auvergne where she, her ex-husband and her best friend all shared the same bed. But I was already beginning to enjoy her as a colleague.

'The other sisters should approve,' said Mr Bethany, with a sideways glance in my direction, 'as long as they don't think we're corrupting you.'

I didn't join in the ripple of laughter. As far as St Cuthbert's was concerned, the Bishop's initiative had failed. Sister Julian would sometimes put her head round the staffroom door; but it was generally agreed she was too much the intellectual to bother with staffroom chatter, and she continued to take her breaks in the library. The other nuns persisted in going to the stockroom, where Sister Bosco presided over a kettle and a box of Tetley's teabags.

On the first day of term I'd simply obeyed the directive, too eager for a cup of coffee to wait for the others. By the end of the first week it was obvious that no other nuns were going to join me; but my breaks in the big, untidy room were the only bright spot in my school day, and I was reluctant to give them up.

'God, I'm knackered,' said Miss Manifold. She yawned vigorously and stretched out her arms, nearly knocking Mr Bethany's glasses off the end of his nose. He was wearing a chunky Italian cardigan, which on another man would have looked stylish and dashing, but made him look old-woman-ish. He winced, and settled himself fussily by the radiator.

I tried not to stare as Margie flung herself back in her chair and crossed her legs. She didn't look 'knackered' to me, with her sparkling eyes and rosy cheeks. It was only last term that she had taken over all the art classes, and already she was nearly as popular as Sister Monica. Popular with the girls, that is. With the nuns, she was definitely out of favour.

At St Cuthbert's, the female staff were enjoined to wear skirts. Anything else was a bad example. So Sister Bosco, as Deputy Head, had told the staff on the very first morning of term. Women teachers in trousers were their own worst enemies – and the enemies of other, more law-abiding teachers. Sister Ursula agreed with her, and so did the Bishop. Of course, what the staff wore in their own time was their own business.

'Big bloody deal,' Margie had muttered mutinously. Sister Bosco glanced sharply in her direction, her face darkening.

'What was that, Miss Manifold?'

'I said,' replied Margie, 'that I shall wear what I like.' She flicked back her mane of red hair. 'If a male member of staff wants to wear a dress, that's fine by me. It's not against the law. Nor is a woman in trousers, as far as I know.' And gathering up her folders, she sailed out of the staffroom, leaving Sister Bosco with her mouth open. So far the Deputy Head hadn't reverted to the topic.

'Goodness knows how you had the nerve, Margie,' said Miss Vavasour. 'Perhaps it's because you're a non-Catholic. You weren't brainwashed like the rest of us.'

'I just don't like keeping rules,' said Margie, yawning again. 'God, I could sleep for a week.'

'Out on the tiles last night?'

'That's right,' grinned the art teacher. 'A whole load of us went on to the Somali. Goodness knows what time I got home.'

'You're burning the candle at both ends,' said the French teacher, as she riffled through a pile of exercise books. 'Not that I didn't at your age.'

'You should come with us one night, Lavinia.'

'To the Somali? I'm past it, Margie. It'll be crammed with randy young men wanting to cop off.'

'Just your scene,' replied the young woman mischievously.

Lavinia snorted as she moved to answer a knock at the door.

'For you, Sister Brigid,' she called across the staffroom. 'There is a girl without.'

'Without what?' said Mr Bethany, as though by rote. Yet another of his little jokes.

Irritated at being disturbed during coffee-time, I made my way to the door. Predictably, it was Selina Boothroyd.

'Er, Miss – I mean, Sister Brigid,' she smirked, 'I shan't be here for English. Mummy says I'm to take the rest of the day off.'

'And why is that?'

'I'm auditioning for the North-West Youth Orchestra tomorrow,' said the girl. 'And I need time to practise.'

'I'm sure your mother said nothing of the sort,' I replied. 'She must know your schoolwork comes first.' Despite the firmness of my tone, I had my doubts. Mrs Boothroyd was one of the school governors, a large, tweedy woman with a strident voice, who considered her daughter a cut above the rest. She had already complained to me about Selina's progress – or lack of it – at the last parents' evening.

'Oh, Miss,' Selina whined, 'why can't I go home? English is a waste of time.'

'Please tell your mother from me,' I said frostily, 'that you cannot be released from English – not today or any other day. I'll see you in class in five minutes.'

By the time I'd finished with Selina, the bell was ringing for the end of break. I swallowed the rest of my coffee in a gulp, to the hubbub of the other teachers washing their mugs and gathering up their books for the next onslaught.

Sister Bosco stuck her head round the staffroom door. 'The bell has gone,' she announced to the room at large.

'Have they nicked that too?' whispered Margie.

Miss Vavasour screwed out her cigarette vigorously and

rose to her feet like an old warhorse, a plume of smoke furling forth from each nostril. The pupils were moving slowly past the staffroom door, like a tide of dirty water. Taking a deep breath, I plunged in.

'Excuse me,' I said every few moments, inching my way against the current. 'Excuse me.' No one took any notice. To my left a scuffle broke out among a group of ominously big girls. An elbow dug sharply through my *pèlerine*, and there was a dangerous tearing sound as somebody stepped on my habit. Already my veil had been tugged in several directions.

Mr Bethany was struggling down the other side. 'Little animals,' he mouthed as a satchel buckle snagged his cardigan. '*Get out of the way, girl!* You've got to show them who's boss.'

Grudgingly the children parted to let us through. On regaining my breath, I jabbed a dawdling fourth-former in the ribs, angry at the unfairness of it all. As a child I'd lived in fear of my teachers, jumping to my feet whenever they entered the room, and moving to the wall when they walked down the corridor for fear of bumping into them – unless they were carrying exercise books, in which case I offered to help. On the way to and from school I'd always worn my hat and gloves, despite the ridicule of girls from the secondary modern. The lay staff were ever vigilant, and would report any rebels to Sister Bosco. A girl from the year above mine had been expelled for eating an ice lolly at the bus-stop, and refusing to apologize.

On returning to St Cuthbert's, I had meant to surprise everyone by being kinder than my teachers had been to me. But things had changed during my absence, and it was me who got the surprise – at how rude the girls had become, and how they shouted and swore even in the presence of senior staff, and disregarded the weaker ones altogether. Nothing had prepared me for my pupils in 3W, who were bored by school and not afraid to show it. Mother Wilfred had been right. They wanted to see how far they could go – and they soon found out.

First I tried cajoling them, then I attempted sarcasm, saying all the things I'd once heard Sister Julian say, and vowed never to use. When that didn't work I tried to frighten them as Sister Bosco had frightened me. That was no good either. When I yelled at them they yelled straight back, and when I dished out detentions, they failed to show up. I was at a loss.

It would have been easy to bring up my difficulties in the staffroom. Miss Vavasour and Mrs Tarn, for instance, were both experienced teachers, and I envied their breezy scepticism about their pupils. But kind as they were to me, I knew how they felt about my lack of training. I'd once overheard Mrs Tarn pronounce it unfair that nuns with no qualifications should be appointed to posts that hadn't even been advertised. And Miss Vavasour was well known to be wry about Sister Bosco's promotion to Deputy Head over her and many another more talented lay teacher.

Although we shared the same pupils, and divided our day by the same bells, a gulf was fixed between us and the secular staff. At four o'clock, when they returned home, we withdrew through the big mahogany door to the refectory. There the lay sisters helped us to mugs of tea drawn from an urn, and slices of white bread and raspberry jam. At five I returned to the now deserted school, pinned up my habit and did my charge – an hour and a half's scrubbing and dusting. After that came chapel, supper, recreation, and then an hour or two for marking and preparation. At eleven thirty – or earlier if Mother Wilfred happened to poke her head round the library door – I would pack up my books and go to bed.

We were all known to work hard. Sister Ursula ran the whole school without secretarial help, and the light in her turret room was often observed by the likes of Margie Manifold on her way home from a party at twelve, one, or even two in the morning. Like the rest of us, the head-mistress would be up again at five thirty. Sister Bosco, as Deputy Head, taught maths to over half the school, besides running the parent–teacher association and the Legion of Mary. As head of English, Sister Julian was also school librarian, in charge of the book club and the foreign student exchange. Even Sister Ligori, long past retirement age, gave piano lessons throughout the school.

By electing to spend my breaks in the staffroom, I had cut myself off from these nuns. None of them tackled me directly – not even Sister Bosco, who could scarcely contain her disapproval. I was, after all, obeying the Bishop's instruc-tions; but they often made pointed remarks about the way my habit smelt of smoke, or how I'd missed an important message.

It would have been easy to confide in Sister Monica. Part of my problem was that 3W had been expecting to have her as their form teacher, and resented being fobbed off with a past pupil. But Sister Annunciata had warned me that the invalid mustn't be worried, so when she asked for news of the girls, I pretended that all was well.

I had always been fond of Sister Ligori, but she preferred the old way of doing things, and would cluck disapprovingly at the very idea of eating or drinking in front of a lay person. But I was growing desperate, and on finding her alone in the music room, I blurted out my difficulties.

'I can't cope,' I told her, fighting back the tears, 'and my lessons are a mess, and I don't know what to do.'

'It will come, with prayer,' said the old nun kindly, looking up from her songsheets. 'Ask Our Blessed Lady to help you.'

'I already have – and things are getting worse. What do *you* do,' I persisted, 'when a child won't obey you?'

'You catch more flies with honey than vinegar,' advised the old nun. 'The trick is to charm them. They'll soon come round.'

Mulling over her advice, I turned down the corridor towards my class. As I passed the library, Sister Julian stuck her head round the door.

'Everything all right, Brigid?'

As the noise from my waiting class drifted down the corridor, I was tempted to tell her my problems. But then I remembered Mère-Maîtresse's warning.

'Yes, fine, thank you.'

'Good. I hope you'd – er – tell me if it wasn't.'

'Of course.'

Her voice trailed away as the ghost of a grimace passed over her features. 'Er – try and keep the noise level down in class, won't you?'

'Yes, Sister.'

'I wouldn't have mentioned it – but Bosco's on the warpath. You don't want her bursting in on you.'

The banging desk lids reached a crescendo as I hurried down the corridor and pushed open the door. Sister Julian was wrong. This was not a level of noise, but a solid wall.

A few of the girls, including Selina Boothroyd, were trying to do their homework, heads bent, but most had abandoned all pretence of work. A transistor radio was playing somewhere out of sight. At the back of the class a noisy little group was screeching and giggling over an object clasped in the hand of Maureen O'Shaunessy.

I remembered her as Lorraine's skinny little sister, begging for an Everton strip for her twelfth birthday. Now she was taller than I was, with Lorraine's fair skin and voluptuous figure. I brought my ruler down hard on the lid of the front desk to attract her attention.

She swung round, glanced at me and then laughed provoking-ly. 'Hey, Brigid,' she called out, 'your headgear's crooked.' There was a guffaw of laughter from her best friend, Linda Renucci.

I had expected Maureen to be on my side, and felt hurt when, early in the term, she started to make trouble – all the more so because she looked so very like Lorraine. When her big brown eyes narrowed in derision, or she sauntered late into class – the O'Shaunessy saunter, I called it – it was as though my best friend had turned against me.

I was stung by her use of my Christian name, and her obvious lack of respect. The other girls might have forgotten that I'd been the sixth-form swot while they were first-years, but Maureen was always on hand to remind them. Goodness knows what else she might have told them – she had often hung around while I was chatting to Lorraine. I tugged nervously at my coif, before trying to restore order.

'Maureen, please return to your place,' I said quietly, trying to remember Sister Ligori's advice. She stayed where she was, still surrounded by a group of girls. The noise continued unabated.

'Turn that radio off,' I said to no one in particular.

'You'll never guess what they've got, Sister,' said Selina, from the depths of *Flush*.

I didn't particularly care. All I wanted was for them to return to their seats before Sister Bosco heard them.

'Girls! Get back to your desks,' I said again, louder this time. Still nobody took any notice.

'Make them stop fooling about,' said Tracey Peach, another of the girls who were doing their homework. 'They're giving me a headache.'

'This is a waste of time,' said Selina, 'I could have been home by now.'

Doubtless Mrs Boothroyd would get to hear about this. 'Girls!' I yelled at the group gathered round Maureen. 'What have you got there? Give it to me at once.'

When they ignored me, I barged down the aisle nearest

the door, determined to confiscate whatever it was. I was
sure it was Linda who had it behind her back; but by the
time I lunged at her she had already passed it to Maureen,
and her hands were empty. Too angry to notice that a hush
had fallen on the room, I grabbed hold of Maureen.

'Get off!' she said. 'I've done nothing wrong.' And she
spread her empty hands. 'Look, Brigid,' she said.

Without stopping to think, I hit her as hard as I could
across the face. Mysteriously the radio had stopped playing.

I felt a surge of pleasure as the young girl gasped with
shock. At last, I thought, I've got my own back. Then her
face turned to putty colour, and she sprang to her feet.

'Watch out, Mo,' called Linda.

To my surprise, Maureen's hand dropped to her side. The
silence had grown intense. And then I noticed that all eyes
were focused, not on Maureen and me, but on the door.

'Where's your teacher?' said the voice of Sister Bosco.

'Over there,' sniggered Selina, pointing in my direction.

I turned round. The Deputy Head stood in the doorway, her
bulbous blue eyes travelling over the class. 'Stand up,' she said
to the girls frostily, 'when a member of staff enters the room.'

They stood up.

Then she turned to me. 'And what,' she said, 'is the
meaning of this uproar, Sister Brigid?'

'They were passing something,' I said lamely, 'from hand
to hand –'

Selina Boothroyd gave a shrill giggle, and pointed to the
floor at the foot of her desk.

Following her gaze, I saw what looked like a small
balloon made of brown rubber.

'And who,' said Sister Bosco ominously, 'does that belong
to?'

Silence.

'Selina Boothroyd, I'm surprised at you – a girl from a
good Catholic home.'

'It isn't mine, Sister, really it isn't.'

'Then whose is it?'

Selina fell silent.

'I'm giving you one more chance, Selina. If you don't tell me straight away who brought this ... object in here, I'm going to send you to Father Gorman. And we'll see what your mother has to say about that.'

Puzzled, I stared at Sister Bosco. Why was she making all this fuss over a balloon?

'It's Maureen O'Shaunessy's,' mumbled Selina.

Maureen's face turned from white to red, the insolent little smile fading on her lips.

'I thought as much,' said Sister Bosco triumphantly. 'The doer of the devil's work.'

The room was so still that we all heard Maureen swallow drily.

'You can pick it up now,' said Sister Bosco. 'No, don't put it in the bin to corrupt some other child. We will need it as evidence. I'll see you outside the stockroom.'

Suddenly the young girl's attempt at sauntering looked pathetic, her feet clumping slightly in clogs that were supposed to look like Miss Manifold's, and her shoulder-blades, still young and thin, sticking out of the cheap jumper.

'You may continue with your ... lesson, Sister Brigid,' said the Deputy Head curtly, as Maureen left the room. I reached for my copy of *The Long, the Short and the Tall*, and, shaking slightly, instructed the class to open their books at the beginning of Act II.

'Scarcely a suitable play, under the circumstances,' Sister Bosco said as she made for the door. 'But you'd better continue with it, for the time being.' She swivelled round to face the class. 'I am teaching in the next room but one,' she warned, 'and if I hear one peep out of you girls, I shall be back immediately. And it won't only be Miss O'Shaunessy that gets into trouble.'

For the first time ever, I gave out the parts uninterrupted, and the class listened in silence as the readers stuttered their way through their lines, no one daring to act the fool. Ten minutes before the end of the lesson I gave them a simple comprehension exercise based on what they had read.

Surveying the rows of bent heads, I thought for the second time that day how unfair it all was. I had gone to school with these girls, and knew them far better than Sister Bosco ever could. Yet they obeyed her, while refusing to obey me.

Perhaps that was part of it, I reflected, as the bell went for the end of the lesson, and the class began to file out of the door. They were letting me see a side of themselves they would never show anyone else, not even – or especially not – their own parents. And they knew a side of me nobody else knew – not the admired Miss Vavasour nor the flippant Lavinia Tarn, not even the nuns in my own community; no, most certainly not them.

As I made my way back to the staffroom, Sister Bosco appeared at my elbow. At the far end of the corridor, I could see Lavinia and Miss Vavasour, both staring in my direction. The Deputy Head drew me inside the stockroom and closed the door.

'Father Gorman is dealing with the O'Shaunessy girl,' she told me. 'I see you look surprised. But you must understand – she may well be in a state of mortal sin.'

'For disrupting my lesson?'

'Ah!' Sister Bosco exclaimed triumphantly, 'despite growing up in the Dingle, you don't know much about girls. But then, you never were very observant. There is a difference between innocence and ignorance, you know.'

I nodded dumbly.

'I doubt if Mrs O'Shaunessy will complain about your treatment of her daughter,' Sister Bosco went on. 'Luckily for you, she doesn't come near the school from one year's end to the next. With another type of parent, you'd have been in serious trouble.'

'I don't know how it happened.'

'You have a lot to learn about teaching, Sister, and the lay staff don't seem to be helping you very much, do they?' said Sister Bosco magisterially. 'Miss Manifold, for instance, is new to us, and a non-Catholic at that. As for Mrs Tarn – well, she isn't a very *stable* person at the best of times.' The Deputy Head stared at me, her blue eyes bulging. When I remained silent she carried on. 'The other nuns share my view, Sister Brigid. From now on you are forbidden to enter the staffroom. Instead, you will spend your breaks in the stockroom, with us.'

TWENTY

—

'Snow was falling, snow on snow,
Sno-ow on snow,'

droned Sister Gonzaga, as she hobbled across the kitchen.
The Superior had given her special permission to wear
bedroom slippers at work, because of her bunions. Often
she would forget to change back into her shoes on leaving
the kitchen, and go shuffling up to the communion rail,
much to Mother Wilfred's irritation. 'A law unto herself,'
she would sigh.

The world outside was wimpled in snow. From my seat
at the big pine table, I could glimpse people's boots through
the area railings as they clumped home from work. It was
late afternoon on Saturday, and my turn to help Sister
Gonzaga with the supper. On the table, a coil of black
pudding was banked up against a string of sausages and a
pile of soapy white tripe, and the air was pungent with
frying onions. It was the warmest place in the convent.

The kitchen was lit by a single bulb hanging from a flex
in the centre of the ceiling. Mother Wilfred wanted to install
a modern kitchen, with fluorescent lighting and an electric
cooker, but Sister Gonzaga refused point blank. 'Married
women have to settle for a fitted kitchen,' she said, 'but not
me.'

One-two-three – the mound of rosy fingers grew steadily
as I stabbed at the sausage skins with my fork. Then I
fetched an old china bowl from the fridge, scraped out some
lard into a frying-pan, and shoved it across to the hot plate.

'Go gingerly,' said the cook, 'or you'll end up looking

like me.' As a young nun she had left a chip pan on the cooker while giving tea to a tramp at the back door. By the time she returned it was smouldering, so she carried it into the damp night air, thinking to cool it down. For a second she thought she was standing in eternity, as the oil blazed up in her face, and the skin slithered off like a tomato's. That was fifty years ago, and the scars on her cheeks could still be seen among the wrinkles.

Summoned by the sound of Sister Gonzaga riddling the stove, the convent tabby – mysteriously called Juno – sauntered in from the snow on his long legs, flicking each paw as he crossed the floor. With his mangy fur and pointed head he bore an uncanny resemblance to the fox fur in Sister Nicole's linen-room. As the heat rose a familiar smell mingled with the frying onions, rankly and aromatically feral. Gonzaga refused to take Juno to the vet's, swearing that he had been neutered as a kitten; but watching him spray the Aga systematically, his preposterously long tail waggling like a rattlesnake, and his hind paws treading as though jerked by an invisible puppeteer, I thought it unlikely.

It was impossible to tell whether the cook had noticed the yellow droplets sizzling down the oven. She had started smuggling Juno up to the dormitory, where he would crawl between her sheets and curl up until the rising bell. Sisters Columba and Annunciata, who slept in the cubicles on either side, complained loudly about the tomcat smell, but nothing was done until Sister Bosco found a flea in her bed on Christmas Eve. She put the matter before Mother Wilfred, who commanded the cook to put Juno out at night. From the occasional scrabbling noises in the dormitory, I surmised she didn't always obey.

'Fetch me that bag of mushrooms,' said Sister Gonzaga, 'from the bottom shelf in the larder.' I opened the door to the right of the range, trying not to breathe in through my nose. The catering, as Mother Wilfred often pointed out, had got too much for the old nun. To the back of the larder shelves lay food in various stages of decay – six-month-old eggs, rotting onions, a packet of slimy bacon. I found the mushrooms, and shut the larder door behind me, breathing out with relief. With the taint of rotting cauliflower clinging to my nostrils, I slid a packet of lard into the bin while Sister Gonzaga's back was turned, and was beginning to clean the mushrooms when Sister Columba, the portress, bustled into the kitchen.

'Pooh! What's that smell?' she said, her bird-like eyes fixing on Juno, who was hooking down a piece of tripe. 'Stop that, you bad cat,' she scolded, seizing him by the scruff of the neck. 'Ouch! He clawed me!' She glared indignantly at the cook before nudging the cat out into the corridor with her shoe. A cold draught swept round the table.

'Leave him alone,' said Sister Gonzaga mutinously. 'I can't turn him out in this weather.'

'I don't see why not. Insanitary little animal. But I didn't come here to fight over Juno,' the portress went on, her head cocked to one side. She turned to me importantly. 'Sister Brigid, you have a visitor.'

'Now?' I asked in surprise, rising to my feet and untying my apron. 'Who is it?'

'An old friend of yours,' Sister Columba smiled tantalizingly.

'Not Lorraine!' I exclaimed. I'd been dreading this visit ever since Maureen had been told not to come back next term. I'd heard that Lorraine was on work placement in Japan, but might be back for Christmas. We'd been allowed six cards each for lay people, and I'd sent one of mine to the O'Shaunessys, but got no reply.

'No, dear, it's not Lorraine,' said the portress. 'This is a man. He's waiting for you in the school library. It's all right – you've got permission from Mother Wilfred.'

A man? I could only think of Uncle David, and he was still in London, spending the New Year with an old schoolfriend. To my surprise, Sister Columba donned my apron and settled herself down at the kitchen table. Impatiently I stood by the kitchen door, waiting for her to accompany me. We were forbidden to stay unchaperoned in the presence of any male who was neither a priest nor a close relative. But Sister Columba showed no sign of moving.

'Run along now,' she said briskly. 'I'll give Gonzaga a hand with the pudding. What is it tonight? Tinned peaches? Oh, well, never mind.'

'Aren't you coming with me?'

Sister Columba gave me a knowing look. 'That won't be necessary, dear.'

So it was Uncle David, after all. On passing the front door I noticed a sheaf of frostbitten twigs shoved through the letterbox, intertwined with a long stem of ivy and some withered chrysanthemums. Heather March had been at work, in spite of the snow. She was one of the parishioners – a good soul, Father Gorman would say, but just a little bit touched. She used to hang around the convent, with her shabby tweed coat gathered tight around her, and straw hair sticking out from under her hat. Every now and again she made what she called one of her bokays – of weeds, grass, and flowers plucked from the park or other people's gardens – to push through our letterbox. In the spotless surroundings it looked incongruous; but there was no time to tidy it up, so I hurried on to the library.

There were the usual shelves of battered classics and outworn paperbacks, shabbier than ever in the shadowless hum of the strip lights, but no sign of any visitor. Then I heard the sound of turning pages.

'So this is where young Brigid got her education.' Before I could identify the drawl, a tall young man stepped out from one of the alcoves.

176

'Jonathon!'

'Not exactly well stocked, your library,' he said, 'which explains a lot.'

'I thought you were in Tangier.' His face looked leaner and harder than I remembered, and his clothes were aggressively casual – tight blue denims, embarrassingly worn around the crutch, lumberjack boots and a donkey jacket. It was the first time he and I had ever been alone.

'Marrakesh. And the shoot is over, so I'm home for the New Year.'

'So what are you doing in St Cuthbert's?'

'Visiting you, stupid. Partly at the behest of Elisabeth, I must confess – who insists, by the way, on being addressed as Sister Elisabeth.' He hoisted himself on to one of the tables. 'I hope you're not going in for that nonsense?'

'Er – no,' I said, glad to be unchaperoned.

'Good. Elisabeth has issued me with instructions to quiz you about St Cuthbert's, and report back to her in minute detail when I go to Rome.'

I had heard from Elisabeth twice since leaving the Mother House, long, chatty letters about the convent – near the top of the Spanish Steps – and how she and a young Indian nun called Magdalena were learning to restore frescoes at the Fioronzine Institute. 'Please write soon and give me all the gossip', she had put as a postscript. But I had never asked permission to reply.

'Do you miss her?' I said.

'She was easy to talk to – not like a girl at all. And I adored her clothes. She always said she was just an Edward-substitute for me, but that was wrong. She was nothing like Eddy.' Jonathon paused. 'And what about you, Brigid? Is the convent all you'd hoped?'

'I manage to keep going.'

'I was sorry to hear about your mother.'

'It's made me grow up – the religious life.'

'I wonder if it will have the same effect on me,' he said musingly.

'On you?'

'My second reason for coming,' he met my baffled gaze, 'is to give you my news. Your portress has wheedled it out of me already. I'm going to be a monk.'

So that was why I'd been allowed to see Jonathon on my own. Of course. And I'd thought it was because ... 'But Jonathon,' I gasped, 'you're –' Once again, I choked on the word.

'Yes, I know I am,' he said calmly. 'Gay as the eighteen-nineties. But that doesn't mean I can't have a vocation.' He hurried on impatiently as I opened my mouth. 'You're about to say that I wouldn't be here now if Eddy had said yes. Perhaps you're right. But plenty of nuns and monks have suffered from unrequited love.' He looked at me closely. 'Eh, Brigid?'

I gulped and nodded.

'Please don't look so disapproving.'

'The Church condemns homosexuality, Jonathon,' I replied. 'It may be condoned in a layman ... as long as he doesn't do anything ... but as a priest ... in a few years' time you'll be saying mass.'

'I've shared all my doubts with Father Anselm, both inside the confessional and out, and he says everything's quite in order.' Jonathon smiled slightly at the accidental pun. 'As long as I forget about Eddy. That should be easy, because he won't have anything to do with me – not in the only way that matters.'

'That's an odd remark for a would-be monk.'

'Then I'll be an odd sort of monk,' replied Jonathon. 'Don't worry about my immortal soul, Brigid. It's not your responsibility.' He leant back on his elbows, knocking over a pile of Sister Julian's catalogue cards.

'You'll never stand it,' I said, with a touch of malice. 'Not because of your – uh, tendencies,' I added, 'but because it's not what you're used to.' I glanced round the sparsely stocked shelves, then thought of his home in Cressington Park, with the oil paintings and Turkish carpets so vividly described by Elisabeth. 'You weren't bred up to it like I was.'

'I'm joining the Aloysians, Brigid – not St Cuthbert's School for Girls. Father Anselm used to be the Master of an Oxford college. I shall go there to read history.'

'Lucky you – doing what you always wanted,' I said, 'living in a college among your peers.' I kept my tone friendly, but took no pleasure in his news. How very like Jonathon to swan into the religious life as though he owned it. Cosy chats with his novice-master, and one of the best libraries in England. Soon he, too, would be an Oxford don, dispensing port as though in his own drawing-room. Like Elisabeth, who would live and work among art treasures in Rome – while I stayed in St Cuthbert's dusting the banisters and trying to teach *The Long, the Short and the Tall*.

'Tell me what the matter is,' said Jonathon.

I shook my head.

'Go on – you may as well,' he said impishly. 'In five years I might be hearing your confession.'

'Over my dead body.'

Jonathon laughed. 'I know it takes a bit of getting used to. It was Elisabeth who made it seem possible. We used to discuss our vocations for hours on end, when we should have been revising for A levels.' He cocked an eyebrow. 'I wonder why she never told you.'

'We Joubertians aren't allowed to discuss the past.'

'Is that so?' replied Jonathon. 'What a bore!' Was it his own accent he was mocking – or my law-abiding nature?

'It's better that way,' I went on hastily. 'People's histories can be very divisive – what with us all coming from different backgrounds.' I gazed round the library. 'Better to leave those things behind.'

'Until awkward visitors pop up to remind you.'

'Nothing ever quite goes away,' I said dismally, 'here in Liverpool.'

'I do,' said Jonathon, sliding down from the table, 'and so has Elisabeth. By the way, what am I to tell her?'

'Please give her my love,' I said, 'and tell her I'm very happy.'

'Will do,' he said, with a mock salute. He pulled a peaked cap out of his pocket and set it on his head at a jaunty angle. 'What on earth's that smell?' he asked as we made our way down the corridor. 'Tripe and onions! Amazing! Takes me right back to prep school.' The steel tips of his boots rang out on the stone flags. When I opened the front door it was snowing hard.

'Goodbye, Brigid,' he called on his way down the path. 'Remember to pray for me.'

On turning away from the door, I noticed Sister Columba hovering on the far side of the hall. In her hand were Heather's twigs.

'Did you enjoy your visit, dearie?'

'Yes, Sister.'

'It's grand news, isn't it – about the young man's vocation?' She stared at me curiously.

'Yes, it's grand news.'

'You were pals at school, were you?'

I nodded. 'He went to All Hallows.'

'And did he have a girlfriend?' persisted the portress.

'He was friendly with Elisabeth Bavidge – that is, Sister Elisabeth of the Trinity.'

'Is that right now?' said Sister Columba, clearly delighted. 'Then she gave him up for God! Now he too has a vocation. The ways of the Lord are a wonder to behold.' She nodded her head. 'Such a handsome young man – and what lovely manners. Soon he'll be a model to us all.' And with that she bustled off down the corridor to ring the supper bell, with Heather's bouquet still trailing from her hand.

TWENTY-ONE

—

'I don't suppose,' said Mother Wilfred testily, 'it is what any of us would have wanted. But we have no choice in the matter. It's part of *aggiornamento*.' She articulated the foreign syllables with distaste.

The rest of us, summoned to the community room for a reading of Mother General's epistle, were watching her intently.

'Our lives are about to change beyond recognition, and many of our most cherished customs will disappear.' She paused to flick through the sheaf of documents on her desk. 'Other less ... stable communities have already joined the headlong rush towards innovation. Only this morning I had a phone call from the Mother Superior of Rouen. Her nuns have shut down their *lycée* without waiting for permission, and gone to live alongside the workers.'

'How dreadful!' murmured Julian sarcastically.

'Our sisters in California have taken to organizing civil rights marches; and in Mexico they're leaving in droves for the *barrio*. Even in Britain,' Mother Wilfred stared icily at Sister Julian, 'the cloister is becoming a thing of the past, with nuns planning to move into council flats to play at being social workers.'

'Living in Tower Hamlets is hardly *play*,' said Julian.

'I, as you know, have opposed change,' Mother Wilfred said, ignoring her. 'Now Mother General is making it mandatory. We must all pray it doesn't go too far.'

'Surely,' said Sister Ursula, 'there will always be room in the Church for women dedicated to God.'

'What sort of change does Mother General want?' asked Bosco suspiciously.

'A greater involvement with the laity – which for us in St Cuthbert's means our pupils, and the secular staff,' Mother Wilfred said non-committally. 'Our school day will be shared with the other teachers as completely as possible.'

I tried not to look smug as Sister Bosco turned brick-red with indignation. 'It'll never work,' she said. 'Look what happened to Brigid.'

'Brigid was in error through being a little too *un*worldly,' drawled Sister Julian, 'not from too much knowledge.'

'Will you please let me finish?' said Mother Superior, before Bosco could answer back. 'Even our Holy Habit has been abolished. Soon we will be dressed like this.' Gloomily she held up a pencil sketch at arm's length.

We stared at a picture of a smiling woman in a knee-length skirt and short veil, stepping out of a minibus. The habit was a well-known source of dispute. On one side the older nuns, led by Sister Bosco, were ready to defend their voluminous brown serge down to the very last stitch. For them it was a bequest from our Mother Foundress, and a link with our beginnings in Berbiers.

In the middle were most of the teaching staff, including Sister Monica, who had come downstairs for the first time that morning to sit with the rest of us, pale but determined. She didn't say much, but I knew her views of old. 'It's so impractical, this medieval garb,' she'd once complained, when Patsy McCann had accidentally knocked a jar of poster paint over the young teacher's skirt. 'And so very extravagant.' She held out the surplus yards of cloth to our gaze, now smeared with orange. 'You see girls, we have a vow of poverty,' she explained, 'yet we use all this material. What we need is a modern habit – something practical, but recognizable.'

At the other extreme was Sister Julian. 'It doesn't matter

what we wear – that's the whole point of being nuns, not dressing to please. I suggest we go down to the nearest Oxfam shop, and have done with it.'

I looked at her with dislike. Did she really expect us to dress like ordinary women? Reluctantly, I agreed with Monica that our medieval garb was unnecessary. But I liked not worrying about my figure, or what to wear in the morning, and hoped the changes would not go too far.

'Where's the new pattern?' asked Sister Ursula.

'We will have to work out the details for ourselves. Sister Nicole in the Mother House has – er – refused to co-operate.'

'I'm not surprised,' said Monica. 'Anything less than *haute couture* and she's not interested.'

'A superannuated district nurse,' Sister Bosco sniffed at the picture. 'You won't catch me looking like that.'

'I don't like it any more than you do,' replied our Superior, 'but it is now a matter of Holy Obedience.'

'Don't worry, Bosco, you'll soon get used to it,' Monica reassured the Deputy Head. 'I'll give you a hand with the pattern, if you like. We can make it quite flattering.'

'We could ask Sister Gonzaga for more salads,' said Sister Ursula, as the old cook moved out of earshot. Her gaze ranged over the assembled nuns. Most of us had lost our figures.

'More salads!' barked Bosco, her eyes popping. 'What do you mean, more salads? We don't get any salads. That's our trouble. We only get stodge.'

Mother Wilfred shrugged. 'What can I do about it,' she asked, 'with Gonzaga grown so old and intractable, and no young nuns to be trained as cooks? Now please don't tie me down to details. I have enough on my hands.'

She swept out of the community room to gather up our wooden refectory platters and bear them off to the lumber room while the rest of us clustered around the picture of our new habit – all, that is, apart from Sister Julian, who stayed pointedly at her desk.

'Look at this, Sister,' Monica called out. 'It'd really suit you.'

'I'd rather discuss *Perfectae Caritatis*,' said Julian.

'I don't know what you mean,' said Monica, looking hurt.

'That's my point. It's the Vatican document on the religious life, and we haven't even read it – just sat bickering about clothes. And in the meantime, Wilfie is running rings round us.'

'Mother Wilfred is only trying to look after us,' said Bosco.

'We're not babies,' retorted Julian, her usual calm giving way to an angry flush, 'to be protected from the big bad world. We've been given the go-ahead.'

'To do what?'

'You heard what Wilfie just said. Other nuns have abandoned their habits to live at one with the poor.'

'And to think,' moaned Bosco, 'we spent all those years praying against communism. Now the religious life is riddled with it.'

'We can live out our vows here in the convent,' said Monica placatingly.

'You call this poverty?' Julian gestured angrily at the gaudy new curtains and upholstered chairs. 'It's time you took a stroll across the Dingle!' And with that she stalked out of the room, leaving the rest of us half-angry, half-shamefaced.

Julian's worst suspicions must have been confirmed when Mother Wilfred summoned a taxi to take herself and Sister Bosco to the city centre. The pair returned five hours later with a complete set of white china plates, matching casseroles, and a large canteen of stainless steel cutlery.

'These are to replace our wooden platters,' announced the

Superior, dumping one of the parcels in the refectory. 'There'll be no more washing up at table. Seemingly it's unhygienic.'

Sister Bosco tore off the wrapping paper. 'They're heat-resistant and dishwasher proof,' she carolled, her temper improved by this excursion into domesticity. 'And you'll never guess what else we bought.' With a defiant glance at Julian's disappearing back, she trotted ahead of us to the kitchen.

Obediently we gathered round in a little circle, all except Sister Gonzaga, who glowered from the larder doorway. There, alongside the Aga, stood a gleaming white dishwasher.

'Gonzaga would never cope with all our dirty dishes,' explained Sister Bosco. 'So we came up with this. I chose a model that rinses three times in scalding water. All we do is stack our dishes on this rack, and pop the cutlery down here. I'll be in charge of the soap powder.'

'I don't want you trailing in here after every meal,' put in the cook. 'It'll only cause confusion.' And clasping Juno to her bosom, she disappeared inside the larder and banged the door.

'Never mind about Gonzaga,' said Columba. 'She'll soon see how much work it saves. I only wish you'd got one of those electric toasters – it would be so handy for Father Gorman's breakfast.'

'And a vacuum cleaner,' put in Annunciata. 'I'm at my wits' end with that top corridor. These gadgets could save us hours.'

Mother Wilfred raised her eyes to heaven. '*Laborare est orare*,' she said. 'To work is to pray. There are great blessings to be gained from manual labour.'

'Even so,' said Sister Columba, 'it would be nice to have a washing machine.'

Unfortunately Monica, who had only just entered the

room, chose that moment to tackle her about the liturgy. Egged on by the parish priest, she'd been learning to play the guitar during convalescence. 'Please may we have a choir practice?' she said now. 'I've got some good ideas for Sunday mass. Father Gorman says it'll soon be open to lay people.'

Mother Wilfred's brow clouded. A former classics teacher at one of the best girls' schools in England, she was a longstanding admirer of Archbishop Lefebvre. If she and not Father Gorman had been our chaplain, we would still have been hearing mass in Latin. 'I'm sure Father Gorman knows best,' she said icily.

'So we'll need our own bidding prayers,' Monica persevered, 'and some modern hymns.'

'We'll have no ear-splitting, guitar-twanging pop songs,' said the Superior sternly. 'I can't bear the sight of nuns strumming away with their legs crossed.'

'It's difficult to sit down and play the guitar without crossing one's legs,' explained Monica patiently, 'and we must learn some hymns in the vernacular. Father Gorman says so.'

'If Father Gorman tells us to be a laughing-stock,' said Mother Wilfred, 'then so be it. But don't expect me at choir practice.'

Over the next few weeks Sister Monica pushed, bullied and cajoled the rest of us out of the Middle Ages and into the twentieth century. Her new role seemed to set her on the road to recovery, and Mother Wilfred soon saw the advantages of leaving the details to her. Under her tutelage we abandoned plainchant to sing our Office in English, and learnt to warble our way through hymns to the tune of 'Let it Be' and 'You'll Never Walk Alone' while Mother Wilfred kept her mouth firmly shut.

Sister Julian disapproved of these changes every bit as much as Mother Wilfred, but for opposite reasons. One day she summoned Ursula, Monica and me to the library. Far from going too fast, she told us, we were failing to keep up, and should experiment with more radical ways of doing things, even if it meant that we – the most open-minded nuns in the community – cut loose from our more conservative sisters.

We never found out what she had in mind. Ursula wouldn't countenance the idea of doing things separately, and Monica backed her up. As for me, I resented the way she was slighting Monica's efforts to experiment, and couldn't see why she wanted to dump our inheritance from the Blessed Anne Joubert at the whim of the last Pope.

After this, Sister Julian isolated herself behind a pile of documents in the school library, where a light burned long after everyone else had gone to bed. Although she stopped trying to discuss things with us, she must have been in contact with other communities, because she was always asking Mother Wilfred for extra stamps. I hadn't forgotten Mère-Maîtresse's warning about Sister Julian's over-eagerness for change, and kept well away.

In the meantime Monica had bought a bale of brown crimplene, and addressed a memo to each one of us individually, reminding us to begin shaving our legs – otherwise the hairs might come bristling through our nylons. She would put a packet of razors in the wooden press at the end of the dormitory. And we would need to start wearing a bra. If we wrote our size on a piece of paper, she would buy them for us at Marks & Spencer.

For Sister Gonzaga it was the last straw. 'I've never worn a brassière in my life,' she said indignantly, 'and I never will. They're made for harlots.'

'She won't allow herself to be measured for the new habit,' cried Monica to Mother Wilfred, waving a pair of cutting-out scissors. 'What should I do about her?'

'Quite honestly, I'm at a loss. She's threatened to stop cooking.'

Monica shelved the problem by getting to work on the rest of us, while hoping the old cook would fall into line. The art teacher still hadn't returned to work, so she was free to spend the remaining weeks of term poised over the community room table, cutting, shaping, putting in darts and letting them out again for women made indecisive by anxiety. By the Easter holidays, everyone's new habit was complete, apart from the cook's.

Mother Wilfred decided that it would be too distracting for Father Gorman if we donned our short dresses for mass. Instead, we adjourned to our cubicles after breakfast. Monica had laid out each habit on the appropriate bed: a knee-length brown dress, a short veil, a pair of nylon stockings in American tan and a white bra shaped like twin ice-cream cones.

I was shivering slightly by the time my habit, *pèlerine*, coif, veil and *serre-tête* were bundled into the bottom of my wardrobe. I pulled down my corset and old lisle stockings, and tore the cellophane wrapping off a new pair. Although they were thirty-denier, they felt unnervingly wispy.

'Jesus, Mary and Joseph, mine are laddered already,' exclaimed Bosco. An awkward little group, we clattered down to the refectory in our unfamiliar court shoes – all except Sister Gonzaga, who, still wearing her old habit, was in the kitchen preparing coffee.

'Don't you worry,' said Monica, 'there are plenty more where those came from.'

'That strikes me as highly extravagant,' said Julian, 'for a change made in the name of Holy Poverty.' All the same, to judge from her elegant appearance, she had dressed with some attention.

'Well, here we are, Sisters,' said Mother Wilfred. With her long legs, and full breasts sagging from three decades without a bra, she resembled a gloomy bird of prey.

'At least,' Sister Ursula consoled her, 'we aren't decked out in powder-blue polyester leisure suits, like our community in Palo Alto.' She turned tactfully to Monica. 'Thank you for your good efforts on our behalf.'

Monica's reply was drowned by Bosco, her iron-grey hair sticking out from her veil in something resembling a crew cut.

'From now on I shan't be taking assembly,' she said. 'Can you imagine – five hundred girls sniggering at my ankles.'

'Whatever's wrong with them?' inquired the headmistress, chafing her hands. It was March, and the central heating had long been turned off.

The Deputy Head stuck out a stout leg of equal girth from knee to shoe. 'I'm a beef-to-the-heel,' she replied, 'that's what. I'd give anything to be you, Julian.'

It was the first time I'd seen the English teacher smile for weeks. It was ironic, I thought, that she cared nothing for clothes, because the home-made dress that clung to the thick waist and bulging hips of Bosco hung on Julian's bony frame as though designed by none other than the great Molyneux. Suddenly I remembered the words of Sister Nicole.

'I once saw your beautiful organza dress,' I blurted out as the other nuns began helping themselves to coffee, 'in the Mother House linen-store.'

Julian's features softened into a smile of reminiscence. 'Ah, yes!' she exclaimed. 'That dress belonged to Sarah – she made me wear it one last time. But such an impractical choice for the journey to Berbiers! She spent half her time unhooking my floating panels from French porters.'

'Who was Sarah?' I said curiously.

'Sister Elisabeth,' she corrected herself. 'Not the one you know – her predecessor, who died in the Congo.'

'Oh, yes,' I said, 'I remember.'

'Funny that I once adored beautiful clothes.' She smiled a

little sadly, and wandered over to the coffee urn, leaving me wondering if I mightn't try and speak to her again. After all, Mère-Maîtresse hadn't said to stay away completely.

'Whatever will the girls say?' said Sister Bosco when we met for lunch.

'The girls,' said Mother Wilfred firmly, 'won't notice the difference. They have their heads of full of – er – the Beatles and Whatsisname Jagger.'

But Mother Superior was wrong. Far from not noticing, thirty pairs of blue, brown and grey eyes were trained on us each lesson, and during break suspicious shrieks and giggles issued from the cloakrooms, to fade away the moment any one of us entered. I was most afraid of 3W. Linda Renucci had been subdued since her friend, Maureen, had been expelled for the possession of what I now knew was a condom, and during the spring term I'd managed to impose a semblance of order, largely by sending any trouble-makers to Sister Bosco. But I still dreaded their scrutiny, and lingered for a few moments in the corridor before my first lesson.

Then, taking a deep breath, I clasped my register more tightly and strode into the classroom. The girls rose to their feet – all but one.

'Linda Renucci, stand up,' I ordered, longing for the protection of my old habit.

'Where's Sister Brigid?' she demanded of the room at large, staring around in mock puzzlement. 'I only stand up when there's a nun in the room.' There was a shocked silence, then one or two covert giggles.

Remembering the O'Shaunessy disaster, I fought to keep my temper.

'Linda,' I said as calmly as I could, 'you may stand or not, as you please. If you don't, I shall report you to the Deputy Head.'

'Do as you like,' smirked the girl, 'because you've got a shock in store.'

Before I could find out what she meant, there was a rapid knocking at the classroom door. Selina Boothroyd, who sat nearest, moved to open it, but too late. It banged back on its hinges, and there in the classroom stood my old friend.

'Lorraine!' I exclaimed.

Gone were the mini-skirt and beehive. Her hair, restored to its natural colour, tumbled to her shoulders, and her woollen skirt was the same length as my own – but instead of brown court shoes, Lorraine wore boots of soft Italian leather.

'Great!' breathed Linda.

The elegant and understated clothes were at odds with Lorraine's expression. 'So what have you got say for yourself?' she yelled, striding up to my desk.

'What's the matter?' I quavered.

'Matter? You know bloody well what the matter is.' Her cheeks were bright with temper as she gripped the edge of my desk, seemingly unaware of the preternaturally still 3W.

'I can't talk now,' I said hopefully. 'As you can see, I have a class.'

'You're going to talk now, Brigid, because I'm not leaving until you do. Here or the corridor – it's your choice.'

'The corridor,' I replied hastily. There was a ripple of laughter from the class. 'Get on with your work, girls,' I said frostily, and mustering what dignity I could, I followed Lorraine from the room.

'How dare you get that poor little kid expelled?' she shouted, without waiting for the door to close.

'I didn't,' I told her, shutting it firmly. For once, the girls were in perfect silence. 'It wasn't my decision.'

'*It wasn't my decision*,' mimicked Lorraine savagely. 'Pontius bloody Pilate! It was your fault she got into trouble, and nobody else's. Your fault because you couldn't control a teddy bears' picnic, and were too proud to ask advice. And you never spoke up for her, not once.'

'I asked Sister Bosco to reconsider – but it was no good.'

'I've only your word for that.'

'What Maureen did was wrong. She was a difficult pupil.'

'Fooling around with a French letter makes her difficult? Don't be soft,' said Lorraine. 'You're so bloody right to dress like an overgrown Brownie, because that's what you are.'

'Contraception is a mortal sin,' I replied. 'And so, for that matter, is sex before marriage. Sister Bosco had to do something.'

'Sister Bosco is a fucking sadist,' said Lorraine, 'and so are you. I didn't think you'd change so fast.'

'You mind your language,' I told her. 'There's a lot you don't know about Sister Bosco.'

'I wouldn't piss on her if she was burning,' said Lorraine. 'Victimizing a child like that. If only I hadn't been away. My mam kept it from me, because she knew I'd come right back.'

'What happened to Maureen isn't the end of the world,' I said coolly.

'A Catholic secondary modern *is* the end of the world,' said Lorraine. 'And you know it. You and I had a chance to get out – even if you blew yours, because you were shit scared.'

'That's a lie.'

'And now you want to stifle other people,' Lorraine pounded on. 'Do you know what the kids call you?'

'No, I don't.'

'Sister Rigid!'

'I wonder where they got that from?' I said acidly. I had a bitter taste in my mouth, and desperately wanted Lorraine to go away.

'Wherever they got it from, you deserve it, because that's what you are. And there's no need to hop from foot to foot in case your precious Sister Bosco overhears – I'm going as fast as I bloody well can, before I murder you, you hypocritical little cow.'

'Go then,' I said coldly. 'And the sooner the better – if that's how you treat your friends.'

I watched her pace down the corridor, nearly knocking over Sister Julian as she emerged from the next classroom. At the bottom she turned to face me once more. 'You're no friend of mine, Brigid Murray,' she shouted, 'and it's lucky for you there isn't a hell. Because if there was, you'd fry there.' And with that she disappeared round the corner.

TWENTY-TWO

So that was how they thought of me. *Sister Rigid!* Lorraine's mocking voice rang in my ears for the rest of the lesson. Surprisingly, the girls didn't take advantage of my failure to concentrate, and even Linda Renucci stayed mute. I, for my part, had no wish to remain in their presence one second longer than necessary. As soon as the bell rang for break, I bolted down the corridor to the staffroom.

'Welcome back!' called Lavinia Tarn in her best contralto. 'I knew it would all come right in the end.' I sat down in my old place, surprised to discover my legs were still shaking.

'Somebody's changed her habit,' sang Mr Bethany.

'Let's give Sister Brigid a moment to settle down,' said Lavinia. 'She's worn out.'

'What's the matter, dear?' said Miss Vavasour as the others went to help themselves to tea. 'You look quite peaky.'

'I've just had a terrible shock.'

'Whatever happened?' she asked, laying down the netball she'd been patching.

'Lorraine O'Shaunessy appeared in my class – in a rage about her sister.'

'Did she indeed?' said Miss Vavasour. 'You and she were pals, weren't you?'

'She was my best friend.'

'A good girl at heart – but what a little trouble-maker!' said Miss Vavasour. 'Couldn't do a thing with her in games. All she wanted to do was smoke behind the bike-shed.

Maureen was a different kettle of fish – a talented athlete, and willing to work at it.'

'You're making me feel worse.'

'Rubbish,' said Miss Vavasour. 'I broke a boy's nose on my very first TP, and wanted to throw in the towel. I still think about him, sometimes – but I made myself carry on. So will you.'

'But what about Maureen?'

'Sister Bosco should never have called in Father Gorman,' said the games mistress. 'No priest knows how to handle a young girl. If left to the likes of us, Maureen would still be here.'

'But she might be giving boys condoms.'

'The best thing she could do, under the circumstances,' said Miss Vavasour, fixing me with her slightly bloodshot eyes. 'None of it's ideal, I grant you. If only they would forget about sex and concentrate on PE. You leave Maureen to me – I coach her for county netball.' She held out a packet of Player's Extra Strong. 'Are you allowed to smoke yet?'

Even though there was no question of nuns being allowed to smoke – and the staffroom was the riskiest place I could think of – my hand moved towards the proffered cigarettes. 'I would love one,' I said impulsively. 'I haven't smoked since the day I entered.'

At that moment the door opened and in walked Sister Bosco, with Sisters Julian and Ligori in attendance. I shoved the cigarette back into the packet so fast that I bent it.

'Oh dear, never mind,' said the games mistress. 'I'll get you a nice cup of tea instead. Good and strong, with two sugars. And don't go worrying about Lorraine. She'll soon calm down.' With that she loped off towards the urn.

'Sister Bosco,' trilled Mr Bethany, fluttering over to greet the Deputy Head. 'How very charming you look! Simply years younger! And here are Sister Julian and Sister Ligori!

This is a great honour. Please sit down, and allow me to fetch you all a cup of coffee.'

Blushing to the rims of her eyes, Sister Bosco allowed him to escort her to the staffroom's only armchair. The other nuns followed, as though in her train.

'The colour's OK, but the length's all wrong,' commented Lavinia.

'You should have let me help,' said Margie. 'I love making clothes.'

'Don't bother Sister Brigid with that now,' said Miss Vavasour, handing me a mug of tea and two biscuits. 'Nuns don't care how they look, do they, Sister?'

'Sister Monica had to follow the guidelines,' I told Margie, on the brink of tears. 'It's not her fault if we look a mess.'

'I hear Sister Monica's getting better,' Lavinia put in quickly. 'She'll soon be back in school.'

Although grateful to Lavinia for changing the subject, I could only nod non-committally. Convent opinion was divided, with the infirmarian and her followers maintaining that Monica was dangerously ill and needed more bed-rest, and Mother Wilfred disagreeing. The doctors, she said, had found nothing wrong. Monica must get back to earning her keep.

'Then I'll be out of a job,' said Margie, cheerfully. 'Oh, well, never mind – I'm getting married in June. Neville says he'll support me.'

'My ex-husband said that once,' warned Lavinia. 'Take my advice, and look for another post.'

But Margie had stopped listening to stare across the staffroom. 'Wow!' she breathed. 'Just look at Sister Julian.'

'What's the matter with her?'

'Nothing at all, now she's out of that wimple,' laughed the art teacher. 'What a bone structure! I wonder if she'll pose for my Mary Queen of Scots. I'm illustrating a children's book.'

After glancing at my head of department as she sat listening to Mr Bethany's chatter, I had to concede she looked better; but I could never like that haughty, aquiline nose and arched eyebrows. 'She's lucky not to look like an overgrown Brownie,' I replied. But Margie had already darted over to accost her.

I was glad to be free next lesson, and, helping myself to another cup of tea, settled down to some marking. Most of the staff had gone back to class, but Sister Julian, I noticed, was lingering on the other side of the room. I bent my head over the pile of exercise books, all too aware that she would have overheard my quarrel with Lorraine.

'I saw your old friend in school this morning,' she said, moving towards my chair.

'That's right,' I said curtly, noting the thick red fringe beneath her veil. She must have been growing it for some time.

'Was that what you were talking about – with Miss Vavasour?'

'We did touch on it,' I replied, hoping Julian hadn't noticed the cigarette.

'Why didn't you turn to me, Brigid? I am your head of department.'

'But Miss Vavasour was here – just after it happened.'

'And I was there at the time,' said Julian, 'but you ignored me. I sometimes wonder why you feel so little confidence in me.' As the green-grey eyes considered me thoughtfully, I began to wonder why myself.

'I'll tell you next time anything goes wrong,' I promised. Sister Julian seemed satisfied with that, and left the staff-room, while I tried to forget about her by getting on with my marking.

But as the term crept towards Whit, I found myself seeking her company. Most of the other nuns, I suddenly saw, were elderly – apart from Monica, who had suffered a relapse and, muzzy from her medication, went early to bed. Sister Annunciata was well over sixty, and slept in the infirmary to be near Monica. Although she was by nature chatty, a pattern of disturbed sleep had pushed her to the brink of exhaustion. I admired Sister Ursula, but as head-mistress she too was overstretched, and had little time for conversation. So when I felt lonely, I would go the library and tell Sister Julian all about Berbiers, and how I missed Lucie and the tomboyish Mary Lou. She never said much on these occasions, so I couldn't see how she might be a bad influence. And besides, I told myself, she was one of my sisters: better talk to her than to the gossipy secular staff.

Summer came early that year; by June the leaves on the trees bordering the park were scorched and dusty, and even Bosco was glad of her lightweight habit. Day after day the glass dome of the Palm House flashed up into a cloudless sky. The high windows of my classroom were tilted open from early morning, and I took every possible class into the garden.

One day in mid-July I had finished school by three thirty. It would have been easy to join Margie and Lavinia, who were chatting out on the lawn; but I was feeling hot and headachy. Soon it would be time for bread and jam in the cool of the refectory. In the meantime I would slip up to the dormitory and read my letter from Lucie.

Even under the new regulations, the dormitory was offi-cially out of bounds during the daytime. But, I reasoned with myself, it was a pointless rule; and Mother Wilfred would be sure to give her permission if asked. Besides, with everybody still in school, no one was likely to see me.

On crossing the hall I noticed another bunch of weeds poking through the letterbox. Dandelions, daisies, and groundsel. I opened the front door, and glanced across the road to the park. There was a storm on the way, with thunderheads piling high above the Palm House, and the swifts screaming among the chimneypots. Predictably, there was no sign of Heather. She was spending the summer riding round and round on the Toxteth Circular, and confined her visits to the early morning. Carefully pulling her bouquet through the letterbox, I shut the door and ran upstairs.

Lucie began her letter by lamenting the change in her patron saint. Lucy, the virgin martyr, was traditionally portrayed holding her eyes in a dish for the viewer's edification. These eyes had supposedly been torn out, then restored miraculously. This event, it now transpired, had never occurred – and nor had the body of Saint Lucy – if, indeed, the saint had ever existed – been unmovable and unburnable, as legend had it. As the Church revised her canon, Lucy and many other famous figures – like Saints Veronica and Christopher – were proving apocryphal.

'It gave me quite a shock, finding that I hardly knew my very own saint,' wrote Lucie. 'And after praying to her for so long! I hope the Church knows what it is doing.'

Passing on to the second sheet of airmail paper, I read about the breakdown of distinctions between lay sisters and choir nuns in Berbiers. Once Lucie would have spent her life as the community drudge; now she was going to catering college – 'and just as well,' she added, 'if I am to teach cookery – I wouldn't know where to begin. I tried to persuade Mother General to let me go to horticultural college instead, and take over from Hercule, but she's very ill, and I don't like to bother her. Hercule himself has had a stroke, and can't water the vegetable garden any more, but he still cares for your dear mother's grave. Mère-Maîtresse is well, and sends you every blessing. The novitiate is a quiet place by comparison with our time. Only five postulants! Remember to pray for vocations. The harvest is great but the labourers are few – fewer every year.'

I wondered why no St Cuthbert's girls had gone to be

nuns since Elisabeth and me. And how could five postulants manage all those charges? At least they wouldn't be harassed by Hercule. Wishing I could revisit my mother's grave, I turned to arrange Heather's daisies in my toothmug. It was then someone else entered the dormitory – someone short of breath, and moving in a hurry. I considered stealing away, but it was too late. The footsteps paused outside my door – then on they went into the next cubicle. Only with the sound of a bed being dragged from the wall, and a sheet shaken out, did I guess that someone was making a bed for Monica. Tapping lightly on the cubicle door, I stuck my head round.

'Good heavens, child, you gave me a fright! Why aren't you in school?' gasped the infirmarian.

'I was free last lesson, Nuncy, and came up here to have a wash. I see you're making Monica's bed.'

'It's not for Monica. She'll be in the infirmary for the rest of the summer, I reckon. Her new medication knocks her for six.'

'Then who's moving in here?'

'Don't ask me – I'm only doing what I was told,' replied the old nurse. 'You'd best see Mother Wilfred.'

'Not likely,' I replied. 'I shouldn't be here in the first place.'

'Then run along before you get into trouble,' said the nurse. 'The bell went five minutes ago.'

I wondered about my new neighbour while we ate our bread and jam. No one in the community had any reason for changing cubicles. Then, at the beginning of recreation, Mother Wilfred beckoned me over.

'Mother General is about to phone, and I can't leave the convent,' she told me. 'You're to meet the six o'clock train at Lime Street. Here's a five-pound note. The taxi's due in half an hour.'

'But who am I to look for?'

'Sister Elisabeth,' she replied. 'I'm sending you to the station because you know her already.'

'Why on earth is she leaving Rome?'

'Curiosity is still your besetting sin, Sister Brigid,' said Mother Wilfred severely. 'You've been told all you need to know. Don't let me down by interrogating your sister.'

Was Elisabeth coming here for good? I wondered. Perhaps one of the Bavidges had been taken ill, I thought, scanning the crowd at the ticket barrier – but then it would hardly be a secret. Soon the flood of passengers had dwindled to a trickle, but there was still no sign of the Joubertian brown. I made my way across the concourse to ring Mother Wilfred for further instructions.

Only one telephone was working, with a slim young foreigner in a royal blue suit on the line. *Ciao!* I heard her say, followed by a flurry of Italian, and then, at last, *Arrivederci!* I moved impatiently, worried about the waiting taxi. The Italian jiggled from foot to foot, balanced on precariously high heels, then started gabbling again. Another five minutes ticked by before she plonked down the receiver and turned towards me.

A heart-shaped face with a dash of bright lipstick, and shiny bobbed hair. 'Elisabeth!' I gasped.

'Brigid! I'm so glad they sent you.'

As we embraced, I remembered fainting outside the Mother House, and how she'd smelt of garlic and the same musky perfume she wore now.

'You should have told me you'd left,' I said, suddenly pleased to see her.

'Left?' She turned towards me as we clacked over to the taxi rank. 'Left what?'

'Left the Joubertians,' I replied, glancing at the tight skirt and sheer tights as she climbed ahead of me into the taxi.

'But I haven't,' she said, settling herself in the back seat. 'In Rome this is our new habit. Can't you see our cross?' She held out a lapel bearing a minuscule gold J.

'Nobody would guess you were a nun.'

'So much the better,' she replied with a grin, rummaging in her handbag. 'Then the conversation doesn't get churchy.'

'Sister Julian will like it,' I offered, 'but I don't know what the others will think.'

'Sister Julian always said she couldn't care less about clothes.'

'She has her human side.'

'That's good,' said Elisabeth, pulling out a packet of Marlboro, 'because from what I remember St Cuthbert's is short on human beings.'

'Are you really allowed to smoke?'

'Mother Maria Goretti turned a blind eye,' she said, with a flick of her little red lighter. 'Judging by the look on your face, this might be my last chance. Have one yourself.'

'Miss Vavasour offered me one the other day,' I told her, 'but I had to put it back. Are you coming to teach?'

'Yes, I am, Brigid – but I can't tell you anything more. Don't worry, you'll soon see why not.' She smiled wanly.

'Elisabeth,' I remonstrated, 'what on earth have you done?'

'Nothing wrong,' she said, 'and if I seem quiet it's because I hated this dump as a girl – and here I am, back again.' She leaned forward to stub out her cigarette as St Cuthbert's lurched into view. 'What a hideous mish-mash of styles. I don't know how I shall stand it.'

'It's not as bad as all that . . .' I told her as we hurried up the path. The words died on my lips. There on the doorstep was Mother Wilfred, drawn up to her full height.

'And what,' she said ominously to Sister Elisabeth, 'is this rig-out you're wearing?' She ushered her in through the front door.

'It's what one wears in Rome,' said Elisabeth.

'Sister Monica! Come here at once,' boomed the Superior.

The young nun appeared at the far end of the corridor,

and moved slowly towards us. She had grown a little stooped over the past few months, and although the night was warm, she was huddled in a shawl.

'Take Sister Elisabeth to the dormitory,' said Mother Superior, 'and find her a veil. Tomorrow you can make her a decent dress.'

Apart from me, nobody noticed the curl of Elisabeth's lip. Suddenly I saw us all through her eyes, noting how our dresses had already begun to sag and bulge in odd places, and our veils were too skimpy to disguise the inexpert haircuts we gave each other to save on bills. Then Monica stepped forward to guide the newcomer to the dormitory, and the moment passed.

But what was Monica staring at so fixedly, and why had she stopped dead in her tracks? Impatiently Mother Wilfred gestured her onwards. But Monica wasn't moving – or not towards Elisabeth.

Her eyes were fastened on a far corner of the ceiling, and her neck was craning backwards as though it must snap. Then suddenly, with a wail, she arched her spine and plunged on to the tiled floor, with a crack.

As the rest of us watched appalled, Monica, her eyes glazed and her mouth toothpasted with white foam, began to thrash convulsively, banging her head on the legs of a hallstand. Her veil had been knocked off by the fall, and a pool of urine grew on the floor beside her.

The door of the community room opened wide and shut with a bang. And then Sister Annunciata was across the hall and down on her knees beside the writhing figure, protecting it as best she could from the furniture.

As the convulsions ceased, the old nun glared up at us. 'Don't just stand gawping,' she said, 'do something useful – like calling the doctor. That goes for you too, Mother Wilfred. If you hadn't overworked her, this wouldn't have happened.'

The Superior drew in her breath sharply, but failed to rebuke the old nurse, who was still crouched over Monica. Then she turned down the hall towards the telephone.

Elisabeth and I faced each other in silence across Monica's unconscious form. 'You told me St Cuthbert's wasn't that bad,' said Elisabeth eventually, her face pale. 'And you were right. It isn't bad – it's terrible.'

TWENTY-THREE

—

That night some of the community stayed in chapel after Compline, heads bowed, praying for the recovery of Sister Monica. Others, including Sister Julian, Elisabeth and me, huddled round the community room door, in breach of the Grand Silence. Nobody wanted to go to bed, and only when Mother Wilfred came down from the infirmary with a face like a thunderclap did we move reluctantly to the dormitory. I longed for sleep to blot out the image of Monica, thrashing on the floor with her veil askew. But it continued to elude me, and the convent clock chimed eleven, twelve, one.

I was just drifting off when the silence was ruptured by the noise of footsteps running down a distant corridor. My eyes snapped open. Total darkness. I was telling myself I'd imagined it when a door slammed shut – louder than any nun would slam it. Elisabeth was turning restlessly, and I knew that she'd been woken too. I was on the brink of whispering to her through the partition, when the telephone shrilled in Mother Superior's study below. It was answered in two rings, so at least someone knew what was going on. My job was to compose myself for sleep.

It was long after dawn when I fell into a light doze, to dream of Monica, not as she had been the night before, but as I remembered her from fourth form, standing solemnly in front of us with her eyes shining.

'And this, girls, is the secret of colour.' She pointed to a giant palette, studded with lakes from cobalt through aquamarine to palest eggshell. Each little lake pulsated with light, magnetic and bottomless.

'It all depends on how you mix them,' the art teacher's voice echoed in my head as the lakes began to overflow and lap across the classroom. 'If you get it right, you've got it made.'

I wanted to ask a question but my hand was too heavy to raise above the turquoise waves. And then the nine long strokes of the rising bell pealed across the classroom, and I woke with my right arm cramped against the wall.

At breakfast it looked as though the others had slept badly, too. Ursula, Elisabeth, Julian – all were pale and puffy-eyed. At the top of the table, Mother Wilfred's chair was empty, and so was Monica's. I would slip upstairs to see her after completing my charge.

Outside the infirmary I hesitated for a second, wondering if she was awake, then raised my hand to knock. But the door swung open before I could touch it, and there was Mother Wilfred.

'Please, Mother, may I . . .' My sentence tailed away as her eyes turned frostier than ever.

'You have no business hanging around here, Sister Brigid. Seeing that you've finished your charge so quickly, you can clear one of the staffroom lockers for Sister Elisabeth. Next term she will have a full timetable. In the meantime she must help out any way she can.' With that she stalked off down the corridor.

I found Elisabeth perched on a classroom windowsill, staring out across the playground. She was still without a veil, and the skirt of her new habit had ridden up above her knees, showing a hint of stocking-top.

'And to think,' she murmured, jiggling a high-heeled shoe on one toe, 'that I've only just got away from this dump.'

'But you were so positive about it all – when I got my *billet-doux*.'

She smiled ruefully. 'That was for your benefit,' she

replied. 'It's easy to be optimistic when you're *en route* for Rome.'

'What was it like there?'

'It's another world,' she replied fervently. 'All the rules and regulations you have here – they're out of the ark. In Italy it's so free and easy. We could get up and go to bed whenever we –' she broke off as Sister Bosco bustled past.

'Let's go the art room,' I said. 'It's nice and peaceful up there.'

'At least Wilfie's forgotten about my new habit,' remarked Elisabeth as she clacked upstairs beside me.

'I wouldn't count on it. Monica will be set to work the moment she's on her feet.'

'That isn't very likely.' Elisabeth gave me a sidelong look. 'Can't you see how ill she is?'

'She's had an epileptic fit before – and recovered. Mother Wilfred wants her back on the staff.'

Although the sunny old attic was deserted, Margie Manifold's clutter had been pushed to one side, and Monica's palette dumped on the teacher's desk. On the easel was a large piece of painted hardboard, still damp.

'She's back at work,' cried Elisabeth.

'She never really stopped,' I replied. 'Look at this picture.'

Gone were the days of the minuscule silver fishes. A giant hand filled the frame, its sausage fingers clenching a paintbrush to a carmine-coloured palm.

'My God, but she's talented,' said Elisabeth.

'She's stopped doing her abstracts,' I remarked.

'That's because she wants to get her point across – and fast. They won't be hanging this one in the front hall.'

'I wonder if she'll finish it this weekend.'

'Doesn't look like it,' said Elisabeth. 'Isn't that her, over there?'

I glanced out of the window. Sure enough, there was

Monica, a tiny figure drifting across the park. Beside her scurried Sister Annunciata. They were clearly heading for the shops.

'I'm glad she's getting better.'

Elisabeth opened her mouth and closed it again, then said after a moment, 'Wilfie told me to make lunch. Apparently Sister Gonzaga's ill, too. This place isn't exactly a health resort.'

'I'll give you a hand,' I said, 'and show you where things are.' After a last look at the painting, we made our way back to the convent. Elisabeth, oblivious of the rule of silence, was chattering about our time in the Mother House. Tactfully omitting anything that might remind me of Madge, she reminisced about our Clothing, and gave me news of Mavis, alias Sister Raphael, now running a home for unmarried mothers in Detroit, and Mary Lou, who belonged to an experimental community in Santa Barbara.

'We are meant to be working in silence,' I reminded her on the basement steps.

'Silence is a thing of the past,' she said airily, as we entered Gonzaga's gloomy domain. 'In Europe everybody's aiming at more communication.'

I prised open a window. Juno, who had been parading up and down the sill, skidded in across the draining-board. The smell in the kitchen had worsened over the last few weeks. As we scrubbed down the big deal table, Elisabeth told me more about the convent in Rome, which was on a single floor of a modern apartment block. 'For meals, everyone sits round a Formica table in the kitchen. And there's a fridge with unlimited Coca-Cola.'

'And we have a larder with unlimited cauliflowers,' I replied, peering into its recesses, 'most of them rotten.'

'Anything else?'

'Three dozen eggs.'

'Bravo! We shall make omelettes,' said Elisabeth.

'We'd better be careful. They'll have been here for months.'

'Then crack each egg into a teacup, in case it's rotten,' she advised. Soon there were two dozen golden yolks swimming like spawn in the big white mixing-bowl, and I was beginning to enjoy myself.

'I wish I could say it's nice to be back,' said Elisabeth as she rummaged in the fridge for butter, 'but I can't. Everyone seems so old.'

'They mostly are,' I replied, 'apart from Monica, Julian and me.'

'We must write to Jonathon,' said Elisabeth. 'He's having a wonderful time.'

'A wonderful time,' I echoed, 'in the novitiate?'

'Certainly. It's a homoerotic paradise – with one of the best libraries in England.'

Before I could ask what homoerotic meant, Sister Columba bustled into the kitchen with Juno suspended by the scruff of his neck. 'I caught him spraying on the infirmary staircase,' she said. 'Filthy little beast.' She put him out of the window, and peered in the mixing-bowl. 'Gonzaga's got flu,' she said, 'and doesn't fancy anything. And don't go cooking for Monica. She won't be eating with us.'

'I'll take hers up on a tray,' I replied.

'You'd best leave that to Sister Annunciata,' replied the portress.

Bowing my head at the implied rebuke, I absent-mindedly cracked an egg straight into the mixing-bowl. The kitchen filled with the stink of sulphur.

'My God,' shrieked the portress, 'it smells worse than Juno.'

'Allow me,' said Elisabeth, as I jabbed short-temperedly at the rotten egg with a teaspoon. Brandishing an eggshell, she scooped up the putty-coloured mess within seconds and dumped it in the bin.

'Aren't you the clever one?' said Columba admiringly.

'A trick my grandmother taught me,' replied Elisabeth, as she twirled towards the stove, frying-pan in hand. 'No, Brigid, don't use rotary beaters, try a fork – or best of all a balloon whisk. Yes, that's excellent.'

'You'd better be quick,' said the portress. 'The bell will go in five minutes.'

'With *omelettes aux fines herbes*,' said Elisabeth, 'you can't start until the last moment.' She poured some of the egg mixture into a small frying-pan. It fluffed up within seconds as she flipped it deftly before sliding it on to a warm plate. Then she did another while Sister Columba scuttled off with first. Within ten minutes the whole community had been served.

'The best meal in months,' pronounced Sister Bosco as we made our way to the community room after lunch. 'This foreign food has something to be said for it.'

'We must now go and say our rosary together,' I told Elisabeth as the others went off to recreation. 'The community said theirs when we were cooking.'

'Surely you don't still say the rosary! It's a prayer for illiterate peasants.'

'Our Holy Mother Foundress had a great devotion to it,' I said, 'and she was far from illiterate.'

'It's like clocking in and clocking out,' grumbled Elisabeth. 'In Rome we could pray how and where we liked.'

'Well, you're not in Rome now.'

'And therefore can't do as the Romans do?' she laughed. 'All the same, I think I'll go into the garden.'

'You have to ask permission,' I said, in the sneaking hope that Elisabeth's strange continental ways would make Mother Wilfred see me in a better light.

'I think I'm the best judge of where to pray,' replied Elisabeth. 'Besides, it's nice and cool out there.'

'Mother Wilfred won't like it.'

'Then Mother Wilfred has got a lot to learn.' And with

that she disappeared through the side door, and shut it behind her with a bang.

I carried on alone to the chapel, which was in gloom apart from the sanctuary lamp flickering at the far end. Kneeling down heavily in the back pew, I began to examine my conscience.

My life at St Cuthbert's was smooth enough on the surface, I reflected. All my classes were now under control, and I got on well with both the lay staff and the community. Even Sister Bosco had grown quite affable. But Elisabeth's babble about Rome, and her tales of the other novices, had made me realize how accustomed I'd grown to feeling slightly miserable since leaving the novitiate. Worse still, Elisabeth's return – her poised demeanour, her culinary skill – had triggered all my old, forgotten feelings of inferiority. Gone was the sense I had in Berbiers that each new hardship was fresh proof of God's favour. I felt more as though He was treating me as nobody very special.

Unable to concentrate on my prayers, I was easily distracted by a faint snuffle from the altar. As I peered curiously through the gloom, a dark outline took shape on the marble floor. Someone was lying prostrate inside the sanctuary.

I had seen southern European nuns praying cruciform; but who at St Cuthbert's would adopt such an exaggerated pose? Elisabeth was flamboyant enough, but she was out in the garden. And although Sister Julian loved Europe, she was too modern for such an archaic custom. Curbing my curiosity, I forced my eyes shut. The penitent must have her confessor's permission, and that was that.

But I still couldn't concentrate, and after a few more minutes I gave up and made the sign of the cross. On rising to my feet, I discerned a shawled figure against the reddish glow. Sister Monica! For a moment I considered approaching her, to say how sorry I was to see her so ill. But no, that would be intrusive. Better wait until teatime.

But at teatime she was nowhere to be seen, and she was still absent at dinner. The next day was Sunday, and at breakfast her place remained empty. I waited until Mother Wilfred was ensconced in her study, and made my way to the infirmary.

The door at the top of the stairs was open, but there was no sign of Monica; only the infirmarian, stuffing some papers into a tea chest.

'Hello there, Nuncy!' I said cheerfully.

'Don't call me that,' snapped the old nurse. Her face was sagging from exhaustion, and her eyes red-rimmed.

Shrugging, I watched her toss a squirrel-hair brush into the box, the paint dried on its bristles.

'Monica won't like that,' I remarked. 'She hates people meddling with her brushes.'

Without replying, Sister Annunciata picked up the hard-board painting of the hand, and jammed it down the side of the box.

'Be careful!' I cried. 'The colours are still wet.'

'That hardly matters,' said the old nun, 'seeing that I'm about to burn it.'

'Burn it!' I exclaimed. 'She'll never let you!'

'She'll have no say in the matter.' Tears were seeping into the nurse's eyes. 'She went home this morning.'

'Home?' I repeated dazedly.

'Mother Wilfred says that Monica isn't meant for the religious life,' said Sister Annunciata as she peeled a sheet off the bed.

I gazed round the infirmary looking for a sign of Monica's presence. None remained. 'But she had a vocation!'

'I said that I would be glad to look after her, but it made no difference. Mother General rang in the middle of the night with a dispensation.'

'I heard the telephone.'

'I still haven't got over seeing her in her new clothes,'

said the nurse. 'I know that our Superior's word is the word of God – but Monica looked so ordinary – just like anybody else in that skimpy little blouse and skirt. It can't be right.'

'You should have told me.'

'Have you ever helped a nun leave her cloister?' asked Annunciata.

I shook my head. No one I knew had left since the novitiate.

'Then you can take it from me it's sad work – and the less you have to do with it the better. And now, if you'll excuse me, I'll take these sheets down to the laundry.'

Too stunned to offer any help, I wandered into the community room. Only Sister Julian was at her desk, correcting a pile of exercise books.

'Monica's gone home!' I burst out.

The English teacher put down her pen. 'I know, Brigid. She left early this morning.'

'But she didn't say goodbye!'

'It wasn't that she didn't want to – she chose to obey the Holy Rule.'

'Where has she gone?'

'Her vows expire at Christmas. Until then she will live at home with her parents in Manchester – in the world but not quite of it. Soon she'll be –'

'What's her address?' I butted in. 'I'm going to write to her.'

'I've no idea,' said Julian, 'and I suggest you don't try to find out. Away from the convent, she might have a chance of recovery.'

Sister Monica had a vocation, so how could being a nun make her ill? I struggled to assimilate the idea.

'She entered as a healthy young woman,' continued Sister Julian, as though reading my mind, 'and had her first fit the night before her Clothing. In those days illness was seen as a sign of God's favour, so no one was bothered.'

'So why did she get well again?'

'She was a born teacher – and if we'd stayed as we were, she might never have had another fit.'

'But she was always pressing for change,' I objected. 'She designed our new habits.'

'Yes, yes, I know – but it's not easy being a modern nun. These changes we've all been fussing about – they're only the icing on the cake. There are deeper things begging for attention, but nobody dares investigate.' She took off her horn-rimmed specs and rubbed her eyes. 'Don't worry too much about Monica – she's an artist, and will be happier out in the world. And if it hadn't been for this, your friend Elisabeth wouldn't be with us now.'

'You mean . . .?'

'That's right. She's our new art teacher.'

So that was the source of the mystery. And I'd been the only one not to realize. 'You can't understand how miserable I feel,' I said, trying not to cry.

'I understand, Brigid – far better than you realize.' Sister Julian's tone grew more gentle. 'When Sister Elisabeth was sent to the Congo – no, not this one, I'm going back years – I thought I was going to die. But as you can see, I'm still here – although I sometimes wish . . .' She turned towards me with a little smile. 'You are luckier than me, Brigid. You'll never hear of her again.'

Before I could ask what was so lucky about that, Sister Bosco bustled into the room, and shooting Julian a reproachful glance, sat down at her desk. As it was the first Sunday of the month I took out my writing paper. We were allowed one letter home every four weeks, but since I had no family apart from Uncle David, and had quarrelled with Lorraine, I usually asked permission to write to another nun. This time it was Bony's turn.

But the words would not come. We had to submit our letters to Mother Wilfred unsealed, so I didn't dare mention the art teacher's departure. After half an hour of crossings out and fresh starts, I abandoned the attempt, and, following Elisabeth's example, went to pray in the garden.

Unlike the Mother House, St Cuthbert's employed no gardener. The flowerbeds were weeded by Sister Columba, who had stacked her wheelbarrow and gardening tools in the shed before the sabbath. I wandered in peace along the narrow path to the grotto in the corner of the playground, and surveyed the statue of Our Lady on her little pedestal, with a bowl of tulips at her feet. Sister Monica had taught us how to sing 'Ave Maria' on this very spot, when we were in first year and she was fresh from the novitiate, her life mapped out before her. Even then I had longed to be like her.

And now she was somewhere in Manchester, and I was standing in her place. Never again would she don her Joubertian brown, or walk up and down the gravel path, reading her Bible. Taking out my rosary beads, I prayed that somehow Sister Monica might return to St Cuthbert's before Elisabeth filled her place as the clever, charismatic young nun, turning all the girls to God and Van Gogh.

After three Hail Marys I stopped short. Sister Julian was right: Monica would be happier out in the world, free from the bells which ruled our day, free to paint and forget about time, and to buy decent clothes. But life at St Cuthbert's looked so blank without her that the thought gave me no pleasure.

I'd grown far too wrapped up in other people, I reflected – the girls, the staff, and most of all in Sister Monica. No wonder I was unable to see this new trial as a special sign of God's love.

But I came here for God, not Sister Monica, I told myself fiercely, knotting the beads around my palm, and starting my rosary again. At last I had realized: it wasn't Sister Monica I should be praying for. It was me.

TWENTY-FOUR

———

I had begun committing a mortal sin, and didn't know what
to do about it. I would have liked to confide in a sister, but
Elisabeth was too close to my own age, Ursula too austere,
and Mother Wilfred, as my Superior the obvious choice, was
distant and unsympathetic. I had thought of Sister Julian,
who had been kind to me since Monica left, but I found the
subject difficult to broach, and the right opportunity didn't
present itself. She had taken to making long phone calls
whenever Mother Wilfred was absent; and when the phone
rang at odd intervals she would skid into the hall to talk in
low tones, without divulging the caller's identity.

So I struggled on, hugging my secret, as one by one
Monica's pictures were taken down from the classrooms and
corridors to be replaced by children's drawings, or reproduc-
tions from the Vatican museum. The infirmarian told me
that Mother Wilfred had ordered all Monica's paintings to
be burnt. I could see no reason for this, so when I discovered
a cache of nearly Finished canvases in the art room, I carried
them in secret to my cell. At the end of an afternoon's
teaching I would mount the dormitory stairs, take them out
from under my bed, and, laying them on the counterpane,
contemplate them in turn. They were a series of close-ups,
painted with such myopic intensity they were an assault on
the retina. Some were of treebark – the mulberry by the
grotto, the lime trees in the park – close and grainy enough
to register every tinge of russet, olive and ochre. Others
were studies of leaves in a green so drenching that the paint
still looked wet.

Monica's last pupils had already sat their O levels, so few

of the girls still asked after her; and the community was forbidden to mention her by the Holy Rule. But far from forgetting her, I felt more closely connected than ever. That month I was acting as sacristan, and after preparing the altar for mass would stand for a few minutes at the chapel door, watching the sun rise through the great monkey-puzzle tree in the garden, and wondering why I'd never noticed it before. Sometimes during a free period I would wander across to the park, and, abandoning custody of the eyes, gaze up at the leaves that Monica had painted, now dusted with summer ochre. It was the first time I'd looked around me since rebuked by Mother General after my First Vows. After all, this was only Liverpool, the place where I'd grown up. To my astonishment, far from being banal, the colours here were just as lovely, the shapes as intricate as in the Midi.

At night, after peeling off my stockings, I would gaze through my skylight at the stars, relishing the air flowing on to my warm skin to bring it out in goose pimples. Then I would don my nightdress, slide between the sheets and stretch out my legs. My stomach seemed to have grown tauter and flatter, and I longed to look in a mirror to see if my shape might not be better than I'd thought. One night I cupped my breasts in my hands, suddenly aware of how full they had become since I was a teenager. Absently I touched one of my nipples – and the effect was so sharply pleasurable that I touched the other one without pausing to consider, and then, using both hands, began to caress them.

The next night, when I did it again, my thoughts drifted towards Jonathon Maule; but I now knew too much about him, and the image failed to excite. I should have stopped straight away – but the activity scarcely seemed sexual, having more to do with the cool of the sheets, the warmth of my skin, and my new-found pleasure in being alive. On the third night I was longing to get to bed, and my nipples felt hot and hard as I slid into my nightdress. It was then other images began flashing into my mind – Hercule turning towards me that night in the vegetable garden, and, even more shamingly, Mary Lou, now Sister Boniface, sprawled in the train with her boyfriend. How could I have been so judgemental? If Mary Lou had felt like this, I thought, all too aware of my hardening nipples, she had done better than me in giving it up for God.

I could no longer hide it from myself: I was in a state of mortal sin, and must go to confession. The pleasure in my newly awakened senses vanished as I thought of confiding once again in Father Gorman. If he couldn't understand me when I was a teenager, he was even less likely to now I was a nun.

'I can't seem to get on with my sisters,' was all I could bring myself to stammer through the heavy grille of the confessional.

'Have you fallen out with them or what?' said the priest testily.

'No, Father,' I replied, with the dismal sense I was prevaricating, and therefore wasting his time. 'It's just that I feel so – lonely.'

'Is your health all right, child?'

'Yes, Father – except that I feel tired and sort of restless at the same time.'

'What you need is a holiday,' he pronounced. 'Ask your Mother Superior to let you lie in next week.'

Ironically, given the nature of my sin, Mother Wilfred agreed to my spending more time in bed, and every morning for the next seven days I lay on while the rising bell tolled its nine strokes, and the rest of the community bumped, snuffled, coughed and thumped their way out of bed and down to chapel.

Although it was quiet once they had left the dormitory, I seldom got back to sleep. My eyes would fix themselves on the hairline crack across my ceiling, as I wondered how to survive another day. Each morning I resolved afresh not to let my hand touch my breasts. And then at night it would seem irresistible – waiting a little while for Elisabeth on my left-hand side and Columba on my right to settle down and fall asleep. Sometimes I wondered if any of the others had ever done what I was doing. I thought not. Elisabeth, Ursula, Julian – in their different ways they seemed so settled and composed, so at home in the religous life. Not until their breathing steadied would I begin stroking my breasts. What was the point of giving this up, I reasoned with myself, before making a proper act of contrition?

I was careful always to stop before I lost control. Then I would lie awake for hours, my mind racing. *My sisters, be sober and vigilant, for the devil your enemy is roaming the earth like a ravening lion*. To think that I had once felt unafraid of Satan. Now, as the night wore on, I knew I would burn in hell for all eternity.

The next morning I would go to Holy Communion as usual, thus committing not only mortal sin but sacrilege, too cowardly to kneel alone in my pew while my sisters moved to the altar. My pleasure in prayer had disappeared, and my mind often wandered during the service. But although God had turned His face away, I never doubted my vocation. Hadn't our novice-mistress told us that feelings don't count? As we left the novitiate she had given each of us the autobiography of the Little Flower, Thérèse of Lisieux. *I am in a dark tunnel*, wrote the saint, *and you have to go through it yourself to understand how dark it is*. At the page where Thérèse describes how her soul was enveloped in what she calls 'the land of fog', Mère-Maîtresse had slipped a bookmark bearing my name in religion, and the date of my First Vows.

'The Good Lord gives us a honeymoon,' she told us. 'Enjoy it while you can. It will come to an end soon enough.' Although I felt no better at the end of my week of late mornings, I replied politely to Sister Annunciata's brisk inquiry and began getting up again as usual. My honeymoon was over before I'd even known it had started. If this was my dark night of the soul, I had better get used to it.

Term came to an end at last, after prize day, sports day and a farewell party for Margie Manifold. The community settled down to its holiday quiet, and within hours Elisabeth was busy clearing out the art room, Ursula was doing the timetable, and Columba was in the garden, weeding energetically. Even Heather had disappeared for her summer holiday on the Toxteth Circular.

I should have been happy to have some time to myself, but could think of nothing better than to mooch around the convent. Luckily there was a lot going on, as the order continued to shudder its way into the twentieth century. We now had permission to write letters whenever we wished, and were under no obligation to show them to our Superior. Each nun was given a small amount of pocket money at the beginning of each month, to be spent as she pleased. On receiving our first instalment, Elisabeth and I went to the shops across the park. She bought a pair of fifteen-denier tights, making a little moue of discontent when the sales assistant said all they had was American tan. I bought a new notebook. I knew these concessions weren't solving my problems, but they took my mind off them for a while.

The most startling innovation came at the beginning of August. As usual when she had something important to say, Mother Wilfred summoned us to the community room after breakfast.

'My sisters,' she said, waiting for us all to be seated, 'Mother General has made an extraordinary announcement.' She paused for a moment while Bosco dropped her rosary beads, stood up to apologize, and picked them up again. 'You are each one to be allowed home on holiday – for one whole fortnight.'

Sister Columba was the first to respond. 'Home on holi-day? To Ireland?' she cried. 'Glory be to God!'

'Home on holiday,' reiterated Mother Wilfred solemnly, 'to your parents, wherever they are.'

'All the old ones are dead,' said Bosco. 'Does that mean I have to stay with Pat-Jo?'

'As long as he's a member of your immediate family.'

'And what will happen to Juno?' asked Gonzaga. 'He can't be left on his own.'

'Sisters Annunciata, Julian and Brigid have, I believe, no close family left.' Mother Wilfred peered at us over her half-moons. 'Is that correct?'

We nodded. Sister Julian had turned, I noted, a shade paler than usual.

'So you three can be our caretakers – watering the plants and feeding the cat,' said Mother Wilfred, a little too smugly, I thought.

'I hope they remember,' said the old cook. 'He takes a bit of looking after.'

'What will we do the rest of the time?' asked Julian.

'You may do as you wish: walk, read or . . . relax,' said Mother Wilfred vaguely.

Columba's face was creased by smiles. 'I'll see Kilkenny again before I die,' she was exclaiming rapturously to anyone who would listen. 'Thank the Lord!'

'Mummy's just off to France,' said Elisabeth. 'Can she take me with her?'

'That is quite in order,' said Mother Wilfred, 'as long as you have your own bedroom.'

'I dare say I'll requisition the conservatory,' she drawled. 'I always used to.'

Mother Wilfred grimaced. She still hadn't forced Elisabeth into the St Cuthbert's mould.

An ill-assorted trio, Sisters Julian, Annunciata and I sat silent as the hubbub rose among the rest. I tried to rejoice in my sisters' good fortune, but underneath I felt cheated. France, London, Ireland – everyone else was going away – and here was I, who had never had a decent holiday in my life, still trapped in the city where I grew up. Luckily, I was kept too busy over the next few days to feel sorry for myself, what with washing, sewing and packing, ordering tickets and making seat reservations for nuns who hadn't used public transport for forty years.

At nine o'clock on the Monday morning there was a ring at the door: Edward Bavidge, come to collect Elisabeth. Sisters Kevin and Ligori left next, flying straight to Dublin from Speke. Mother Wilfred was travelling by train to Fishguard, and Sister Ursula was going to stay with her brother the Monsignor in Ealing. The rest were travelling overnight on the Irish boat. Just before the arrival of the taxi, Gonzaga disappeared into the kitchen to cook a special bit of tripe for Juno. The smell, which pervaded the front hall, was making Columba turn paler than ever. She had woken everyone at five that morning by dragging her suitcase out from under her bed, to unpack and repack it for the fifth time. Bosco was trotting aimlessly up and down stairs. 'Do you show them your passport on the boat?' the portress asked her, 'or do it beforehand?'

'How would I know?' snapped Bosco. 'We'll see when we get there. Now stop moithering me.'

By the time Sisters Annunciata, Julian and myself had waved the last taxi off to the docks and set the house to rights, it was long past our usual bedtime. Exhausted by the bustle, we bolted the front door and crept to chapel for a silent Compline. Mother Wilfred had insisted on Annunciata moving back from the infirmary, where she'd continued to sleep since Monica's departure, and on getting undressed I could hear her making her bed in the next cubicle but one. Soon after lying down she was snoring heavily, and at the far end of the dormitory Sister Julian turned restlessly. Despite these noises, the house seemed preternaturally quiet.

The next morning we attended mass in the parish church because Father Gorman too had gone to Ireland. 'I know this isn't the holiday any of us might have chosen,' said Sister Julian at breakfast, 'but I think we should make the best of it.'

'What can we find to do?' I asked. I hadn't slept well the night before, and was feeling tired and lacklustre.

'Wilfie has left us quite a lot of money. We could go into town – or to Southport – or for a nice long walk.'

'Don't ask me to go traipsing around,' said the little nurse. 'I want to put my feet up.'

'Then we'll stay here, to make sure you do,' said Julian.

'Of course we will,' I said, disappointed. Unable to resolve my personal problems, I was longing for distractions. After lighting a fire in the community room for Sister Annunciata, I trailed up to the library to read *The Power and the Glory* for my O level class in September while Julian catalogued some new books.

After a lunch of some leftover macaroni cheese, Annunciata returned to her fire and Sister Julian and I carried our cups of tea out in the garden and sat on a bench by the grotto. It was a mellow August day, its heavy silence broken only by the starlings chattering over the ripening apples.

'What's the matter with Annunciata?' I asked. 'She says she's cold – but it's sweltering with that fire in the community room.'

'She's never been right since Monica left,' replied Julian. 'Not having a proper holiday is hardest of all on her, because she's tired out.'

'She seems so grumpy.'

'That's because she doesn't like me – not since I voiced my views on Monica's epilepsy.'

'I hope she feels better tomorrow,' I said tentatively, 'then we could all go out.'

'You try and persuade her. She's fond of you, Brigid – because you were fond of Monica.'

'You never said what you would like to do,' I remarked.

'I'd like to forget about being a nun for a bit,' replied Julian surprisingly. She was still looking tense from the bustle of the day before. 'Read some new books – enjoy some sunshine.'

I nodded. Even if we couldn't get out, there would be a welcome break from routine.

'Margie Manifold was right,' I said as the sun glinted through the branches of the monkey-puzzle tree. 'You look nice in your new habit.'

As though catching my mood, Sister Julian reached up to pluck the veil from her head. 'There's no one around to see,' she grinned. 'Annunciata's fast asleep.'

I stared in surprise at this new, devil-may-care woman – then gazed at the statue of Our Lady of Lourdes, her rosary beads hanging from her right hand and her blue sash bent by an imaginary wind. 'I suppose you're right,' I said, and pulled off my own veil.

Giggling at the incongruity, we entered the kitchen bare-headed for a second cup of tea. Juno gazed down with narrowed eyes from his perch on top of the dresser. 'He looks quite scandalized,' said Sister Julian. 'I hope he won't report us to Wilfie.'

We stayed out in the garden for the whole of that afternoon. Every now and again Julian would look up from the airmail letter she was writing and comment on the warmth of the weather, or some bird that had alighted on the rockery. Happy to be in her presence, I knew it was the perfect opportunity to tell her my secret.

The sun dipped below the level of the rooftops while I stalled for time by gazing at the lights coming on in the backs of houses across the playing-field. An old lady was leaning on an upstairs windowsill to water her geraniums, and next door to her a woman and a man sat chatting on the top step of a fire escape. Soon it would be supper-time.

'Do you ever feel tempted by life outside the convent?' I said at last.

To my relief, Julian didn't seem offended. 'The road not taken,' she smiled. 'Yes, I do – frequently. There's a lot about the religious life I don't agree with.'

'You mean you regret – being a nun?'

'Not at all. It's part of my vocation – to be aware of what might have been, and still turn my back on it.' She packed away her pen and paper. 'And what about you, Brigid? Do you find it a struggle?'

I paused to consider. 'I can't imagine not being here,' I said. It was only half a lie.

To my disappointment, Julian didn't seem disposed to continue. 'Then you're one of the lucky ones,' she said lightly. I was still struggling to formulate my next question when Annunciata appeared at the kitchen door. 'Come on, you two,' she called. 'It's nearly dark.'

There was some bacon in the fridge, and some eggs, but none of us felt like cooking, so Julian and I made sandwiches while the infirmarian fed Juno. Then we went to chapel for another silent Vespers. A little wind had crept up from the river by the time we locked the front and back doors and went upstairs.

I had no urge to touch myself that night, but lay quite still with my mind tracking back over my conversation with Sister Julian. She had seemed to invite my confidence, and I'd been on the brink of making a confession when Annunciata appeared. Perhaps there was a purpose in this holiday, and I'd get another chance tomorrow. I prayed that she wouldn't be disgusted, but would advise me on how to gain absolution without going to Father Gorman. If she could, my problem might not be as big as I'd thought.

—

TWENTY-FIVE

Next morning it was raining, so coaxing Annunciata into town was out of the question. I stoked up the community room fire and watched her doze over the *Catholic Herald*, to be joined by Julian at coffee time.

'Still reading *The Power and the Glory*?' she asked, sitting down beside me. 'Can't you find anything less worthy?'

'You're the librarian,' I replied. 'It's your job to make a recommendation.' I was beginning to enjoy teasing this new, engaging Sister Julian.

'I recommend that you forget about books for a bit,' she replied. 'Why not take some of the money Wilfie left us and buy yourself a bathing costume? When Nuncy's better we might go swimming.'

'Oh, I couldn't,' I said awkwardly. 'I might never use it.'

'Take it, for goodness' sake. There's plenty more.'

I caught a bus into town and, plucking up my courage, dived inside the nearest chainstore. I felt an incongruous figure making my way upstairs to the ladies' wear department, but nobody seemed to notice anything unusual. I had just spotted some regulation swimming costumes in among the minuscule bikinis and Hawaiian prints, when a voice behind me said, 'Can I help you, Sister?'

I swung round to face a tall young sales assistant in a pink overall.

'Maureen!' I gasped, staring at the pixie face with its snub nose and freckles. 'Maureen O'Shaunessy!'

'That's me,' she grinned. 'Large as life, and twice as natural.'

'I hadn't thought – when I came in –'

'You needn't look so guilty, Sister. I was asking to be chucked out.'

'Well,' I said awkwardly, 'I hope this isn't too bad.'

'Not for a Saturday job. And in September I'm going on a training course.'

'How's Lorraine?' I asked next. 'I've been meaning to get in touch . . .' My voice trailed away.

'Obstreperous as ever. She's threatening to call and see you on her next visit home. Oh, don't worry – she's calmed down a lot. Heading straight for middle management, if you ask me. It was just that she felt – betrayed, you know – when you let them throw me out.'

'I know,' I nodded, 'and I'm sorry. I was doing what I thought best. I would act differently now.'

'What's this, then?' asked Maureen suddenly, turning her attention to the swimsuit in my hand.

'I might be going swimming,' I explained. 'I'm on holiday.'

'Here in Liverpool?' she said incredulously.

'That's right. Most of the others have gone away. I'll be looking for things to do.'

'All on your own?'

'Sister Julian and Sister Annunciata are here too.'

'I wouldn't buy one of them,' said Maureen. 'They cling to your shape the minute you step in the water. Leaves nothing to the imagination.'

'Then what's best?' I asked helplessly.

'Try one of these,' she replied, selecting a turquoise halter-neck. 'Much more flattering.'

'Are you sure?' I stared doubtfully at its ruched bodice dotted with scarlet flowers.

'Positive – just your colour.'

'Can I try it on?' I asked.

'Sorry – we don't have changing-rooms here. What size do you take, Sister?'

'I don't know,' I said helplessly. 'Er – Sister Monica used to decide that.'

'I think you've put on weight,' said Maureen, gazing judicially at my hips. 'You'll need a fourteen at least. Bring it back if it's not right.'

'It looks as though I need the exercise.'

'That's three pounds fifteen and ninepence to you, Sister Rig – Sister Brigid,' said Maureen cheerfully. 'And cheap at the price.' She took the five-pound note I offered her, and popped the swimming costume into a carrier bag. 'Cheerio, and have a good time.'

I returned to St Cuthbert's to find that Sister Annunciata had retired to bed. 'She's got a sore throat,' said Julian. 'She needs lozenges – and honey and lemon.'

The rain still hadn't cleared after lunch, so we shrouded ourselves in old waterproofs and splashed off across the park to find a chemist.

'If only Nuncy would get better,' I said as we tramped past the Palm House, 'we could start enjoying ourselves.'

'It's hardly a dream holiday.' Sister Julian's green-grey eyes were bright with amusement, and her haughty manner had disappeared. 'But I've known worse.'

'Do you have no family left at all?' I asked, keen to establish the right note of intimacy.

'Never did have,' said Sister Julian cheerfully. 'I was brought up in an orphanage.'

I was taken aback. 'But you sound so –' I wanted to say middle-class, but was afraid of sounding rude.

'Go on, say it,' urged Sister Julian. 'I know I sound over-refined. In the beginning my accent was meant as a camouflage. Then the camouflage stuck.'

'When did you decide to enter the convent?'

'At nineteen years old. The orphanage was run by Joubertians. I envied their security and sense of purpose. And I knew they would train me to be a nurse – or a teacher.

I'd already spent a year in the typing pool, and didn't like it.'

'Couldn't you have gone to university instead?'

She shrugged. 'There was no one to support me. The nuns were willing to train their own sisters – but they couldn't subsidize every brat who'd been dumped on their doorstep.'

'It must have been the Lord's will for you to enter.'

'Maybe so, maybe not,' said Julian laconically. 'For me it was a route upwards and outwards. Or that's what it seemed like at the time.'

'And now?' I asked timidly.

'And now – well, that's a long story. I envy nuns like you, who seem to enjoy the religious life. And even Mother Wilfred. Yes, I know she's got her limitations –' said Julian as I opened my mouth to speak, 'that's my point. She hasn't got the imagination to see what she's missing.' She peered at me sideways under her rainhood, eyes bright. 'Oh, dear – I seem to have implied that you're unimaginative, too. I didn't mean to.'

'I am, but never mind,' I said, not wanting her to stop. 'Did you ever –' I stepped aside for a gaggle of tourists heading for the Palm House – 'have a boyfriend?' My heart was pounding.

'I never had the least interest in boys,' she replied calmly. 'I find it so irritating – teaching bright girls and watching them fail their O levels because they're scared of doing better than some pimply little lad.'

'At least I didn't do that.'

'You had me worried at times – mooning around that boy from All Hallows.'

'I hardly ever think of him now,' I told her.

'I'm glad to hear it.'

'But I do think of sex sometimes.' Having blurted it out, I could go no further.

'And?' Again the bright-eyed scrutiny.

Ahead reared the sandstone pillars at the entrance to Lark Lane, gleaming in the by now sheeting rain. In a few moments' time we would be jostling the other shoppers. It was now or never.

'And something's gone wrong – it's ever since Monica went home . . .'

The blood was singing in my ears as I groped for ways of explaining what it was I'd been doing. In desperation I turned to Julian, aware that my cheeks were aflame. But to my surprise her attention had been caught by a black and white cat curled in a shop window.

'Sister Julian?' I said, rebuffed by her lack of interest.

With seeming reluctance she withdrew her gaze from the cat. But instead of turning towards me, she stared stonily ahead.

'In that case,' she said distantly, 'I suggest you confide in your confessor.'

Too miserable to tell her that I'd already tried, I opened my shopping bag and fumbled for change. By the time we'd reached the chemist, and she still hadn't met my gaze, my misery had turned to anger. Why had she suddenly turned so frosty – it was worse than being at St Cuthbert's. And she had encouraged me to speak! I was right about her from the start. She was moody and unjust.

After paying for the medicine in silence, we trailed back across the park, and, as she had promised before we set out, stopped at the little café for afternoon tea. While we were eating our éclairs, Sister Julian, perhaps regretting her sternness, struck up a conversation about landscape gardening, and I replied as best I could. But it was no good. Our camaraderie had evaporated, leaving us back where we'd started – but with me more resentful than ever. And there's a whole fortnight ahead, I thought dismally, with nothing to do but read Graham Greene and nurse Sister Annunciata. Suddenly I longed for the rest of the community – Elisabeth, Columba, and even Bosco. At least they were chatty.

TWENTY-SIX

'My nightdress is drenched in sweat,' said Annunciata from her pillow next morning, 'and my head's pounding. I must have a temperature.'

She certainly looked ill. Dark circles had appeared under her eyes, and her normally rosy cheeks were sallow. 'I'm going to call the doctor,' Julian told her.

'I know what to do better than he does,' grumbled the infirmarian. 'All I want is to be left alone.'

'That may be – but Wilfie would never forgive us if anything – if we didn't look after you properly.'

'Then you'd best move me to the infirmary. We can't have him coming up here.'

After breakfast Sister Julian and I made up her old bed, and helped the little nun down two flights of stairs.

Doctor Reilly diagnosed bronchitis, and prescribed bed-rest. 'She's exhausted after nursing Sister Monica for so long,' he said once we'd got downstairs. 'What she needs is good nursing. On no account let her move around.'

'I'm really sorry,' she moaned after he'd gone. 'This will ruin your holiday.'

'Nonsense,' said Julian, 'look at the weather!'

After our first drenching we had lost our enthusiasm for braving the rain. Having failed to confide, I felt constrained by Sister Julian's company, and wished she'd disappear to the library. Instead, she sat hunched in the community room over endless games of solitaire – a surprising pursuit, I thought sourly, for so intellectual a woman. In between looking after Annunciata, I tried to get on with *The Power and the Glory*, glancing up now and and again to search hopelessly for a break in the clouds.

It wasn't until the weekend that things began to get better. The weather was so damp we'd taken to lighting a fire on our own account, and had pulled in two armchairs from the priest's parlour.

'Would you like me to make you a hot drink?' I asked Sister Julian after an hour or so. She had put away her solitaire set, and was rummaging irritably among a pile of jigsaws.

'Oh, well, suit yourself,' I said brusquely when she failed to reply. 'I'll make one for Nuncy and me.'

'Sister Brigid.' A new note in Julian's voice made me turn back.

She straightened up and took a couple of steps towards me. 'I've been unkind to you over the last few days, and I want to apologize. Spoiling your holiday like this.'

'I wish you'd tell me what I did wrong.'

'You did nothing wrong,' she murmured. 'Nothing at all.'

'Then why did you go all quiet in Lark Lane,' I persisted as we made our way to the kitchen.

'I'm going to take a risk and tell you,' said Sister Julian, watching me put a pan of milk on the stove. She paused for a few seconds and then said abruptly, 'I was downright jealous.'

'Jealous?' I echoed in amazement. 'Jealous of me?'

'Of you and Monica,' replied Sister Julian, reddening slightly, 'You had such a rapport.'

'I was very fond of her,' I replied, more bothered by the other nun's discomfort than my own, 'but I don't really miss her.' This wasn't strictly true, but it seemed tactful. I turned away, ostensibly to keep an eye on the pan.

'I always thought – that you might follow her.'

'Certainly not,' I said, taking refuge in indignation. 'I'm not a puppy. Besides, I don't know where she lives.'

'You're so literal-minded,' laughed the other nun, her good humour seemingly restored. She slipped her arm round my waist and gave me a light hug. 'Now let's forget about this embarrassing subject, and have that cup of coffee.'

I felt too awkward to quiz her any further on the subject of my old art teacher, but later that afternoon, when the rain had cleared and we strolled down to the promenade to watch the tide turn, her words reverberated in my mind. Could it be that she wanted to be my role model, as Monica had once been? I considered the possibility. As a girl, I had thought Julian too clever, cold and sarcastic. But now I was beginning to like her more – her honesty, her intelligence, her unusual way of looking at things.

'What did you think of me – when I was a pupil?' I asked her suddenly.

She paused to watch an especially long and creamy wave.

'You reminded me of myself at that age', she said. 'So intense – and so enthusiastic. I always wanted to mother you. In fact you were lovely,' she added suddenly.

'Me? Lovely?' I burst out laughing. 'I used to think you despised me!'

'Not in the least,' said Julian. 'And I wasn't a bit surprised that you had a vocation – although I must confess I was hurt when you didn't confide in me.'

'There is something – I've been wanting to say.' Suddenly I felt sure this was the right moment.

'Go ahead.'

'I've started . . . touching myself – in bed at night.'

'Masturbation!' exclaimed Julian. 'I wouldn't worry too much – we've all done it. After all, it doesn't harm anyone.'

'Even though it's a mortal sin?'

'Surely God has bigger things to worry about. But if you're anxious, why not go to confession at the cathedral?'

'Now?' I said. 'On holiday?'

'Of course – we'll go tomorrow.'

To think how easily my problem could be solved! This could be the answer for me – someone at St Cuthbert's to advise me and share my thoughts. Suddenly I realized how lonely I'd been since leaving the novitiate.

'There's no one I'd rather be on holiday with,' I told her impulsively. 'You've been sent by God to make life bearable.'

'Let's hope I don't make it worse. It's a serious thing, friendship.'

Mère-Maîtresse had been wrong, I decided as we strolled along the prom. That was because she only knew Sister Julian by reputation. Clearly her high intelligence made people over-suspicious, because she wasn't really in favour of change at all costs – she thought things through carefully, and wanted the best for our order. I knew now how honest and scrupulous she was – look at the way she had acknowledged her feelings about Monica and me – and to one of her own past pupils – and encouraged me to go to confession. I was flattered that she'd mentioned the word friendship, and longed to live up to her expectations.

The fine weather settled in, and Annunciata's temper improved with her medication. The next morning she urged us to explore the city centre. 'I don't want you young ones hanging around,' she said. 'What I need is some peace.'

We left her a thermos flask of tea, and a packet of biscuits, then set off down the boulevard. The sky was high and blue, and a light breeze came whispering up from the Mersey. We went first to the Anglican cathedral, and as I wandered round its dark interior with Sister Julian at my side, I felt happier than ever in my life before.

'It's the last Gothic cathedral in Europe,' I read from the guide book, as we gazed down the nave. 'And I like it better than ours.' It was only recently we had been allowed to visit non-Catholic churches, so it was our first time inside. I stared up at the huge sandstone pillars, and the multiplicity of arches and inner stairways. 'More sense of history.'

'I disagree,' replied Sister Julian amicably. 'It looks as though they stuck on every detail they could think of – and the effect is too heavy. Let's have a look at ours.'

We climbed the cathedral tower to look at Paddy's wigwam, as we used to call it, beckoning at the other end of Hope Street. Although its concrete was discoloured, the stained glass beneath its spiky coronet was glowing bravely in the sunshine. 'See – it's more in tune with the times,' said Sister Julian. Chinatown was at our feet, and out across the Wirral we could see Moel Fannau, outlined in silver. 'I used to hate living here,' I told Sister Julian as we passed the big cathedral bell on the way back down. 'Now I think I might like it.'

'Then why don't you go to confession to mark your fresh start?'

We strolled along Hope Street, and up the Catholic cathedral steps into the sunny round space beneath its dome. A young African priest was hearing confessions, and when my turn came I only mentioned the one sin. I must have sounded confident, because far from interrogating me the priest gave me absolution straight away. I don't think he even knew I was a nun. Sister Julian waited while I said my two Our Fathers, and then we celebrated by going on the Birkenhead ferry. Nobody came to take our fare, so as the boat plied back and forth across the river we stayed talking on the top deck, and I told Sister Julian how I'd done this with Lorraine, in imitation of Jonathon and Edward, without ever enjoying it.

On our fourth crossing we landed, and strolled along the riverfront to Birkenhead Priory, to gaze up at where the sun came glancing through arches where once there'd been stained glass. At teatime we sat on a broad stone wall to share a bar of chocolate and speculate about how the others were spending their holidays.

'Mother Wilfred will exhume her old habit,' laughed Sister Julian. 'The streets of Cork will see her swathed from head to foot in brown serge.'

'And Sister Bosco will make each member of the family kiss the floor if they are late for meals. Even the children – no, especially the children.'

'And Elisabeth will go topless – while smoking Balkan Sobranies.'

As we wandered through the little streets back to the ferry, I wondered why I'd once felt afraid of Sister Julian. We returned home and prepared a meal to take up to the infirmary and share with Annunciata while telling her about the two cathedrals, and our trip on the river. When the old nurse began to doze, Julian and I went to chapel and on up to the dormitory, tired after so much sightseeing. The summer darkness had already fallen, and we lapsed into silence while getting ready for bed, instead of chatting across the empty cubicles.

Instead of calling goodnight, I slipped in between the sheets and lay in the glow of my bedside light, watching the storm clouds racing across my skylight. I felt happy and replete at the day's events, and had almost fallen asleep when there was a flash of lightning, followed by a light tap on my door.

'Sister Julian?' Although the infirmary was down on the first floor, I lowered my voice to a whisper.

'You've forgotten to turn your light off,' said Julian. Somehow it wasn't surprising that, instead of flicking the switch, she moved quietly to the edge of my bed and sat down.

'Don't you think it's about time you stopped calling me Sister?' she asked gently.

I shifted a little to the left. 'But you are my sister,' I told her. 'More than anyone else.'

'That is what I should like, Brigid,' she said. As she murmured my name, I glanced up at her heavy auburn hair, grown longer than I'd ever seen it before. When she reached down and took my hand, her grasp felt strong and dry. Suddenly the little room seemed warm, almost stifling in the golden light, and I knew something was going to happen.

It seemed the most natural thing in the world when Julian slowly leaned over and kissed me once on the forehead, and once, very gently, on the lips. My blood began to pulse faster, and my hands and arms felt limp. So this, I thought, is the reason for all those rules – against particular friendships, against talking in twos, against visiting the dormitory during the daytime. And here we were, I thought, with a surge of elation, together in spite of them all.

As she began to stroke my hair I struggled to speak before it was too late. 'This is wrong,' I murmured, my lips feeling swollen and slightly tender. 'We'll be in a state of sin.'

'Let's not talk about sin now,' said Julian. Another flash of lightning lit the skylight, and a door slammed two floors down. She folded back the sheet, switched out the light and lay down quietly beside me. I had never been so close to anyone before, and stretched out my hand timidly to touch her arm. She felt fragile under the white cotton nightdress, and softer than I expected. Her skin smelt faintly of musk, and her hair had come loose from its knot on the nape of her neck, and was curling on to her shoulders.

'This will be the first night we spend together, and if you say so, it will be the last,' said Julian. By now my whole body was tingling, and without realizing it I had pressed up against her, longing for her to kiss me again. She put both arms around me, and held me to her. By the glimmer of my skylight I could see that her eyes were closed, and her lips slightly parted.

'There will be plenty of time to think about sin tomorrow,' she murmured.

TWENTY-SEVEN

But we didn't talk about sin the next morning, or, indeed, on any of the mornings that followed, and in no time at all it was the end of the first week. I moved through the days in a trance, not dwelling on the nights, but revelling in my new-found happiness. I'd found everything I'd ever wanted – and here in the convent, where I'd least expected it. It was providential.

The weather stayed fine and, apart from looking after Annunciata, we spent most of our time sightseeing. We strolled through the sunlit rooms of the city art gallery, lingering over Giaquinta's Venus and her Cupids, and Cranach's nymph of the fountain with her sly smile and plump thighs. We had only been there once before, on a community outing, with Mother Wilfred instructing us to close our eyes every time we passed a nude. All I could remember was Van Dyck's shrewd-faced Infanta Isabella-Clara-Eugenia, dressed in the habit of the Poor Clares, because she reminded me of Mother General.

Day after day we wandered round Liverpool together. Occasionally – walking along the promenade at Otterspool, or exploring a parish church – Julian would let her hand brush against mine, or risk a brief caress of my breast. More often I would stand entranced, pretending to gaze at the clouds over the Mersey, or the marine light on the famous waterfront, aware of nothing but her breathing gently by my side.

But mostly we just talked, swapping endless details of our childhoods, convent gossip, tales of the novitiate and the religious life, our views of Father Gorman, Mother Wilfred, and all our sisters. I told Julian about the death of Madge, and how guilty I felt about not speaking out and insisting that I stayed behind in Berbiers instead of going to the château. She reassured me, saying that my mother's lonely death was Mère-Maîtresse's responsibility, not mine, and that I could have done no different.

She explained in her turn about her friendship with Sarah Cunningham, who later became Sister Elisabeth of the Trinity. Although Sarah was rich and she poor, they had loved one another as girls and had entered the convent on the same day, far too innocent to disguise their feelings.

'Sarah had a nightmare one night in Berbiers,' Julian told me. 'I was in the next bed, and when I heard her cry out I climbed in beside her, and held her till she fell asleep. We were shattered by Mother General's summons, because neither of us could see what we'd done wrong.'

'Did Mother General punish you?' I asked.

'She wanted to send us home, but our novice-mistress begged her to let us stay. Sarah was moved straight to the Congo, under strict orders never to contact me again. They say she was happy as a missionary; but I know her spirit was broken – otherwise, why would she have died so young?'

After parting from Sarah, said Julian, she'd never wanted to grow close to anyone again. But she'd felt drawn to me even when I was a girl – and this time knew better than to show it. She was thrilled when I returned to St Cuthbert's – and to teach in her department. Yes, she knew things soon went wrong. It was just that I was so determined to do things my own way; and so friendly with Monica, with Miss Vavasour, with Mrs Tarn – with everyone, in short, but Julian. Sitting at the kitchen table, out in the garden, or dawdling along the promenade, we tracked back over every aspect of my first year as a teacher. The only thing neither of us ever mentioned was what we were doing in bed.

Every evening at nine o'clock we would take Nuncy a

cup of cocoa, and tell her about our day. Then, after settling her for the night, we would go up to the dormitory. By tacit consent we would get undressed separately. After giving the old nurse plenty of time to fall asleep, Julian would slip down the little corridor to my cubicle. Usually she would spend a few minutes sitting on the side of my bed, stroking my face and hair. Then, turning back the sheet, she would climb in.

Once we heard a creak on the stairs, and thought it must be Annunciata. Julian flitted out of my bed and back to her cubicle in seconds – but it proved a false alarm, and she rejoined me after half an hour. Sometimes she would lie on top of me, kissing my face and neck; at other times she would stretch outside beside me, her small rounded belly pressed against my hips as she murmured in my ear or buried her face in my neck.

There was nothing to disturb our peace. Annunciata, whose temper was improving with her medication, dozed during the day and slept soundly at night; the new term still seemed pleasantly remote, and as the GCE results hadn't yet come out, there had been no awkward phone calls from the girls or their parents. Whenever a postcard arrived from France or Ireland we stuck it on the back of the dresser without reading it. 'We'll be hearing about their holidays soon enough,' said Julian.

The outside world didn't intrude until our very last day, when we got back from mass in the parish church to find Nuncy still asleep. We had exchanged the refectory, with its dark oak tables and frosted glass, for the priest's parlour, a cosy little room with French windows on to the lawn. When not on holiday, Father Gorman had breakfast in here after mass. I had set the table and flung open the windows while Julian made breakfast.

Already the sun was hot, and a couple of cabbage whites were pursuing each other round the buddleia. We settled down to a special breakfast of coffee and croissants while trying to decide whether to visit Speke Hall or the Russian Baths for our final afternoon.

We had both cast our veils aside on returning from mass. Normally we would have left the parlour door open so that we could hear the front doorbell. But we had been overtaken by the sense that our holiday was rushing to a close, and were absorbed in our plans to make the most of it.

'Or perhaps we shouldn't do either,' said Julian, 'when the weather's so hot.' I was leaning over Julian's shoulder to look at the guide book, with my hand resting lightly on hers, when there was a tapping on the French window.

'So there you are,' came a voice, 'I've been searching all over.'

I snatched away my hand and gazed out at the stick-like figure with its shabby coat and straw hair.

'Heather,' breathed Julian.

Desperately I looked round the room for our veils. No sign. We must have left them in the kitchen.

With admirable calm Julian rose to her feet, and advanced towards the window as though it was the most ordinary thing in the world for two bare-headed nuns to be taking a late breakfast in the priest's parlour.

'Yoo-hoo,' said the woman.

'How did you get into the garden?' demanded Julian.

'I rang and rang at the front door – but no Sister Columba. So I scrambled over the wall – down there, by the grotto.'

'Sister Columba's on holiday,' said Julian.

'Yes, I know,' replied Heather inconsequentially. 'I brought you these flowers.' From behind her back she produced a bouquet of tea roses. 'For the twosome,' she said with a little bow and a sly grin.

At this even Julian looked flustered. 'Good heavens – Heather – where did you –'

'I bought them – what do you think?' said the old woman, leering up at us with a sudden switch of manner. 'Better than all those weeds, eh?'

'Well – that's very kind – but really – you shouldn't have bothered.'

'Nothing's too much bother for you, Sister Julian.'

'Thank you – and now let me show you out – no, come this way – no need to scramble over the wall.'

As Julian ushered the old woman through the hall, I cleared away the dirty dishes, my pleasure in the breakfast gone.

'How much do you think she saw?' I asked when Julian returned.

'Nothing at all,' she said airily. 'And if she did see something, she's too cracked to know what it was.'

'I'm not so sure,' I replied. 'Those flowers weren't coincidence.'

'No one ever believes Heather,' said Julian decisively. 'We're safe enough, take my word for it.'

I longed to believe her, but still felt rattled; and when a letter arrived that same morning from Berbiers, saying Mother General was gravely ill, I could no longer forget I was a Joubertian. Even if Heather never told the community about our misdemeanours, how would Julian and I contrive to behave normally?

Julian seemed unaware of my anxiety. 'Good thing if she goes,' she replied to the news from the Mother House. 'We need someone in tune with the times.'

Despite my new respect for Julian, I was troubled by her casual attitude to the holy old nun. Mother General had steered our order through difficult times, and now she was dying, far from her native Poland. She deserved more respect.

Shoving the letter back in its envelope, I resolved for the sake of Mother General to stop sinning with Sister Julian.

After dumping Heather's roses in the pantry, I put on my veil, took Annunciata her breakfast, washed up, and persuaded Julian that we should leave for the Russian Baths straight away.

We paid with the last of Mother Wilfred's money. 'That's well judged,' said Julian, pleased at her budgeting.

I had never been steaming before, and wasn't quite sure what to expect after I'd struggled into my new costume. 'Don't you like it?' I asked on emerging from my cubicle.

Julian stared at the turquoise and scarlet flowers. 'Where on earth did you find that?'

'Woolworth's. Maureen O'Shaunessy sold it to me.'

'The little madam,' laughed the other nun. 'Her idea of revenge, I suppose.'

I looked down. With its ruches puckering the red petals festooned across the bodice, my swimsuit might have belonged to a 1950s bathing belle. Even so, I resented Julian's laughter, and for the first time that holiday wished to be alone.

Without another word I moved towards the pool, plunged in and began ploughing up and down. The time had come to forget about the touching and the kissing, so vivid and yet so vague, as though I'd been dreaming. How I wished I had.

Gasping from the first proper exercise since I was a schoolgirl, I clung to the rail in the deep end. From the other end of the pool Julian waggled her hand cheerfully before diving into the water, a trim figure in her regulation costume. Ignoring her, I returned, thoughts churning, to my dogged breast stroke.

At first, I had resisted the idea that what we'd been doing was a sin. Her hands never strayed lower than my breasts, so what was wrong with hugs and kisses? If Julian thinks it's all right, I kept telling myself, then it must be.

I had never dared ask her if she felt worried too. But as

our holiday wore on, I could no longer deny to myself that we were committing a mortal sin. If the merest caress of one's own breast was enough to send one hurtling down to hell, then what did it mean to stroke the breast of another nun? My whole body ached for her to continue, and the place between my legs was warm and wet by the time we fell asleep. She must know as well as I that any sin against chastity was a mortal sin. If forced to admit it, she might have stopped doing it.

I had confessed my sin of masturbation without a firm purpose of amendment, I thought feverishly, my face stung by the over-chlorinated water. Far from gaining absolution, I had compounded my guilt many times over by going to Holy Communion every morning. At night I was too distracted by the prospect of Julian leaving her bed for mine to say my prayers. I'd been worried about my salvation at the beginning of the holiday. Now, emerging from my lustful daze, I felt miserably aware that my last state was far, far worse than my first.

After half an hour Julian beckoned me to the side. 'Are you going to thrash up and down for ever,' she asked, smiling, 'or come with me to the steambaths?'

I clambered out, exhausted, to follow her upstairs. A female attendant helped us stow our clothes in a locker. 'Not often we have sisters in here,' she commented.

'No,' said Julian suavely. Without a flicker of embarrassment she peeled off her wet swimsuit, wrung it out and put it in her locker.

'Do we have to go without clothes?' I hissed.

Julian nodded. 'Don't worry – it's women only.'

Clumsily I dragged off my wet suit. Two of the naked women in the room were chatting under a shower, and took no notice. But the third, reclining on a wooden bench, was eyeing me up and down. Trying to forget about my flabby white thighs and bottom, I put my clothes in a locker and slammed the door.

Julian's little breasts were bouncing, and her pubic hair stood out against her pale skin in an auburn triangle as she led me across the tiled hall to a green door. The steam hit me in the face like a hot, wet towel. Even though I gasped as the moist air poured down my throat, I headed straight for the far end, ignoring the discomfort in my anxiety to be invisible.

Julian plopped down beside me on the wooden bench. 'It was meant to be a surprise,' she said. 'Don't you like it?'

'Yes, it's lovely,' I replied politely. Through the steam I was beginning to discern two women opposite me – a stringy blonde, adorned with sovereign rings, and beside her one of the fattest women I had ever seen, roll after roll of flesh balanced on a minuscule pair of bikini bottoms.

'I could have kept my costume on,' I whispered to Julian in irritation when the other women had gone.

'Why bother when you look so beautiful?' She stretched out a hand to place it lightly on my belly.

'Stop doing that,' I said angrily. 'We've already been caught once today.'

Already I was sweating profusely, and my stomach was covered in red blotches. Gazing down at my glistening body, I imagined all the impurities gurgling down the channels under our benches. I stayed there as long as I could – far longer than I should, according to Julian – and not till I was on the brink of fainting did I stagger out to a shower built like an Iron Maiden.

The swimming must have clarified my mind, I thought, as I angled the cold water jets at every part of my body, standing there until I felt steely and pure. By the time I reached out for my towel, I'd resolved never again to let Julian touch me.

'I don't want us to do this,' I said coldly as she sat on the side of my bed that night. 'It's a sin.'

The moon was just rising, a thin white crescent through

my skylight. Instead of replying the other nun stroked my arm. Praying for the strength to be firm, I lay back on the pillow and closed my eyes.

'I can't believe that any more,' she said at length, 'but if you still do, you are right to tell me to go away.'

What had been so clear when I was standing in the shower now seemed cruelly perverse. To my dismay, my body was responding of its own accord as my breasts grew hot and tight. 'I don't know what I believe,' I wailed, willing her to leave at once. But her grip on my arm had tightened. Unable to resist any longer, I reached out and pulled her face down to mine, kissing her over and over again. Somebody's skin was wet with tears, but I didn't know whose.

'This,' I told her, 'will be the very last time I touch you.'

I believed I meant it.

TWENTY-EIGHT

—

Elisabeth was the first to return, strolling slim and tanned into the community room where Julian and I sat without speaking.

'What's up with you two?' she said cheerfully. 'Fallen out?'

'Welcome back.' Julian rose hastily to her feet. 'I'll make you a cup of tea.'

I filled the silence with random chatter about Annunciata's bronchitis, and what we'd seen in Liverpool. Ignoring me, Elisabeth gazed round the community room. Could it be that she sensed something? I glanced anxiously at her face. 'Heavens,' she said, 'I'd forgotten how bleak this place really is. One grows inured. Mummy sends love, by the way.'

She was followed a few minutes later by Sister Ursula, and soon after that by the Irish nuns. They all seemed tired and out of sorts. Instead of sitting down for a cup of tea, or going up to see Annunciata, Mother Wilfred strode around the ground floor tight-lipped.

Luckily we'd cleaned and dusted, and set the priest's parlour to rights, putting Heather's bunch of roses in the bottom of the dustbin. 'Did you have a nice time?' I asked, trotting after her. Perhaps Nuncy had heard something at night, and written her a letter – or Heather had met her off the boat. No, that's impossible, I kept telling myself. Nobody will find out.

Gonzaga went straight to the kitchen without greeting anyone, only to emerge a moment later.

'Where's Juno?' she said accusingly.

Julian, entering the room with a teapot in her hand, glanced at me in alarm. 'Did you feed him last night, Brigid?'

'Er – no. I thought you had.'

Julian could remember feeding him on the Wednesday – and might have put down a bowl of milk on Thursday morning – but neither of us felt sure.

'He would have yowled if he'd been hungry,' said Julian as we hurried down to the kitchen.

'Maybe,' I replied. The truth was that, blinded by sin, we had forgotten the little animal.

The tears were rolling down Gonzaga's face. 'I knew something was wrong,' she croaked, 'or he'd have been waiting for me at the gate.'

After checking in the infirmary and searching the outbuildings, Julian and I combed the neighbouring streets, calling his name and looking under parked cars and in the gutters, praying he hadn't been run over.

'Don't worry, he'll turn up when he's hungry,' said Julian.

'He's not that sort of cat,' said Gonzaga. 'You'd better go to the mortuary.'

'The what?' said Julian, appalled.

I already knew the cats' mortuary, having gone to the damp Victorian terrace as a little girl with Madge on the disappearance of my kitten. We'd clambered down a flight of slimy stone steps, with the brackish water of the Mersey lapping at the bottom. There had been no sign of the kitten, and Madge had come to the conclusion that he'd been stolen to make a Davy Crockett hat. But the smell of disinfectant and dank fur had haunted me ever since.

Julian and I set off straight after supper. The doorbell was answered by an old lady in a floral pinafore, with her grey hair in a bun.

'Looking for a pet, are you?'

'A tabby tom,' said Julian.

'Oh yes,' said the woman, 'a lot of them get into trouble.'

She led us down to a basement where the air was cold as ice. Round all four walls ran a stone slab. On it were stretched rows of little corpses, three deep. With their flattened, nondescript coats, and stiffly extended hind legs, they looked more like rabbits than cats.

'I think this might be him here,' said Julian, her voice rising.

'Are you sure?' I said doubtfully. 'It looks a bit small. This one's more his size.'

'But those aren't his markings,' said Julian. 'He had a black butterfly shape on the back of his neck. This one over here's more like him.'

'That one's a her,' said the old woman.

We continued to wander up and down the rows of corpses, peering at this one and that. There were dozens of dead tabbies, some drowned, others run over and crushed beyond recognition. 'I don't think he's any of these,' said Julian despairingly.

'Can't we say we found him,' I asked, 'just to put her mind at rest? If the real Juno turns up, she'll be so thrilled that she's sure to forgive us.'

'Impossible. She wants us to bring him back and bury him by the grotto,' said Julian.

We returned empty-handed to the convent kitchen, where Gonzaga was hovering over a pile of clinker. The Aga had gone out days ago.

'He had a happy life,' offered Julian.

'You can't have been looking after him,' sniffled the cook, 'otherwise he would never have gone out the gate.'

'It must be God's will,' said Mother Wilfred, appearing out of nowhere. 'You were far too attached to that cat.'

Ignoring her, Gonzaga shuffled off to the pantry, and banged the door behind her, leaving the Aga unlit. We arose next morning to find the weather turned sharp and blustery, and the radiators cold. I knelt in chapel with my head in my hands, irritated by the fidgeting of Elisabeth on my right, and Bosco, who had caught a cold in County Cork, wheezing behind me. When the time came for Holy Communion, I rose from my knees automatically; and so, I noted, did Julian, looking serene as ever. Perhaps she, like me, was too far gone to worry. I felt numb and lifeless – and when Father Gorman arrived on Friday to hear our confessions, I rattled off a list including every sin except the crucial one.

It was all Julian's fault, I reflected, after completing my six Hail Marys. She had, after all, come to my cubicle on that first night, knowing she would climb into my bed and initiate the kissing and touching. I began to wonder if she'd ever done this before – and at times I even worried that she'd been luring me on, only to report me to Mother Wilfred.

Had I been out in the world, Julian was not the sort of person I would have wanted to get to know. As I girl I had thought her too remote to be likeable. Now I was beginning to find her repellent. That pale, slightly shiny skin – how could I have brought myself to kiss it, while those tapering fingers slid underneath my nightgown? Then, just when I was feeling most repelled, I would be shaken by a wave of longing, and roam around the convent, hoping to catch her alone. On finding her, I never mentioned mortal sin for fear she would agree, and refrain from kissing me gently on the lips, or brushing her hand softly against my breast as we parted.

Worst of all was my sense of something incomplete. Until the holiday, touching my own breasts as a teenager had been my keenest sexual pleasure – and the ensuing guilt had convinced me it wasn't worth it. I had thought myself above Sister Bosco's O level biology class, when she used the reproductive system of the rabbit as a starting point for a lecture on what she called the facts of life. 'Never forget you're high school girls,' she'd tell us, her colour mounting. 'Sex is for the secondary moderns.'

Privately, I agreed. When I heard Lorraine whispering with the other girls in the cloakroom about going too far, and getting out of control, I knew that only a fool would risk pregnancy. It was Jonathon's mind I loved, not his body.

Now, having taken a vow of chastity, I could see how naïve I'd been with my bus-stop talk of Beethoven, when all Jonathon wanted was to be alone with Eddy. Julian's hands had never strayed below my waist, but I lay in the dormitory at night wondering what it would be like if she went further, while the place between my legs grew wet and slippery.

Elisabeth asked me several times why I was so preoccupied, but I fobbed her off with excuses about the approaching term, and hoped that nobody else had noticed my absent-mindedness. I wanted to be in bed with Julian just one more time – after all, it could hardly compound the sins I'd been committing, and if I did everything I'd imagined, once and for all, it might put an end to this obsession. After that it's confession, I told myself, and no more sex for the rest of my life.

On the last Saturday of the holidays I asked permission to go to the dormitory to change a laddered pair of stockings – and there was Julian, just emerging. Reading my glance, she followed me to my cubicle.

'Why now, Brigid?' she murmured as I shut the door. 'I thought it was all over.'

'I can't explain,' I said hoarsely, as she began to kiss my face and throat. She had just undone the top three buttons of my dress when we heard Sister Bosco bustling upstairs, and sprang to our feet, to emerge dizzy and red-faced. If the

Deputy Head hadn't paused on the landing to pick up a dust-ball, she would have known the worst.

Undeterred, I found another opportunity next day, when the rest of the community went out for a walk. 'Come with me – please,' I whispered to Julian on finding her alone in the library. I was breathless by the time we reached my cubicle, and a bell was shrilling in my ears. I shut the door behind her, and pulled off my veil.

'Brigid,' she murmured, 'are you sure?'

For answer I pulled her towards me and kissed her on the mouth. It was the first time I had taken the initiative, and she responded eagerly, sliding her tongue between my lips. Far from being revolted, I was eager for more, and cradling her head with my hand pressed my mouth hard against hers. It was she who detached herself first.

'Lie down,' she said out loud. I lay flat on the bed and raised my hips so she could slide off my knickers, knowing we were going to go further than ever before. Glancing at her face as though for the first time, I registered her flushed cheeks and parted lips. When she moved on top of me I moaned out loud and noticed with a distant part of my brain that my legs were spread and my knees bent, and my hand was guiding Julian's hand between my thighs. She knew what I wanted by instinct, and began to rub me with the palm of her hand.

Unable to lie still any longer, I forgot about the dangers of making a noise, or the others coming back from their walk. Whatever was happening, I wanted it to go on for ever – but it was so intense I could bear no more. Someone was moaning with pleasure – could it be me? – and I become aware that my hips were thrusting of their own volition – then suddenly I was out of control, my whole body heaving in unbearably pleasurable spasms, and Julian's hand was clamped over my mouth.

'Ssshhh,' she said, more as an explanation than a command, 'you'll have the whole house up here.'

Gradually the sensation waned, the room steadied itself and my breathing slowed. Sheets and blankets were in a tangled heap on the floor by my discarded veil, and my dress was rucked up round my waist. Julian was still caressing my cheek with her hand, which smelt unpleasantly of the place between my legs, like yesterday's knickers. Could that have been me, pressing my pelvis against her and begging her to continue?

'What do we do now?' I said tonelessly.

She seemed not to have noticed my dismay.

'Do the same – to me,' she whispered.

Do that – to her – to Sister Julian? I suddenly saw how grotesque we looked with our short hair and shapeless dresses, bumping up and down in a travesty of sex. 'I have to go now,' I whispered. 'I promised to help Sister Gonzaga.'

'I don't believe that for one moment,' said Julian. 'You're fobbing me off.'

It was the first time I had ever heard her raise her voice. 'I'm sorry,' I murmured placatingly. 'It's just that I've never felt like this before.'

Julian seemed not have heard me. 'You're a hypocrite, Brigid,' she went on angrily, 'turning all pious the moment you got what you wanted.'

'It's just that – I think we ought to stop – all this.'

'We need to talk about it – not just pretend it didn't happen.'

'It was a moment of weakness,' I said as distantly as I could. My clothes felt clammy, and my head was throbbing painfully. 'I can only ask you never to refer to it.' The front door slammed down below, and the voice of Mother Wilfred boomed out in the front hall.

'Let me know if you change your mind, Brigid,' said Julian, rising to her feet. 'There are many ways of being a nun.'

'I don't agree,' I said, beginning to make my bed.

At that, Julian put on her veil and left the room in silence. For the rest of that day I avoided her eye. Term was beginning next morning, and I was glad to be underprepared, because it meant forcing myself to work hard. Released by that last, degrading experience, I felt able to concentrate for the first time in months.

Over that autumn I seemed to become two people. During the day I was Sister Brigid, the teaching nun, able to enjoy my pupils' fresh faces, and the golden colours of the park outside the classroom window. Julian had been as good as her word, and made no particular effort to speak to me. But sometimes, on looking up at recreation, I'd catch her eye and turn bright red at the memory of her flushed face and parted lips.

I still couldn't face going to confession, and didn't know where to start. After dark, as I lay listening to the foghorns blowing across the Mersey, I was often invaded by a sense of hopelessness. One night over half-term I felt more feverish than usual. For a dangerous moment I considered creeping down to the far end of the dormitory where Julian slept. Then I drew back, ashamed. She had taken me at my word, and had not spoken once unnecessarily since term began. Why begin again now?

Everyone else seemed to be sound asleep. I felt for my habit, hanging neatly behind the door, and got dressed as quietly as possible. Although the hall clock showed only ten past one, we had gone to bed so early that it felt much later. I knew that what I was doing was forbidden, but it seemed so trivial by comparison with my other sins that I scarcely gave it a second thought once the dormitory was out of earshot. I had been taught how to move silently in the novitiate: now it was coming in useful. I slid back the big bolt on the front door and, making sure to slip the key in my pocket, walked down the garden path and across the empty road into the park.

The air smelt sour with the end of autumn. Most of the leaves had already fallen, and the branches formed bony haloes round the street lamps. In the middle distance the Palm House lantern glimmered in the moonlight, and beyond it was the little lake, with its row of boats rocking eerily in the middle. I strolled across the deserted grass to the pavilion where, as a child, I used to spend my pocket money on ice-cream. Down one side was a palimpsest of tattered posters, only three or four of their slogans still legible. To judge by their dates they were advertising long-gone poetry readings: Black Sabbath, Procul Harum and, most mysteriously, Ten Years After. Pondering their meaning, I headed towards the aviary.

A figure I identified as Heather was scurrying down the path ahead of me, a bunch of rhododendron leaves in her hand. At her heels bobbed a little cat, its tail erect.

'Juno!' I called out suddenly. 'JUNO!'

The woman either didn't hear or took no notice, and hurried on, head bent. The cat paused for a second to gaze in my direction, then trotted after her. Soon they had vanished round the far side of the aviary. I wondered if it really was Juno, and how I could tell Gonzaga without incriminating myself.

Soon my feet were soaked with dew and my body was chilled from walking without a coat. But as I tramped over the acres of sodden grass, one thing was becoming clear: I couldn't go on the way I was. Julian was right: I was a hypocrite. Better to have stayed in the world than to live a life under broken vows. But I still believed I had a vocation. My envy for Monica's new life had evaporated, and I dreaded returning to the world in disgrace. A famous Franciscan was to lead our end-of-term retreat. Perhaps he would be able to help me. There must be somebody, I thought desperately.

On hurrying up the convent path I glimpsed a pale face at

the first-floor window. Although it disappeared when I paused to draw the key from my pocket, I waited in the hall for several minutes, half expecting Mother Wilfred to stalk downstairs and confront me. But all stayed silent, and when, soon after two o'clock, I slipped into the dormitory and got undressed, all my sisters were sleeping as peacefully as ever.

TWENTY-NINE

—

For the second time that year Heather kept quiet about my wrongdoings, and community life carried on as normal. I no longer feared that Julian and I had been detected; she was still leaving me alone, and the other nuns continued to treat me much as usual. I kept going to Holy Communion every morning without being struck down for sacrilege, and told myself that my prayers had been answered and I would survive until the end-of-term retreat. Then I would confess my sin to the as yet unknown Franciscan, and by Christmas the whole shameful episode would be over.

I began spending more time with Elisabeth, who was working on a backdrop of the Liverpool skyline for the carol concert. In the evenings I would climb the stairs to the art room, much as I had in Monica's day, to help her paint scenery. To my surprise, we were getting on well. For the first time Elisabeth told me about her past, confessing that she'd longed to be friends with Lorraine and me, but was scared by our brains. Her father had been so angry when she failed her O levels, and Edward and Timothy always made her feel stupid. In Rome she'd scarcely been able to keep up with the course – and now Mother Wilfred was threatening to send her back there to get a degree.

She enjoyed gossiping about the other nuns – Wilfie, Gonzaga and Bosco – and on occasion made remarks so apposite they made me blush. 'And then there's Julian,' she'd say. 'A woman with a past.'

I wondered if Elisabeth remembered admiring Julian's organza dress in the novitiate linen-room – and Sister

Nicole's disapproving comments. 'I hardly know her,' I'd mumble, my cheeks hot.

'Oh,' Elisabeth would reply brightly, 'I always thought you were good pals.'

I was sometimes tempted to repay her confidences, and tell her what had happened over the summer. Elisabeth was, after all, known to be worldly, and hadn't been shocked by Jonathon Maule. By way of sounding her out I introduced the topic of my old flame, who had apparently been assigned to the monks' community farm, and was developing an unsuspected talent for rearing chickens.

'Does he not find some things about the religious life – er – irksome?'

'He always knew it would be hard,' Elisabeth replied, putting down her paintbrush, 'but it's better than life out-side. After all, homosexuality is a sin – and luckily he can confide in his novice-master.' She smiled at me. 'It's impor-tant to share your troubles, don't you think?'

I could only nod, and absorb myself in tracing the two birds on top of the Liver Building, while Elisabeth rattled on about the young monks. One night they had all hitched up their habits and danced to 'Please Please Me' and 'Love Me Do'. The head infirmarian had come downstairs half-way through, to stage an entrance clad only in a jockstrap.

I remembered Julian's flushed face and parted lips with shame. My behaviour looked tawdry by comparison with Jonathon's openly acknowledged love for other men, no less racy now he was a novice, and I was glad not to have risked confiding in Elisabeth.

The term was drawing uneventfully to a close when, one Friday evening in December, Elisabeth was called away to a props meeting with some parents in the school hall. I stayed behind to colour in the silhouettes of the two cathedrals, alone for the first time in several weeks.

Dance, dance, wherever you may be,
For I am the Lord of the Dance, said He.

I had grown so absorbed in my job of distorting the topography a little to allow the wigwam pride of place, that it was a while before I realized it was snowing – large white flakes tumbling earthwards, the first of the season. Humming contentedly, I began pencilling in the spiky coronet on the cathedral roof, too busy to do more than register a faint thud on the stairs. By the time I glanced up, Sister Julian was standing in the doorway.

'What are you doing here?' I asked angrily.

'It's time we had a talk,' she said, shutting the door.

'About what?' I asked, keeping my face blank.

'You know what about. It was part of our lives – and you're pretending it didn't happen.'

Her face was pale and she was staring at me fixedly. Perhaps the strain had been too much, and she was hatching some crazy plan to tell the community. 'It's not part of life,' I gabbled, 'it's something private, it's a sin, we set a bad example.' My voice was trembling, and I had to lean against a desk. 'What we did was wicked and pointless.'

Julian moved a step or two closer. 'That's not what you thought when you asked me up to your cubicle.'

'You're older than me,' I shot back, 'and should have known better – instead of showing me what to do.'

'You were willing enough to learn.'

'Go away!' I cried, as the car doors of departing parents began to slam in the car park below. 'Elisabeth will be back any moment.'

'Elisabeth!' said Julian. 'A zealot if ever I saw one. Don't trust her too far.'

'You're jealous!'

'I'm not,' said Julian, 'I'm saying we can't carry on like this.'

'I'm sick to death of you,' I hissed, 'and I hate everything we did.'

'You're lying to me, Brigid,' she said, 'and that's understandable. But please don't lie to yourself.'

'I wish I'd never met you,' I was stung into shouting back, 'and believe me, that's no lie.'

'So that's your last word on the subject?' Julian moved towards the door.

'Sister!'

She paused, her hand on the knob, and then turned back to face me. 'Yes?'

'You won't tell anyone – about us?'

She shot me a look of contempt.

'If they find out,' I continued feebly, 'they'll expel us both.'

'Yes, they will – and we might count ourselves lucky. Two Spanish nuns were burned at the stake for doing what we did.'

'That was during the Inquisition!'

'Then what about that sister in Kansas?'

'When?'

'Last year. After telling her superior that she loved another nun she was given six months' electro-shock therapy,' said Julian. 'Then she killed herself. Now don't you see?'

'I didn't know we'd been so wicked!' I wailed.

'Who says it's wicked? Not me.'

'It must be – if they punish it like that.'

'They must be scared of it, you mean,' said Julian contemptuously.

'Leave me alone – you've no right to frighten me like this.'

'I'll leave you alone, if that's what you want,' she said. 'But remember: I tried to show you a way forward, and you didn't want to know.' With that she left the room and shut the door.

I began cleaning some brushes in the corner sink. My heart had scarcely stopped pounding when Elisabeth dashed in, ten minutes later.

'What's up with Julian?' she asked. 'She's gone charging off to Wilfie's study.'

'Who knows? Some sort of end-of-term crisis,' I lied. It was obvious that Julian, motivated by some desperate need to draw attention to herself, was going to expose us both.

Elisabeth stared. 'You're looking pale, Brigid.'

'Let's lock up,' I said quickly. 'The bell for Compline went ages ago.'

Luckily Elisabeth followed me downstairs without any more questions. Having pleaded unsuccessfully with Julian to remain silent, all I could do was struggle to behave as normal. When we met the following day, Mother Wilfred gave no sign that anything was wrong, nodding graciously whenever our set for the carol concert was praised, and chatting over coffee and mince-pies in the staffroom at the end-of-term party. I had begun to think Julian had thought better of her plan, and the expected summons might never arrive when, on the first day of the holidays, Elisabeth poked her head round the community room door.

'Wilfie wants to see you in her study.'

Ordinarily I only knocked on her door when I needed to ask permission to take the girls on a school trip, or to see an educational film. Then she would glance up to proffer me a brusque yes or no, and carry on writing. Today, however, she nodded me to the chair facing the window, and sat down behind her big oak desk. The late afternoon sun was shining uncomfortably in my eyes, while the old nun's face was in shadow. Ignatian techniques, I said to myself, but the knowledge didn't make me feel any less uncomfortable.

'Sister Brigid,' she said without preamble, 'there's something you haven't told me.'

'I – I –' I stuttered, wondering where to start.

Silence. I was conscious only of the old nun's eyes fixed on mine, and the watery sun topping the plane trees.

'Hurry up, Sister,' she said curtly, 'my time is limited.'

'What do you want to know about?' I asked in desperation.

'I want to know,' said the Superior, 'what you were doing on the second Sunday in September.'

It felt as though an ice cube was melting in my stomach. 'I couldn't sleep,' I told her, 'so I went for a walk in the park.'

'That disgraceful escapade was in November,' said the Superior frostily. 'I am asking what you were doing in September – with one of your sisters.'

I stared down at the pale green lino, my heart hammering.

'I am giving you this chance to explain yourself against my better judgement – so make the most of it.'

'I don't know what you're talking about,' I said, my cheeks burning.

'I suggest you stop telling lies and tell me about yourself and Sister Julian,' Mother Wilfred said disdainfully.

'I – I – ' I stuttered again. What, exactly, had Julian said? 'It meant nothing,' I said.

'Don't prevaricate,' she said. 'I've been told all about it.'

I'd known that evening in the art room that Julian would take her revenge, but I hadn't foreseen the wave of hatred that swept over me now. First she'd seduced me, and now she'd betrayed me, ruining my life in the process – and all because I'd rejected her.

'So you're going to send me home,' I said.

'I must confess that would have been my solution – but the decision belongs to Mother General. Luckily for you, she is too ill to be troubled. The matter was referred to the Provincial Council.'

Ursula, Bosco and Ligori – they were all members. What had they decided?

263

'Sister Julian is older than you, and more to blame,' pronounced Mother Wilfred, 'so after several days' debate we agreed to give you a second chance.'

So I could remain a Joubertian. Despite my unhappiness I felt a tide of relief.

'We've all been praying for a sign of repentance,' Mother Wilfred went on silkily. 'Had you even told Sister Elisabeth . . . who set out to make it easy . . . but there was nothing. As the weeks passed you seemed to grow ever more silent and self-absorbed.'

So my old rival knew too – worse and worse.

'If only I'd listened to Heather I would have acted sooner, but I dismissed her tales out of hand. I should have known better than to leave a naïve woman like you with Sister Julian.' The Superior stared balefully across her desk as I sat wondering who'd told Elisabeth, and what she thought of me now. 'Goodness knows how far this scandal has spread. Heather could have told anyone.'

'I don't know how I could have been so sinful.'

'I've known you since you were a little girl, and can see that a background like yours is . . . unfortunate, to say the least.'

I stared at her, wondering what she meant.

'Your father left home when you were so very young,' elaborated the old woman. 'The loss must have been great. Your mother was brave, after her fashion – but with no instinct for motherhood. As a result you are for ever casting about for surrogate parents – Monica, your novice-mistress, and now this latest . . . disaster.'

'Sister Julian was not a surrogate mother,' I said hopelessly, 'she was a –' I wanted to say passion, but didn't dare.

'Sister Julian is an evil, self-indulgent woman, too proud even to admit she's done wrong.'

'I'll never speak to her again,' I promised. 'Not alone, that is.'

'You will never have the chance,' said Mother Wilfred, standing up abruptly to signify the interview was over. 'Sister Julian is no longer one of us.'

So she'd been sent home, and I hadn't. 'But that isn't fair,' I blurted out.

'I take it that you don't want to follow her, Sister Brigid?'

'No . . . but it's just that – I wanted her to do what she did . . .'

'You may save the details for the confessional,' said Mother Wilfred coldly, ushering me to the door. 'You have committed a terrible sin against purity, Sister Brigid, an affront to Our Blessed Lady.'

I remembered Mère-Maîtresse warning me about Sister Julian before I'd left Berbiers. Once again, I'd disregarded the advice, and gone my own way.

'I know I need guidance, Mother,' I said. 'I want to begin all over again.'

'Then you may start by praying to the Blessed Anne Joubert to help you overcome these unnatural urges,' said the Superior as I stepped out into the corridor. 'You think I'm harsh – and perhaps I am; but I've the good of the order at heart. You are not the first young nun to be corrupted by that woman, Sister Brigid – but with God's grace you will be the last.'

THIRTY

—

Far from rebuking me for what I'd done, or treating me with disdain, my sisters were at pains to welcome me back into the community. They fussed around as though I was recovering from major surgery, taking over my charges and showering me with little presents. I never found out who had been told what, but everyone seemed to know the reason for Julian's departure.

'If I'd been on my feet it would never have happened,' said Annunciata, beckoning me over at recreation. 'I wish you'd let me know, dear – I would have put a stop to her goings-on.'

'Brigid is a good girl,' said Columba to no one in particular, 'and best off with us.'

'I never did like Julian and her lah-di-dah ways,' Bosco chipped in. 'It's good riddance, if you ask me.'

And so the waters closed over my friend's head, as though she never had been one of us. Only Sister Ursula seemed doubtful. 'They shouldn't have let her go,' she said sombrely as Bosco bustled off to make the Stations of the Cross. 'She was the cleverest of all of us – and besides, loving someone is not a crime.' Clearly the headmistress didn't know the kind of love Julian and I had gone in for. Too embarrassed to explain, I nodded vaguely, and followed Sister Bosco to the chapel.

As instructed by Mother Wilfred, I went to see the priest in private on the first day of our retreat. He must have been told quite a lot about me, because he didn't seem at all surprised when I stammered out my story.

'It's natural to want affection, Sister,' he said kindly, 'but we must sublimate our sexuality. That's what a vow of chastity means.'

'I don't know how I could have done it.'

'You must forgive yourself, just as Our Blessed Saviour has undoubtedly forgiven you. You have a very special part to play in His Church.'

I stared at his bony hands, as they fidgeted with a packet of Benson & Hedges. When Mère-Maîtresse had said the same thing in Berbiers, I had agreed unthinkingly – now all I could aspire to was hanging on.

The priest sensed my unease. 'In the intensity of your attachment to another nun, you neglected community life,' he told me. 'Your sisters are here to love and support you. You must learn to trust them – and support them in return.'

He absolved me there and then, as I knelt before him in the little parlour where once I'd breakfasted with Julian. On rising to my feet I thanked him for his advice. With his shaggy hair and beaky, intelligent face he reminded me vaguely of Jonathon Maule, and I was pleased that he patted me on the shoulder as I left the room.

From then on I was determined not to think about Sister Julian, consigning to the furnace the holy pictures she'd given me, and her postcard of the nymph of the fountain. My relationship with her was over, and it was time to get on with the business of being a nun. As the priest had predicted, soon whole hours passed without my thinking about her – then days, and then a whole week. I was on the road to recovery.

Yet sometimes I found myself down on the promenade, gazing out across the tide, and then I would remember how we'd stood that August day, side by side. Now and again a girl would ask after her – but she had not been popular with her pupils, and besides, they were too well used to our comings and goings to comment much. Night-time was worst, when, unable to sleep, I relived our friendship stage by stage in the haunted dark. Only then could I bring myself to acknowledge what I'd hidden from Mother Wilfred, and even from the retreat priest: how much I'd loved Sister Julian and, even though that love had waned, how hurt I'd been by her betrayal. And then that hurt would give way to anger: by going to Mother Wilfred, Julian had not only thrown away her own vocation, she'd tried to ruin my life too, and they'd done right to expel her.

There were rumours that Julian was still on Merseyside – that she had returned to County Kerry – that her new home was just across the park – but it was only Linda Renucci who said that, and, as Sister Bosco reassured me, she was nothing but a trouble-maker. I yearned to put the past behind me, and hoped for once that Sister Bosco was right.

As an aid to spiritual recovery, I now had weekly interviews with Mother Wilfred. During the first I tried once again to explain that Sister Julian had not forced me into doing wrong – I'd acted of my own free will. There was clearly a lot of evil to be rooted out of my nature, said Mother Wilfred. She made forgetting Julian all the easier by reminding me that she'd once seduced another young nun. At the very next interview I was told the whole story. Far from being dispatched to the Congo against her will, Sister Elisabeth of the Trinity had begged to be sent as far as possible from Sister Julian and her impure proposals. She asked her new community never to mention Julian's name in her presence, and even on her death-bed she'd implored the infirmarian to ensure that none of her keepsakes went to her one-time friend. I listened to Mother Wilfred in silence, but inside I felt humbled by my lapse of judgement. My childhood instincts had been right all along: Sister Julian was a cold, manipulative woman, eager to get her way and careless of others.

That winter held Liverpool for a long time in its grip. The boating lake was frozen over for four and a half weeks, the giant yuccas at the entrance to the park drooped and died, and some panes in the Palm House were cracked by frost, causing the death of several rare plants. Since Juno's disappearance we could safely feed the birds, but at least one froze to death each night on the kitchen windowsill.

One morning during half-term the rising-bell went as usual, but I failed to raise my head from the pillow. A lump of gravel blazed at the back of my throat, and sickly-coloured shapes fanned out before my eyes. I lay through Matins, in too much pain to worry about asking permission. And then, just before breakfast, Annunciata stuck her head round my cubicle door.

'Was that you, moaning all night?'

'I can't swallow.'

The nurse put her hand on my forehead, then peered down my throat. 'Good heavens, child – your temperature's right up and your tonsils are meeting in the middle. We'll move you to the infirmary.'

Doctor Reilly was called, and prescribed bed-rest and a course of antibiotics. Day after day I lay flat on my back, too tired to turn over, or even reach out for a sip of water. At breaktime I would hear the unearthly shrilling of the children in the playground. When the tears oozed out of my eyes to trickle down my temples and on to the pillow, I was too fatigued even to ask myself why.

It was a fortnight before I felt strong enough to sit up. 'Thank goodness you've stopped crying,' said Elisabeth, plumping up my pillows and discreetly plucking a rotten apple from the bowl on my locker. She had kept me well supplied with fruit bought out of her monthly allowance, but so far I'd had nothing to eat.

I smiled feebly. 'I feel such a fool.'

'Nonsense,' she said. 'You must have been through hell. No wonder you collapsed.'

I smiled at her brisk voice. 'I'm glad it's all over,' I said. 'I'm ready to make a fresh start.'

'If only you'd confided in me,' said Elisabeth reproach-fully. 'That night in the art room – I was saying everything I could think of to pave the way.

'How soon did you realize what was going on?'

'The moment I came back from holiday,' she replied, 'with the two of you sitting in that darkened community room – you could have cut the air with a knife. And then there was Julian trying to get next to you at recreation, while you turned bright red and looked the other way. Some of the others noticed, too. I tried not to think about it too much – but then one day I heard you both in the dormitory.'

'What?' I gasped, 'but we hardly ever –'

'It was that time the others went out for a walk,' explained Elisabeth. 'I too had got permission to stay behind and write a letter. I was just running upstairs for envelopes.'

I groaned at the thought of the noises we'd made. 'And I was so shocked about Jonathon Maule.'

'It was easier for him, because he came to terms with it before he went in,' replied Elisabeth. 'You were so innocent about it all. I thought it was dying down – but when I heard you together, I knew I must go to Wilfie.'

'What?' I gasped. 'You told her first – before Julian . . .?' I stared in resentment at the composed little figure at the foot of my bed, and struggled not to yell out the first words that sprang to mind: you interfering little bitch. I still had a lot to learn about humility.

Elisabeth nodded soberly. 'Forgive me, Brigid – it was my duty. She hadn't suspected a thing.'

Suddenly I remembered the novitiate Chapter of Faults, and the high, confident little voice denouncing Sister Bon Pasteur. Elisabeth's principles had remained high. 'So Julian needn't have bothered going to Wilfie,' I remarked.

'Julian never dreamt of it. She didn't even feel the need to go to confession.'

'But that night in the art room . . . she was threatening me . . .'

'Trying to brief you, more like. The Provincial Council was about to meet, and Julian had been warned by one of her contacts in London.'

'She was so sure of herself,' I said.

'Let's say she had a strange idea of the vow of chastity. You should never have been left alone with her.'

'It was disgusting. I don't know how I got entangled.' All the time Julian had been thinking ahead, while I stumbled on with my eyes shut.

'It could have happened to anyone,' said Elisabeth. 'The important thing now is to do like Jonathon, and rededicate yourself to God.'

I lay back against my pillows and closed my eyes, lest any more tears leak out. 'You can depend on me to give you support,' I heard her add quietly. 'We Joubertians are moving into the twentieth century, and need nuns like you – who've fought against temptation. God always tests his best vocations.'

I nodded feebly. 'And now,' she continued, pouring out a glass of orange juice, 'I'm going to go and get you some lunch, before Gonzaga takes over. She was threatening to cook you tripe and onions.'

The next day I was well enough to get out of bed and sit at the infirmary window. Waiting for my poisoned throat to clear, I gazed out across the park, watching the March wind ruffle the daffodils. My crisis was past, and the future lay in front of me like a blank canvas, said Mother Wilfred. It was for God to fill it in as He pleased.

At the end of the week, Elisabeth brought me a note from Lorraine. She was back in Liverpool, living at home with her parents and working at Littlewoods. She had decided to bury the hatchet, as she put it, and wanted to come and see me. Would I be there over Easter?

I was too weak to write a reply, but found myself getting

dressed for the first time on the day she'd suggested for her visit. It was a warm spring afternoon, and my body felt so light and thin that I anchored myself to the banister as I teetered downstairs to the parlour.

Lorraine was already waiting, one high-heeled foot tapping against the fender, her scarlet sweater dress aglow.

'Brigid – you've gone so skinny! More of a twiglet than a Brownie!'

I smiled at the joke. 'Thank you for coming to see me. I've been wanting to put things right.'

'You should have written,' she said gruffly.

'I know – but somehow I didn't have the guts – and then I was ill.'

'That's obvious,' said Lorraine. 'You look like death warmed up.'

'Never mind,' I replied. 'I'm getting better.'

'Listen, Bid,' she said, pulling her sheepskin coat around her a little more tightly, 'I can't relax in this atmosphere, so I'm going to take you for a run in my car. Don't worry – I've asked permission. Old Wilfie seems to have mellowed. She says it will do you good to get a bit of sunshine.'

Lorraine's red mini was waiting by the kerb. I collected my coat from the row of pegs by the front door, and within seconds we were roaring round the park and on to the dual carriageway. The other traffic looked bright and far away, like Dinky toys. 'Where are we going?' I said.

'I may as well tell you now,' said Lorraine. 'I'm taking you to see her.'

'See who?'

'Surely you can guess,' Lorraine shot me a swift glance.

'No,' I said. But my heart was pounding, and my breath was coming in short, shallow bursts.

'Now don't you realize?' said Lorraine triumphantly as she accelerated down the dual carriageway towards the Dingle. 'We're going to see Julian.'

THIRTY-ONE

___

'What does Julian want?' I gasped.

'She wants to see you again, idiot. We all do. God knows why.'

'Where did you meet her?'

'She's taken a house a few doors down from ours. Yes, in Moses Street. I was shocked at first, I can tell you – my old English teacher moving in. I was afraid the rest would come flocking after. I don't think I could have stood living in the same road as old Bosco.'

'How much do you know about – what she and I – why she . . .?'

'The lot,' said Lorraine. 'She says it's no secret.'

I winced at the thought. How many more people were going to know what I'd done?

'Don't worry, Bid – I'm not going to phone the *News of the World*.'

'It was a mistake,' I said, my voice rising above the sound of the engine.

'Well – if you say so.'

'Stop the car,' I said, clutching at the door handle. 'I'm going back.'

'Oh, no, you're not,' said Lorraine, accelerating past a Volvo and executing a sharp left-hand turn. Within seconds we were threading our way through the maze of streets towards the Holy Land.

I began to panic. Ever since that day in the infirmary when Elisabeth had told me that she, not Julian, had gone to Mother Wilfred, I'd wanted to revise my judgement of the banished nun. But I'd obeyed their instructions to put her out of mind. Now I was about to see her, and didn't know what to think.

'I shouldn't be here,' I wailed as we swung past the Wellington Vaults. As usual on a Sunday, the curtains were drawn for a stay-behind. I wondered abstractedly who was sitting in Madge's corner by the fruit machine, and if the big television set was still flickering out the latest unimportant world news. Life had been carrying on for a long time without me.

'We're here,' said Lorraine, pulling in to the kerb.

I stared at my old home. It had changed over the years since I'd left. Transom windows had replaced the old sashes, and it looked brighter and more prosperous, with hanging baskets and wrought-iron gates. Several other façades were newly painted in bright pastels – lemon, terracotta and aquamarine, seaside colours. Lorraine had parked outside the O'Shaunessy house, but it was number 23 she was pointing at, the one with green paintwork and a window-box filled with winter pansies. I glanced nervously up and down the street.

'You can't sit there all day,' said Lorraine. 'Get out and knock.'

I eased myself out of the car and began walking across the pavement, then stopped half-way. Someone had seen me, and was moving across the room.

'Ring the bell, idiot,' said Lorraine as she locked the car. 'I'll give you a lift back later, if you want one.'

'How long did you say we'd be out?'

'One and a half hours,' she replied with a grin. 'If you want to know, we've gone to Otterspool.' With that she winked, and disappeared into her house.

There was silence for several long seconds, and then the door swung back – not on Julian, but on a slim woman of about my age, with dark curly hair and red jeans. She looked oddly familiar.

'Brigid!' she exclaimed in a Texan drawl. 'Long time no see.'

'Bony!' I cried, as the memories flooded into my mind – the hippy on the train to Berbiers, the convent rebel, the slim and serious young nun.

'It's Mary Lou now, not Boniface, thank goodness. I've heard the last of that old man.'

It was the first time I'd seen an ex-nun – not that I would have guessed from Mary Lou's carefree air that she had ever worn a habit. She was glowing with life and health, like no one I'd ever known in the Dingle. 'What on earth are you doing here?' I asked as she beckoned me inside.

'I've come to be with Julian – she needs a bit of support.'

'Come from where?' I asked. 'The last I heard you were in California.'

'Julian will explain the minute she gets back,' she said as she ushered me into the little front room. 'She's gone to the store for coffee. I'll go put the kettle on.'

She was still the same frank, open Mary Lou that I remembered from Berbiers – but firmer and more resolute. I gazed round nervously while she filled a kettle in the kitchen. Everything betokened a fresh start: the smell of paint, the posters on the bright, white walls, the stripped pine and big paper lampshade. In my baggy pinafore dress and old brown shoes I felt dingy and out of place.

'Why don't you relax?' said Mary Lou, poking her head round the door. I made for a chair in the far corner, carefully removing a pile of ironed T-shirts. 'Put a record on and make yourself at home. You look tuckered out.'

'Who does all this belong to?' I asked, aware that after years of convent austerity I'd been looking too greedily for good manners.

'Julian and me,' said Mary Lou. 'We're setting up house. That poster was done by your old friend Monica.'

'Is she here too?' I asked, staring in bewilderment at the

image of a woman in green dungarees waving a sheaf of corn in the air.

'Let's just say she's in touch,' grinned Mary Lou. 'The poster was a moving-in present.'

With her words came the sound of footsteps in the street, and a key turning in the lock. 'I'll go fix that coffee.'

She brushed past someone who was entering the room. Feeling too weak to struggle to my feet, I stared at the woman who had once been Sister Julian. She'd put the weeks since leaving St Cuthbert's to good use. Gone was the ragged convent hair-do; her professional-looking shingle made her green-grey eyes, subtly enhanced by make-up, look larger than ever. She too had lost weight; but where I looked gaunt in my flapping pinafore, she was a woman of the world in black velvet jeans and a sweater in colours by Mondrian. I had a sudden, desolating sense of having been left behind.

She smiled briefly and sat down on the sofa across the room. 'I heard you were ill,' she said, 'and that Elisabeth was looking after you.'

'She's been very kind,' I said defensively.

Julian sat up straighter. 'You have the cheek to tell me how kind she's been,' she said. 'when she denounced me to Mother Wilfred?'

'She thought we were doing wrong.'

'So running to an old bigot was going to put it right?' Julian's eyes narrowed.

I was taken aback by her strength of feeling. 'She was acting for the best,' I protested.

'The best! It's zealots like her who make convent life unliveable – creeping around spying on other women.'

'She's really quite liberal,' I said, 'and she's still friends with Jonathon Maule . . .'

'Another hypocrite. Leering at other monks during the week, and asking for absolution every Friday. All those two are good at is disguising their ambition.'

We glowered at each other across the spider plants, while outside the sun tilted over the rooftops. The visit was going wrong. 'Forgive me, Julian,' I begged. 'I've been a coward.'

'You've come to see me,' she said, relenting. 'That wasn't cowardly.'

'Lorraine didn't tell me until I was in the car.'

The tension between us dissolved as Julian burst out laughing. 'Typical,' she said, 'after all our instructions about giving you the choice. And to think I once blamed her for holding you back.'

'We've been nuns too long,' said Mary Lou, entering the room with a tray. 'We've forgotten that other women take decisions.' She put down her tray and raised one of the sash windows for a tabby cat running up and down the sill.

'Juno!' I cried.

'I thought so, too,' said Julian. 'She was lost one night in Sefton Park, and answered to the name – so I brought her home.' She caressed the cat's bulging flank. 'It was only then I saw she was going to have kittens.'

'From the sound of it you two have a lot to talk about,' said the American. 'I'm taking my coffee upstairs. I have to finish that article.'

'Mary Lou's freelancing for the *Echo*,' said Julian with a touch of pride, 'to pay the mortgage.'

I nodded, unable to utter a word, as she handed me a mug. 'Why did you come to live here?' I asked as the American shut the door behind her.

'It was cheap,' she replied. 'And the house was for sale at the right time.'

'I thought you might have gone home to Ireland.'

'Ireland isn't home any more,' she said, 'not since I was eighteen.'

I still hadn't asked the question I needed to. Feeling as though something irrevocable was about to happen, I took a deep breath, moved across to the sofa, and sat down beside her. My limbs were as heavy as lead, and in my ears was a noise like a chainsaw.

'Julian,' I burst out, 'what is Mary Lou doing here?' My temperature must have shot up again, because my throat was dry and my cheeks hot.

'She came over as soon as she heard I'd decided to leave St Cuthbert's.'

'Decided?' I echoed. 'I thought you were sent home.'

'If Wilfie says that, she's lying,' said Julian. 'Of the twenty nuns on the Provincial Council, twelve voted that I should be allowed to stay, along with you. Reluctantly, Mother Wilfred informed me of their decision. To her surprise and relief I chose to leave instead.'

'Without giving me a word of warning,' I said reproachfully.

'I was trying to tell you that night in the art room,' said Julian sharply, 'but you wouldn't listen.'

Glancing down, I noticed her small hand clenched in her lap, and touched it lightly. 'I haven't been saying what I want to say,' I said in a low voice, while my hand closed over hers of its own volition. 'I've missed you – and nobody makes up for it.'

She remained still under my touch for a second before gently detaching my grasp. 'Brigid, you mustn't.'

'Mustn't?' I cried out, 'after all we've done together?'

'Those times are gone. You must think what you're doing.'

I remembered how numbly I'd listened to Mother Wilfred, to the retreat priest, to Sister Elisabeth, conceding their points, agreeing to do what they said. 'I've been thinking all my life,' I cried. 'It's time to begin feeling.'

'But I can no longer feel for you,' said Julian, 'not at the moment.'

'You're punishing me, aren't you? Rejecting me as once I rejected you?'

'That is not why I – why we – asked Lorraine to bring you here,' said Julian quietly as she rose to her feet and walked across to the fireplace.

'So what are you trying to do? I asked. 'Taunt me with Mary Lou?'

'We want to know if you'll leave St Cuthbert's to come and join us.'

'Here in this house?' I asked, watching her light the gas fire.

'Why not?' said Julian. 'We have enough room and enough money.'

The future rose before me as the little flames wavered and spread. So Mary Lou and Julian wanted me to be with them, and were offering me the chance of leaving St Cuthbert's behind. How bleak it suddenly seemed by comparison with this cosy little home. How could I return to the carpetless floors and cold, polished surfaces? To live a life of routine, forever having to ask permission, haunted by the memory of my disgrace, and grateful for Elisabeth's condescending kindness. Instead I would return to the streets of my childhood, where I too would find work to do, and begin again.

'I've backed down twice when I should have spoken out, first over Madge, and then over you,' I cried, turning again to Julian, 'but this time I've learned my lesson. I want to start a new life here with you – and Mary Lou.' In my excitement I rose to my feet and began pacing up and down the little room. 'My vocation is a sham.'

Julian sat watching me in silence for a moment or two, then smiled sadly. 'But mine isn't,' she said.

I gaped at her. 'Then why leave the order?'

'A vocation is more than bricks and mortar, Brigid,' Julian corrected me. 'I may have left St Cuthbert's – but I'm every inch a nun. Luckily there are others who feel the same way, including Mary Lou. By the time I came here our plans were well under way.'

'You mean you're going to live here as a nun without permission?'

'They are voting this week for a new Superior General. The Italians and Dutch all support Mother Maria Goretti. If she gets in she will defy the Pope, and let us live among the people.'

'But you're in a state of mortal sin!'

'According to Father Gorman maybe,' replied Julian, 'but not everybody thinks like him. I too have a vocation – and no man will ever take it away from me.'

'You can't dash off and form a splinter group – they never last.'

'St Cuthbert's is dead,' replied Julian. 'All those old nuns in a dark house.'

'Only a few weeks ago you were sleeping in my bed,' I expostulated. 'What sort of behaviour is that?'

'There's more to our vows than who we sleep with,' said Julian. 'The real sin against chastity is failing to love enough – and that's why I took your hand away.'

'But I can't walk out of St Cuthbert's just like that,' I exclaimed, 'without even knowing if – if you would put me first.'

'You let me down, Brigid – and I can't forget it. In the future – who knows? If we were living and working side by side, my feelings might change. In the meantime there's Mary Lou to consider – and those who are coming to join us.'

I thought of our Holy Rule, and the Chapter of Faults, and the nun in Kansas who was given electric shock treatment. 'They'll never let you get away with it.'

'The world is changing, Brigid, despite their attempts to stop it.'

I gazed perplexedly at Julian's face as a car door slammed outside, followed by the sharp beep of a horn. Lorraine was getting ready to leave. 'But you might never love me again!'

Julian rose, touched me gently on the forehead. 'I'm making no guarantees, Brigid – and I'm not saying our new life will be easy. There are only ten of us so far – and the Pope is threatening excommunication. Only you can decide what you will do.'

'I can't face it,' I cried. 'I went through hell over what I did with you – until I got to confession. I'd be living in mortal sin again.'

'That's what they say. But I say you've got to grow up sooner or later.'

'I am growing up,' I flashed back. 'A vocation means keeping vows of poverty, chastity and obedience – not rushing off to live as you please when the going gets rough.'

'If that's your belief you should return to St Cuthbert's. It's almost time for supper, and they'll notice your empty place.'

Lorraine's car horn beeped again, and the engine coughed into life. I pictured the convent on the far side of the park, where I'd first met Sister Monica and found out I had a vocation. It was there Madge and Uncle David met Mother General, setting out from the little house two doors down the street. And because I'd joined the Joubertians, Madge had departed from that same house on her one and only journey to France.

I pictured her quiet grave in the Mother House cemetery, and the peace and order of the convent day. Could I really give that up to return to this narrow street? To be in the world but not of it, one of a bunch of odd women set apart from the neighbours by their neat clothes and middle-class ways, going to mass every morning in the concrete parish church along the dual carriageway?

Then I thought of the convent refectory, where the refectarians would now be moving quietly up and down the long table, laying our places for supper, beneath the little lamp flickering under the portrait of the Blessed Anne Joubert on the end wall. Outside was the convent garden, with the grotto where Monica had taught us to sing 'Ave Maria', and where Julian and I had first sat. As I thought of those things the little room, with its cheap lampshade and piles of ironing, seemed trivial and impermanent. Far from being changeable, or easily influenced, I was a Joubertian through and through, I realized at last, destined to live and die within my cloister walls.

By the time I rose to my feet I felt quite calm. 'It's time for me to go home to St Cuthbert's,' I said to Julian.

She followed me through the darkened hallway. 'If you have any regrets later on,' she said steadily, 'you can console yourself with the thought that, for a rather unloveable woman, you have been loved a lot.'

Before opening the front door I slipped my arms round her waist and held her tight. It would be a long time before I saw her again, if ever.

'I'll never forget you,' I said, stepping out into the cold spring air, 'and I'll never again deny what we did.'

Mary Lou, her curls haloed against the light, waved a wooden spoon from the kitchen.

'Goodbye, Mary Lou,' I called, 'and good luck with your new life.'

'God bless you, Brigid,' said Julian, squeezing my hand.

'Goodbye, Julian.'

'All the best, Brigid,' called Mary Lou as I trudged down the path towards the waiting car. She sketched a cross in the air with her wooden spoon. 'You'll be back.'